BETSY ROBERTS

by N.G. Neville

Published by
Llyfrau Cambria Books, Wales, United Kingdom.
Cambria Books is a division of
Cambria Publishing.
Discover our other books at: www.cambriabooks.co.uk

For Caroline and Edward

Acknowledgements

The author would like to thank Patricia K. Meyer, Elizabeth Burke, Sam Ashton, Edward Burke, Rita Watson, Jane Pearson for their support and encouragement.

BETSY ROBERTS

A tale of survival in the early American West!

This story is set in the early pioneering era of late eighteenth and early nineteenth century America. It is a gripping, horrifying tale based in part on true historical events and characters.

The central character, Betsy Roberts, was kidnapped, abused, then was caught up in the evil, murderous activities of the notorious Harpe brothers, Micajah and Wiley Harpe, The Terrible Harpes. She later became a perpetrator, unwillingly at first but later complicit in their heinous crimes.

How she survived this truly appalling experience, even eventually prospering later in New York during the eighteen hundreds, and creating a successful business and family dynasty there as depicted in the second part of this story, is illustrated through her extraordinary courage and determination – but at a cost!

CONTENTS

PROLOGUE

On a downcast day in April 1773 in Orange County, North Carolina, two young boys were hiding in bushes. They were watching tentatively through gaps in the branches, in growing horror, as both their parents were dragged out of their modest log cabin by a mob of local men but with some women also in attendance, all shouting and screaming with great ferocity. The couple watched the arrival of this mob with nervous trepidation but believed that everything would actually be settled amicably once they had a chance to speak with the ringleaders. After all they had lived in their home for many years with the two boys, surely reason would prevail. Alas this proved not to be the case.

As the crowd got closer shouts of vengeance and hate were heard.

"Traitors, hang 'em both!!"

Thankfully the two boys had gone out to collect some firewood for the simple stove that the family possessed. On returning they were stopped in their tracks by the sight of this mob of mostly men, armed, shouting and hollering, all determinedly heading for the modest log cabin which they had lived in until now. They both shook with fear desperately clinging to each other with the younger of the two, a tall lad, clutching the sleeve of the older, smaller one. Of the two boys one was a tall sturdy, swarthy looking young fellow, the other shorter and leaner. Their parents, William and Elsie Harper originally from Scotland, owned this cabin and modest

1

farmstead, they had worked hard since their modest plantation had been seized by locals, which at the same time had aroused the dislike and suspicion of the local American patriot residents due to their loyalty to the British King George. This was viewed as a most traitorist thing by their neighbours.

Now this local angry mob, aroused by the many accusations which were circulating around the territory, especially of them spying for the British Government so the colonies could be taxed more, and other vague treachery plots, had decided to take matters into their own hands. Passions had become inflamed so much that with little encouragement or alcohol, usually fanning the flames as is a normal consequence, action was now demanded, especially by certain vociferous self-appointed spokesmen who whipped up passions in and around the local neighbourhood.

Ignoring protests of innocence and pleading for mercy the two Harpers (or Harpes as their sons became known as) were dragged to a nearby tree, ready made nooses made from a long rope, thoughtfully brought with them then thrust over their heads, and to the delight of the mob they were pulled up high by two pairs of local, burly Patriot men. Kicking desperately, dancing the macabre dance of death, William due to his greater weight ceased dancing first, Elsie, a little longer, until she too hung lifeless. The process was not mercifully quick, but took at least five minutes before Elsie was choked to death, this was a cruel form of execution but that did not worry the mob.

The old couple had both fought for their lives but when death came, inevitably, the two who had been joined together in matrimony over twenty years before, now hung limply together in death in a macabre way, resembling neglected and ragged manikins.

During their dance of death, observing the perverse

humour of this terrible spectacle, one of the mob shouted.

"Look at them Royalist bastards now haha!!"

Few really responded to this scornful comment and gradually the mob fell silent as they looked on at the two lifeless bodies which were now gently swinging in the morning breeze. Some felt a tinge of guilt, others took pleasure in their work and felt justice had been served, as they saw it, crying out.

"Death to Royalist traitors!"

Gradually the mob dispersed after a while with some looking around and wondering where the two boys were.

"Where are those two young critters?"

One of the crowd muttered but none were interested enough to pursue them. They had had enough, revenge lust had been satiated and whatever happened to the boys was now in God's hands, or maybe the Devil's.

"To Hell with them, they won't be lasting long out in the forests, if bears don't get 'em then brigands or Indians will!"

Someone called out representing the general feeling of all.

All the time watching this horrific spectacle the older, smaller of the two boys, kept pulling the other boy further back into the bushes.

"We'll have to go to Old Baldwin's place and see if he will take us in. There's no other choice brother" he said wiping away the tears in his eyes with his ragged sleeve.

Stunned, the older boy just nodded.

They made their way stealthily from this horrific scene, looking back all the time hoping that no-one would see or come after them. Terrified, they ran deeper into the safety of the dense woods which they hoped would give them sanctuary, heading South, not knowing what fate lay in store for them.

PART ONE

CUT ON AND BE DAMNED!

Map of Eastern United States around 1780 where the Harpes and their family pursued their outlawry.

CHAPTER 1

Early March, 1789

In a clearing by Beavers Creek, near Knoxville, Tennessee, a fierce, icy wind ripped across the small farmstead of John and Mary Roberts sending remnants of branches, assorted debris, snow flurries and leaves, all swirling around in a vision of chaos. A few crows occasionally ventured into the blasts of air, but then quickly sought safe havens among the bare trees. The winter had wreaked its' usual havoc and clearly had not completed its' work yet.

There in a modest but well-kept log cabin lived a family of three with their dog, a mangy retriever who they referred to as 'Smoky' due to it's blackish colour. The family, originally from Devonshire, England, had toiled hard for several years building a life for themselves in this wilderness which gave little reward to neither man nor beast. It's natural beauty and richness belied the many dangers which existed, whether from man, wild animals or simply the weather. But this had not deterred the Roberts family who worked hard to create something of which they had begun to take pride, and even begun to think of a more permanent legacy which they could leave to future generations.

However this cold, forbidding day in February didn't start well for the youngest daughter, Betsy Roberts, their only living child. Their other daughter Susan had vanished when she was out looking for wild herbs and flowers in the woods nearby some seven years ago. After searching for her in the inhospitable wilderness of those times, assumed she had either come to grief from roving renegade Chickamauga or Cherokee Indians, a wild bobcat or a bear maybe, or outlaws, who God forbid, had possibly kidnapped and murdered her. The hated Tory rape gangs consisting of disaffected, mostly Royalist brigands, murderers and various desperados, still roamed menacingly around the country even as late as 1798. They robbed from, destroyed the homes of local American settlers, stole their livestock whether they had fought or supported the revolution or not, kidnapped women and even children or murdered them all. No mercy was shown by these desperate brigands who also had neither loyalty or concern for each other.

The forces of law and order in the form mostly of the army but also vigilantes or posses, sought out as many of these gangs as they could but it was a far from easy task given the vast wilderness and stealth of them, many of whom had worked for the British as guides invaluable with their deep knowledge of the country. There were many possibilities and people quite often disappeared never to be seen again. Either that or she had been robbed by a neighbour or so called neighbour, of the little money she had on her in her purse, possibly kidnapped and killed.

Pa had in fact tried desperately to find her, scouring the territory near and far, often at considerable risk to himself, sometimes with the help of his neighbours, honest God fearing Christian folk who joined forces with him on occasions, but alas mostly on his own. This meant he was away from home for days at a time which naturally worried him greatly, his thoughts returning as they would to his dependents back at the farm. How would they manage without him in this wilderness? Unfortunately it rapidly became clear to him as he increasingly became more vulnerable while he was alone, feeling all the time that he was being watched, that there was no sign nor hope of finding Susan. Therefore with a heavy heart Pa had to admit defeat and called off his search for the poor girl much to her mother's distress, but not so much Betsy who expressed or rather feigned sorrow, but in reality felt little emotion at her sister's disappearance.

"You don't seem too upset Betsy at Susan's loss?" her Ma said one day while sat down peeling potatoes for the broth that was being prepared for supper.

"Sure I do Ma but she's gone now. We must get on mustn't we? Surely the good Lord will watch over her?" Betsy replied somewhat diffidently.

Ma stared at her in some surprise but dismissed any thoughts of Betsy having no regard for Susan, so she preferred to keep any further such thoughts to herself. Betsy was needed more than ever now as being the only extra pair of hands left so, as Ma decided, it was best not to probe too deeply. Betsy could be a truculent girl but valuable to them at the same time. And Betsy knew it.

It was freezing cold this particular day. Her Ma and Pa unusually had scolded her for not feeding the hogs early enough as it was now around 11.30am, much later than normal for these few beasts to receive their food.

"I'm seventeen years old." she had said, "not a child."

"Then grow up and take responsibility for yourself." Pa had said in his usual calm but irritated tone.

Betsy was prone to bouts of insolence and casual unconcern on occasions, even as young as she was, and consequently she was well aware of her unique position in the family as the one remaining offspring of John and Mary Roberts, which caused her parents to treat her with less severity than they otherwise might have done.

The events of this day were so far tense and confrontational for them all, but things were to get much worse for Betsy Roberts.

CHAPTER 2

Seventeen years old Betsy Roberts, an attractive, slim, blond haired girl of medium height, physically mature for her age, was making her way this late morning to a hog sty where the family kept a few miserable hogs, in order to feed these animals. As she got close to the sty, they grunted, snorted and moved toward her in expectation of food, or what passed as food – leftovers, scrapings and whatever else there was from the kitchen. But hogs are not fussy creatures and will eat pretty much anything, even each other given the opportunity if hungry enough, and the sight of the fair Betsy climbing over the fence aroused their interest and expectations as she came closer to them.

In their haste to be fed the hogs on their way to the swill knocked Betsy to the ground.

"Jesus, Goddamned hogs!" she shouted, annoyed.

She looked up from her prone position, got up, and walking slowly to the feeding trough in the distance, she noticed out of the corner of her eye two strange, small speck-like shapes, both figures on horseback and coming toward the farmstead. Observing these two mysterious shapes, a feeling of foreboding hit her immediately.

"Pa!" Betsy called out.

"Pa!!" shouting more loudly.

Pa appeared at the door looking out to see what Betsy was shouting and by now gesticulating demonstratively.

"Goddamn it girl can't ye do anything right?" Pa yelled from the cabin.

"Pa!!!" Betsy gave a final call.

Betsy's concerns grew in urgency as the two men came closer, looking even more menacing especially the larger of the two, who even from a distance, exuded an aura of latent evil which Betsy sensed straight away.

Her father now came out of the cabin to see what she was shouting for. He too now saw the two riders and also felt a tinge of danger potentially emerging from the woods.

The two specks were now to be seen in full view, two figures on horse; one a huge, rough looking figure, a well set man, the other shorter but quite sinister looking man. Betsy and her father, who had come over to her aid, helped her to her feet, both stood watching curiously as the two men dismounted, tied up their mounts on the fence and approached at a steady, walking pace.

"I don't like the look of those two fellas Betsy, go and get my rifle from the cabin quick!"

Betsy ran as fast as she could into the cabin brushing past her Ma who was becoming concerned herself at what was going on, sensing something was not right. Then Betsy returned with an old loaded musket her Pa had from the War of Independence, ready for action as Pa always had it...just in case.

The two strange men approached the cabin where Betsy and her father stood waiting to see what they wanted.

"Can you two kind folks give two weary travellers some food and maybe sit by your fire for a while?"

The shorter of the two men asked calmly with a smile.

Betsy's mother from inside the cabin, looked out through their only grimy window, watching both men closely. She studied them both, the two of them appeared wild looking, unkempt and dressed in buckskins. The shorter of the two looked threatening in a way, the bigger brutish looking man, looked downright murderous with a smirk on his face as she could make out. They were dressed in their rough skins with beaten hats, the bigger man wearing what looked like an animal's head as a hat, in fact it was wolf's head, not too uncommon headware amongst some pioneers and fur trappers.

"Oh God." she whispered to herself, her fears for her two loved ones becoming more intense now as she looked on.

"Ain't got any food to spare fellas." said Pa, "You can have a warm by the stove and some coffee, it's all we can offer you."

"That's Christian of ye sir." said the shorter of the two men.

Ma now moved cautiously outside by the door and was watching the larger man. She then heard her husband say.

"Come inside." Pa generously offered.

At that moment as Pa looked to offer shelter, Ma saw the larger man level his rifle which he had swiftly taken from his horse, and shot Pa in the chest. Pa dropped to the ground groaning, his musket falling away now impotently. Blood seeped from the hole which could be seen in his chest. Betsy and Ma screamed as the two men come closer, the large man then struck Betsy with the back of his hand knocking her to the ground rendering her unconscious. Smoky, barking wildly and attempting to bite the smaller man, was dispatched expertly and efficiently by the smaller man with his knife. The dog lay dead, blood seeping from and into his thick fur. The larger man then strode into the cabin grabbing Ma, who had vainly tried to defend her home with a kitchen knife, by the throat, then struck her once forcefully on the head with his tomahawk.

Ma fell dead, her head cleaved open by Micajah Harpe's favourite weapon. Mercifully she had died instantaneously.

A scene of dreadful mayhem ensued destroying the relative peace of this once calm homestead. The two men proceeded to ransack the cabin in search of anything useful they could find but what little of value there was, was of little value to these two vagabonds. They took a few items of clothing, Pa's rifle, some food which they stuffed into a saddlebag strung over Micajah's neck, some coins, the rest they left behind having no use for any of Ma Robert's nor Betsy's clothing. Wiley grinned then called out to his brother.

"Let's do the lassie!"

Micajah smirked.

"Aye!" he replied casually.

Acting quickly as if this was a not uncommon occurrence, both men then went outside and dragged the semi-conscious Betsy back into the cabin laughing as they moved her along. They then threw out her mother's lifeless body outside near to her dead husband, the two corpses lay forlornly close to each other, as they had been so close to each other during their lives.

These men, the Harpes, two infamous Harpe cousins, some say brothers, Micajah or 'Big Harpe' and Wiley or 'Little Harpe', as they were known by many folk who were aware of their terrible reputation, and by then known as notorious murderers and robbers, brigands of the South Eastern American wilderness, had made themselves feared and hated by all who knew of them throughout Kentucky and Tennessee.

By the time of this incident Betsy's parents were their

twentieth and twenty first victims. Their campaign of murder had been waged for some time before, it was reaching it's peak at this time spurred on by hatred, vengeance as they saw it for previous wrongs done to them. Both the Harpe brothers (as we will refer to them now rather than cousins) had become totally immune to the pain that they caused. The Roberts family, especially Betsy of course, were just one more example of the trail of horror and destruction committed by them both.

Alas there were many more horrors to come.

Betsy Roberts aged 17

CHAPTER 3

When Betsy came to, a feeling of sheer visceral, terror overcame her, aware of the appalling situation which now existed around her, and gradually realising that her parents were both dead, she struggled to move herself away. She breathed desperately, trying in panic to control herself, though tears streamed down her face.

Micajah Harpe, the bigger (he was at least six feet four inches), and the more brutish looking of the two men, threw her roughly on to the bed of her parents, ripping off her skirts, and underwear, all the while poor Betsy screamed in terror.

"No, no, please, no!!"

Micajah just paused very briefly, laughed and continued the brutal assault without any concern for Betsy's desperate pleas.

When he was done it was the other man's turn, Wiley Harpe. He forced his way upon Betsy but not as brutally as Micajah, she was by now in an almost catatonic state mercifully, only barely aware of what was happening to her and said.

"Keep quiet girl and you might just survive."

Wiley looked at her before he began the rape of Betsy and he murmured to her, putting his hand over her mouth and whispering strangely as if some hidden thought had taken root within him. Betsy being a brave, intelligent girl grasped some desperate meaning from what he said despite her numbness. A glimmer of hope flickered midst the horror of what had, and what was happening to her, and perhaps what was to come she feared. She had an almost instinctive animal like ability to grasp the main elements of a situation, even as young as she was, to work out ways of dealing with situations bad or good, and living in this dangerous wilderness, it served her well.

When this brutal sexual assault was over the two Harpes laughed and pulled Betsy up from the bed as if nothing of great significance had happened. Micajah looked at her with contempt and snarled a vicious grunt at her, as if she was some piece of rancid meat.

"Done with ye now bitch." he muttered contemptuously.

He looked at Wiley whose countenance gave little away, but nonetheless aped his younger brother in a less convincing manner.

"This lassie could be of some use te' us brother." he said.

The significance of this comment was completely lost on Micajah who then left the cabin beckoning to Wiley to follow him, dragging poor Betsy, who groaned imploringly in agony, behind him.

A traumatised Betsy Roberts shook with fear as she was being dragged along but somehow with enormous effort, steadied herself mentally and fixed her thoughts with monumental willpower on dealing with this dreadful situation and more importantly, what was going to happen to her next.

When they paused briefly, which was to allow Micajah to hastily return to the cabin in order to drag the two bodies from outside and into it, then set fire to the building thereby destroying any evidence of their nefarious deeds. They completed their task which was in fact their usual modus operandi. Betsy tidied herself as much as she was able, wiped the tears from her face and though shaking with a fear that she had never experienced before in her short life, and desperately tried to compose herself using every ounce of her strength and courage. She had no idea of what was to happen yet.

While Micajah was away setting fire to her home he turned to Betsy and spat out.

"Just do as I damned well tell ye, if ye don't you'll die, understand wench?"

Betsy weakly nodded.

So began Betsy's ordeal with the two infamously known Terrible Harpes, two of the very worst outlaws in American history, not as well known as the likes of Jesse James, Billy the Kid and John Wesley Hardin but in many ways much worse.

CHAPTER 4

Within a short time of Betsy being dragged outside, she was tied to Wiley's horse, the two Harpes then started to casually ride away at a steady pace pulling her along with no care for the poor girl. She struggled to stay on her feet but despite falling two or three times, she managed to keep up. Her willpower and the fact that she was a strong, fit young woman saved her from what could have been a terrible, agonising death, though Wiley's intention to keep her alive might just perhaps have saved her.

Later that day though, after what seemed an eternity being dragged by the rope from Wiley's horse, stumbling at regular intervals, and beaten along a trail through dense forest, Betsy fell and called out.

"I can't go on no more!"

Micajah turned, dismounted, aimed a kick at her but Wiley sensing that this might finish her off or at the very least injure her badly, motioned and shouted for Micajah to stop.

"Why the hell?!" the giant said.

Wiley grinned and muttered.

"She has value brother, we don't want damaged goods now do we?"

Micajah nodded picked her up roughly.

"Git!" he bellowed and thrust her onwards.

Wiley quickly pushed her on to the back of his horse, this time saving her from further punishment. He did this not so much out of a sense of mercy, but simply because he had thoughts of using the girl himself and what use would a corpse be, or at the least a misshapen, crippled thing.

The two men and Betsy, now thankfully being given some water by Wiley, carried on, and fortunately for her they soon came to a modest clearing which revealed a shack, partly broken down, abandoned some time ago by settlers just off the trail which was by now known as the Wilderness Road. It was late now, darkness was descending and rain started to fall.

After tying up the two horses they entered the shack which from it's outward appearance would offer but poor cover and comfort.

***

Stumbling into what seemed like a cave but was in fact a rough cabin or more accurately a wooden shelter hastily constructed by the two men from some long past pioneer's deserted cabin which had been left to rot. The three of them searched through the darkness to make out a few ambiguous forms. The figures were difficult to make out but gradually Betsy recovered her senses as she began to feel just a little bit more like herself. Betsy recognised a thin waif like figure in the gloom tending a baby and sitting alone, but was soon distracted as Wiley Harpe flung a piece of wood at the figure.

He then shouted.

"We're back bitch now get makin' some dinner we have a guest!"

He grinned and proceeded to light a simple oil lantern which slowly revealed a grimy hovel, made as tidy as the mysterious woman could make it. There was little more than a few old stools, a broken table, a stove and some grimy straw mattresses to be seen. In fact the run down cabin had been used in the past by various travellers but had now become neglected and forgotten by all who passed through these parts, except of course the Harpes. It had become abandoned, falling prey to the worst type of humans and wild beasts who had no interest in repairing this pitiful place.

Just then the thin dark haired woman got up and looked at Betsy, who was too stunned to say anything, the woman merely stared momentarily at her, smirked and went about the business of preparing some food from what was available – some rough meat, potatoes and the like and began to make a stew from these meagre morsels.

After a while pausing from her chores the woman said in a gruff voice.

"Got anythin' for us Micajah?"

Micajah ignored her and as the baby then began crying shouted.

"Shut the damned bairn!"

He turned away and went outside to relieve himself with Wiley seated on one of the stools filling his pipe in the gloom.

The woman who seemed unconcerned carried on making the stew which smelt foul, it's black colour within a grimy cooking pot, a most unappetising sight but Betsy, by now was hungry since she had not eaten anything since early morning. It was now approaching sunset and when Micajah returned, kicking the door open violently, the stew was ladled out on to four wooden bowls. Wiley and Micajah grabbed their own portions which were large but the two women had to make do with what was left. Micajah shouted scathingly.

"Be grateful lassie yer getting' anythin', if ye ain't no use to us we'll be cookin' you for dinner!"

"Just eat, we need you healthy so ye can work." Wiley added.

They both spoke in a strange dialect which was a blend of guttural Scots passed on from their parents as well as other Scottish relatives, but also the more local accents which had begun to emerge in the South. Betsy herself spoke in a more Kentuckian accent, but an English West Country lilt could still be discerned to an ear familiar with that beautifully rustic part of England.

Betsy ate in silence drinking some water offered to her by Wiley but she was so exhausted from her traumatic experience that day that she fell into a deep sleep. It wasn't long before the rest of this unholy group also took to their rest, with Wiley Harpe sleeping next to Betsy, perhaps offering some protection for her in case Micajah decided to violate her again. The woman with her baby settled in a corner feeding the mite intermittently as well as keeping it as quiet as she could so as not to provoke another violent assault from Micajah.

CHAPTER 5

It was another two days before a traumatised Betsy regained some semblance of sanity. She was put roughly on horseback with the smaller of the two men putting her in front of himself, as they travelled along a trail to somewhere unknown to her. The other woman with child was forced to walk most of the time until Micajah, in a rare moment of concern, allowed her to ride on his own mount. The child's wailing tested his nerves so that he preferred going off ahead on foot occasionally to see if the trail ahead was safe.

Betsy's time during the preceding two days at the cabin had been spent mostly sleeping and also groaning occasionally from the pains of her brutal treatment. She tended to keep a low profile as much as it was possible, saying little, obeying any instructions given and eating whatever scraps were served up by the other captive woman who had to keep her child quiet especially when Micajah, the baby's father, was about. Luckily he spent much of his time out in the forest looking for prey or checking one of the traps he had set. Both the Harpes ignored her and Wiley also went off on the second day with his brother to hunt. Despite their efforts, in actuality nothing of much use was killed, only a bobcat which wasn't something edible, but the unlucky cat had wondered into the sight of Wiley's musket and paid the price. A clean kill.

On the second day Betsy began to ponder to herself what was going to happen, uncertain and confused as she was, she also possessed a glimmer of hope combined with a purposefulness which she believed, against all odds, might see her through this terrible situation. At certain times Betsy wondered to herself about her situation as she was huddled up against the wall of the cabin.

"Lord." she thought… "why haven't they killed me? There must be some reason."

Her fear of death or abuse was ever present but because neither of the Harpe brothers had killed her, at least for the present, she entertained the promise of getting out of this situation somehow. Suddenly amidst such thoughts Micajah called.

"Here!" he shouted.

They dismounted, and the big, brutish man pulled Betsy off the horse roughly.

"Gather some wood for a fire." he ordered.

Betsy just looked at him askance.

"Do what I say bitch!" he shouted at her.

"And don't try to run off do ye hear? There's nowhere for you to go anyway." the smaller man said.

He then spoke to the large man who terrified Betsy.

"Micajah see if you can shoot us up some food while I make us a shelter."

"Aye Wiley." he replied.

Micajah took up his long rifle, filled it with powder from his pouch and set off to the forest to look for prey.

Betsy thought the large man "Micajah" as she realised was his name by now, simple minded, and was maybe controlled at least to some extent by the other smaller man, 'Wiley' as she knew now.

She collected some dry wood nearby as instructed and brought it back to the makeshift camp which Wiley was putting together.

After summoning up some courage Betsy edged closer to Wiley and inquired tentatively.

"Are you two brothers?" she asked Wiley as confidently as she could.

"Yes or half brothers in fact lass, but raised together as proper brothers, why do ye ask?"

He answered this in some surprise at Betsy's questioning. Wiley looked at her with not a little consternation, completely taken aback but intrigued at a girl like this asking him questions so early in her captivity. Her next question took him by even greater surprise.

"Is he right in the head mister?" she asked looking straight at Wiley.

"As long as he is content." replied Wiley for the moment entertaining this unusual young woman.

Wiley then smirked thinking this girl was either mad or quite a brazen wench as he thought of her. Like his brother he was used to women simply complying with anything they both commanded or at least they remained mutely unobtrusive, the only way any of them could survive.

Betsy shuddered at Wiley's advice to her and thought that she had better avoid Micajah if she could, and make herself get closer to Wiley. She might last a while longer until she could escape when the opportunity arose. It was a strategy she would adopt as it seemed to offer the best hope of staying alive.

Suddenly a shot was heard, Micajah then soon returned with dubious cuts of meat hacked off a young deer he had killed and roughly butchered out in the open.

"What's that?"

Betsy looked at the bloodied pieces Micajah brought, then asked him directly, standing erect for the first time since her ordeal began.

Micajha turned looked at her with a frown of contempt mixed with surprise.

"Put it on the spit and shut up!" Micajah growled, becoming more irritated.

It was the first time he had encountered a girl who asked so many questions and didn't seem as intimidated as the others, or at least that is what it appeared. Wiley then hastily took Betsy away toward the crude makeshift spit he had made, and proceeded to show her how to put the meat on to it, crudely spearing it with a sure hand. He then turned to Betsy, took her by the arm and pulled her closer saying.

"Don't cross him girl" he said quietly looking into her eyes.

Betsy pulled back but realised the significance of this and saw that Wiley had at least a little concern for her, or so it seemed to her naive nature at this time. She then gradually and surreptitiously began to consciously but subtly fade into the background when Micajah was near – it was a good way of ensuring a better chance of avoiding possible harm or worse.

Night drew near and after eating this rough meal Betsy sat carefully away from the two brothers and the other woman, whose name she did not know yet, unobtrusively observing both men, but at the same time avoiding eye contact with either of them. Already Betsy had resolved to survive in any way, and gain revenge for her parent's deaths. Hatred burned within her, subsumed periodically by her grief at what had happened to her Ma and Pa, the inevitable tears and burning rage vying for priority within her. Her emotions at this point were in a kind of crucible of competing forces which were to be forged ultimately into something quite extraordinary and fearsome. At the same time she began to think of ways that she might make her escape and be rid of these two monsters, easier said than done no doubt, but Betsy was a tough girl and if there was an occasion to make her escape she would be ready to seize the opportunity. There was certainly no doubt in her mind about that.

Micajah 'Big Harpe' and Wiley 'Little Harpe'

CHAPTER 6

Now the two Harpes; Micajah, originally christened Joshua, and Wiley originally William, or 'Big Harpe' and 'Little Harpe' as they were often referred to, had similar and yet contrasting appearances and indeed differing personalities.

The bigger one, Micajah, standing a massive six feet four inches, had the appearance of some fearsome bear, dressed as he always was in skins. In Winter he wore bearskin usually or wolfskin, often with a wolf's head fur headcover atop. He had black curly hair, was heavily bearded, and of swarthy, dark looks and countenance. It was rumoured that his father had had an illicit liaison with a Negro slave girl against her will in the past, she subsequently became pregnant and had given birth to Micajah, a difficult birth needless to say.

After some soul searching his father decided to keep the child despite the protestations of his wife who he confessed to after much interrogation by her, and who then threatened to quit him. The young child engaged both parents as only a beautiful, innocent babe can. They kept him as a supposed orphan with the slave girl told to keep quiet if a she knew what was good for her. The poor girl had little or no choice, being as she was, the property of both husband and wife.

Micajah grew up loved but aware that he was different and so quickly learned to use his size and power to deal with any baiting from other boys that he encountered. A tendency towards brutality and even cruelty became quite natural to him, he thought nothing of beating mercilessly any unfortunate foolish boy who crossed him in any way either verbally or physically.

In one instance he beat a certain boy, the son of a neighbouring farmer, so badly that the lad nearly lost his life, such were the wounds inflicted on him. The stage was therefore set, he would inevitably grow up as a huge and menacing individual. Micajah was not going to put up with any ill-advised nonsense from neither man nor beast and when aroused his temper was both unpredictable and volcanic.

Wiley, the shorter of the two Harpes, presented a contrasting figure and personality. He was much smaller, lithe in build also with black hair, though with tinges of reddishness in it, he was of straighter, and paler visage, and with a personality which if you met him you would realise that there was a clever slyness about him. He had an inclination towards learning, which was totally lacking in Micajah, and he would actually read books which he found from his parent's modest bookshelves, his father taking some pride in this seeking for knowledge and betterment. Even the Bible was regularly delved into, it was a source of wisdom with the many stories, psalms, proverbs therein from the Old and New Testaments, to which Wiley became fascinated.

The boys attended church or what passed as a church during those times. A shack more like, ministered by a firebrand Calvinist preacher named the Reverend Abraham Cole, whose services and homilies became hotbeds of wrath and dire warnings of sin. The Old Testament was Cole's favoured book, he rarely referred to any passages of mercy and forgiveness in the New. At times he raged against sin quoting passages usually from the Old Testament, Hell awaited those who did not repent! There was little hope of salvation in Cole's sermons which even saw him thumping the lecturn, shouting at the top of his voice, and gesticukating wildly in his attempts at putting the fear of the Lord into his congregation.

Like Micajah, Wiley was not averse to vicious, violent actions and would deal with other boys quite ruthlessly when necessary. He too was now dressed in skins with a bedraggled beard and usually wore a raccoon skin hat. Also, like his half-brother, he enjoyed the business of slaughtering hogs and cattle when the chance occurred, as it did on their farm, actually using his knife skilfully to cut the poor beasts' throat.

Their father had taught them well using the most effective methods of killing, bleeding and eviscerating the animals. Gradually they both became more and more adept at this with Micajah using a hammer to stun the animal first and Wiley finishing off the hog or cow with his exceedingly sharp knife. Wiley as the natural son of the Harpers always felt a touch superior and benefited from an instinctive intelligence lacking in his younger half-brother.

These qualities, that were the mark of the two boys, became something of a template for future nefarious, criminal activities and made them eventually known as the most hated, feared bandits in American pioneer history. Thus the 'Terrible Harpes' were created and they would indeed bring terror to the whole territory. Their reign of murderous terror would leave a legacy like no other for many years to come.

A map of the territory from the 1700's where the Harpes and their women operated.

CHAPTER 7

Unaware of all this information concerning the Harpe brothers, Betsy sat with her legs hunched up in the makeshift shelter contemplating her situation, and then suddenly became aware that Wiley was watching her closely. His steely eyes were focused on her intently, watching her as if she was some helpless prey.

She shivered, thinking to herself.

"Good Lord I've got to keep on the good side of him no matter what he does to me or I am doomed."

She braced herself and stared back defiantly.

Wiley noticed her staring and so got up and approached her and standing over her for what seemed like an eternity to Betsy, he smiled, nodded to her in an odd, knowing manner, his eyes glinting, stroked his beard then turned away and then settled down for the night leaving her alone. After this strange and uncomfortable event, Betsy lay back nervously at first but eventually she fell into a deep sleep, totally exhausted, both physically and mentally.

***

Dawn arrived and as the sunlight penetrated gently through to the cabin and nature's lively and reassuring noises became apparent, Micajah and Wiley were already moving around instructing the other woman, who Betsy had not paid much attention to until now, so far away was she normally that she seemed at the other end of the shack, but now appeared again with her baby in her arms. They told her sharply what to do, though by now she was well drilled and utterly subservient. She had that ability unique to many mothers of being able to carry on with chores with her baby tied in a sling at her front, the poor infant often muzzled.

Her name was Sally Rice, her infant, a swarthy looking boy, almost certainly Micajah's, was given the name of "Ban" by Micajah, after the Harpes' former British commander, the infamous Lieutenant Colonel Banastre Tarleton. Sally herself as Betsy could see, was a pale brown haired woman of some thirty years old, her clothes mostly torn and unwashed, a grubby shawl her only real comfort. She was thin and pockmarked due to the harshness of her life so far, not surprisingly the poor diet they ate had contributed to her ill looking appearance. Scurvy was a not uncommon ailment due to the limited diet available, with little chance of anything more than meat and a few wild berries, nuts and even carrion on occasions.

Sally was the second 'wife' of the two Harpe brothers, the previous one a certain Maria Davidson, had managed to escape while Micajah and Wiley were drunk one night not far from a small group of travellers – immigrants from Holland, who were heading West in search of a better life through the recently created Cumberland Gap, but had camped with their three wagons for the night nearby just off the trail. The Harpes had observed their movements and now planned to take the group by surprise and rob them of all their possessions, also murder the whole group leaving no witnesses and simply for the hell of it! This they were well capable of doing, having done this before on more than one occasion. Fortunately Maria escaped with her child, stealthily making her way to the Dutch party and

34

warning them of the Harpes' intentions. They initially took some convincing but soon believed her due to her genuine pleading and total veracity of the story she told them, it was hard for anyone to make up such a story let alone a woman with a child in her arms.

In gratitude, but also knowing that it was their Christian duty to help this poor woman and her child, the leader of the group, a Dutchman called Ruud, offered her a place on one of their wagons, which she gratefully accepted and Maria was never seen or heard of again. She travelled West and thankfully made a new life for herself.

On discovering Maria's absence the next morning the Harpe brothers furiously set out to find her, but as the Dutch group had left hours before and were now in no doubt as to the Harpes' evil intentions arming themselves accordingly, Micajah and Wiley reluctantly called off their search and instead decided to find another 'wife' or two at the first opportunity.

Ready now to depart, Wiley and Micajah packed up the horses. Betsy drifted in and out of her sleep but was quickly awoken brutally by the larger man. Micajah kicked her, shouting.

"Get up bitch!"

Betsy jumped up startled and wincing in pain from his kick.

"No need to kick me like that!" she protested.

"Ha! I'll cut your damned head off if you backchat me like that agin'!"

"Leave her be Micajah, we can make use of her later." Wiley said wishing to avoid further damage to his new possession, as he increasingly saw her.

Wiley turned to Micajah and gently advised him that this yong girl could be very useful to them both.

"How?" Micajah replied.

"You'll see brother, I have plans for her." he gestured crudely toward him. Wiley grinned and looked knowingly at Micajah.

A feeling of dread overcame Betsy on hearing this and she stumbled as she walked over to the horses looking at Wiley as if he had let her down.

Quickly mounting their steeds with the two women now mounted on freshly stolen mules, Sally holding on to the baby, they travelled along the Cumberland Gap trail for two days with little rest or pause, only snatching sleep whenever a suitable sheltered clearing was found or a in deserted cabin. On the second day Wiley pointed to a trail off the main road and shouted to Micajah.

"Down here, come on! We'll get some supplies there Micajah, remember that miserable critter called Cutter?"

Micajah responded positively remembering as Wiley did that there was a place that might provide something of use to them both. They turned and moved along the trail at Wiley's behest, when eventually they came to a small trading post which appeared some distance away in the forest clearing.

"We'll get supplies here brother." said Wiley pointing to it.

"Aye." replied Micajah.

Betsy looked on hoping that something better will come of this and at least they might have some decent food and provisions. She felt dirty and longed for a little piece of civilisation which until now had been non-existent.

36

Arriving at the trading post, no more than a ramshackle cabin or shack displaying the name 'Cutter's Stores' crudely painted on a sign outside, a not uncommon sight in these parts, Sally was told to stay outside with her 'bairn' and keep an eye on the horses.

"Ye ain't any use to us here galla!" Micajah shouted to her, Sally merely nodded compliantly.

Then walking inside with the two Harpes, Betsy was shocked at the darkness, as it seemed there was no light except from a small, grimy window which allowed the most meagre light through. Despite this as soon as her eyes adjusted to the darkness, she noticed an array of disorganised provisions which caught her attention, some in sacks, some on shelves, some in boxes, some in tins.

A fat, greasy, unkempt man called Cutter (he didn't seem to have a first name but was known simply as Cutter to everyone), with a matted black beard appeared wiping his stubby fingers over a filthy apron that partly covered his bulging stomach. He stood behind a simple counter which was little more than a table.

"Gooday folks can I help you?" he grunted, adjusting his breeches underneath his apron, then pulling his braces over his shoulder. He looked at the three figures screwing up his beady eyes.

No sooner had he moved or said these words than Micajah jumped over the counter in a flash which was quite amazing given the size of him, made a dash to him and drew his tomahawk from his belt, bringing it down as fast as lightning until it split the man's head in two. All this before Cutter could even move. Betsy on witnessing this screamed in horror thrusting her hands over her face.

The man now lay dead on the floor, a trail of blood drained beneath the floorboards, his skull expertly cleaved in two.

Women's voices now were heard from the gloomy rear of the store, a dull muttering apparent.

"What do we have here?" Wiley remarked with a grin.

"Come out and show yourselves or it will not go well for you women!"

Two bedraggled women, slowly emerged nervously from behind a curtain at the rear of the building. One appeared quite stout and tall, raw boned with dark brown hair, the other thinner with brownish, dark hair. Both women were in an unwashed neglected state which shocked Betsy on first sight.

"Who are you two?"

Wiley looked at them both after inquiring of them. He stared at them now and sought to make out if they might be of any use to them. Micajah at the same time was sitting on a barrel smoking his pipe contentedly rather like some predatory animal pleased after a successful kill.

"Come on speak up. You fatty, what's your name?" he said pointing to the bigger of the two women.

"Susan."

The bigger of the two women replied in a dull, monotone voice which seemed to reflect her large size, though she would not be considered fat today as Micajah had commented disparagingly. She had a downcast look about her which suggested that here was a woman who had endured so much that it had drained her of all feeling.

"And you woman?" Micajah continued, pointing at her

with his long clay pipe, then looking at the other woman continued his interrogation of sorts.

"Sarah sir." the other woman of thin appearance with filthy and unkempt fair hair muttered in reply.

"Speak up bitch!" shouted Micajah suddenly.

"Sarah!" she cried.

"How would ye both like to come with us, we could have some fun eh? It's going to be better than this shithole!" Wiley said.

The two women look at each other.

"Alright, we been here seven years against our will. Cutter used us as whores for some of the customers who hadn't seen a woman for long time, filthy scum they were, he made extra money for himself but gave us nuthin'. Cutter said he'd kill us slow if we ran away." Susan replied.

Wiley and Micajah laughed.

"Oh did he? Ain't gonna torch anythin' now." Micajah said pointing to the bloodied corpse lying on the earth floor.

Wiley grinned, and turned toward Micajah.

"Let's set fire to this dump." he snarled.

Micajah nodded agreement and the two men started to set light to the place smashing oil lamps, whale oil, taking delight in their work and then watching the flames gradually seize hold of the building and consume it greedily. They poured much of the oil over Cutter's body and set light to it.

They all then quickly moved outside the cabin.

Micajah especially enjoyed this destruction knowing that Cutter would be reduced to ashes along with his home.

"Goddamned Yankee can burn in Hell!" Micajah shouted.

Both men turned away and the group departed with Betsy looking back and in reality taking some secret pleasure in Cutter's destruction. She was glad that he would be erased from the world. What did she care if another brute was dead?

Susan and Sarah

CHAPTER 8

A way from the trading post as they awaited the start of their journey along the trial, the two women now in the daylight, looked unsure if their decision was a wise one on seeing the two men clearly. They could not, or would not speak to each other, Sarah especially, but they contented themselves with furtive glances to each other, reading each other's thoughts as they had done so much over the years. They had lived in fear for most of the time with Cutter, aware that one wrong word might bring death to either or both of them. Cutter was as vile a creature as one could find in this wilderness, merciless and ready to abuse either woman for his own pleasure. Unsurprisingly they were both relieved to be rid of him though they were both uncertain as to what the future held; better or worse or perhaps just the same?

Betsy looked on in some surprise at Susan and Sarah's secretive communication but was unconcerned. The two bearded Harpes cut a frightening sight, one a huge monster of a man clad in filthy clothes, skins mostly, and armed with a tomahawk, musket rifle and knife attached to his waist, the other one also grimy, complete with rifle, two pistols and two large knives displayed in leather sheaves. Both men stared at the women and pointed to the women to start moving, and so with no alternative the two women packed some provisions together which had previously been got from the cabin as could be located in the brief time available to them, turned to go, each also with a few meagre belongings now wrapped up.

They knew it was too late and pointless however to change their minds. Betsy looked at the large woman called Susan quizzically.

"Something familiar about her." she thought.

The men moved off on horseback having stuffed their bags with provisions from the trading post but there was no room for Betsy on Wiley's horse this time, so she had to walk with the three other women.

"Keep up or you'll be left behind. You won't last too long I promise you, if bears, wolves, coyotes and the rest don't get you there's plenty of real bad folk and Indians that will ha!" said Wiley, and turned away.

Betsy felt almost betrayed and even this early she resented the company of the two women who could become a problem for her. She looked accusingly at Wiley who rode ahead unaware. Both he and Micajah had all the provisions which were kept in saddlebags tied to their horses, they then looked back to make sure the women were keeping up, shouting at them.

"Git movin' quicker 'fore I take a whip to ye all!" Wiley threatened from time to time. Inevitably little or no allowances were made for them during the whole of the journey.

CHAPTER 9

After a long and arduous journey back, which involved delays along the trail due to the women falling and having to be threatened, beaten and cajoled, and Wiley at last taking Betsy on board his horse, they arrived at their retreat. The two other women by now were utterly exhausted and begged for water and some food. Sally said nothing and had taken to sickness. She looked in a terrible state with her baby limp in her sling. She suddenly collapsed and fell to the ground with her child falling lifeless beside her. The two tragic figures lay side by side, a sight that would in normal circumstances illicit sympathy and shock, but these were by no means normal circumstances. Sally gasped and then lay still, she could not be moved even with the brutal promptings of Micajah. Wiley looked at Micajah and said.

"She's done for Micajah, 'tis best to finish her off here as there's no way we can carry the bitch, nor the wee bairn either."

Micajah glared at her and without any hesitation took out his pistol, cocked it and shot her without any expression of regret, just cold bloodied killing. This was not so much an act of mercy but a matter of fact and necessity as one might dispatch a wounded animal. No niceties of feeling existed in Micajah Harpe. The baby was already no longer of this world, taken mercifully before any act of violence could harm him further.

The women looked on in some shock with Betsy too scared to make any comment, by now realising that this would be futile and merely arouse further trouble, She stood there and merely observed the shocking, poignant event.

Betsy then muttered beseechingly to Wiley about wanting something to drink.

"Shut up and ye'll get somethin' when we're ready!" shouted Micajah as he turned to the women.

Wiley pulled Betsy down from his horse telling her.

"Don't get any ideas I give a damn about you girl but you ain't much use to me dead."

Betsy nodded not wishing to create any discord in this uneasy, uncertain relationship. She looked across at the other women who lay on the ground. One of them looked across at her and squinting her eyes and seemed to stare at her in a jealous, vengeful way. It disconcerted her initially then aroused her curiosity, why was she staring like that, she wondered?

***

It seemed to Betsy that the woman who she now knew was called Susan looked at her in such this strangely bitter way for some reason unknown to her at this point in time. Thinking more deeply she suddenly thought in a flash of recognition; 'could it possibly be THE Susan, her sister, who she remembered from nearly eight years ago and had disappeared mysteriously?' Confused thoughts raced through her mind creating a mixture of consternation, shock and some suppressed elation at the thought that this scruffy and ill looking figure could be her long lost sister, Susan. Betsy looked again but Susan turned away suddenly, not engaging in any way with Betsy's attentions.

Later Betsy watched the two wretched women carefully and thought to herself.

"I can use these two to my advantage."

Pondering further she concluded.

"Maybe they can take the brunt of Micajah's wrath and violence while I can get closer to Wiley? It's my only hope."

Betsy was from now on more and more thinking of her own well-being and survival and less about empathising or joining forces in some way with Susan and Sarah, who she viewed unfortunately as lost causes as was the case with poor Sally, with perhaps little to offer by way of any use to her in her struggle to keep alive and even prosper ultimately. As time progressed Betsy grew some strength from surviving each day and even scoring small victories along the path, occasionally getting the better of Wiley and Micajah.

Her thoughts concerning Susan and Sarah turned to a distant slightly contemptuous attitude, which she had first thought on seeing them both appear in Cutter's Stores dressed in rags. Why on earth did they not try to overcome him and escape? After all there were two of them against an obese degenerate. Betsy figured that if she had been in their position she would not have hesitated to kill the brute, her youthful exuberance was still in evidence despite all that had happened so far, she felt that she had a good chance of freeing herself.

After considering these points she decided that her path was now set, Betsy Roberts was going to survive and gain strength in whatever way she could.

CHAPTER 10

The Cumberland Gap which overlapped Kentucky, Virginia, and Tennessee, and surrounding territory at this time, was a wild and inhospitable place, inhabited until comparatively recently around the 1790's by wild animals and native American Indians, mostly Ridgetop Shawnee, Chikamouga as well as renegade Cherokee and Creek tribes. These tribes had at first fought with great determination and bravery against the new white settlers who had appeared as if by some inexplicable, supernatural force beyond their experience. The tribes had realised eventually after many damaging clashes with the settlers which involved loss of life especially their young braves, that some necessary pragmatic co-operation had to be agreed with their new neighbours on some occasions, notably when war broke out between the French and British, and then later between the British and American Revolutionary forces.

Wiser councils in the tribal factions realised that gains could be made with a more co-operative relationship, even if this co-operation was to be abused by some of the white settlers who viewed the natives as heathen savages to be exploited or even killed. Many settlers indeed organised themselves, especially when there was no protective military presence in the territory, into bands of vigilantes who killed any natives they could find. There was a steely determination to stake their claim and brook no opposition. Only a few brave, far-sighted pioneers, attempted to come to any genuine agreements with the various tribes as Daniel Boone had years before. He was the exception, others included Davey Crockett and Simon Kenton from Kentucky, who was a friend of Boone, who fought against the Indians, though Kenton later was taken in by the Shawnee tribe and shown a degree of respect due his bravery and endurance.

Through this vast wilderness, early pioneers such as the great, respected Daniel Boone had forged a route through it for settlers to follow on their journey west. This was the Wilderness Road, though it was little more than a trail just wide enough for a wagon to pass. It was perfect ambush territory for the likes of the Harpes and other brigands to fall upon unsuspecting travellers and settlers who usually lacked the instinct and wherewithal to defend themselves effectively. Many of these bands of travellers were families seeking a better life, religious groups seeking to preach, convert and bring the word of the Lord to these heathen natives as they considered them. These groups were mostly ill-equipped to deal with ruthless, murdering bandits, whether Indians or such outlaws as the Harpe brothers. In the many valleys, ravines, riverbanks and even left in the open, there could often be seen the poignant remains of wagons, broken and burnt, dead horses and even corpses usually having being stripped and eaten by buzzards, vultures and other larger scavengers which naturally included bears, bobcats, coyotes and wolves.

Most of the native Indian tribes had fought for either the British or French forces as they struggled for ascendency, and then either or both the British or American forces during the War of Independence sometimes changing sides if it was advantageous to do so. What care had they for either of these foreign forces British or French or American for that matter? All were interlopers who had generally wreaked havoc and destruction in a short period of time on their sacred way of life.

Surprisingly Micajah and Wiley had actually lived with the Chickamaugas at their settlement at Nickajack around 1794 before they kidnapped the women, Maria Davidson being the first, then others who became their followers and "wives". They participated in Indian raids and even massacres during this time. Therefore murder and pillage was not something new to them, indeed they remained generally on good terms with the renegade Indians who viewed the Harpes as outsiders like themselves, bent on revenge and destruction.

Ill-fitting but likely allies. The chaos and killing wrought by the Harpes was something that many of the Indian natives viewed as a good service which they themselves would engage in. The more, the better, if it rids the territory of this white scourge. It was in this ferment of violence, exploration, great optimism, death, cruelty and occasionally extraordinary examples of mercy and courage, that Betsy Roberts, along with the Harpe brothers and their other women, existed. They were not an exclusive band of men and women in the territory by any means, but their actions created something unique.

CHAPTER 11

A few days later after resting up in their new makeshift home, which was now a cave, one of many around this part of the country which gave at least some modicum of cover and some protection, they laid up for a while. They had travelled along the nearby trails, including the Wilderness Road, for several more days making camp along the way in clearings off the beaten track. Betsy had now more and more taken control of Susan and Sarah, telling them both that Wiley and herself were together, as married, thus sowing seeds of fear into their dulled minds. This was a somewhat exaggeration of the situation to say the least.

Later after they had taken something to eat and sat together, Susan turned to Sarah and muttered grimly.

"This bitch thinks she has the right now to tell us what to do."

Sarah nodded sadly.

The next two days saw a kind of truce brought on by the need to rest and recuperate, only the restless Micajah wondered off to search for prey and set traps, both which brought some fresh meat. Wiley focused on checking their considerable collection of weaponry; cleaning, sharpening and maintaining the effectiveness of these items so that their deadly effectiveness would be ready on hand to use at any given moment. There was no second chance in most situations whether against their human prey who they wanted to rob, or defending themselves against a posse out to get them or the vigilantes hell bent on killing them. Betsy watched, fascinated as Wiley went about his tasks but she had to be on her mettle when he took to taking his pleasure with her, something she was able to manage to some extent since Wiley, thankfully for her, was less brutal, even possessing less libido or so it seemed.

Susan and Sarah became less fortunate as Micajah, more impulsive carnally, would simply grab one of two women and without any restraint force himself on them, the only solace was that it was a quick procedure.

The whole family as well as two dogs who had attached themselves to the group, left the sanctuary of the cave after two days, with the Harpes wishing to keep on the move. After a day's trek through forest and across brooks, they eventually came across an abandoned shack, another not uncommon ruin left by either settlers going on their way west, or outlaws using it as a base for their activities pretty much as the Harpes had been doing. There were other brigands operating in the territory as well as the Harpes, but none had the appalling notoriety of these two fearsome men.

"We'll stop here for a while Micajah while I figure out what to do and where to go." said Wiley.

"For a few days maybe." replied Micajah, leering at the three women, with the usual thoughts on his mind.

Sitting down in the cabin, Betsy moved closer to Wiley for safety.

Ignoring her on this occasion, Wiley got up quickly and instructed the three women to clear the shack which was in a bad state with the remains of one or two dead animals and some rubbish and other detritus left behind. They then gathered firewood and started preparing food. A deer had been previously shot by Micajah whilst on the trail, an opportunist incident which Micajah took full advantage of, creeping up on the creature and taking it by surprise. It was prepared and readied for cooking. His skills in this respect were second to none having learned it during the War and before, as they both used whatever means to survive. Living with the Chickamauga Cherokee Native Indians for several years had taught them much, especially hunting and survival skills.

Micajah was indeed the better shot of the two as Wiley was the better at using a knife. It was he who skinned and gutted the deer expertly and efficiently. No meat was wasted since they knew not when another opportunity for a kill would occur.

Soon after, to Betsy's surprise after they had eaten, the two Harpes started talking as normal folks would in a normal situation. They began reminiscing about their past, both had filled and lit their pipes and were sat smoking with undeniable pleasure.

She could not believe what she was hearing and concentrated carefully on what they said, while at the same time appearing not to be noticing this discourse, sitting in the shadows and making sure they could not be aware that she was eavesdropping on them. If caught she knew it would spell danger!

They spoke of a time when they fought for the British in the Revolutionary War and how, under the command of the infamous Lieutenant Colonel Banastre Tarleton, or "Bloody Ban" as he was known, due to his reputation as a bloodthirsty soldier and commander, who showed no mercy or compassion for any of the American Patriot enemy nor indeed any of their civilian sympathisers. He was known often to take no prisoners, killing them instead and burning homes down even with the families of men, women and children in them, if they showed any semblance of resistance.

"Do you remember that group of dirty Yankee prisoners that Bloody Ban asked us to dispatch Micajah?" Wiley asked.

"We tied them up real tight first" he continued.

"You'd cleaved four heads before even they knew what was going on." laughed Wiley looking at Micajah.

"Aye but the other eleven knew what was going on and knew what was a comin'."

Micajah growled in amusement, a rare smile crossed his lips.

"The look on their miserable faces when they saw your axe!"

Wiley was now laughing out loud.

"Please sir I've got a wife and three children." mimicked Wiley, "...well they're orphans and widows now says you...haha!"

"You were quick with the knife Wiley, five of them quick as lightening!" said Micajah.

"Bloody Ban shouting I told you to dispatch them not butcher them boys!'

"And you saying 'one was as good as another Sir'."

"Yes I must agree with you Harpe" Ban said "...now finish up and join the rest of the men as we are breaking camp, and off he rode on his fine black stallion."

The mood then changed to one of poignancy as they both thought back to a time before the War. Betsy observed from her position, listening intently.

"Aye but the one thing I regret not doing was killin' Old Baldwin." Micajah nodded agreement..

Micajah turned to Wiley and bitterly said.

"You have no idea how many times I took your turn Wiley!"

He spat out vigorously a stream of tobacco.

"You never told me." Wiley answered in some shock.

"Why would I? The way he treated everything on his plantation, from niggers to pigs, we should have left him sooner."

Micajah went on.

"If we'd known them natives treated us so well we could have gone to them first. I liked living with them Wiley."

Micajah hung his head.

"Me too." Wiley replied.

"Tis too late now brother."

"Aye."

Wiley agreed sadly thinking he had some guilt or brotherly responsibilityto admit.

The two of them recounted other memories from their past which occasionally caused amusement but more often than not bitterness, sadness and hatred especially of the "Yankee scum" who had driven them out of one place after another, viewing them both as traitors and the murder of their parents. It was this resentment that caused the brutal murdering and banditry that they turned to, more than anything else. That combined of course with actually witnessing both their parents being hanged, especially at such a young age.

Upon hearing these tales of bloodshed and hatred, Betsy shuddered and thought to herself.

"God, they are madmen!"

When the talking was over between Wiley and Micajah, Micajah slumped between Susan and Sarah but soon fell asleep much to the relief of both women. Wiley lay down beside Betsy then turned to her saying quietly.

"Did ye hear any of that lass. Best if ye did not."

Betsy feigned drowsiness, shook her head suggesting to him that she had heard nothing, but as Wiley took to sleeping she thought further, considering her options but also shedding a tear when thinking back to that terrible day when the two monsters appeared destroying everything she had cherished, most of all of course her dear Ma and Pa. She found it difficult to restrain her despair but also her hatred of the two villains as she lay there by the side of one of the two perpetrators, but Betsy was made of strong stuff and before long she had recovered her confidence.

This was the moment more than any other that she now decided she would survive no matter what the cost would be.

Old Baldwin

CHAPTER 12

We must now return to the events after the death of Wiley and Micajah Harpe's parents, William and Elsie, who were hanged as well as events thereafter to some extent. Their experience with 'Old Baldwin', their uncle, will hopefully enlighten the reader regarding the subsequent behaviour of the two outlaws. It was a defining, experience, one which scarred them both.

***

After witnessing the horror of their parent's execution at the hands of a mob of revengeful local Patriots, the two brothers made their way to their uncle's place some eighteen miles away. They walked along forest trails which they had become familiar with since an occasional visit occurred with their parents, who with some reluctance went to see their father's cousin, one John Baldwin or 'Old Baldwin' as he became known.

When they arrived at Old Baldwin's cabin which was a rundown wooden place, Wiley knocked on the door, frightened and trembling since John Baldwin had a reputation for cruelty and was someone who both boys were reluctant to seek help from. Unfortunately their choices were limited with no-one else to turn to at this time so when Old Baldwin appeared their reception was one of cursory greeting.

"What dee ye want?" he shouted in his still evident Scottish accent.

Wiley told him what had happened expecting at least some sympathy and pleaded with him to let them both stay with hin as they had nowhere else to go.

"Damned fools, serve 'em right, Willy was always a fool!" he scowled... "he shoulda' stayed wi' me after the war. Nay married that dumb bitch!"

Wiley said nothing, Micajah at this time was a subdued lad who let his elder brother do the talking.

"Well get in, ye can make yerselves useful, ye scallies!"

He then pushed the two boys inside giving them both a kick on their way.

John Baldwin was a skinny, slightly stooped, ugly creature when the boys met him but also before then it has to be said, he had never been blessed with good looks that was for sure. Most of his teeth were missing except for a couple that remained, plus a few stumps, his head was balding with what hair he had left, it was greasy, grey and usually matted. He had come to America with his cousin William Harper on a British merchant ship, looking, like so many others for a better life, but also it must be said to flee the attentions of the law, who had been looking for them due to allegations made against them by some neighbours who had accused them of the theft of livestock primarily. Warrants had been issued for their arrest. Escape was therefore a necessity if they were to avoid execution by hanging, the penalty for such offences at that time.

Both men were of similar age but William, a little younger and more presentable, met and married a local girl in what is now Ashville, North Carolina, named Elsie. The two prospered and as we have seen produced the two Harpe boys. John left aggrieved at being abandoned, as he saw it, and began his career of rustling, rearing hogs and abusing anyone smaller or younger than him whenever he got the opportunity.

Both cousins were loyal to the British cause and being Calvinists were antagonistic towards French as well as local patriots who were their more numerous neighbours. Their loyalties were often tested and where William Harper was more diplomatic in dealing with any trouble, John often got himself into difficulties on more than one occasion.

It was into the home of John Baldwin that the two young brothers, who were not even in their teens, found themselves. So began a period of the most appalling abuse, cruelty and exploitation of them both as Old Baldwin was often drunk from liquor he brewed himself and let loose violent assaults, both sexual as well brutal attcks often wounding the boys. It was, however, Micajah who bore the brunt of these assaults. Being less clever than Wiley, he was unable to extricate himself from Old Baldwin's attentions and more often than not exacerbated an already dangerous situation by mumbling, or staring dumbly at his perpetrator. This made the situation worse and Old Baldwin would fly into a rage as he assumed Micajah was exhibiting defiance towards him. Wiley on the other hand, as the more articulate and devious of the two boys, was usually able to deflect the drunkard's attentions or talk him out of an assault, though not always, as he too was often beaten, more often than not with Micajah.

The abuse by their 'uncle' extended to forcing the two boys to do all the dirty, unpleasant jobs that had to be done at his grimy cabin. These included cleaning out the pig sties, an especially disgusting job, cooking, whatever Old Baldwin had stole or grown in his vegetable patch, mostly potatoes, washing clothes, cutting wood, clearing out the latrine then digging a new one as well as anything else Baldwin demanded they do. He forced them to slaughter hogs which was something they were familiar with doing anyway, but to make the task mor unpleasant he would torture the poor bound beasts before Wiley slit their throats, poking his own knife into their eyes to hear their squeals. He laughed dementedly whilst doing this, then after the hog was mercifully dead the two boys then had to butcher it in a simple shed outside, the odour there almost as bad as the latrine hut.

The time of the day they both dreaded most was in the evening as their uncle became progressively more inebriated casting his lewd attentions at the two boys. He had never married not unsurprisingly, but his inclinations became progressively more degenerate as time went on, even extending to occasional copulations with the hogs, even these unfortunate creatures seemed to know what was about to happen and seemed to avoid his attentions as much as dumb beasts can. Wiley would endeavour to make himself scarce if he could but Micajah, lacking the innate intelligence of his elder brother, merely sat in the most depressed, abject manner. It was then that Old Baldwin would turn his attentions to the boy, grabbing him and then forcing Micajah to do what anyone of either sex would wish to avoid if they could. This sexual abuse would usually be followed by a beating which involved both boys (there was only so much Wiley could do to escape attention as well) with both boys being kicked into their corner of the cabin where they slept or simply shivered in terror. It is hard to imagine a more dreadful situation for two such vulnerable young boys to endure.

But endure they did until one day Wiley said to Micajah.

"I can't take this any more brother, we must kill this

bastard, anythin' is better than this."

Micajah who had recently been on the end of a particularly brutal assault nodded in agreement and said.

"Aye, cannae tak' more o' this Wiley."

Wiley then made plans to rid themselves of this beast, 'uncle' or no.

The plan was simple; they would wait until Old Baldwin was well and truly drunk, then with an axe, one that Micajah had kept for himself recently, hiding it under their straw bed, finish off the beast.

The plan was initiated in the evening as John Baldwin downed his home made brew, luckily he swiftly became drowsy with Wiley even taunting him over his inability to… "tak' his hooch" to which Baldwin lurched forward attempting to grab Wiley, but as he did he stumbled and fell. With this Micajah took his opportunity by bringing down with immense force, the axe he had ready which he now thrust right into his back. Baldwin fell heavily to the floor groaning in agony, which then enabled Wiley to finish off the brute with his knife, slitting Old Baldwin's throat.

The boys stood there for a while looking at the motionless body of their uncle, Micajah shaking with hatred, Wiley relieved to be rid of this diabolical monster for good. They slept in some peace for the first time in so long and next morning gathered together what things they could, and escaped, not before setting fire to the cabin with Old Baldwin's body left as it was from the night before. It was many weeks before a neighbouring farmer discovered the remains of him which were skeletal by then, but took little notice, not caring to report the incident. No-one mourned the passing of John Baldwin.

The two brothers headed for a nearby encampment of Chickamauga native Indians near Nickajack, who they had become acquainted with through their uncle Baldwin who sometimes traded with them. Baldwin, like the Indians, also shared their hatred of the local settlers and through this empathy, gave the boys the only favour he was able to, indirectly of course. Thankfully the Chackamauga's headed by their chief Dragging Canoe, took them in and soon they joined their raiding parties, hunting expeditions, numerous murders of men, women and children, all of which became their first source of pleasure for many years. The Indians taught them much and became valuable allies to the two Harpes.

CHAPTER 13

Some months later as Betsy, in a relatively short time, became more and more hardened and had become used to the Harpes modus operandi which involved getting her to act as bait due to her natural good looks, ("she could charm the coat off a coyote Micajah!" Wiley proudly boasted), luring travellers, especially lone travellers, into the hands of the two Harpes, mainly Micajah initially. It was he who finished them off with ruthless efficiency normally involving his tomahawk, while she acted out her then usual ploy of dissembling the lost, frightened maiden seeking succour. The trepidation and horror she initially felt at being forced to do this work as with any unpleasant task, gradually became something quite routine and unremarkable.

This process of dehumanisation has been witnessed with people for many years in many extraordinary situations. It is easy to judge and condemn such people whether they be truly evil, or unwilling tools but no-one really knows exactly how one would react in such extreme circumstances. 'There but for the grace of God...' Betsy's options were limited in the extreme and she had no time to contemplate the consequences of this work, she just got on with it as a matter of survival with considerable tenacity. Feelings of remorse for what she had been involved with would have to wait, if they would ever concern her that is.

On a dull day in the Fall of 1798 on this particular occasion Betsy, as arranged by the Harpe brothers, appeared by the side of the road disguised as a distressed lone female, her hands covering her face, she looked the picture of vulnerability. After a short period of time she was seen by a lone traveller on horseback coming steadily towards her, with a mule trailing behind him carrying some bags of goods.

The man was of rough appearance as was usual, though dressed well with tricorn hat, he was of heavy build and bearded. He was a Virginian named Stephen Langford who had previously, days before, foolishly boasted of his wealth to many others in an inn where he stayed the night. The interested listeners included the Harpe brothers, who happened to be at this particular inn known then as Pharris' Inn near Crab Orchard, Kentucky, run by a John Pharris and his mean, shrewish wife, Jane Pharris.

The two of them kept what was much like a rowdy or bawdy inn regularly populated by a collection of drifters, travellers, brigands, loose women and other odd characters. Fights often broke out there leading occasionally to death, as one customer took offence or imagined some slight from another. It did not take much for violence of this sort to erupt which Pharris and his wife would then deal brutally with in such a situation. It usually involved beating either man mercilessly with cudgel or even musket, or ejecting them, much to the amusement of the other drunken customers, the women especially taking delight at this foolishness. A rough moonshine and other spirits were on sale there along with ale brewed by the landlord which had the consequence of rendering many of the customers pretty senseless within a short period of time. Sensibly, as a deterrent, John Pharris had near to him at all times his trusty pistols, cudgel, and a wife not averse to dealing out violence even to him if he so much as looked at one of the women in the inn!

Jane Pharris trucked no nonsense as far as her husband

was concerned, she was at least as proficient with pistols, cudgel and anything else she could get her hands on or she would make do with her fists which could deal out as much punishment as could any man, as many found out to their cost. On several occasions she fired warning shots when things were getting out of hand. It always did the trick, together with her fearsome voice which boomed across the inn.

"I'll kill you scum, damn y'all!!" she bellowed furiously a sound which reverberated throughout the confines of the inn.

Stephen Langford in this environment became very drunk on the local brewed moonshine which he took a liking to, encouraged by Pharris's wife who made one of the serving girls pay him attention. He ill-advisedly let it be known to the men, mostly locals that night, that he was a man of wealth and substance who could buy any woman he felt inclined to. He even flashed his thick, bulging leather wallet as his tongue and behaviour became more loose. It did not take long before Langford's loud boasting gained the attention of the Harpe brothers, which then encouraged Wiley to question the man with some fake bonhomie buying him another drink and more, and finding out where he was heading to, which he soon discovered from the foolish Langford.

"I'm heading West friend and woe betide anyone who tries to get in my way!" Langford exclaimed, becoming more unsteady as he lolled around in his chair, his head leaning toward Wiley as if he were informing him of some great secret information. Soon after he became so drunk that he started falling around and talking more incoherently, Langford then with the "help" of Wiley, eventually took a room at the inn which Jane Pharris arranged for him.

"Let him sleep it off, he'll be fine come mornin'" she promised Wiley who pretended some concern for his new acquaintance.

Langford was shown to his room, a modest affair with chamber pot, bowl of water and creaky bed for comfort. He slept deeply as Jane predicted and in the morning, despite a thick head, after taking some breakfast and coffee, he set off with no memory of the preceeding night's events or of Wiley and Micajah Harpe. He was unaware that his route was known and his fate sealed.

One of the bags he carried contained silver coin which Wiley knew from his talk with Langford was on him. This proved too much of a temptation for the brothers to miss out on, Micajah needed no encouragement to play his part in the robbery and Betsy was told what to do, though she was fully cognisant of what her role was in this criminal action. The Harpes followed Langford from a distance as he left the inn, they had instructed Betsy where to lie in wait. She was also promised a reward if she played her part correctly. Betsy by this time cared little of the dreadful fates of these men saying to Wiley.

"They're stupid and I've no concern for them."

This was true now, she exhibited little emotion or concern for what she was about to do.

Wiley grinned and Micajah merely told her to get moving.

"Git!" he growled.

The two brothers began their task.

***

As planned out on the Wilderness Road, Betsy, stood alone, appearing distressed, she caught the eye of Langford, and looking surprised at first he glanced around to make sure he wasn't being seen, then dismounted by the trail, and walked over to her. He had decided to see what this attractive girl was up to and despite a thick head, he had enough sense about him to take any free pleasure on offer.

"Now missy what the Hell you doing here, what's happened to you girl?" he enquired.

Looking closely at Betsy he soon realised that this was, to all appearances, an attractive vulnerable woman and why not take advantage and have his pleasure? If she resisted then his knife would deal with the situation and he would dispose of her in the forest where wild animals would leave no trace of the girl.

"I'm lost Sir can you help me?" Betsy replied appearing innocent and looking at the man and beginning to guess that he had bad intentions.

Quickly he grabbed her around the throat and pushed her on to the raised grassy roadside ground feverishly pulling up her skirts in the process.

"Get off me you bastard!!" Betsy instinctively yelled, spat at him and scratched out at his face.

Just then as a now disconcerted Langford was about to strike her, a sharp pain in his ribs jolted him, followed by several more stabs into his ample body.

Betsy had managed to locate her knife with her other free hand and with extraordinary speed, determination and without a second's hesitation, stabbed Langford with all her force.

He limply fell away towards the ground which was then followed by a kick from the rising Betsy.

Wiley ran to them from behind the dense forest trees,

finished off the man with his knife, stabbing him in the throat, as Micajah also appeared, quickly burying his tomahawk into his back, the tomahawk lodged there.

Langford lay dead as Betsy kicked him again with full force into his head. He now looked a sorry sight as he lay on the road his bloody head back and side revealing the force of stab wounds and kicks.

"He deserved his fate." thought Betsy as she looked on at this wretched sight, Langford who had desired to take his pleasure on a vulnerable girl, had now paid the ultimate price!

Wiley who was chewing some tobacco by now, spat out a stream of this dire black liquid on to the corpse contemptuously saying.

"Another fool gits his."

Micajah pulled the body away down the side of the road and proceeded to strip away the coat and shirt that Langford was wearing. He then gutted him with an efficiency quite remarkable but borne of endless practice initially from the hogs on the farm, then eventually humans. Rocks were collected from the adjacent riverbank, then expertly pushed into the cavity of the body to weigh it down. After this procedure Micajah then simply threw the body down into the river below.

The three of them stood together and watched as Langford's body sank mournfully to the bottom of the slowly moving Dix River.

While this was being done Betsy turned to Wiley who looked at her then somewhat reluctantly muttered.

"Guess I owe you some gratitude for helping me kill that pig when you did. Though I would have done it all by myself."

He spat contemptuously toward the river.

Betsy pulled out the bloodstained, small, sharp knife which she had kept on her person and smiled.

"After all maybe I didn't need your help Wiley."

"Just do your Goddamned job, you hear." Wiley retorted angrily.

He looked at the knife and then at Betsy, and stroking his beard grinned at her with a feeling of some little admiration for this unusual young woman. Composing himself he said with some irritation and awareness that maybe Betsy was something a bit special. Not like other subservient women. It made her attractiveness all the more alluring to Wiley who had never met a girl like this before. Little did he know that a lot more was to come. Wiley turned away now and made his way down the valley side to where Micajah was.

"We don't want to leave any traces Micajah, this critter was known by many round here."

"He won't be tellin' anyone nuthin' now Wiley." Micajah muttered.

They both climbed back up, picked up the bags belonging to Langford, took hold of his horse and mule and motioned to Betsy to follow them.

"Let's get back to the cabin and show the other two bitches what we got." Wiley grinned.

Betsy simply nodded and followed.

***

Langford's body was found a week later by the side of the

Dix River. It was a truly terrible sight which shocked even the hardened men of those times, used as they were, to witnessing death in all its forms. News spread around the whole territory of this horrific murder bringing renewed fear as many suspected the Terrible Harpes of being responsible. A reward was put out offering three hundred dollars for the capture of the two Harpes, dead or alive, and this news filtered through to them.

"Three hundred dollars Micajah, t'aint enough, we need to do more to make it more, as befittin' the two most fearin' outlaws. That's what I say brother!" Wiley exclaimed.

And so as if to justify the price offered, Micajah and Wiley Harpe determined to pursue their work with renewed gusto.

CHAPTER 14

The Harpe 'family' returned to their latest hideout which was another cabin originally, the home of a man named John Graves from Clinton County, Kentucky, who they had brutally murdered along with his young son just a few days before. Their bodies had simply been thrown into the woods by the Harpes and left for the buzzards and other wild creatures to finish off. Micajah, Wiley and Betsy entered the cabin and sat themselves down.

Susan, Sarah with their infants, born recently to the evil Harpes, followed, they were by now totally brutalised and subservient to the extent that Betsy became growingly contemptuous of them both. She still wondered if Susan was her sister but had dismissed the idea and refrained from speaking to her about this.

Micajah shouted.

"Get some coffee made Susan!"

Susan immediately set about this without any hesitation, knowing full well the consequences of delay. Micajah threw the bags taken from the wretched Langford down on to the floor, motioning to Susan.

"There's some food in the bags we brought, so you and Sarah take it out and get cooking for we're alla' hungry."

Micajah gestured aggressively to the two women. Sarah duly obliged and pretty soon coffee was made and some food courtesy of Langford was cooking on the iron stove heated by

71

sticks of wood collected on their journey before they arrived at the cabin. The food consisted of mostly beans, a regular staple diet as well as a few scraps of meat which Micajah had retained in his saddlebag. The two men then sat down next to each other, commenced smoking their pipes with some of the stolen tobacco and after a while ate the meal Sarah and Susan had prepared. Betsy sat alone, after a while all five had eaten, Micajah's child began crying with hunger.

"Shut him up!" Micajah yelled.

"Ain't so easy Micajah, he's hungry and ailin' for somethin'." Susan replied.

"I said shut him up woman!!"

Micajah reared up threateningly, his immense form casting a shadow over the women. At this Susan went outside and after a while returned with the poor child sleeping in her arms. How she managed this stilling of the infant time after time no-one was certain nor for that matter really cared, least of all Micajah.

Wiley and Micajah grabbed Langford's bags and took them outside with the intention of taking a good look at the contents which included much money, silver and other items of value, they then hid them somewhere near the cabin that only they knew. Betsy though had begun to realise that this and other stashes were where considerable amounts of money, valuables and such like were being hidden for future use. She had begun to make a mental note of every location which the Harpes appeared to hide their loot. As a young woman in her prime, her memory was sharp, as was her quick wittedness and reactions which left the other two women far behind. Betsy had also gained the protection of Wiley who increasingly wanted Betsy for himself, he had no intention of sharing her as they did with the other women they had kidnapped over the years.

She cultivated this bizarre relationship to her advantage and once again that night Micajah contented himself with the company of Susan and Sarah, who whilst pleasing the brute had also to tend to their babies, one of which was definitely Micajah's due to his black curly hair, the other, a girl, was not so easily identifiable as either of the two brothers due to her having brownish/reddish hair. Wiley though reckoned it was his but had no interest in claiming parentage.

**

Next day the three women were together in the cabin while Wiley and Micajah went out hunting, looking for a deer or wild boar hopefully which would provide at least for a few days good food. Venison or pork were particular favourites with the Harpe brothers and Sarah being the best cook was well able to make a tasty stew. It was a rare event when Micajah actually made a grudging compliment to Sarah, but it was frequently followed by a violent rebuke to Susan and Betsy, who rarely cooked in actuality, as to their 'uselessness'. They returned this time however with a wild boar which Micajah had shot and then finished off by Wiley with his trusty sharp knife. The creature was tied to a stave carried by them both over their shoulders, with blood still dripping from it's neck and belly. Micajah had gutted and scrubbed the beast so it was almost ready for cooking. Every part of the boar could be eaten, including the head and trotters which made this animal a very welcome catch.

Later after eating, and after a spell of muted conversation, Betsy stared at Susan and began to wonder again if this was in fact her long lost sister. Susan merely tended to her sleeping baby, not making eye contact with her. She had had another child by Micajah a year ago but lost it through an unknown illness which made her determined to keep this one safe from the violent attentions of him. As Betsy mused she tried hard to remember what Susan was like before she disappeared and if there was anything especially memorable she could recall or any particular incident involving her that stuck out. Her main memories were that Susan and she did not really get on and Susan even bullied Betsy without any warning. Susan, she remembered, had a temper which she used against her sometimes in a violent and spiteful way as sisters were prone to be quite often. Such thoughts and recollections inevitably diminished the urge to speak with her and reconnect. Susan was a big raw boned woman as she appeared now, and even as a girl she recollected, she was not someone to argue with, so Betsy avoided conversation as much as she could.

Despite this later in the afternoon the following day the two women were forced to prepare some more victuals together as Susan's son was sleeping. This was for Sarah to do primarily, thankfully she was already busy preparing to cook the meal when the Harpes eventually returned again.

Betsy looked at Susan and caught her eye and suddenly said.

"It's you ain't it Susan, you remember me don't you? It's your younger sister Betsy Roberts, same surname as you."

Susan froze briefly, barely looked at her then replied.

"I don't know. All I know is that I was taken by Cutter and no-one came after me you hear!" she said sternly.

"Good Lord Susan it is you." Betsy's eyes lit up.

"What does it matter now bitch?" Susan spat out.

This angry comment hurt Betsy but she brushed it off not entirely successfully. She nevertheless continued.

"Ma and Pa went looking for you Susan, you know, they even got a posse with neighbours to go after you. Pa spent days and weeks trying to find you risking his life out in the wild and often as not on his own. You know, it wasn't easy to get other folk to help back then"

Betsy looked intently at Susan. Susan after a short while replied with some discomfort.

"I said it don't matter now Betsy, so shut up about it. Pa never liked me much so I doubt that he spent too much time goin' after me. Anyway I belong to Micajah now as his wife and if I were you I wouldn't say anything about this you hear." Susan glared at her.

"Micajah is just as likely to give you a beatin' or worse if you go saying things like that you dumb wench." Susan continued.

She turned away from Betsy in irritation thus making further talk unwise and impractical.

Betsy got up and went outside to collect some wood for the fire. She mused about what she and Susan had said and resolved not to bring up the subject again. The response to her by Susan with its dismissive contempt made her now believed that Susan was in reality no longer her sister as such, and she even felt some contempt for her. The fact is that they never got on and if she was Micajah's wife there was no point in further discourse on the matter. Betsy would seek to look after herself and use every means and tactic to preserve herself and to Hell with the other two women, what did she care if they survived or not?

According to Betsy's thinking even Sarah was a dumb bitch with little to commend herself, she was little more than a slave who was shared between the two men in every way imaginable. There was no way Betsy Roberts was going to go the same way, she was going to get through this come what may.

At this point a sudden hardening of Betsy's heart occurred which was now becoming permanent, as if some concrete wall had now set hard enclosing it from those feelings which would undermine her resolve. She was always a tough girl well able to look after herself, and in this wilderness and hard life she had become quite a resourceful woman. Not so unusual at this time with so much danger around every corner. Nothing much worried her...except of course the two Harpes, but even there she started to believe and figure that she would be able to outwit these two monsters. Men are men and Betsy reckoned she could get the better of either Wiley or Micajah in some way or other. She knew though that she had to tread very carefully especially with Big Harpe who was liable at any time to go into a violent rage, and Wiley too who could be sly and sadistic whenever and wherever the mood took him. There was rarely any time when Betsy could feel completely safe from his attentions.

The one thing Betsy had cultivated cleverly was to keep on Wiley's good side even providing him with sexual services, but also appealing to what goodness there was in him however meagre it was. She had witnessed that Wiley also had a level of control over Micajah which had got her out of tricky situations more than once. She had as yet been able to avoid Micajah's advances and she wanted to keep it that way. There is little doubt that Wiley was, as we have seen, no way he was going to share this fascinating and attractive young women with his brother.

Susan at this time became pregnant again and later on she suddenly turned to Sarah, speaking secretively, she motioned her toward her saying.

"I never would have stayed with Micajah but I was taken by force you know."

Sarah replied, a little confused.

"We both were but it's too late now we just gotta make the best of our situation and maybe try to get away if the opportunity presents itself Susan. I don't know how though."

Betsy overhearing this comment laughed so that both women could hear her and blurted out contemptuously.

"You can dream if you want but I reckon we'll be with these two for a long time yet."

Sarah and Susan both turned to Betsy and Susan with irritation, replied to her sternly.

"Why don't you get out of here if you can, I won't miss yer moanin' for one."

Betsy looked contemptuously at her and scoffed.

"I ain't as dumb as you, you'll see if I ain't." and she looked away.

Susan got up suddenly and went for Betsy with the intention of striking her but Sarah grabbed her arm saying.

"Now steady on Susan we got to stick together and fightin' among ourselves won't do us any good that's for sure."

Turning to Betsy she said with rare feeling.

"You Betsy, why don't you do something useful instead of provoking Susan here?"

"Oh sure I'll get on." Betsy muttered.

At that point the two Harpes suddenly came in and Wiley, noticing some discord amongst the three women, shouted.

"You damned women shut up before I tie all three of you up and roast ye!"

Micajah then pulled out his knife and pointed it at them threateningly.

"I'll do the three of you if you don't stop squabbling, ya hear!"

Susan and Sarah sensibly turned away and got on with their work while Betsy seated herself and smiled. She was unworried at this stage about Micajah since she had noticed Wiley watching him for any violent response toward her, and undoubtedly he would have intervened to prevent him harming Betsy...though maybe not the other two, who the brothers viewed to some extent as expendable.

Such was the situation in this dysfunctional 'family'.

CHAPTER 15

Two weeks later a traveller called Jakob Bekker was making his way along the Wilderness Road with his wife and son in a wagon with one horse tied to it. The sun was shining that day and the family were looking forward to starting a new life out West. They were second generation of Dutch immigrants who had travelled across the Atlantic Ocean on one of the many trading ships of the period. Suddenly they pulled up as Bekker felt the need to answer a call of nature. He jumped down from the wagon and going to the edge of the road, he noticed down in the valley by the river on the gravelly side, what appeared to be some human remains. Bekker stared in some surprise at this sight and made his way down the valley side to investigate until he got up close to what now became clear was the skeletal remains of some unfortunate person, just a few bits of cloth and rocks strewn by what was his stomach.

"Hell!" he called out in shock and rushed up the side of the valley back to his wagon.

"There's someone's body down there Emily, we need to get to Stanford and tell Captain Ballenger."

"Are you sure Jakob?" Emily replied.

"As sure as I'm Jakob Bekker." he said confidently.

Bekker set off to the small settlement which was within the stockade of Stanford where a certain Captain Joseph Ballenger was stationed. They had intended to lay up for the night anyway and Ballenger was the only law, or what passed for law, in these parts.

It took around four hours of travelling to get to Stanford, turning back along the trail from whence they had made their way, and on arrival Bekker made straight for the Captain who fortunately was in his office, to report his grisly find.

After telling Ballenger, (a man who was now in his fifties, grown stout with brownish hair and his beard showing flecks of grey in it, a veteran of the War of Independence who still wore his uniform proudly), where and what he had seen, the Captain immediately determined to investigate and then suddenly turned to Bekker saying.

"I've a feeling I know who is responsible for this, in fact I'm damn sure I know who it is."

"Who do you reckon?" Bekker replied.

"Those evil scum the Harpes and their Godforsaken women. Soon as it's light tomorrow I'll get a posse together and get after them. I heard just yesterday that they were now staying near Carpenter's Station so it shouldn't be too hard to find them."

Ballenger continued, becoming excited at the prospect of finally capturing the evil villains and their women. He also remembered that there was a three hundred dollar reward attached to their capture, dead or alive. He cared little which it would be. He continued looking at Bekker with a determination to succeed.

"These vermin have been robbing and murdering poor folk for some time, stripping the bodies and even fillin' their guts with rocks to weigh them down in the river, can you believe?!"

Ballenger scratched his head and carried on.

"It's high time they were dealt with but even in this country we need proof, well damn it I think we have enough to hang the lot of them!"

With that he advised Bekker, his wife and son to be careful and lay up for a day or two within the fort, until they captured the Harpes. Bekker gratefully agreed and Ballenger arranged for them to have lodgings for the night within the stockade.

***

Next morning after getting together a posse of around seven or eight men the Captain set off in pursuit, and it was not too long before reports came to him that a strange and menacing group, or family more accurately, of two men and three women had been seen by a cabin near Carpenter's Station as he had thought.

Ballenger dismounted ordering his men to do the same.

He instructed them to follow him on foot as he reckoned, given the information he had which he figured was reliable, that the Harpes and their brood were holed up at the Groves cabin. He had recently heard that he was missing, together with his son. This was not unusual in those parts but it made sense now that seemingly foul play was the cause of their disappearance.

As the posse got nearer they could see movement and hear voices especially the voice of Micajah who suddenly shouted something indecipherable.

"That's them." whispered the Captain to his posse and gestured for them to spread out and surround the cabin. All eight men felt a nervousness as they became aware that these two Harpes with their fearsome reputations were more

81

dangerous to deal with than any usual brigand or band of renegade Indians.

Muskets and pistols at the ready, on the order of Ballenger, they stormed the cabin bursting in by kicking open the door off it's rusty hinge. Taken totally by surprise Micajah and Wiley froze where they sat, as both men were unable to get to their weapons quickly enough, and without any choice, held up their hands.

Betsy broke away from the other two women who held on to their infants, appearing suddenly and ran over to the Captain.

"Thank the Lord we're saved." she cried, and fell to her knees dramatically before Captain Ballenger.

Wiley looked on askance.

Betsy was shaking, with tears running down her face and hands held out imploringly.

"Look further into the cabin at the rear and you'll see the other two women, We've been held captive for so long!"

She cried and somehow more tears streamed down her face.Looking angrily at the two Harpes, Ballenger shouted.

"You murderin' scum!"

Micajah merely scowled but Wiley with his hands in the air replied sarcastically.

"Now what gave you that idea Captain?"

Susan and Sarah appeared from the back of the cabin dishevelled and somewhat frightened, rather like caged animals who were now uncertain and unsure of what to do. The prospect of freedom had arrived but how to deal with this new situation was something they both were not able to comprehend.

Betsy though, unlike Susan and Sarah, then seized her opportunity saying confidently.

"Us women have been forced to do whatever these two evil fiends told us. You can't imagine sir."

Betsy looked at Ballenger with sad but slightly alluring eyes and the Captain's suspicions were soon replaced by sympathy and not a little attraction for this blond, blue eyed young woman.

"Bind these brigands but leave the women, I can't see them running very far with their babies. You come with us." he instructed the women… "but you would be unwise to try anything." he warned.

The posse seized the two Harpes and tied their hands, two men doing the job roughly on each Harpe while the others pointed their rifles threateningly at them both just in case of any resistance. None of the posse would need any encouragement to blow away these two killers.

"I am the Wolf and I will kill you all!!" screamed Micajah who suddenly reared up, desperate to attack them all.

"Shut that bastard up!" shouted the Captain.

Big Harpe was then gagged, clubbed with rifles, and violently kicked. It seemed to have no effect such was the hardness of his body, well used to brutality. Wiley on the other hand looked on with contemptuous hatred toward the posse men.

"Ye will regret this, I promise ye all." he said as he twisted his torso round to look at them all.

Betsy seeing this and smiling secretively to herself then motioned to the two other women to follow, and the party set off back to where their horses were tied, with Big and Little

Harpe the objects of some more rough treatment on route. Unlike Betsy, the other two women said very little but merely obeyed Ballenger's commands. He looked at them with some consternation, wondering what they had endured but at the same time his eyes and most of his thoughts were for Betsy. Like many men before and after he had fallen under the spell of this beautiful, bewitching girl who seemed to possess something that even he, an old experienced man, found difficult to completely resist.

They set off soon after and returned to the stockade with Micajah and Wiley linked together then mostly dragged by a rope along the trail all the way back. All the while they were the objects of curses and threats which merely caused Micajah to shout profanities at them, unafraid as he was of pain. He looked to all intents and purposes, like a wild animal frothing at the mouth.

"Yaargh I'll kill ye Yankee scum!!"

He shouted this and other expletives defiantly, growled and threatened more murder as well as revenge, which some of the posse, especially the younger men with families, believed could possibly happen.

Captain Ballenger

CHAPTER 16

On returning to Stanford, Captain Ballenger instructed that the Harpes be incarcerated in a makeshift jail, more accurately a wooden blockhouse with no natural light and merely straw mats to sleep on. Two buckets were left, one pail as the toilet, and the other with water in it. Two men were placed as guards outside with instructions to keep a close eye on them both. The two Harpes scowled, shouting occasional threats and abuse at the guards, Micajah even challenging the whole force to take him on.

"Yankee cowards!!" he raged then challenged... "any one of ye cowards to fight me, I'll kill ye an' eat ye over a spit haha!!"

Wiley laughed and instead of provoking further retribution thought about how they could escape and then later seek revenge. They were left to themselves in their cell from then on with only dry crusts of bread with maggots within, thrown in for them to eat, the slop bucket purposelessly kicked over at one point much to Micajah's further threats of violence. The sergeant in charge laughed and shouted.

"You are filth so filth you will have more of!"

The effect of this was largely wasted on the two Harpes who were well used to living in squalor and filth, Micajah even threw faeces at the sergeant when he appeared briefly at their cell door.

Two days later Captain Ballenger arranged for the party to

be removed to Danville some distance away, where a proper arraignment and trial could be arranged. He was unsure about what to do with the women especially Betsy, who had spoken of the murder of her parents and her kidnapping.

It did not seem right to Ballenger to punish her for the crimes of the Harpes. As for the other two women, Susan and Sarah who had their babies tucked away, they seemed so traumatised, indeed brutalised, and incapable of much useful communication that he became pretty much indifferent toward them. They were pitiful objects, dressed roughly, saying little which suggested a certain degree of complicity to his mind, it did little to endear themselves to him.

Ballenger noticed that Susan even seemed to have a certain loyalty toward the bigger man which caused some consternation and even amusement, Sarah too asked dumbly what was going to happen now and when would they be able to see their two "husbands".

"In Hell!" one of the posse shouted at her.

Sarah turned to Susan and the two women stared blankly.

Meanwhile Betsy explained to Captain Ballenger that both women were what she described as "wives" to the Harpes and had borne children, Susan had given birth to two, of which just one survived, and Sarah who also had two babies, one of which had sadly died probably due to Big Harpe's rough, intolerant treatment.

"Hard to believe that any man can behave in such a cruel way." Ballenger stated, stroking his beard in consternation as men tend to. This was a trait Betsy had noticed among the Harpes as well as her own father though not surprising as most men sported beards of every shape, length and size.

"You need to know that they have done some terrible things to many innocent people. I was even forced against my will to act as bait to lure poor people to their deaths."

Betsy whimpered, feigning distress but suggesting some genuine feeling of remorse and guilt. She had clung on to thoughts of her parents and how she could gain revenge for what had happened and now an opportunity had occurred which might bring her the freedom she desired, and even the chance of revenge on the two monsters now lying, incarcerated in a guarded cell.

She looked at the Captain with pitiful eyes, his resolve apparently weakened she discerned, he then moved toward her and patted her tenderly on her shoulder.

"Now don't you go blaming yourself child."

Betsy wiped her tears with her sleeve and nodded.

At this Captain Ballenger rose from his seat and went outside, soon after making arrangements for the entire group to be transported to Danville.

He was not going to take any chances. The Harpes would be bound up tightly and put into a secure wagon with an escort of six men to ensure that there would be no escapes. Their women would be placed in another wagon so that they would not have to endure any abuse or threats from the the two brothers. The court there could sort out the rest, he had done his duty.

CHAPTER 17

O n arrival at Fort Danville which in reality was little more than a slightly bigger than usual stockade, garrisoned by American Patriot soldiers under the command of a Colonel Walker, an older man, tall with white wispy hair and a fine moustache which he often twisted whilst in the act of contemplation. He was a veteran of the recent War of Independence, and so the Harpe family were handed over to him.

Walker had distinguished himself at the Battle of Cowpens in 1781 which the Harpes had participated in on the British side under the command of the Harpes' former commander Lieutenant Colonel Banastre Tarleton. Now, after the war, the major was seeing out his days as commander of this frontier fort. A curmudgeonly old man he was, but his sense of rightness and humanity were not in doubt, qualities all people in the territory recognised in their dealings with him. His steady leadership, diplomacy and tact had helped things to quieten down in recent times, and rarely were they attacked by any of the native Indian tribes. Some trading and exchange of information even had begun to take place between the two sides.

At the same time on arrival at the fort the Harpes and their women plus two infants were duly handed over to Colonel Walker, and the two men were then swiftly manacled and led away to the jail house. Micajah Harpe on route, shouting.

"Ye yella' bellies I'll take two or more of you on and knock

89

yer damned brains out!"

At this he was given a severe battering by three of the accompanying guard who struck with their muskets then kicked at the bound villain.

"We'll hang you two bastards you'll see." the same company sergeant retorted glaring at them both.

Wiley merely stared with eyes that glared hatred at them, but he had more sense than Micajah to provoke unnecessarily, a similar beating. Micajah, built like a grizzly bear, could take such punishment but Wiley though hardened, was not as indestructible as his bigger brother. Simultaneously the three women were taken to a separate building where they were locked up together in comparatively more comfort. The cell contained three separate beds, with fresh water and two buckets.

On entering the cell, Betsy felt distinctly uncomfortable and asked to see the Colonel. Susan and Sarah glared at her with malice and jealousy raging through them both, especially Susan. Her request was refused by the sergeant but soon after he returned and shouted to Betsy.

"Come this way, follow me!"

Betsy followed him and was presented to Colonel Walker who sat at his impressive desk, which had no doubt been shipped over from the East, New York exactly. Walker wore his uniform from the War of Independence proudly with its epaulettes neatly displayed on his shoulders. His sword was placed against his desk. He looked thoughtfully at Betsy as she entered the room gesturing for her to be seated. He began.

"Captain Ballenger mentioned to me that I should go easy on you girl. Why, please explain?"

Betsy looked him in the eye and whimpered hesitatingly but at the same time convincingly. She replied nervously.

"Sir if you only knew what I have been through these last years it would shock you to the core sir. I have been abused by those two monsters, made to do things which fill me with shame...but I had no choice. Sir...please have pity..." she implored, tears beginning to trickle down her cheeks... "I want to leave them and find a new life for myself and become a true God fearing woman again, as I was before my poor parents were murdered and I was kidnapped."

She burst into tears and fell down sobbing uncontrollably.

Colonel Walker suddenly felt pangs of pity for Betsy, then arose from his seat and helped her to her feet saying. "Dear Lord I understand my dear, you are safe now and we will deal with those two brigands to be sure."

"Thank you". she mumbled, wiping away the tears which seemed to be turned off and on conveniently.

"What about the other two women, can you tell me if they were involved with these heinous activities or not complicit like yourself?" asked the Colonel.

Betsy continued with great feeling. "Please don't say anything to the others but both women are wives to the two men, they both carry their children with them. Susan the tall one is married to Micajah, Big Harpe and Sarah married to Wiley, Little Harpe. They don't have much choice 'tis true but they scare me almost as much as the Harpes with their rough ways and threats toward me sir. I've lived in fear for all this time! Please Colonel Walker can you help me, a poor innocent young girl? I'm begging you!"

Betsy full of emotion turned away dissembling her hurt.

91

Colonel Walker was taken aback at this outburst then thought for a while and suddenly decided, looking at Betsy directly but with a certain compassion in his eyes. He announced softly.

"I will give assistance to you all so that you can all search for your lost families, least any that are left alive, naturally I hope some might still be safe, though from what you've told me seems unlikely. I can't see no purpose in holding any of you ladies as it seems to me that none of you had much choice but to do whatever those two devils told you, even the two other women as you describe, though I do agree with you that there is some cause for doubt regardin' their roles in all this, so I will set you all free tomorrow, meanin' the other women once I'm satisfied as to them not bein' a threat from now on. You Betsy are free to leave now if you wish. The men will stand trial as soon as we can arrange things and get Judge McBain over and hang the pair of 'em." he ended with a resolve to do things right as he saw it which pleased Betsy.

"Thank you Colonel." she said and sat down feeling a huge sense of relief and satisfaction at her performance.

Soon after Colonel Walker, giving further thought away from the lure of Betsy with her story implicating Susan and Sarah, all three women were duly released, even given some provisions and a horse to help them find a place to live. Word then spread around the fort that Colonel Walker had decided that they were innocent and as much victims as any of the many poor unfortunates who had come to grief previously at the hands of the Harpes. This caused a degree of consternation with some within the fort, including several of his own men, complaining that he was being too lenient and was losing his wits. Mutterings went around such as.

"He's lost his wits."

"The old critter ain't up to this anymore, that young girl turned his senses!"

These were some of the comments uttered away from his hearing. They believed that the women had serious questions to answer along with the Harpes. Nonetheless orders had to be obeyed.

Consequently the newly released women were soon after sent out to return along the trail, making their way back to their camp. They were a sorry group, bedraggled, hungry and frightened but at least they were free and had some food thanks to the kindness of the Major at the fort who provided them all with some basic provisions and clean water poured into skins. Betsy though had already made her mind up as to what to do. As soon as they were back and sat around a fire she spoke to Susan and Sarah in a firm voice.

"We are going to have to get Micajah and Wiley out of jail you realise that don't you?"

Sarah stared in some shock and disbelief.

"Why I can't go back to that!" she called.

"Me neither, you do what the Hell you want to but me and Sarah will go our way with or without you, better still without you Betsy." Susan added threateningly.

Betsy smiled to herself.

"That's fine but when I get the Harpes out of that jail first thing they'll do is come looking for you and I'll guarantee you'll both be gutted and dead soon as anything." she said looking at them both straight in their eyes and in earnest. She continued.

"Another thing you forget is that they have stashed away a lot of money and valuables, and I for one want my share, so s'far as I see it this is the only choice." And with that Betsy finished speaking.

Susan and Sarah looked at each other and after some thought and whispering to each other in desperation, Susan spoke.

"Alright we do what you suggest but mark this you bitch, soon as we're free from all this I don't ever want to see nor hear of you ever again hear me, sister or no you can go to Hell!"

Susan's pent up fury and envy came to the surface.

"That's fine Susan I'm going back to the fort now to get Micajah and Wiley out as I've figured out a plan, so I'll take the horse and see you ladies later. You got your infants to tend to anyway."

Without further ado Betsy made her way out and set off back to Fort Stanford on horseback as she intended.

Left behind, Susan and Sarah felt helpless and spoke to each other of their mistrust and dislike of Betsy who had become more and more powerful, especially as she seemed to have won over Wiley's affections and protection.

"She ain't Wiley's wife, I don't know of any weddin' Sarah, she's just some schemin' whore that's what she is!" Susan called out to Sarah angrily.

As for Micajah he seemed almost indifferent and simply took out his frustrations on the two women and children whose lives were often at risk from his unprovoked rages. They had no choice but to accept whatever fate and Betsy would bestow on them.

CHAPTER 18

Betsy returned to the stockade early that evening after a long and dangerous journey back, careful to avoid any potential trouble by keeping her wits about her and taking two loaded pistols with her. She entered the fort without any delay since she was recognised by the sentries on duty, and quickly made her way to Colonel Walker's office who welcomed her with obvious surprise.

"Betsy what are you doing back here?" he asked, getting up and dismissing another soldier who was with him.

"I must ask you Colonel Walker if I can stay awhile for the other two women have threatened me with my life and I have nowhere else to go."

Betsy once again feigning fear, implored the Colonel.

Colonel Walker stared at her, twisting his famed moustache and shifting uncomfortably in his armchair.

"Dear me this is a pickle, yes of course dear at least until after the Harpes have been hanged and we can help find somewhere for you to go, maybe work here?" Walker mused.

"That is most kind Colonel."

Betsy move toward him stumbling as she did. Colonel Walker stood up, grabbed her and held her gently, and as he did Betsy rested her fair head into his arms.

"You are a most considerate man Colonel and I am grateful."

She looked up into his eyes and Colonel Walker fell under

her spell immediately caressing her until with a start, he felt the pistols under her topcoat.

"Goodness girl what are you doing with these?"

"For my protection Sir." Betsy replied quite innocently.

"I understand, hope you know how to use 'em.""I do, my Pa taught me well." Betsy said casually.

"Best get some rest Betsy." Colonel Walker replied and pulled away from her with some unease.

He then showed her where she could rest for the night pointing to a sofa in the corner of another room adjacent to his.

"I hope you will be comfortable there my dear...but if you should need anything please do not hesitate to call out, I'm a light sleeper you know."

Colonel Walker stared at her for a short while thinking things he had not done for many a year, especially since his wife had passed away, then bid Betsy goodnight and left leaving her to ponder her next move. She had already partially worked out her strategy but was glad of the opportunity to reflect a little more. She felt a satisfaction at having got so far by using her wits, especially as none of the other women, or even the Harpe brothers themselves to some extent, had anything like her single mindedness and imagination. This was her belief.

Betsy Roberts was becoming a determined and resourceful woman who would use any means to achieve her goals, most importantly to survive.She made herself comfortable arranging some blankets that Walker had provided for her and settled down for the night, coming to a decision regarding her next move, all the while keeping alert for any disturbance. A fort full of men, many of whom had not seen or been with a woman for such a long time, was always a potential danger as she well knew.

***

At Fort Danville across what served as a parade ground and common area, opposite the Colonel's quarters was the jailhouse where Micajah and Wiley were held, and so later in the evening Betsy decided to make her move. Around midnight Betsy crept into Colonel Walker's room next door, where he slept alone, noisily and soundly – whisky and his pipe by his side on a small table by his bed. Betsy had noted that he kept the keys to the makeshift jailhouse in his coat pocket and without any delay and stealthily, she took them, making sure that no noise was made by carefully handling the two large keys.

Closing his door, she quickly made her way in the darkness across to the hut and as there was no permanent guard outside she was able to unlock the door and gain entry. The noise of her entering this gloomy place awakened Wiley who called out.

"Who is it?"

Betsy shushed him… "Shh keep quiet Wiley, we don't want to alert them guards."

Wiley could not quite believe his eyes as he regarded the familiar shape of the young woman who he considered his wife. He smiled at her and looked at Micajah ready to stop him making any sound. Betsy continued cautiously.

"It is me, Betsy, I've come to set you both free."

And with the other key she unlocked the jail door, untied Wiley's ropes and then Micajah's who had stirred from his slumbers, growled ungratefully.

"What took you so long woman?"

Betsy ignored this and finished her work releasing the two Harpes with her trusty sharp knife. Without any further delay, they made for the door and seeing no-one near in the pitch darkness, escaped from the stockade, Micajah brutally knocking out a sleepy sentry on route with his bare fist. Wiley then took the keys from Betsy and quickly ran to the stockade armoury such as it was, and with a piece of luck, found that the second key he tried, opened the door. Wiley grabbed two rifles, three pistols, Micajah's tomahawk, all of which he recognised as their own weapons and ran back to the group.

"Got them Micajah." he muttered.

Micajah nodded approvingly and Betsy grabbed the keys from Wiley throwing them on the ground.

"We don't want another reason for them to come after us, we're in enough danger as it is."

Wiley simply ignored her remark and joined his brother. It was a fairly clear evening outside away from the fort, with the moon providing sufficient light for the group to make their way to freedom.

In the semi darkness punctuated by various noises from creatures of the night, the three of them made off to their hideout. They had untethered two horses with Micajah aboard one and Wiley and Betsy on the other. The Harpes were accomplished horsemen and soothed the two horses expertly making sure little or no noise was made as they made good their escape from the fort.

It was dawn before they arrived at their destination tired and wet from the heavy rain that had started soon after they set off, much to the irritation of Betsy who had appreciated the clear sky until then. But such is the unpredictable nature of the weather, especially at that time of year. The rain had progressively gained in force during their journey making their journey especially unpleasant. Wiley had thanked Betsy surprisingly, in a rare moment of genuine emotion which took her aback, but she suppressed any feelings toward this man who after all had abused her for so long. Betsy was not about to go soft.

"We can't stay here too long as they will work out where we are hiding." said Wiley moving to more pressing issues.

"Let's get movin' then." Micajah agreed.

Wiley turned to Betsy looked at her closely and said.

"You're a clever girl who knows the right thing to do don't you?"

He stared at her in an inquisitive way.

Betsy, without hesitation, replied.

"We are a family aren't we Wiley and you look after us women, right? I always was going to get you men out of there, what do I care about Yankee rats?"

"Good girl, you did the right thing...just as well you did though lassie." Wiley added, reverting back to his usual threatening nature.

Micajah merely looked at Betsy with some dislike and mistrust but said nothing more.

Soon after the two other women with the infants were collected then moved on taking the few possessions that they had with them. Micajah and Wiley were especially relieved to have their reclaimed trusty weapons and powder.

CHAPTER 19

The weather next morning was fair with few clouds to be seen, the ground still damp from last night's rain but firm enough to travel on especially as the trails that Wiley and Micajah intended to travel on were covered by the vast forests of trees which provided cover. And so the group set off with all their belongings, the two infants, complete with the two stolen horses from the fort. This made travel much easier since Micajah and Wiley each had a horse, Wiley with Betsy aboard, Susan and Sarah shared with the two babes, and the fourth a mule was used as a pack horse with all the bags tied to it and the mule itself tied to Micajah's horse in tow. They moved on away from the vicinity of Stanford, riding as quickly as possible given the two Harpes had Betsy and the two women and two infants in tow with them. They travelled day and night without rest along obscure trails which avoided the main routes to escape the posse. When the horses were rested all three women were forced to walk behind, then beaten and threatened if they lagged behind much to Betsy's growing anger and annoyance. The Harpes intended to keep their mounts fresh in case they needed to make a fast escape so the women including Betsy had to walk for much of the way.

Suddenly to Betsy's shock Wiley turned on her when she muttered some complaint, as he was sometimes prone to do, and beat her quite unmercifully as if to demonstrate to his brother his contempt for all the women including Betsy, and his undoubted loyalty to him. It also served to dispel any thoughts that Betsy might have, that he was going soft and becoming vulnerable. She had to know who was boss.

"Damn these Harpes, Wiley will pay for this!!" she thought to herself as she recovered from his blows.... "I'll have my revenge sooner or later and be rid of these devils!"

His latest behaviour merely served to reinforce her hatred and determination to gain her revenge and be free at last.

They headed deep into the wilderness of Kentucky since Micajah had decided that they would be welcomed at a location on the Ohio River by a certain Captain Mason and his band of river pirates at the now notorious Cave In Rock, which was a huge cavern set deep into the cliff overlooking the river. It had become a near perfect hideout for those outlaws such as Mason and his river pirates and was a constant danger to river boatmen and travellers, especially those with goods, who fell prey to these avaricious and bloodthirsty brigands. Over the decades it had been used regularly by various outlaws but was nowadays permanently occupied. It is thought that even the notorious outlaw Jesse James later took refuge there while he and his brother Frank were on the run from the law.

Before arriving there though they came upon a cabin in a clearing with a lone woman and young boy tending a meagre vegetable patch late in the afternoon.

"This will do for the night." said Wiley, looking on.

"Aye." replied Micajah then adding menacingly... "I'll do away with those two and we can move in."

Moving quickly and quietly as the woman and boy were busily digging, up root crops, Micajah swiftly dispatched them both, the woman first with his tomahawk and then, as the boy shouted out loud in terror, he twisted then snapped his neck as easily as wringing the neck of a chicken with his huge bare hands and with as little emotion. Betsy looked on with some shock but also with a certain admiration at this efficient method of killing, as if he was dispatching a hog, cow or more appropriately a chicken, with no emotion felt

On entering the cabin the women soon found food from a well stocked larder and set about preparing dinner with eagerness.

Looking at Wiley, Betsy suddenly asked boldly.

"Can't we stay here for a while? We're all done for Wiley."

Wiley stared back and replied with some irritation.

"No we'll get caught if we linger here too long. You should know that by now lassie."

Betsy understood further discussion was futile but that didn't stop Micajah glaring at her in a threatening manner all too familiar to her, so Betsy turned and beat hasty retreat outside to collect some firewood to place under the cooking pot hung beneath the crude fireplace vent.

They stayed one night.

CHAPTER 20

Next morning after eating well and packing some food, Micajah set light to the cabin using the oil lamps which he smashed first before setting them alight, and after admiring his handiwork briefly, they set off for Cave In Rock, something of a sanctuary as they saw it. Betsy turned round as they were leaving and watched the fire take hold with smoke billowing away and the two unfortunates, mother and son lying dead by their sorry vegetable patch. She felt little sympathy but instead hardened her heart and focused on her own well-being, as the group made it's way through rough trails and on the lookout for dangers at every mile.

After a hard journey through backwoods trails and forest still keeping off the known roads, the party had reached within two miles of Cave-In-Rock when Micajah called a halt.

"I'll go on from here and see Mason and his hounds first, to see the lay of the land....Mason likes me." chuckled Micajah.

"Lord above." thought Betsy in some surprise looking at Susan and Sarah who made no response.

"I wonder what he means by that." she wondered somewhat perturbed. "Mason's most likely terrified of him and who wouldn't be?"

Wiley then ordered that a camp of sorts be made in a small clearing and Micajah motioned to Wiley that he was leaving, quickly mounted his horse and rode off.

Soon after as they sat around exhausted by their journey

and worried about what was going to happen, Betsy went over to Wiley sat beside him and asked.

"Who is Captain Mason, Wiley?"

Wiley looked at her, smiled and replied.

"A bit of a river pirate...lives in a large cave by the river with his men, you'll like him and his cave Betsy!" laughed Wiley.

Betsy considered what Wiley said and Micajah before, and thought to herself. "This isn't going to end well."

She looked at Wiley and said in a pleading voice.

"Now I trust you Wiley to look after us women especially me, you hear." Wiley turned and muttered.

"Careful what you say girl or who you trust"

Betsy decided not to push things too much and moved away leaving Wiley to smoke his clay pipe which he had carefully lit and cut at a piece of branch. He had a skill in carving and would occasionally surprise the women and make something interesting, usually fashioning the rough shape of an animal either a bear or wolf, especially a wolf. He was also adept at making a makeshift shelter from wood collected, if there was no cave, ruined cabin or suchlike. In the cold winters in Tennessee, Virginia, Carolina and Kentucky any shelter was welcome; skins were used as cover and for warmth, clothes stolen from the Harpes' victims were particularly welcome and the women and infants sometimes benefitted from bonnets, shawls, coats, dresses, shoes, blankets...all taken from these unfortunate people.

Most of their victims were in fact men travelling west or going about trade, but occasionally whole families were slain mercilessly by the Harpes usually with Betsy's sly assistance, and it was then that the women were able to take advantage of the booty. Needless to say Wiley and Micajah took whatever they wanted first. A large armoury of weapons grew as well as coins, jewels, loot of all kinds.

There was little room for sympathy from Betsy and the other women in such a harsh, unforgiving environment.

CHAPTER 21

About an hour later after carefully making his way through dense forest and working his way carefully down the valley side via Rock Creek, all the while keeping his horse steady, Micajah approached Cave-In-Rock , dismounted and made his way around to near where the entrance of the cave could be seen. The River Ohio before him slowly and casually moved onwards and Micajah could feel the refreshing, barely perceptible, gentle spray, even as far as he was from the shores.

The Ohio River which got its name from the Native Indian Iroquois word O-Y-O which means great river, in fact it flowed easily through the present day states of Pennsylvania, Ohio, West Virginia, Kentucky, Indiana and Illinois, before it joined its sister river the mighty Mississippi. It had been long used as a means of transporting goods down river by Native Indians, then later pioneers and tradesmen who used it regularly. Its easy flow and shallowness made it ideal for rafts and flatboats especially, where heavy goods could be moved with comparative ease. Unfortunately at the same time there had always been a threat of attack from various quarters and especially from the inviting and ominous Cave-In-Rock, a perfect vantage point for surprise attack and refuge for outlaws and river pirates of every description.

Soon though, Micajah while approaching this cave, heard a commotion and moving nearer to have have a better view of what was going on, could see that the pirates, about six of them who apparently had captured a young man and were roughly dragging him along. The bodies of the rest of the crew, two others, lay by the shore, their flatboat (for they were transporting goods) lay moored.

"Hallo the camp, it's the Wolf!!" yelled Micajah suddenly appearing out of the treeline.

One of the pirates quickly turned and saw him. Looking more closely he said looking back at the others he thought.

"Damn, one of the Harpes." he muttered under his breath as he recognised the unmistakable visage of Micajah Harpe looming closer.

The pirate then turned and shouted to Mason.

"Captain, Micajah Harpe's here!"

Mason approached from the cave, looked at Micajah and said in a gruff irritated voice.

"Well Micajah Harpe, now what do you want here?" he asked Micajah.

"Looking for a safe haven for me and mine for a while Mason." Micajah replied standing still in front of Mason.

"How many of you?" Mason inquired.

"Seven of us Captain."

Mason looked at him for a moment and said.

"You can stay for a while but no trouble, not like the last time you hear." he added staring fiercely at Big Harpe.

"No trouble Mason." grinning at him and then going on.

"I'll go and get 'em then."

Micajah turned away and went to get his horse, mounted

the steed, turned around and headed back, retracing his steps back.

***

Later as darkness drew in, the family of seven made their way along the trail back to Cave-In-Rock with Micajah and Wiley urging the women on with threats and curses all the way. Susan with her baby found the going particularly difficult and instead of any assistance, was ignored by all except Sarah who with her infant, a girl of two, shared her predicament. It is hard to imagine a more desperate and heart rendering sight than these two poor women who were made to walk with their infants trying to keep up with the Harpes, who cared for nothing but themselves, hardened as they were to brutality and dehumanised to such an extent that even young children and their cries had no effect on their wicked, granite hearts.

Betsy, riding with Wiley Harpe by now, cared little for her erstwhile sister and her offspring, who she gave scant thought to. Survival was the focus of her thoughts, nothing else mattered and as they drew nearer to Cave-In-Rock she began to feel even a shimmer of excitement about this new adventure or even how she might gain some extra advantage for herself. Anything was possible and she had to be ready at all times, at a moment's notice, to seize any opportunity which might arise.

When they all reached the shoreline Micajah stopped and looked at the cave which was a huge wide opening into the cliff which overlooked the Ohio River.

"We're here, you women follow me and Wile...and keep

your mouths shut, 'specially you Betsy!" he said threateningly.

Acknowledging the presence of one of the pirates who was guarding the entrance they entered the cavern leaving their three horses to be taken away by another pirate. Slowly the women moved forward fearing the worst.

"Get in there!"

Wiley shouted and pointing to the inside of the cave, the women quickly obeyed.

Inside the cave they saw an enormous chasm before them which went back deep into the cliff, it was broad with the opening slightly narrower as one got nearer to it from the inside. It had been fashioned over centuries by wind and water erosion, and as they moved further in, they were observed by a motley collection of pirates, brigands and a couple of Negro slave women who had been taken captive to provide amusement and menial work for the gang. Some of the pirates bore the wounds of previous skirmishes, some from the war just as Wiley bore his chest scar. One pirate, MacSwain, who had lost his left leg as well as an eye, hopped around menacingly, while his erstwhile companion, an old grizzled, heavily black bearded, thin specimen named 'Old Toke', so named due to his Scandinavian roots, could only make odd noises since most of his tongue had been cut away when he was captured by British soldiers during the War, and who did not take kindly to his shouting and swearing at them. Colonel Banastre Tarleton had ordered the removal of his tongue to…

"Quieten this blessed rebel!" he demanded…then adding… "It will teach him some propriety." mused the Colonel.

It was Wiley Harpe who cut most of Toke's tongue out but his victim was unaware of who did it since Wiley punched the fellow hard in order to render him at least semi-conscious. The procedure worked and Old Toke, though he screamed with pain, was so consumed in his agonies never knew who his tormenter was.

Both men frequently were drunk and were always willing to torture any poor captives who they thought might have had allegiance previously to the British King George. It was Old Toke's way of gaining some revenge for what had been done to him. Mason tolerated these two old dogs with some patience, especially as they were easily persuaded to do any unpleasant tasks with the usual promise of some of the stolen grog or bootleg whisky.

Entering Cave-In-Rock the darkness inside turned to blackness for a moment as they moved further in, but then a reddish glow was perceived from a little further into the cave. This glow grew stronger and appeared around a slight bend in the cave as a large fire, which was burning fiercely, became visible. Some oil lamps too illuminated the cavern mostly filled with whale oil, but the smell was pungent and made the women squirm with disgust.

Captain Mason came forward looking fearsome with his unkempt blackish beard, bedraggled clothes, two pistols, three daggers hung from his belt, and wearing proudly an old tattered blue uniform also from the War of Independence where he had served in the Virginia militia with Old Toke and MacSwain. He looked at the Harpes and their women and proclaimed sternly.

"You're here now so you'll do as I say and make yourselves useful."

He grunted, then leered salaciously at the three women. Betsy felt a shiver but ignored him. Micajah and Wiley were tempted to say something but kept quiet and the family found a part of the cave which was unoccupied which they quickly made their own place. Their assortment of belongings were scattered on the cave floor, makeshift beds were arranged by the women with Betsy making sure she placed herself near to Wiley, more for safety than any feeling of affection.

Next day Wiley volunteered Betsy to act as bait to lure any unwary passing boatman to the cave, dumb enough to be tempted by this seductive young maiden.

"Betsy is good Mason and has been useful to us. She can get any damned fool to come over."

Wiley nodded to Mason who was sceptical regarding this young woman's use but thought she might be of some use. Wiley then grabbed Betsy then pulled up her skirt revealing her left leg to Mason.

"Just lookee' Mason now ain't that as finer piece o' fresh meat as y'll see anywhere?" he laughed salaciously as Betsy broke free.

At this Betsy stared angrily at Wiley but then smiled and decided to do what was called for as it would further reinforce her crucial role in these situations.

Mason nodded approval, then told Wiley she could do her job straight away. Sure enough later on two men whose boat, or raft more accurately, came near to the shore of the river spied Betsy standing near to the cave waving in apparent distress.

"Help me!"

Betsy wailed and the two men, one older and a younger lad of no more than around sixteen or seventeen years, manoeuvred their raft with their long poles, then stepped ashore in expectation of rescuing this pretty blond haired maiden.

As they came ashore Micajah and Wiley appeared as from nowhere behind a rock, and Micajah immediately dispatched the older man with his trusty tomahawk. The man fell to the ground like a heavy sack, standing no chance of defending himself against such a brute.

The young boy, seeing this was shocked to the core, then called out in panic.

"Oh no please don't kill me I'm his nephew and we mean no harm. There's goods on the raft and it's all yours if you let me go!" he pleaded in desperation.

Wiley turned to Micajah and grinning said.

"We're takin' it boy and don't need your damned permission, haha!"

Micajah then was about to smite the lad when Mason appeared from inside the cave and shouted.

"Leave him be, might be useful to us ya hear, as ransom or at least as another slave!"

He grabbed hold of the boy and with two other pirates dragged him off to the cave.

Micajah was furious but under Wiley's influence held his temper.

"Plenty of time and opportunity to get even with him Micajah."

He said intending to keep his brother calm for the time being. He then turned to warn Betsy who merely stood there and said nothing, feeling little or no pity for the terrified young fellow, keeping her own council and thinking to herself that anyway she was now becoming more and more invaluable to these two monsters. What did she care about some young boy who could just as easily have abused her maybe later in life as a man? The process of dehumanisation and survival instinct was now set and Betsy's only concern was her own welfare and potential gain from these events when eventually she could find a way to escape.

"Old fool got what he deserved, nice work Micajah"

Betsy shouted at Micajah, at which Micajah looked with some amazement at this bold statement of affirmation, it left him speechless for a while, incapable as he was of articulating anything much more than the usual threats, grunts and annoyance.

Wiley merely grinned.

CHAPTER 22

Next day the three women busied themselves, as instructed, within the confines of the cave with various chores, keeping their distance all the time from the glances of Mason and his gang, even going down to the shore and washing themselves and their clothes in the gentle waters of the Ohio River, which in the midst of all this horror, was a beautiful and calming sight. The river broad and easy flowing gave some measure of comfort at times like this, any amelioration of such a dire situation was welcome. However later in the evening events turned to a troubling nature as the two Harpes and their pirate 'friends' took to drinking the rough liquor seized from the raft.

Susan looked at Sarah and Betsy and with a worried countenance and said openly.

"This is not good."

Sarah too concerned for her infant's feeding did not hear properly but Betsy replied.

"Look out for yourself sister." and merely smirked at Susan who hardly contained her detestation for her and moved away nearer to Sarah.

"Never thought I'd say this Sarah but I hope those pirates do somethin' bad to her...bitch!"

Sarah nodded in agreement this time replying under her breath.

"I don't give a damn about her Susan."

The feelings of resentment had increased over time and actually brought Susan and Sarah closer together, more so than when they spent the awful years with Cutter.

Meanwhile as the women were engaged in this discourse Micajah shouted over to Captain Mason.

"What you doin' with the captive laddie eh?!"

"Don't know yet, maybe hold him for ransom somewhere, he ain't goin' anywhere anyways."

Mason replied then took another swig from his liquor bottle, a better quality whisky, stolen of course, which he had kept for himself.

"You'll get nothin' for him you fool. Do him in and have done with it!" Micajah called to Mason with something in mind.

"Shut up!! I'm damned if I take any suggestions from you Micajah Harpe!" Mason shouted threateningly, bolder now with the effects of drink.

Micajah started to rise with intentions of seeing off Mason but Wiley grabbed him by the shoulder saying.

"Easy now, we need somewhere to stay for a while."

Micajah replied snarling.

"Aye for now."

He sat down barely concealing his fury.

As the night progressed and the pirates all became more and more drunk, amusing themselves with the two unfortunate Negro women who barely survived the appalling mistreatment meted out to them during this drunken revelry, they either passed out or bedded down for the night with Mason and his lieutenant taking the two women to bed with them. He had first call on these two captive slaves who were forced to please him in the most debauched ways. Mercifully on this occasion it was not too long before he and the other brigands were snoring loudly in their drunken haze.

The Harpes continued drinking and smoking their clay pipes but in a more measured way so that they kept their wits about them, at least to some extent. Betsy remained awake near Wiley who she would bed down with, and observed cautiously what was being said.

"Let's let the boy go Wiley." said Micajah.

"We could have some fun with him." replied Wiley with a devilish grin.

"We could and will. To Hell with Mason!" Micajah exclaimed and slapped his thigh with his fist.

***

The two Harpes suddenly got up and made their way stealthily to the back of the cave where the captive boy was held, tightly tied up and half asleep. Seeing suddenly the two men approach him, he quickly sat up.

"Well lad, shall we set you free?" said Wiley showing consideration for him and looking at the boy.

"I won't breath a word about anything if you let me go." the young man said imploringly.

Wiley smiled replying.

"We'll set you free and give you a horse to boot boy. Won't

116

that be good laddie?" and Wiley nodded.

Micajah smiled at him revealing his rotten teeth which appeared through his matted beard. It was not a reassuring sight for the youth.

"Come boy." Wiley said soothingly and the youth did indeed feel some reassurance.

Cutting his bonds efficiently the two Harpes then took the boy through the cave quietly, avoiding the attentions of the sleeping pirates, their snores and grunts all too audible, and made for where the horses were tied to a tree just outside by the entrance to the cave.

It was a quiet moonlit night with just a few sounds in the distance of nocturnal creatures going about their usual activities unaware of what was about to happen. The Ohio River gently rolled by, the soft sound of it's waves and currents gave some comfort to the boy as he was led along.

All this time Betsy watched events unfold with a growing nervousness mixed with some undoubted sense of excitement. She arose from her bed then followed the group keeping her distance, not wanting to draw attention to herself at this stage either from the pirates or the Harpes themselves. She sensed that one of the slave girls saw her but thankfully remained quiet, perhaps hoping that Betsy might alert the law and have them rescued.

Suddenly as the youth was being led along, Micajah without any warning struck the boy about his head with the flat of his tomahawk rendering him seemingly unconscious as he fell to the ground. Wiley nodded to Micajah and the two of them stripped the boy naked.

"Throw him on that nag Wiley and tie his feet under it."

instructed Micajah.

"Ha, I see." he replied knowingly.

With the boy bound to the horse and flopping around on it they led him up to the top of the cave overlooking the river's shore, a height of about ninety or one hundred feet depending on which part of the cave's summit you would be positioned. With a strip of cloth Wiley then blindfolded the horse which became agitated and soon after the boy began to regain consciousness.

All this time Betsy followed at some distance away, looked on in some shock barely thinking about what was about to happen.

"No good if he doesn't wake up." muttered Wiley to his brother.

"He will. Watch."

After saying this he slapped the boy to awaken him fully.

"What's goin' on?" the lad mumbled nervously.

"We're settin' you free boy!" laughed Wiley.

"Aye on your way laddie!" and Micajah brutally struck the blindfolded horse repeatedly hard on the rump with the flat of his tomahawk. The horse screamed in pain becoming increasingly agitated, rearing and flailing it's legs.

"Gid up there you nag!!" Micajah roared giving the beast a mighty kick.

Realising that something terrible was about to happen the youth screamed in terror.

"No! No!!"

The screeching horse then bolted to the edge of the cliff

with the boy desperately attempting to free himself but to no avail. Wiley lashed the poor beast one last time with his broad leather belt making both Harpes roar maniacally with laughter at this perversely shocking sight. They slapped each other on the back as they roared with laughter, having no regard for the wickedness they had done to this poor, innocent boy.

Betsy stood nearby hiding behind a rock but observing in shock, some unashamed excitement, but fascination as the horse with the screaming boy aboard careered over the edge of the cliff and plunged down to the shore of the Ohio River to both of their deaths. It's calm waters disturbed, it's shoreline rocks now spattered with blood. The shattered and broken body of the boy and horse smashed at the bottom of the cliff against jagged rocks, as the gently lapping and flowing of the Ohio river passed by on its' long easy journey to join up with the Mississippi River, it's bigger cousin.

Such blood curdling screams of terror from the poor boy shook Betsy to the core and yet despite witnessing this horrific scene, a part of her kindled a sense of excitement and even pleasure until then only briefly felt with other atrocities that she had participated in. There was something totally shocking at what had been done to this unfortunate boy which caused Betsy to fully realise the extent of evil present in these two monsters, disguised as men. She felt some shame at her obvious sinful feelings which were mixed with the perverse pleasure she experienced, it caused her to stop momentarily in some shock, but Betsy dismissed her conscience in favour of the former thrill that she had felt when watching this horror unfold.

The commotion awoke Mason and some of his men, bleary eyed but aware that something dreadful had happened.

"What the Hell?!"

Shouted Mason and quickly pushing away the Negro woman who had clung to him for some comfort, he arose and ran outside with four of his men now awake, following behind.

Once outside of the cave the horrific sight of shattered boy and horse was revealed, the boy's body beginning to drift slowly away from the shore, the horse beneath the river's waters. If any life had remained within the beast it was now extinguished. Mason on hearing the hysterical laughter of the Harpes above him then said to his men.

"Holy Jesus I knew they were mad but this is beyond madness. These two devils will get us caught and hanged. We must get rid of them." he added determinedly looking to the other pirates who like him could barley believe what had they had seen.

"Aye!" said some of his men, one of them adding.

"Now!"

Soon after the Harpes returned still laughing to the cave with Betsy following at a distance, neither Harpe yet aware that she had witnessed this horror so wound up and absorbed were they in their nefarious activities. On arriving inside the cave, Mason and all his men, now awoken sharply where necessary, stood collectively to meet them, all bearing arms and pointing them at the two villains.

"Pack your stuff and your women and get out!" yelled Mason aiming at them with his two pistols.

Micajah instinctively drew his axe but Wiley grabbed him by the arm once again seeing at least seven guns pointed at them.

"Now!!" yelled Mason..."get out of here you madmen before I blow you all to Kingdom come!!"

Realising they had no choice, Wiley and Micajah, who slowly put away his tomahawk, turned to the three women and shouted at them to pack up and get ready to leave. Betsy already knew that this was inevitable and had begun this process. She looked at Wiley and smiled a strange smile.

Soon after the seven of them set off into the night making their way up the riverside without horses now, into the forest which was the refuge they knew well.

Just before departing Micajah growled venomously and stared menacingly at the pirates who had escorted them out.

"I'll be back for you Mason, the Wolf will kill ye!" he roared

Wiley remained silent.

At this Mason fired a shot above their heads.

"The next one will hit you Micajah now get!" he shouted.

The other pirates were also aiming their muskets and pistols at the two brothers and it was clearly evident that the threats would very quickly become reality if they tarried much longer, Wiley was especially aware of this threat. The Harpes moved slowly as if in defiance with the three women following as if in some holy procession, taking their belongings and infants with them. They left Cave-In-Rock however clearly relieved that they were still alive.

Despite all this excitement, Betsy was soon thinking a little more rationally now after the events she had witnessed. She realised that she and the other two women were in even greater danger. Not only were they fugitives from the law, but even other bandits would hear about this, and with the likely event of a reward on their heads, 'Dead or Alive', their days would be inevitably numbered. Then there were the Harpes themselves, an ever present threat with no warning or reason to their actions which could erupt any moment into a deadly rage, Micajah the most dangerous of the two of them.

"We have to get away from these two Sarah, Susan." Betsy advised when a brief opportunity presented itself. Betsy, showing an unusual concern for all of them continued

We need to act together for once, understand?"

"How?" replied Susan in some surprise.

"We'll see, I'm thinkin' on it." she said finally with some ambiguity in what she had advised.

Betsy then returned to her own thoughts, and with this the group soon embarked on their next journey along trails, through forest and woods, not knowing what awaited them.

Such was life with the Harpe brothers.

CHAPTER 23

After making their way for what seemed like an eternity away from Cave-In-Rock, Wiley called a halt and instructed that they bed down for the rest of the night or what was left of it, as dawn was approaching and the first very faint glimmers of light could be perceived through the trees, gradually the gentle glow from the morning sun was making itself present. Wiley quickly constructed a makeshift shelter for the night using his well known bushcraft skills, gathering wood, moss and leaf cover from the forest with Micajah cutting up the wood accordingly with his trusty axe.

Next morning after an unsettled night, Micajah mentioned to Wiley that there was a cabin not too far and was sure it was occupied by someone they had once known, however briefly, and in different circumstances.

"How do you know?" asked Wiley.

"You'll see." mumbled Micajah.

Later on that day after being on the lookout for any posse or Mason and his men seeking them, Micajah fell down on to the ground, immediately falling asleep. Exhaustion had caught up with them all so another night under the stars and shelter was needed. All three women soon after took to sleeping though Susan's child became restless and it took all of her abilities to quieten the girl fearing the wrath of Big Harpe, though she slept so soundly that her fears on this occasion were unfounded.

Before taking some sleep, Betsy turned things over in her mind concerning what had happened and how it might be of some use or advantage to herself. In a moment of conscious clarity she baulked at the thought that she had actually witnessed something so awful and not been overly shocked or felt any guilt herself, nor sympathy for the boy that had been so cruelly murdered. She had even found the whole experience thrilling and invigorating to a large extent, participating albeit from a distance, in the horrific event with some relish. Was she as evil as the Harpes?

Thinking back to her own upbringing she had, from an early age, been taught how to slaughter a hog or chicken with knife or with her bare hands wringing the neck of poultry, and how to handle a musket, indeed becoming a genuinely proficient markswoman, as good as any man. Her Pa entrusted her as she got older to go hunting by herself, nearby in the woods, mindful of Susan's disappearance, but believing that Betsy knew how to take care of herself more than her unfortunate sister. Susan demonstrated little inclination to do anything more than menial chores, so accordingly Betsy became more and more her father's favourite especially with no son around. Pa had taught her well and his harsh lessons on survival now stood her in good stead. Death and suffering in this environment was not an uncommon event in her life, it hardened her to cope with the privations and harshness of this wilderness which showed no pity to anyone man nor beast. Even in such evil and desperate situations as witnessed over the last days in Cave-In-Rock, she had become accustomed to all of the daily horrors of life with the Harpes, and now regarded this as the norm and even reckoned that something of benefit could be gained for her ultimately. A certain undeniable bloodlust had taken root within her soul.

Her appearance now was one of a mature woman, no

longer a girl. Her hair though unclean and matted in parts, still had that fairish sheen and her eyes bright and penetrating, unlike the other two women whose whole demeanour had been dulled with little or no trace or remnant of femininity remaining. They looked much older than their actual years. Susan and Sarah were both shared as wives by both of the Harpes though Susan considered herself as Micajah's wife. Sarah on the other hand had lost the will to dispute this and cared little who she belonged to.

Betsy presented a contrast of sorts; her clothes, though shabby and torn in places like the others, she kept as best as she could and whenever the Harpes brought back any goods or women's clothes stolen from the unfortunates who had crossed their path, she was the first to take what was of value. Sometimes whole families with women's and girl's clothes were taken, it was Betsy who had first choice on what to select, especially as she had usually been part of the operation to ambush these poor travellers.

All this was to Betsy's liking and enhanced her feeling of superiority, her sister was of no concern to her, and had indeed become even of no consequence to her. What did she care about this embittered, sullen woman who had displayed no sisterly feeling at all to Betsy right from the beginning when they first met? No Betsy was as hardened and self-reliant as she could be and perhaps there would be more opportunities to benefit from all this madness.

She was soon to be proved right.

CHAPTER 24

Next day was a bitterly cold one, snow had begun to fall, tentatively at first but soon the flurries gathered pace. It was the onset of Winter and the landscape took on an appearance of greater hostility with the birds and animals of the forest wilderness making preparations for the oncoming winter months when times became harsh, and survival precarious and haphazard. Bears prowled around looking for any food they could find to store away, carrion as well as anything freshly killed before their usual hibernation took place. Any meat however old, as well as vegetation would see them through, and as the Harpes well knew, it was not wise to tarry too long in one place nor go off alone. The forest trees gradually lost their leaves revealing a bareness with hostile needles which sometimes gave a threatening appearance.

Wiley instructed the women to break camp and they gathered their few belongings and slowly set off, the two Harpes now strangely subdued and seemingly in no hurry. They wrapped themselves with layers of shawls their feet wrapped in clothes to defend against frostbite which was going to become a present danger. Furs as well as buckskins were now employed, especially by Micajah and Wiley to give added warmth as the weather became more hostile and temperatures dropped to below freezing. The howls of wolf packs and coyotes could be heard in the distance always heralding a menacing ever present threat. Crows cawed and flew about the sky silhouetted as black demons, harbingers of doom.

With no horses now, progress would be slow and painful, sapping the strength of them all even Micajah to some extent, though he seemed to possess an almost unearthly power of survival which no-one else had. A power which made him seem indestructible at times, much more than his smaller brother, Wiley.

Betsy sidled up to Wiley and whispered in his ear.

"Where are we going now?"

Wiley looked at her and snapped back.

"Just follow and you'll soon find out!" adding "…me and Micajah reckon there is a place not too far that could be useful to us but wait and see."

And with that he moved up to his bigger brother and they began discussing something which only aroused Betsy's curiosity more.

About an hour later as the group was following an old trail further into the forest, sounds were heard and shapes appeared through the trees. Wiley signalled for them all to stop and suddenly as if by some mysterious means, a party of seven Native Indians appeared looking menacingly and with tomahawks and bows at the ready.

Both groups stood for a while staring at each other with Micajah and Wiley pointing their two muskets at the Native Indians, when suddenly Wiley recognised the elder of the party whose name he remembered was Dragging Canoe from their days when they lived with them. He glanced at Micajah who also knew this man and nodded to him. Dragging Canoe who was a tall, impressive, older brave, was the leader of the diminishing Chickamauga tribe, an offshoot of the Cherokees who had fought with the British during the War of

Independence and were continuing their campaign of terror against the Patriot settlers who they viewed as before, as enemies and usurpers. Like the Harpes they knew Lieutenant Colonel Banastre Tarleton and that the Harpes had lived amongst them for a time, and like the Harpes they brought terror to settlers wherever they found them, no prisoners were ever taken and the land lay witness to their burning of homesteads, corpses left in the open, often scalped and mutilated. Dragging Canoe and his tribe of native warriors had almost wiped out the early white settlers at the "Battle of the Bluffs" in Middle Tennessee, Fort Nashborough, the land was soaked with the blood of both natives and settlers. Such was Dragging Canoe's skill as a leader and strategist that his influence on battle tactics were long used even at West Point much later.

The modus operandi of this ruthless, skilled tribe was pretty much identical to the Harpes. Their desire for revenge just as great as it was their land that was being taken from them by these white devils, who had appeared as if from nowhere from lands which they knew nothing of. This strange alliance indeed came to the rescue of the Harpe family as Dragging Canoe moved forward to exchange greetings, which consisted of raising hands in a sign of peace and Wiley muttering a few words in their native tongue. The sight of Betsy did not escape the attention of the younger braves who looked on with looks of some lustfulness, even in her state of dishevelment she still cut a desirable sight. It was as if this was involuntary and that it was no fault of herself, such was the condition of a young woman, who despite the privations and suffering she had endured still managed to rise above it all and maintain a natural pride in herself. One thing Betsy could not hide was her now womanly figure, which try as she might on occasions when caution was called for, she was not able to conceal. However she would not be defeated by this, whatever she had to put up with. Susan and Sarah attracted little or no such interest which was fortunate for them ironically.

Soon after a few short words the Indian party moved on and Wiley and Micajah moved back to the women.

"Close shave." he said.

"Who were they?" asked Betsy.

"No concern of you girl, just be thankful me and Micajah knew them from past times."

"Ah, I remember you telling me about that." Betsy replied.

With that the two Harpes motioned the women to move on and before long the family were on the move again, with Wiley and Micajah keeping a close eye open for any sign of danger.

CHAPTER 25

After about three or four miles of moving through forest which now was becoming more difficult with the cover of snow taking an increasingly greater hold, Wiley decided to take shelter from the weather in a huge cave named Mammoth Cave in Kentucky, which was deep enough for a large group to shelter for as long as they wished, indeed may travellers as well as bandits had done so. Some remnants of fires were left and bones, as well as other detritus could be seen scattered around the floor of this enormous cavern.

After a couple of hours respite though, Wiley and Micajah instructed the women to get up and move along to continue their journey. Some grumbling occurred but was quickly dealt with in the usual harsh fashion. After a short while, Wiley signalled for them all to stop as Micajah had motioned to him that he could see someone coming along the trail near to the cave with a mule, obviously with some bags attached, though this was hard to ascertain accurately from where they were.

"Looks like we got someone here." he said to Wiley.

Wiley nodded and took out his knife.

Micajah turned to Betsy and pointed at the man or maybe it was a boy, it was hard to tell, he signalled for her to go down to the trail and do her 'usual job' of seduction. Betsy quickly obeyed and on reaching the pathway road below, she suddenly ran out toward the person who to her surprise was no more than a black boy of around fifteen or sixteen years old.

"Hey can you help me!?" Betsy called in the pretence of some distress.

Seeing her the boy almost fell off his mule in surprise but before he could even get down Micajah quickly came up behind him, and felled the unfortunate youth with one mighty blow of his tomahawk.

Betsy by now was used to this especially after witnessing the events at Cave-In-Rock, but for a moment as she looked down on this forlorn sight and a momentary pang of pity welled up in her seeing this young boy lying bleeding on the ground, his head cleaved brutally. Micajah and Wiley in contrast wasted no time in removing the bags to see what was inside, and discovered that the bags contained beans.

"Ha ha well we've got us some beans Micajah!" laughed Wiley.

"Yep beans is good." Micajah grunted and they took the boy's body throwing it over the mule with the bags tied again and set off without another word.

A little further on Betsy had noticed a sink hole by the road and drew the attention of Wiley to it.

"Good this'll do."

Wiley smiled at Betsy appreciating her initiative.

It was not uncommon in these parts to come across sinkholes, and Micajah without wasting any time pulled the boy's body off the mule, swiftly and efficiently stripped the lad, then proceeded to hack his body to pieces in an expert, proficient manner. He then threw the dismembered parts of his body, with Wiley's help, down the sinkhole.

"First black 'un for a while eh Wiley." Micajah muttered.

Wiley merely grinned.

Susan and Sarah looked on indifferently, but Betsy took an interest in this process, as by now she knew it was vital to hide any bodies or dispose of them. Often the Harpes weighted the bodies with rocks and threw them in a river or creek but a sinkhole would do today. Even the desperate, evil Harpes were reluctant to leave traces of their butchery if they could help it for though the evidence against them was immense by now, they still reasoned that it was insufficient given the largely lawless nature of the country at this time in its history. It was an arrogance of minds so beyond the normal comprehension of ordinary folk.

Betsy's residual feelings of pity for another poor victim were soon gone and her focus returned to simply getting by as best she could, it was the only way she could exist in this horrifying environment.

Later Wiley signalled for them all to stop and make camp by another cave which was cut into the side of a huge rock. They would use this chasm as shelter from the cold.

"We're havin' beans so get cooking you two women." he pointed at Susan and Sarah.

"Micajah and me will rest easy for a while and smoke."

Totally unconcerned the two Harpes sat down, took out their pipes, filled them from tobacco stolen previously and lay back against the cave entrance to relax.

Betsy set up a pot and collected some sticks for a fire which she quickly lit, the ignited flames bringing welcome heat to her cold limbs. Susan looked on tending to both infants who cried mournfully with hunger. Soon enough Sarah was cooking supper on the open stove.

After eating they moved into the interior of the cave and lit another fire, settling down exhausted for the night, but after an hour or so Wiley came over to Betsy, and unusually she responded to his rough advances in an almost lustful manner pulling his buckskin coat apart, pulling his breeches down roughly in her eagerness to engage carnally. Sex was an ephemeral affair rarely lasting more than a few minutes with no foreplay, nor tenderness after the activity had taken place. The two Harpes had never developed more than a basic knowledge or appreciation of the finer pleasures to be enjoyed from it. Indeed a life of the most extreme harshness had given them no time to develop such niceties, sex like everything else in their world was a swift brutal affair.

"How did you get that scar Wiley?"

Betsy asked Wiley after they had finished their peremptory sexual activity.

"In the yankee war." he replied with some surprise then continued with some eagerness to explain to her.

"Goddamned Yankee cut me bad, Leiper was his name, I'll not forget the bastard, I owe him for this. I'm hopin' I get the chance to run into that runt"

He emphasised his anger by rubbing at the wound.

Betsy touched the wound which had never healed properly with some tenderness. It was red with rawness. She was to be thankful of this information in the future. For now she merely looked at Wiley and smiled.

"No more questions woman I'm off to sleep. We got some miles to do tomorrow so you get resting." he said looking at Betsy with some consternation.

Betsy lay down and thought for a while about everything

that had happened recently, and for a moment was disturbed to think that she was involved directly in these evil activities. She quickly dismissed this and fell asleep.

CHAPTER 26

Next morning the Harpes and their women broke camp and set off along the forest trail with the two brothers laughing to themselves about the incident at Cave-In-Rock. They took pleasure with the attitude of Mason and his pirates to their pranks with the boy. Micajah becoming agaitated with mirth, stopped to urinate against a tree and shouted to Wiley.

"Let's find that fine house not too far away that we saw back in the Spring, you know the one that Moses Stegall owns with his pretty wife and kid!"

"Aye just what I was thinkin' Micajah, that Yankee rat and his friend Leiper damn nearly killed me."

"He would Wiley if I hadn't got to you and sent them vermin fleeing. You were lucky to escape with a cut."

Wiley took out his pipe filled it and smoked while the women looked on. Micajah followed suit and they both stood smoking awhile with the smoke from their pipes trailing into the cold air, then nodded to each other and resumed their journey setting off further into the forest.

Later after around three hours of fairly tortuous walking along primitive trails, made mostly by local native Indian tribes and the occasional pioneer who had discovered these rare pathways. They at least gave them some sense of where they were in this wilderness, then Wiley spotted a house beyond the next valley about a mile away.

"There it is Micajah!"

He pointed to where there was a clearing in the forest.

Betsy moved forward and looking at this house, no mere cabin but a finely constructed property with veranda at the front and some cultivated land around it exclaimed.

"Well I ain't seen anything like that for a long time Wiley, maybe three years or more when Pa took us all to Lexington to buy provisions for the Winter I saw me a fine house - just been built too!"

And she marvelled at the fine, imposing building, which stood out in this landscape as if a handsome gentleman of some stature was standing proudly and defiantly. It gave a glimpse of the more permanent structures which were to spring up as the territory gradually succumbed to the encroachment of the new civilisation descending on this vast wilderness. Changes which, within a century, would set the seal on the future of this land of America irrevocably.

Unaware of this Betsy stroked Wiley's arm and said almost seductively to him.

"Can we go and settle there Wiley at least for a while? I'm tired and would love to tend to you dear." she smiled.

Wiley looked at her grinning and motioned to Micajah and the Susan and Sarah to get moving.

As they got closer to the house Wiley signalled to Betsy, Susan and Sarah with their two infants to stop.

"Here will do." Micajah said to Wiley.

Wiley nodded and the two of them, having noticed an opening in a nearby rock just off from the trail which jutted out, went over and after looking in, agreed that it would do as cover for the three women for the night. It was near enough a cave which seemed unused.

"You women take cover for tonight and we'll come back in the morning and bring you down to this house as you can see, ya hear?"

Micajah gestured and instructed gruffly.

Susan and Sarah looked on askance but without any say in such matters, went over wearily to the cave such as it was with their babies now sleeping whilst Betsy remained with the men. She looked at Wiley and said barely suppressing her annoyance.

"I'll come with you...you know how useful I can be. Anyway I'm not staying with those two bitches Wiley."

This amused Wiley but not Micajah who heard her and was about to explode when Wiley intervened and said laughing.

"You're right girl, you can come. I have plans for tonight and I'm sure you'll be part of them." and looking at Micajah, he nodded smirking at him.

"Let her come along she has her uses eh?"

Micajah grinned slightly and nodded approval.

Betsy discerned what was meant by this, but undeterred she went with the two Harpes, keeping just behind as they made their way toward the house.

Susan and Sarah together with their two infants made their way wearily to the cave and settled down wondering what was going to happen next. Susan turned to Sarah and said.

"Just wait 'til I get a chance to fix her Sarah. She has it comin'."

Sarah looked at Susan with a frown and replied.

"She is your sister when all is said and done Susan. Maybe you two can forgive each other someday?"

"Forgive?! She ain't no sister of mine Sarah, you're a fool if you think that. I hate the bitch!"

Her pent up anger and frustration exploded as she cried in frustration leaving Sarah concerned even for her own safety. Only her baby's cries brought Susan out of the rage she had.

Susan sat there still shaking with fury and Sarah realized it was best to leave her to her own feelings, gently shifted away tending to her own child more closely than before whereas for a while Susan seemed indifferent to her baby's cries.

A more pitiful scene it would be hard to find but it was a scene not uncommon amongst poor folk who had nothing, and who had no alternative life open to them. Susan and Sarah simply had to endure for as long as their situation remained as it was.

CHAPTER 27

The house of Moses Stegall was a fine example of late American Seventeenth century architecture, it being constructed of wood with a slate roof with sash windows adorning the front. It had a simple but fine veranda for Moses and and his wife, as well as guests to sit out on, especially on those balmy Kentuckian evenings when all seemed right with the world and a pipe, coffee and good company made life worth living. Such scenes sadly were fairly rare as their own lives were one of toil, uncertainty, fear and worry about the future, but Moses had worked hard, made a good income so far, which enabled them to enjoy their proud new home set alone in a lovely meadow complete with the most colourful flowers in the Spring and Summer months.

Moses had fought on the side of the American Patriots in the War of Independence and even fought against Colonel Banastre Tarleton's men at the Battle of Cowpens in Cherokee County, South Carolina in 1781, where he and his friend John Leiper encountered the Harpe brothers and wounded Little Harpe, as he was then referred to more commonly, during the ensuing battle itself. They managed to escape the attentions of Big Harpe, who came rushing at them by fleet of foot and made their way back to the main force of the revolutionaries. The battle ended in victory for the Patriots and the two Harpes were forced to surrender after Tarleton had made his escape leaving his defeated army to its own devices. But they too would escape soon after killing a sleeping sentry, and another, both who were not paying due attention to their prisoners. This action enabled them to make their way into the wilderness unscathed.

After the War Moses Stegall made a success of trading in various items, mainly from fur trapping; mostly beaver, bears, raccoons, deerskins, wolf, coyote that he caught, which meant he was away for long periods of time leaving his wife and now his young son at home. Luckily his friend from the Independence War, his former superior who he respected, commander Major William Love, usually stayed with them as added protection for his wife and baby son when he was away. Major Love had retired from the army and was content to lend a hand to Moses when he was absent, especially as Mrs Stegall was a fine cook and he had somewhere to stay without being on his own which he was usually. The arrangement worked well but was soon to be tested to the limit by events which spread fear and horror throughout the territory.

It was thus on a cold day in November that there appeared three figures walking across the clearing toward the Stegall house, one of whom was a female, the other two, one a huge tall man, the other a shorter leaner individual. All three appeared to be in a bad state.

Jane Stegall observed the three and went out on the veranda to see who they were and what they wanted. Being a good hearted, Christian woman, she always liked to think the best of people even though she was aware of the dangers present, and being warned by her husband not to allow any strange characters to come into their house. Major Love was asleep in the spare bedroom at this time as he often did during the day, resting his weary body which sported various wounds from his days of fighting battles against the British. So Mrs Stegall without thinking too deeply, and not wishing to disturb the old man, greeted the three travellers with a smile and said

140

on their approach.

"Hello, what can we do for you three? My, my good Lord you all look tired and hungry."

She looked over the three of them noting the young woman particularly who seemed to stare at her and the house with a look which disturbed her slightly. Arriving at the front of the house Wiley moved forward and replied politely to Mrs Stegall.

"Indeed ma'am we are extremely so, as you correctly observed. My younger brother here and my young niece Betsy are most weary. Our wagon was raided by Indians, Cherokees most likely, maybe that Dragging Canoe and his murderers, but with God's help we managed to escape."

Wiley breathed deeply whist Micajah and Betsy looked on casually. He continued.

"Unfortunately we now have nothing left until we get to the nearest settlement. I figure maybe twenty or thirty miles away. Would you be so kind to provide us three with some food and we shall be on our way?"

"Where you headin'?" Mrs Stegall inquired looking a little perplexed.

"Lexington I guess." Wiley replied.

Jane Stegall by this time had growing concerns about the nature of these three starngers, especially the huge, raw boned man who said nothing but seemed to just scowl in a worryingly disturbing manner. The young female she had noticed looked as if she was once a pretty young lass with blue eyes which betrayed a cunning look. All three appeared dirty, even Betsy, spattered with mud and filth but most concerning were the apparent blood stains on the giant especially, more so than the shorter man.

Torn between wishing to show Christian compassion and her concerns about these three strangers, she made a fateful decision. She breathed deeply then continued.

"You are welcome to come in and rest awhile and I will most gladly feed you three and see what I can do to help you on your journey by way of some provisions, though we are not rich people, mind. Do come in now and take your ease."

She motioned for the three to enter the Stegall house.

Betsy looked at Wiley as Mrs Stegall turned to go inside and smiled knowingly, Wiley smiled back to her and then nodded to Micajah who followed menacingly inside.

On entering Betsy felt a pang of jealousy at such a lovely home, which though not endowed with many fine trappings, immediately gave the impression of it being a house which was cared for and welcoming to all and sundry. Betsy had never seen so fine a place before and it hurt her all the more, especially as she had been with the two Harpe beasts for three or more years, and who cared nothing for any style or comfort. After all this time she still retained a sense of the finer appreciation for such a home and furnishings, which though modest by comparison to the more opulent houses in the East, Boston and New York so she had heard, and in England and France, was impressive by the standards of the time. There had to be money and valuables also, she thought.

Mrs Stegall was dressed in simple plain dress with a white apron over it. She was a woman of around thirty-five, fine greying hair, but she looked older. Hard work and worry had aged her as it did most folk.

After a short pause she decided to invite the group to take

supper with her as it was now nearing dusk. She had prepared food which was in a large cooking pot hung over the fireplace. The smell of good food was almost overwhelming to Betsy but also to the Harpes who were relishing supper, a rare, hearty meal beckoned. A brick chimney provided escape for the smoke and the fire which she now lit, it started to bring welcome warmth in the home. This was not unappreciated by Betsy especially who said to her smiling.

"Haven't seen such a fine fire for a long time Mrs Stegall, sure looks good."

Mrs Stegall nodded sympathetically.

"Take a seat, you look as if you need some rest and you fellas..." pointing to a couple of wooden chairs... "take your ease too."

Betsy and Wiley expressed gratitude but Micajah merely sat down, took out his pipe and glared, saying nothing.

"Much obliged to ye ma'am." said Wiley who also took out his pipe, filled it carefully with tobacco and looked across at Micajah with a knowing look.

After seeing to her baby son who was sleeping upstairs, Jane Stegall set about finishing cooking the meal, when suddenly a stranger walked in from an adjoining room. He stopped and looked quizzically at the new arrivals. It was Major Love who was dressed in the worn uniform of a Patriot officer and still stood erect despite his age which was sixty-two. He was surprised to unexpectedly witness such a disparate group, two rough looking men together with a young attractive looking girl.

Wiley and Micajah looked on in surprise at seeing a hated enemy from the War and Micajah exclaimed.

"Who the Hell...?!"

143

Wiley swiftly took him by the arm, intervening to prevent Micajah rearing up and not wishing to start any trouble as yet.

Wiley smiled at the major then spoke to him directly.

"Good evening Sir, we are just staying overnight to rest afore we continue with our journey. We mean no harm but were surprised as we were unaware of anyone else's presence in this good lady's house."

Mrs Stegall interjected immediately turning to Wiley.

"Oh I do apologise as momentarily I forgot that out dear friend Major Love is staying with us 'til my husband returns."

"Indeed Jane." Major Love confirmed.

Straight away Love tipped his hat respectfully, removed it, then placed it on an adjoining table.

Betsy, seated comfortably, smiled at Major Love, who noticed the attractions of this young woman even in her poor, lowly state.

"I see you were in the War Major Love?" Wiley asked with a hint of irony.

"I certainly was Sir, and fought alongside General Daniel Morgan, a fine commander." Major Love smiled proudly.

Wiley nodded in acknowledgement but said nothing more, seeing Micajah seething with a barely concealed hatred like some time bomb ready to explode. They knew of Morgan who had led the Patriot forces at the Battle of Cowpens and other notable skirmishes against the British. He was a hated figure to Micajah and Wiley Harpe, along with many other officers from that time, though not Major Love it seemed.

Betsy observed this with growing concern. The last thing she wanted now, when some decent food and rest were on offer, was for Micajah to get into a violent, murderous rage and destroy this brief period of respite.

Her concerns thankfully were allayed as soon after Mrs Stegall put out the promised food; a stew she had cooked made from vegetables grown herself, with some venison left by her husband, on the large table. The meal was dished out proportionally and eaten with due pleasure, if not with any appropriate good manners from the Harpes, who gulped down the food and some wine with greedy relish.

After eating Mrs Stegall showed the Harpes and Betsy where they were to sleep that night.

"I can give you the spare room up in the loft, if you all don't mind sharing." she said and looked at Betsy to see if this was alright. Betsy merely smiled and nodded acceptance.

"I could put a screen up for you dear" Jane offered.

"Not needed." Wiley interjected quickly. Betsy nodded in agreement somewhat shyly.

With that as the night drew in, they ascended the steps up to the loft and on their way up discovered a well kept room to the left which belonged to Mrs Stegall and her infant son, a baby of less than one year old, with what was Major Love's room to the right.

As it was late Micajah slumped down and Betsy placed herself next to Wiley away from Big Harpe for the usual reasons. It was not long before they all fell asleep in the darkness of an early Winters night.

Major Love soon followed after some discussion beforehand with Mrs Stegall concerning the three strangers and what they were up to.

"I don't like the look of 'em Jane, you have a good heart

my dear but I would not entertain them if it was up to me."

"Oh I'm sure all will be fine Major, anyway they'll be on their way in the morning, it's the least I can do 'specially with that young girl with them. Why she mustn't be a day over seventeen I would think."

Major love paused then continued.

"I hope you're right Jane, I do indeed." he said gently shaking his head.

Jane Stegall smiled at him, then trying to reassure her friend, she replied patting him on his arm affectionately.

"Now don't you be worryin' I'll see you in the mornin' when we'll have a nice breakfast. Sound good?"

Love nodded and bidding her goodnight went to his room upstairs. He settled down but kept his pistols nearby and his sword by his side as a precaution, looking out from his small window at the still, moonlit evening punctuated with the usual sounds of numerous creatures but especially the hooting owl which was perched as usual on a nearby oak tree. It's hooting pierced the freezing air. The major drifted off into a deep, comfortable sleep.

CHAPTER 28

After a while Micajah was awoken by a loud snoring coming from Major Love's room which consisted of a series of humongous snorts, interspersed with grunts and groans. These disturbing sounds proved too much for Micajah and he muttered to the waking Wiley.

"I'm gonna still that Yankee bastard once and for all."

Betsy too was aroused and wiping her eyes asked what was going on.

"Nuthin' we got some business to attend to woman so relax." Wiley replied brusquely, motioning to her to be quiet.

Before she could say anything Micajah was up quickly, grabbed his tomahawk and immediately rushed into Major Love's room like a man possessed. With great ferocity, he slammed his tomahawk into the back of Love's head. The major lay sound asleep never wakening during this assualt, and so knew nothing about what had happened mercifully, and with no chance to move or do anything to defend himself, he now lay dead on the blood-soaked bed. It was a sad end to a loyal soldier of the American Revolution. He had had no chance to defend himself, Micajah Harpe had taken his revenge.

Jane Stegall on hearing the commotion feared the worse and grabbed a pistol calling from the bottom of attic the steps.

"What's going on, is everything alright!?"

Wiley and Betsy, who was now acquainted with what had

happened, was now in a state of excitement, screamed at Wiley.

"Kill the bitch Wiley...DO IT!!"

Betsy suddenly shouted these words to Wiley, words which took him by surprise, in an involuntary fit of rage and hatred.

Jane Stegall had become a figure of loathing to her as someone who had what she had sorely missed for so long. Why should she have all this when me, Betsy Roberts, had suffered greatly and was more worthy than this wretched sanctimonious woman?

Wiley responded quickly, needing no encouragement, he quickly grabbed Jane Stegall, pulled her head back, then brutally but efficiently slit her throat before she could raise her pistol even with it ready cocked. His swiftness and expertise in the art of killing were an impressive but horrific sight. Blood gushed into her nightdress which now became a vision of horror with vivid scarlet red spattering all over, becoming like some slaughterman's apron. Betsy's eyes lit up seeing this, she was almost aroused by the limp figure of Mrs Stegall falling to the floor, gasping very briefly before lying still, a ragged, lifeless shape before her, now bereft of all humanity.

Mrs Stegall's baby son by now was crying loudly in the bedroom next door and after hesitating momentarily, Betsy called out to Micajah in a voice which even he had to obey, such was the unearthly sound she made.

"Finish it off Micajah!!" she screamed at him.

He looked slightly confused at first since this was the first occasion Betsy had actually instructed him to do anything. It would have been unheard of before, a much too dangerous thing to even consider let alone say to him. Now though Micajah responded without thinking, and rushed into the child's room quickly annihilating the child in a flash by picking it up by it's ankles and dashing it's head against the wall. The child knew nothing, it's life extinguished in an instant like so many before it, at the hands of this most evil and monstrous man.

An undisguised feeling of power came over Betsy. This was a sure sign of the changing situation between the three of them and Wiley recognised this straight away. Before he would have struck her for her insolence, and Micajah would certainly have done something violent toward her, even possibly causing her to die violently, but not now. Wiley turned to Betsy and grinned knowingly, saying nothing to her, but acknowledging that she had shown some extraordinary initiative. He viewed it as coming from him; she was his creation, she was as bad as they were now, with the potential to be of even greater usefulness or so he conjectured.

Three people, two adults and a baby lay dead, slain in the most brutal manner, but none of this 'family' of brigands cared so much as a fig. After wiping blood from their clothes, they eventually resumed their night's rest in the Stegall's house, returning to their beds exhausted after the excitement of what had happened. In the morning all three took food left out considerately by Mrs Stegall, thereafter they ransacked the house, taking with them anything that could be of use.

Wiley and Micajah then set about collecting combustibles including oil, papers, garments of all kind and set fire to the house, as a strangely satisfied Betsy looked on outside. The blaze quickly became an inferno with Betsy grinning with satisfaction at this terrible sight. Wiley and Micajah laughed and Wiley shouted.

"Burn ye Yankee bastards!!"

Grabbing two frightened mules belonging to the Stegall's

which were tethered, they mounted them expertly, with Betsy as often before seated behind Wiley, and set off back to where Susan and Sarah were hiding.

***

Within a short time news of this horrific massacre spread throughout the territory and shocked citizens began to feel that the time was well overdue to do something. There had been too many of these appalling outrages where so many innocent folk had been robbed and murdered in the most terrible way.

Bad enough to be murdered but the butchery and carnage which accompanied these killings was too much. Hardened war veterans looked on with horror, having not seen anything like this even in battle or afterwards when sometimes prisoners were dispatched rather than be taken behind the lines. Most men later regretted this action but excused themselves by saying it was done in haste and of necessity. It was one thing to kill an enemy in the heat of battle or shortly afterwards, but the gratuitous murder of innocent men, women and children done by the Harpes was something which was hard to comprehend or to stomach. Enough was enough.

Strangley, though not surprisingly, Moses Stegall was unaware of this atrocity, he was deep in the forests on his quest for furs.

The Terrible Harpes however had to be dealt with once and for all.

CHAPTER 29

The three outlaws, as Betsy had now incontrovertibly by default become labelled, along with the two Harpes, soon returned to the cave hideout and were greeted sullenly by their two neglected womenfolk, who had spent a fearful night even scaring off a curious bear who was as surprised, as they were, to discover it's shelter occupied. Susan, bearlike in stature almost, shouted and gestured wildly as well throwing rocks at the bear, managed to scare off the beast. By morning Susan's baby was crying loudly with hunger and thirst.

The trio of outlaws entered the dark cave, the opening lit by daylight, the interior lit by a solitary oil lamp, one their few domestic possessions.

"Where you been?" Susan asked Micajah who glared at her in response.

"Still that bloody bairn wench!" he yelled angrily as the baby continued to cry.

"She's hungry Micajah, I got nothing for her, ain't no milk left in these breasts damn you!"

The baby cried even more loudly as if to emphasize the point.

Micajah spat and cursed. In a rage he picked up his baby daughter by her ankle and slammed her against the wall as he had the Stegall's infant.

"That's settled her squeelin' and if you start woman I'll

151

settle you agin' the wall!"

Susan screamed in horror.

"No! No! You bastard, may you go to Hell Micajah!!"

"Hell's good enough for me woman." he scornfully replied, then turned his back on Susan. Then he looked at the bloodied child for a short while, stopping momentarily in what might be interpreted as regret, but said nothing.

Wiley looked on at first surprised then amused, adding sarcastically.

"At least we'll get some peace round here now."

Susan, totally distraught and overcome with grief, sat down and wept bitterly. Sarah came over to comfort her but Betsy feeling nothing, sat down and breathed easy, looking away. This was her niece but to her it might just have been a rag doll, so little concern or feeling did she have for Susan's child. Sarah with her own son in her arms asleep, said gently to Susan.

"Don't be grievin' now Susan, the child never knew nuthin' and will go straight to Heaven you know that."

"And Micajah to Hell, won't he Sarah!?" Susan said with tears streaming down her weather worn face.

"Sure enough, I think Hell's too good for the pair of them but there's nothing else to be done."

Sarah comforted Susan as best she could, keeping hold of her own baby who slept in her arms unaware of the dangers it faced. Suddenly in a fit of rage Susan shouted out to Micajah across the cave.

"I hate you Micajah you killed my baby and you will pay!!"

At this unusual outburst Micajah arose, went over to Susan

and kicked at her thigh violently, saying.

"Shut up woman I told you once I'll do for you like your squeelin' brat!" he continued staring wildly, his black curly hair dishevelled, then looking at all three women continued… "and you women all of you, another word and Wiley and me will be puttin' you all in the river with rocks in your guts....ha!" he added.

Micajah's eyes blazed maniacally as he stared at them all barely was he able to control his rage.

At this Betsy thought to herself that no-one not even Micajah would do her harm, she would kill him or Wiley for that matter, first before that happened.

Later Susan and Sarah buried the poor child, placing a simple cross above it's grave hastily dug from the cold ground. Micajah noticed this, walked over and for a moment felt a pang of remorse,

saying to Susan.

"You done right woman by the bairn." he muttered as he looked on at the makeshift grave.

Susan too traumatised to respond, ignored him. With that Micajah went away without another word spoken between them. Susan remained at the graveside weeping softly, her large frame shaking with grief, Sarah by her side giving comfort as much as she could with her own child lay next to her. Betsy remained where she was.

CHAPTER 30

L ater that day Moses Stegall met up with his friend John Leiper. They set out together on their journey home from a meeting of local settlers who were now roused into action to form a posse with the intention of locating and capturing the Harpes dead or alive as instructed, and their women once and for all. Feelings were running high even before the news of Moses's wife and child. Calls for something to be done had fuelled the need for action at the meeting, there had ebeen so many atrocities which had come to the attention of the good people of Kentucky. It was high time these murdering devils were dealt with in the only way fitting; death must be dealt out in any way they could administer it, whether via hanging or killing them both as soon as the opportunity presented itself. The frustrations and anger expressed during the meeting which was at a location near Lexington were palpable. Unfortunately the calls for actual action in terms of raising a posse, were met with a series of excuses ranging from the predictable… "I can't spare the time." "It's up to the law to catch' em not us." or "I got a family to protect and me being away is risky."

There was a collection of other, less convincing arguments all met with some degree of disbelief, but when they considered the problem then the difficulties of being away from their families for any length of time when such murdering rogues as the Harpes roamed the territory, along with other bandits and renegades, was enough to deter some for quite understandable reasons. Their family's safety was their priority, so the early enthusiastic responses to the call for vengeance were steadily fading away.

Moses Stegall and John Leiper lived with their respective families close by to each other, and Leiper, who had become close friends with Moses since they fought together in the War of Independence, had joined with him in their trading business dealing mostly dealing with the furs they trapped themselves and ones bought from trappers who operated throughout the territory. It made sense to limit risk and work with someone you could trust but their frustration at the waste of time and impotence displayed at the meeting was becoming a source of real annoyance.

"Moses!" Leiper called to Stegall as they commenced their ride home together side by side. As they neared Stegall's homestead he continued.

"I can't believe these lily-livered men back there can you? How long are we to put up with those Harpes with their murder and mayhem?" he continued.

"It would be different if they had been affected directly John, you know how things work – if it ain't you or your family's business then leave well alone." replied Moses.

"I suppose....what the..!!" John called out.

He suddenly saw over the tops of the forest trees ahead, a pall of smoke rising from the clearing below. It bellowed thick black clouds which rose up into the valley above the trees. Seeing this Moses exclaimed.

"Oh Lord, That's coming from my home John!!"

Stegall and Leiper looked at each other and without any further hesitation kicked their mounts into action and set off at pace toward the smoke down in the valley, having a suspicion as to what was most likely to be the cause of it.

After what seemed like an eternity, riding at full speed, urging their horses down the twisty trails to the bottom of the valley and on to Moses Stegall's home, they arrived at the scene of the rising smoke. The clearing where his home was revealed the terrible sight of his house burnt to the ground.

"No!!, No!!"

A piercing scream came from Stegall and with John Leiper close by, he soon discovered the remains of his wife, baby son and Major Love, all charred and victims of a brutal death. It is impossible to imagine the emotions felt by Moses as he walked over and cradled his wife's head, a macabre vision with her body barely recognisable. Within seconds he imagined how his wife had come to her end at the hands of the two Harpe monsters who he knew were responsible for this atrocity.

"Jane!" he shouted in abject horror.

Moses then saw his son's body next to her. A wail of abject despair emitted from him, he slumped to the ground amid the still smouldering remains of his once proud home. John Leiper looked on speechless and stunned. After a while he called to Moses.

"Only the Harpes can have done this Moses, it's not the work of Dragging Canoe or any of them Indians for sure."

These words had no effect on Moses as he slowly rose up from this horrific scene and looking around taking in the devastation both human and material, called to John Leiper.

"I know, I know. I'm going to bury my wife, son and Major Love so please help. We can't leave them like this....revenge can wait a while."

"Of course Moses." Leiper replied feeling shaken.

And with that both men undertook the dreadful task of

burying nearby to the remains of his house, the three bodies as best they could, making a cross for each and saying a prayer over each grave. Wiping tears of grief away from his eyes Moses muttered to John Leiper in desperation.

"I can't go on, I'm nothing without Jane."

Leiper put his arm on Moses's shoulder and said to him softly, looking for any words of comfort or solace.

"Be strong Moses, don't let them murderers do this to you. You owe it to your wife, son and yourself to set things aright. By God Moses if they don't form a posse now after this I'll go after them myself, they can't be too far away yet."

Moses listened but did not reply.

Leiper who was still shocked himself continued.

"I'll go back and tell them all what's happened here, most of them will still be around in Lexington, wait 'til I return and please Moses, don't go off on your own." Leiper implored.

"I'll be as long as it takes to finish writing something on these graves, then I'm gone...so you be quick John Leiper."

"I will."

With that John Leiper mounted his horse and made off as fast as he could muster, pushing and whipping the beast vigorously get it to going back up the slope of the valley, through the trees and back along the trail from whence thay had come.

After his friend had gone Moses stood there in shock before undertaking the poignant, heartbreaking task of burying his closest kin alone. After completing this he said a prayer silently to himself, then sat down and waited, his head in his hands.

CHAPTER 31

When John Leiper got back to the meeting place back in Lexington, most of the posse were fortunately still there smoking their pipes and discussing sundry parochial matters.

"He's right 'tis time them critters were seen off. I heard that they killed more than thirty good folk, cuttin' 'em up and dumping their bodies in the creek." so said one of the group spitting out tobacco.

"Aye women and bairns too" said another.

"They ain't humans but beasts, the women too, three of 'em I believe. Work of the Devil and you know what? One of the women is a young pretty thing, daughter of them Roberts family few years ago, who were murdered. Betsy I think her name was."

"You don't say Silas?" said another in some surprise.

And the talk continued with more tales recounted, getting more and more lurid all the time. Just as things were getting more exaggerated John Leiper burst in and quickly informed the men what had happened. Outbursts of more horror and outrage ensued.

"Poor Moses! They killed his wife and baby son as well...and Major Love?"

"Hang 'em, or better still shoot the devils – save us time and trouble!" one of the other assembled men called echoing earlier thoughts but now having greater force.

There was universal agreement to this suggestion and soon after all the men signed up for the posse there and then, this time without prevarication or excuses. Some suggested that they go to Captain Ballenger at Fort Danville and enlist his aid. A few of the men present expressed concern that "…the Harpes were a most dangerous and murderous foe and be best to wait for more men before embarking on any mission to capture these villains."

It was thus left for John Leiper to allay concerns pointing out that he and Moses had served in the Patriot army, as had most of the men assembled and there were others not present who would join them. They would easily overpower and deal with the two murderers, it wasn't as if they were not aware of the threat they posed. They would also have the element of surprise if they tracked them using the skills that many of them possessed from their army days and hunting experience. As for their three women followers, they should be easy enough to deal with though some were aware that one of their number, the younger, fairer one, was devious and would need restraining as soon as she was captured.

Becoming impatient with the procrastinations of some of the assembled group Leiper said shortly.

"I've got to get back to Moses so get you're muskets and gather the others who have left here and join me at Moses's place. One of you ride off and inform Captain Ballenger as to what has happened and where we will be, I'm sure he'll want to join us with some of his men. Dammit it's high time the law did somethin'!"

Agreement was made and Leiper set off back to see Moses, hoping that he would still be there. The remaining

159

assembled men wasted no time grabbing their weapons, saddling up their mounts, and one of the number Nathaniel Greenway, previously a scout with the Revolutionary army, took on the job of riding at top speed to Fort Danville to inform Captain Ballenger.

***

John Leiper rode hard and arrived back at the Moses home or what was left of it, dismounted, looked around immediately to see where his friend was. There was no sight of him worryingly, except for the three freshly dug graves with simple plaques on them that Moses had obviously nailed on to the partly blackened crosses, which he had made from the few pieces of unburnt wood he had gathered from the fire.

The house lay still, burned out with just the odd remnant smouldering still, the large timbers blackened and fallen like corpses. Only the brick fireplace, as well as the brick chimney, remained virtually intact, defiantly resisting all the accursed efforts of the inferno. This house which Betsy Roberts had admired and coveted so much, was no more, it's remains now a poignant reminder of what was once such a fine building amidst the wilderness.

"Damn it, the fool!" Leiper muttered to himself, realising that Moses had headed off on his own.

Fortunately the posse, hastily put together, arrived shortly after as John was looking around. On seeing the men Leiper shouted.

"Come on men we must catch Moses before he finds the Harpes. He's no match for those two fiends!"

The posse of around eight or nine men, armed with pistols, muskets and blades, some dressed in their Revolutionary blue coats and tricorn hats, others dressed in their pioneer long coats and wide brimmed or racoon fur hats to stave off the cold air, shouted their enthusiasm to go after the notorious brigands.

"Kill 'em!!"

Straight away Leiper mounted his horse and they all set off in swift pursuit of the Harpe family hoping to catch up with Moses, or seize them before Moses got to them, no doubt with dire consequences for him. After a short time, riding at full pace, Leiper soon caught sight of Moses who was riding at a steady pace along the trail within a few miles down the road fro his home.

"Moses...wait!!" he shouted.

Moses on hearing Leiper's voice hesitated but stood his horse still. He was torn between wanting to go and get to the Harpes first dispensing justice and more to the point, revenge or wait for help. He considered his options but realised that it might not end well for him if he went on alone and so he wisely waited. This went against the grain but he resisted all the pent up hatred and frustration, combined with the burning desire to seek vengeance, and thought to himself.

"Leiper will end this once and for all, or be damned trying." he said to himself then called out to John reiterating the promise.

"We will end this John!"

"That we will Moses!"

And with that John Leiper signalled to Moses to wait until they had all arrived by his side and then instructed all the posse

161

to make haste. They set off with great determination down the forest trail in pursuit of the outlaws.

CHAPTER 32

Meanwhile Betsy Roberts sensed that all was not well with Micajah and Wiley. Her concerns stemmed from observing the agitated nature of their behaviour and perfunctory private conversations that took placed with greater frequency. Gone was the usual Harpe confidence and arrogance, replaced now with uncertainty and even recriminations with Wiley pointing out the impetuosity of Micajah's actions at the Stegall house.

"You didn't need to kill the Major and Stegall's child so quickly Micajah, not to mention leavin' me to finish the bitch. Could've waited while I decided what to do."

"Shut yourself Wiley! It's no good tellin' me now. Anyway they got what they deserved!" Micajah retorted angrily.

Wiley ceased criticising his brother as he knew well that Micajah was not one to listen to reason. An angry bear or tiger should be left alone and not provoked. Instead he began thinking about their next move.

"That bitch of yours is no good, I plan to deal with her soon!" Micajah suddenly added, feeling a resentment which had been building up over the months since she had first shown signs of the confidence which had manifested itself at the Stegall home. Her, issuing downright commands to him, Micajah Harpe! Then menacingly he turned to Betsy said.

"You think you're smart lassie...we'll see about that!" he added glaring at her.

Wiley frowned in anger knowing that his brother hated his 'wife' as he referred to Betsy, but said to Betsy shortly after when Micajah calmed down a little.

"Don't worry woman I'll take care of ye, he's just lettin' off steam"

Betsy stared straight into Wiley's eyes, then she replied.

"Don't look like it to me Wiley, I ain't ending up like one of your helpless victims. That's damn well for sure, I promise you Wiley he'll regret comin' after me with that tomahawk of his if he does. I'll stick this in him before he breaths!" she added firmly pulling out knife and then stroking her fair hair with an air of defiance.

Wiley smiled shook his head not knowing what to say or how to react at this outburst from Betsy Roberts. He knew that Betsy was more than able to defend herself, her wits had sharpened over the time with him and Micajah.

Susan and Sarah kept quiet during this interchange but all at once Micjah in a fit of temper, struck Susan about her head and shouted.

"Who you lookin' at bitch?!"

Susan now pregnant again, shook with pain but bravely held on to Sarah's baby who she was holding and was now crying loudly. Sarah had her other baby wrapped tightly to keep the cold wind at bay.

Micajah becoming progressively out of control, pulled out his tomahawk intending to do something terrible. Susan screamed a scream of unearthly intensity.

"No!! Micajah don't...please!!" she called, attempting to protect the infants from his rage.

Micajah stood still and slowly put the weapon away and in a moment he became quiet. It seemed as if the memory of killing his daughter before had struck him to the core. Thankfully it prevented him from doing something he would possibly later regret even more.

After a short period of relative calm as Betsy kept her thoughts to herself and made sure her short, sharp knife was well placed under her skirts to use at any given moment, they then continued their journey as Wiley led the way along the trail, stopping only briefly to check if they were being followed.

Betsy, as she walked along behind Wiley, began to consider her options and came to the conclusion that she must seize any opportunity to rid herself of these two evil beasts with their useless, doomed women. This was a woman who had grown so formidable and strong, even to the extent of out-thinking and outsmarting the two Harpe brothers, as Wiley had gradually come to realise.

They now were, or at least Wiley was, aware that time was running out, with a posse surely after them and that something needed to be done pretty quickly if they were to avoid a sticky end. Sensing this was the case and that time was indeed running out and also that the endgame was approaching, Betsy decided that at the first opportunity she would play the victim for all it was worth and use her charms to fool her hoped for rescuers into thinking that she, Betsy, had endured years of utter misery and abuse, completely innocent of any involvement of their heinous crimes. She should be be treated as a victim not as a criminal.

After all it was this strategy that had worked well for her before, notably with both Ballenger and Walker. She realised that most men were stupid enough to fall for her charms and do as she wanted.....all except Micajah Harpe whose behaviour seemed to suggest someone who defied all the rules of normal existence. This was partly true of course, but Betsy was determined to come out of this whole terrible experience the stronger, and rid herself once and for all from the terrible Harpes. They could both swing from the highest tree for all she cared and Wiley's self-serving concern for her meant nothing to her now. It merely served her purpose in one respect, and the only thing that mattered to her...survival.

CHAPTER 33

Meanwhile as the Harpe family continued their attempt to escape and Betsy pondered her options and possible fate, the posse rode up to the edge of the valley looking down at the trail below.

Moses took out his trusty monocular and recognised the five figures below, a relatively short distance ahead of the posse. The leafless trees now helpfully revealed the group to be indeed the Harpes, and their women.

"Look John, there they are, I'm damned sure it's those murderers." he pointed to Leiper who just made out the figures.

"Well John it looks like we found them." Moses said with tears welling up in his eyes. He quickly wiped them away and suppressed the emotions he felt.

John turned to him placing his hand on his shoulder.

"We need to be careful Moses - now is our chance to deal with them." John said still concerned regarding Moses and the danger that in his current state of mind, he would do something rash.

Leiper turned to the posse and gestured for them to follow him, and so they stealthily rode down to the valley to the trail where the Harpes were moving some distance ahead. They were careful not to arouse the attention of them yet whilst Leiper organised their next move. No use in allowing the Harpe brothers time to defend themselves. A sudden rush attack was the best way to take them dead or alive, and at that time even the women and their two infants were of little concern. If they had to perish in this action then so be it.

Luckily the cold Winter's wind was blowing with severity into them against their faces, which helpfully masked the sounds of the posse coming from behind toward the Harpe brothers.

***

Ahead the women all walked along following Wiley and Micajah who were both mounted on mules that they had taken from the Stegall house.

Betsy dropped back to the rear of the group keeping an eye open for any sign of any potential rescuers following. She soon noticed movement in the distance behind. She heard the faint distinctive noise of horses' hooves on the trail, softly betraying their riders' whereabouts. Betsy's spirits rose as she realised that an opportunity might be soon coming her way and as she was pondering this possibility she tried to contain her excitement.

"Could this be a posse come to get Micajah and Wiley?" she thought, but no sooner had she begun to wonder, when Wiley turned and looked back checking if anyone was following.

Betsy reacted swiftly by distracting him.

"Wiley when is Micajah goin' to stop and give us all some rest?" she enquired calling out loudly to him.

Wiley looked ahead and ignored her.

The posse was thankfully gaining ground and without any warning to the fugitives, suddenly charged at speed, which

168

allowed Betsy to fall intentionally down to the ground, rapidly pretending injury to her leg.

"Help!!" she screamed.

Panic ensued as Micajah and Wiley became aware of the danger.

"Look out Micajah it's a damned Yankee posse!!" he shouted alerting Big Harpe.

They grabbed their muskets, but too late as John Leiper had stopped, then took careful aim, fired his new carbine first, before either Harpe could respond. The shot hit Micajah in his back!

"Arrgh!!" he yelled in agony and fell heavily from his mule onto the ground.

Seeing this fate befall his brother, and judging correctly that there was nothing he could do to assist him, Wiley immediately jumped off his own mount, ran up the side of the valley into the upper reaches of the forest itself, seeking cover as fast as he could, and as the posse arrived on the scene, he made good his escape. Before heading away he fired at the posse group hitting one of the men in the arm. He smiled to himself, and with the expertise he had acquired, he disappeared into the dense undergrowth of the trees and bushes. His experience of escape which had been used on many occasions fleeing from vengeful pursuers, stood him in good stead. That together with the steepness of the ridge's side by the road, made it hard for horses to get up the incline. Much to the frustration of Moses and John, they both realised that catching him would be difficult to say the least. Shots were fired upwards in desperation, hoping to at least wound Wiley, but to no avail – he had vanished to all intents and purposes.

"Goddamn it!! I'll come after you Wiley!!" shouted Leiper.

Moses Stegall without hestitation ran to Micajah Harpe who lay writhing in pain on the ground feeling for his wounded back, and soon Betsy came up to him aiming a kick right into where she thought the wound was.

"You bastard Micajah for what you done to all those poor folks and me too!" she screamed, her eyes ablaze with loathing for her tormenter.

Micjah mouthed something but the pain he felt and the paralysis which began to restrict him, as he frantically tried to crawl away, prevented any intelligible word coming from him.

Susan and Sarah, both actually pregnant again as well as carrying their two infants, with Sarah's surviving infant in a sling and in obvious distress, stood aside in shock, unable to escape and unable to assist in any way. Even these two poor wretched women, however, now saw their freedom becoming a possibility.

John Leiper looked at Betsy and pulled her away to one side saying.

"You're safe now lady, we'll take care of him." He said gesturing to the fallen Micajah Harpe.

Unable to move Micajah regained his speech momentarily and glared at Leiper and Stegall, his eyes fiercely glaring at the two of them in total contempt.

"Damn ye all, Yankee scum!" he slowly but ferociously spat out like a snake spitting venom.

"Give me water before you do what ye have to do will ye?" he suddenly pleaded.

Leiper being a Christian, God fearing, humane man took

170

his canteen and poured some cool water into the wretched man's mouth. Micajah slurped some and in an extraordinary moment of clarity, he summoned up some last residue of strength and muttered.

"I ain't sorry for anythin' we done... Old Baldwin caused this...daned bastard....but my own daughter...I do regret..." he gasped.

Micajah winced in agony but held fast as he looked up to Moses and glared at him.

Betsy hearing this knew what he was referring to, and smiled to herself, pleased though surprised, that even this monster was aware of at least of some part of his guilt. She watched in excitement and anticipation.

Quickly Moses Stegall took Micajah's large, bladed hunting knife from his belt, grabbed hold of Micajah's black hair, then plunged the blade carefully into his neck.

Blood spurted forth on to the white, frozen ground, spattered in a grim macabre way, as if on a stark, white canvas.

"This is for my wife and child....you murderin' villain....you can go to Hell now where you belong!" Moses shouted at him with hatred in his eyes, all the pent up loathing coming to the fore now.

Moses stopped briefly as Micajah moaned in pain and knew his time was short, but in a last display of defiance Big Harpe turned his grizzled, bearded face to Moses Stegall and growled defiantly.

"You are a goddamned rough butcher....cut on and be damned!"

He gasped for air one last time, then added... "...I am Wolf!" in a final outburst of spent up hatred.

171

He fell back seemingly dead at last.

Moses needed no more encouragement from Micajah's last words and expertly finished cutting off his head, the blood spattering his leg and seeping into the ground. The most feared and hated man in Kentucky, Carolina, Tennessee and way beyond; Micajah Harpe, lay dead!

The posse stood motionless for a while, speechless until Betsy Roberts said almost accusingly to Leiper.

"He's dead thank the Lord, but you let Wiley Harpe get away."

Betsy then added, looking straight into his eyes.

"You all should have caught both these monsters years ago and Wiley's still free!" she called out accusingly.

John Leiper looked at her unable to respond immediately but gathered his thoughts together saying with some sense of guilt.

"Don't you worry my dear, we'll catch that villain soon enough." Leiper replied apologetically.

He lay his hand on her shoulder to reassure this strangely attractive and strong woman. He already felt a growing attraction for her. Betsy knew what he was thinking and decided there and then to exploit his feelings.

"Can you help me? I have nothing and am homeless now." she implored desperately.

"I will, don't worry dear, I will take care of you." Leiper replied with determination then looking at his friend Moses, he turned away to support to him.

Moses quickly took Micajah's severed head from the ground and put it into his saddlebag, the gruesome object just fitting in and bulging with black, matted hair defiantly hanging out.

"This bastard's head is going somewhere as a warning to any other villains John." he asserted.

There was no argument to that promise and all the posse present nodded in agreement.

"Place it in that tree fork." shouted Silas.

Later Moses and John, in fact, hung the head on a tree at a crossroads known later as "Harpe's Head" or Harpe's Head Road in Webster County, Kentucky. It remained there for several years gradually eaten away by wild beasts and birds, to eventually reveal a grisly, macabre sight; the skull seeming to grin menacingly at any passing travellers who stopped to look at it. Most shivered with trepidation at this awful spectacle. Rumour has it that Micajah's voice can be heard at night still threatening violence to all and sundry!

Susan and Sarah meanwhile, observing these events, begged Leiper and Stegall for mercy explaining that they too were victims and had no choice but to remain with the Harpe brothers. The fact that Sarah was carrying her poor infant, and that Susan was also carrying a child and was obviously pregnant with Micajah's child, as it turned out, helped their cause. Sarah though again pregnant herself and aware she was, displayed no physical signs as yet. Questions however were inevitably asked as to why they did not try to escape when opportunities arose, but Susan explained that they would have been killed for any act of betrayal and they had bairns to care for.

"What could we do? Good Lord we are only two defenceless women at the mercy of those wicked men." Susan said to John Leiper, taking care not to include Betsy in this explanation.

Leiper took pity on them and decided that they should all make their way to Fort Danville with Captain Ballenger, who had just arrived with five men shortly after the slaying of Micajah. The law should now take its' course.

Captain Ballenger, who with his men, had briefly attempted to locate Wiley Harpe but without any luck since Wiley had made considerable progress getting away. He then took charge of proceedings, issuing commands for the next stage. He had recognised Betsy and took the opportunity to make himself known to her, reassuring her that she would be dealt with fairly… "so long as I have anything to do with it."

So the party with Susan and Sarah hitched behind to two of the posse's, with Sarah's child and Susan's childen secured, though crying ungratefully. Betsy now behind John Leiper, taking the time to put her arms around his waist, rode off leaving the bloodstained scene behind on the Wilderness Road. It would become a ghoulish place of curiosity in the weeks and years to come.

Moses Stegall felt little or no relief at what he had done in revenge, the pain was too raw and no amount of suffering inflicted on Micajah Harpe would ameliorate his own suffering.

The whole party made their way to Fort Danville which took the rest of the day, indeed it was nightfall when they arrived there. On their arrival Ballenger was initially slightly concerned at what had happened, since it hardly seemed right for Moses to kill Big Harpe in such a brutal way, but on reflection decided that justice was served, if a little unorthodoxly. He was as relieved as the rest, that this violent monster was dead at last. It also saved him the onerous duty of bringing one of the feared brothers alive back to Fort Danville, thinking back to the last time he had had to deal with Big Harpe. Who knows what folk would want to do with Micajah

174

once he got back. No doubt they would want to lynch the fiend straight away before any trial could be arranged. The sooner news of the death of one of the Harpes was confirmed then folks would at least feel a little easier.... at least for now.

Micajah Harpe

CHAPTER 34

On returning to Fort Danville, Captain Ballenger, when he recovered his surprise at the events that had taken place, ordered that the women must be sent to Russellville to face possible trial for their complicity in the crimes of the Harpes. On refection he had reasoned that it was the right, judicial thing to do.

"Folks will demand that they answer all questions about their involvement." he decided.

Ballenger insisted this course of action was the only way forward in dealing with such an extraordinary series of events, but no sooner had he made that statement, John Leiper intervened and said that he knew positively that Betsy Roberts was an innocent victim of these villains, and he promised that he would look after her until she was ready to decide her future. The other two women he could not vouch for so Ballenger should do what he thought right and proper with them.

When they received this news Susan and Sarah were confident that justice would prevail, they were unaware that Betsy now had an advocate in John Leiper, and assumed that eventually, when all the evidence was presented before a court of law, they would all be freed. They were duly informed about their fates and in three days, after all of the women had been to Russellville then fed and washed, the three of them had begun to look and feel human again. Susan and Sarah recovered their senses to some extent, they then made ready to depart whilst consistently declaring their innocence to Captain Ballenger, and also to certain others who questioned them about their part in the heinous crimes committed by the Hapres.

On the morning of their departure Susan looked at Betsy who she had not spoken to all these days and said accusingly.

"I hope I never see you agin'. You are a lyin' evil bitch and you ain't no sister of mine!"

Betsy said nothing in reply but smirked in contempt, turned away and left her to go to John Leiper, who had taken it upon himself to care for her. She did not wish her sister any farewell, goodbye or good luck wishes. It was the last time that they ever spoke or met each other again, both going their separate ways for good.

And so Susan and Sarah were accompanied to Russellville, where after six days of questioning, it was decided to set free the two unfortunate women as no definite, corroborative evidence of complicity could be found to convict them. In a strange way both women had grown a little in strength, having survived an experience so extreme in it's horror and deprivation, that it would break the vast majority of people, whether men or women.

Susan and Sarah had supported each other throughout the time of their ordeal with the Harpe brothers, realising (especially Susan) that Betsy was not going to support them and was only concerned for her own well-being and survival. Indeed she appeared to them both, unfairly perhaps given the desperate conditions which they all shared, to relish the situation as time went by.

Consequently they turned to each other for succour, managing as best they could. At the same time it is a disturbing fact that they did nothing to hinder the Harpe's murderous activities, and made no effort to escape from them even when

178

the opportunity arose. Amazingly they had even helped them escape incarceration, with Betsy's connivance of course, on more than one occasion, stealing a boat and rowing it near to where the Harpes were imprisoned, then engineering their actual escape. This was another time, not recorded in our story (it would take a thousand pages at least to record all the events of the Terrible Harpes and their women) when the two brothers were imprisoned.

Their complicity or innocence remains something of an open question and a mystery to this day.

CHAPTER 35

After Micajah's demise at the hands of Moses Stegall, Wiley Harpe made good his escape through the forests and valleys of Kentucky and Tennessee using all his wiles and experience, he moved as fast as he could, keeping a watchful eye open for any sign of the posse or any pursuers, covering his tracks expertly. He was brilliant at surviving in the wild, his life of hardship with its extremes served him well yet again, though without Micajah he felt a loneliness that was new to him. The thought of his brother's death filled him with sadness and some guilt having escaped without him. He determined to seek revenge on Moses Stegall if ever the opportunity presented itself to him, but for the moment he had other priorities.

Soon after, within two days travelling, he came upon a group of Native Indian braves who he managed to convince were his friends and allies, mentioning Dragging Canoe who they straight away acknowledged as their Chief. He was then taken to their camp a few miles away, where he was given food and water, and stayed there for several days while he recuperated and planned his next move. The Indians, knowing his past as an outlaw, asked him if he wanted to join them as they were planning raids on settlers themselves and they knew full well that Wiley and his brother, "Big Harpe" hated these newcomers as much as they did. He would be useful to them for sure. Wiley went along with this ostensibly and enthusiastically for his own safety, but he was in reality undecided.

Soon after a raid was done on a group of travellers making their way through the Cumberland Gap, which ended up with the Indians slaughtering all five of the family including two children, Shortly after this Wiley made his mind up to depart and make his way to Cave-In-Rock where he reckoned that he could talk Captain Mason and his pirates into having him back now without his hated brother Micajah, who was the real crazy one of the two brothers. He figured that no posse or law could reach him at the cave and it would give him safe haven, while at the same time enable him to plunder riches with the pirates from river boatmen as before.

Wiley decided that this was the best plan for himself and after bidding farewell to his Indian friends, who expressed some disappointment at his decision to leave, (they even tried to pursued him to remain with them, offering him a young, not unattractive looking squaw, as well as generous gifts and booty) but to no avail. Wiley Harpe therefore set off early one morning bidding a fond farewell to his Indian friends, taking a deep breath before pushing his horse onwards, a fine stallion which had been given to him by none less than Dragging Canoe as a token of friendship. And so commenced the long, arduous journey to Cave-In-Rock, Southern Illinois, complete with provisions and armed to the teeth in case of threats from any pursuing lawmen or dangerous beast.

His course was set.

CHAPTER 36

In Kentucky and the surrounding territories, with the death of Micajah Harpe and the disappearance of Wiley, life took on a more settled appearance with trade and travel along the Wilderness Road a safer proposition, except of course for the occasional Indian raids. Though even here the growing strength of the forces of law in the form of Captain Ballenger's forces at Fort Danville and others, had subdued and driven away much of this threat. But not completely.

All this meant that John Leiper and his now widowed friend Moses Stegall were able to grow their businesses with some confidence. Moses remained alone now and found himself a small cabin some fifteen miles from Lexington out in the wilds, in which he hid his grief and lived out his days as a solitary figure, but one who was always on hand to help. Drink became his solace as time went on, he was prone to bouts of drunkenness which sometimes led to fights when he ventured to other settlements, but which also saw him forgiven and helped, especially by John whenever he got himself into trouble and ended up in the lockup. The terrible happenings which had scarred Moses as well as his killing of the feared 'Big Harpe' always brought a degree of sympathy from the majority of folk. There was considerable gratitude shown toward him from these people but he was unable to claim the reward of three hundred dollars from the Governor of Kentucky, James Garrard, who reasoned that, the action was achieved not by one person alone. He preferred to give greater credit to Captain Ballenger, although he too was denied anything due to the fact that

Garrard figured that; "he was just doing his job for which he received generous pay anyway."

Moses would return to his home a broken man but with at least one loyal, true friend in John Leiper.

***

Betsy Roberts soon blossomed again and regained fully, her former attractiveness, which now was combined with a steely determination never, for the rest of life, to be taken prisoner, or abused again. She had become strong, devious and manipulative and when John Leiper proposed that she become his wife and move into his substantial log cabin, she decided in her own interests naturally, to accept his offer. Little did Leiper realise what he was taking on, smitten as he was with this beauty who he figured would succumb gratefully to his kindness and generosity. He reasoned that Betsy would become the dutiful, loyal wife he had longed for all these years. Unfortunately for him Betsy Roberts was a different proposition with plans and a wilfulness all of her own, but who was quite capable of playing the game for as long as it suited her.

They got married by way of a simple ceremony at the newly constructed church in Lexington, Moses was best man to John Leiper, and within twelve months they moved permanently to Lexington which was growing into a town of some substance. Leiper had purchased a newly built house which lay on the edge of town but stood in it's own modest grounds. Soon after Betsy gave birth to a son, they named Joshua, who was a healthy boy but strangely looked nothing like Leiper having reddish hair and features which confounded him.

He bit his tongue, keeping his suspicions to himself, since if he so much as gently questioned Betsy, she was liable to let loose her temper, which was volcanic. It was a fearsome blast which was almost as frightening as her erstwhile captor Micajah Harpe! John soon discerned that his new wife was not someone to be provoked or taken for granted, and so he sensibly decided to accede to her wishes in pretty much everything, thereby avoiding confrontation in any way. Life should be much easier to cope with this way, or so he figured.

Betsy said nothing but doted on her child as her possession. She knew full well that his real father was a local man named James Weller, a young, good looking blacksmith who Betsy had taken a shine to, and thereafter secretly met purely for sexual relations. James possessed a fine physique, slim in build, with an obvious strength, not just physical but expressed in his character. This with his dark red hair and swarthy complexion attracted a desire in Betsy that she had not felt since she was a teenage girl with her hormones at that time, like most young females, going crazy. The affair did not begin immediately as James never imagined that he would be making love to such a fine, beautiful lady who was married to the respected Mr Leiper who possessed a spotless reputation. He was obviously aware of her beauty and it may have crossed his mind imagining some sexual liaison with her but he quickly dismissed such notions as overtly scandalous.

It was Betsy who made the first move subtly exposing a finely turned ankle, and then teasingly making further suggestive remarks, then asking him to pick up a deftly dropped lace handkerchief which he dutifully obliged her. He spontaneously gave way to his sexual impulse which was met with surprisingly affectionate responses from Betsy. From there, events moved quickly and whether in the stable, out of town or even in her own home, the encounters became regular and passionate with Betsy in particular gaining excitement, something she had not experienced for so long. James was an almost perfect lover, tender but masterful when permitted, but ultimately it was Betsy who was in control and James knew it.

John Leiper on the other hand was sadly not too good in the arts of lovemaking, being unused to a woman's needs (not uncommon with most men at this time), and Betsy as we know, had physical, sexual needs which he was not capable of fulfilling. Having put up with the rough approaches from Wiley for so long, she had found someone other than her husband, who had the ability and knowledge of how to please a woman, something which her secret lover possessed, but which Leiper sadly lacked. Poor John Leiper remained blissfully unaware of his wife's adulterous behaviour but she sometimes wondered if he suspected and yet chose to ignore it, satisfied that she was his wife, and to some extent it relieved him of the burden, surprising though this may sound, of keeping her satisfied.

Three years passed and Betsy became more and more dissatisfied with her life with John Leiper. He was often away on business, sometimes with his friend Moses Stegall who he wished to help get back on his feet after his terrible loss, but sometimes on his own. Sensing her unhappiness Leiper tried his best to please her with generous gifts some he could ill-afford, and often excessive praising of her beauty, but his efforts had the opposite effect. Betsy was not going to be satisfied with the humdrum life of a typical wife who was expected to run a home and rear children, all the while doing what her husband wanted. Not for her this monotonous domestic life where the other wives in Lexington spent their time in petty gossip, which merely had the effect of disinterest in her.

"I'm bored here John, why don't you do something and get

us away from this terrible place and go somewhere which is civilised!" Betsy complained one day.

"I'm sick and tired of the same routines." she added.

"What do you suggest my love, that we move?" he suggested but immediately realised his error. John Leiper had no intention of uprooting and leaving his home, business and most of all his dear friend Moses who needed his support still.

"Yes moving North where there's a better life. I hear New York offers so much and we would prosper there my dear." Betsy replied.

Leiper hesitated, horrified at this suggestion, then said firmly for once sounding as if he spoke with some authority.

"Sounds fine but we've got a good home here my love and I ain't throwing away my business which has served us well enough these past years. Anyway most wives would be happy with what we got. The good Lord has provided for us well Betsy my dear." he added bravely, becoming irritated at her comments.

Betsy left off and returned to her daily chores giving further thought about what she was going to do next.

CHAPTER 37

A week later something happened which gave Betsy Roberts the chance to erase one last strand of suspicion that might one day arise about her past. On a warm day in early June when Kentucky had burst out in beauty with all the trees, flowers and wildlife abundant with so much life, she went into the town to get some provisions and maybe treat herself to a new hat at the same time. Joshua was often looked after by a young teenage girl who Betsy had befriended and used for her own convenience to help around the house. Apart from that the girl was fond of Joshua and was good at looking after him while she, Betsy, took her pleasures, whether shopping, or whether carnal pursuits, with James her young lover.

Betsy suddenly noticed two rough looking men riding into town. As they came nearer she recognised one of them to her horror was none other than Wiley Harpe, the other she knew not who he was. The unmistakable shape of Wiley rode past Betsy, unaware that she had seen him, and headed for the Sheriff's office and jailhouse.

"What the Hell is he doing here and what is he up to?" she mused.

She followed the men keeping a distance and observed as they dismounted by the jailhouse. Taking a deep breath she made her move decisively and went up to Wiley, who she called out to firmly.

"Wiley Harpe!!"

Wiley, surprised by a woman's voice knowing his name, spun around and not recognising Betsy yet, tipped his hat and greeted her.

"Why good day ma'am." he said politely but on inspecting this woman more closely it dawned on him who she was. He was astounded to see his former 'wife' again.

"Well I'll be...."

"Yes Wiley Harpe it's me Betsy...what are you doing here?" she enquired staring straight at him.

Wiley paused briefly then sneeringly replied.

"Not your business you cheatin' bitch..."

Before he could say any more Betsy went right up to him and said in a threatening voice.

"I'll see you hanged, I know who you are and you will do as I say do you hear, you evil scum?"

"Who the Hell..!?" Wiley replied, becoming angry now that he realised the danger he was in as the Sheriff's office was behind him with three armed men all around, looking at him with increasing curiosity and suspicion.

Betsy in a flash stopped him doing anything else which would thereby spoil an opportunity that she had realised and said.

"You'll tell me where the stashes are that you and that sick brother of yours hid and I'll say nothing, I don't know what you're plans are and I don't care, but I'll have what's mine. If you don't I'll see to it that you get hanged!" she said firmly.

Wiley in a state of confusion realising the danger he was in, something he had most certainly not bargained for, agreed and promised to tell her where the stashes were in return for her keeping quiet. He seemed to lose his sense of perspective and gave way to this powerful force in front of him, named Betsy Roberts, who again had the upper hand. He was also aware that she was more than capable of pulling out her sharp and trusty knife and seeing to him there and then. Wiley then whispered in her ear the locations of the three main places where he and Micajah had stashed the majority of the loot they had stolen.

"You'd better be tellin' me the truth Wiley or I'll see to it that they'll do more than just hang you. You hear me!"

Wiley nodded, his whole persona now wilting under the fierce gaze of his erstwhile captive and former 'wife'.

Wiley moved on, now paralysed with fear, told his accomplice, a feeble man named James May who he had befriended at Cave-In-Rock, to say or do nothing if he knew what was good for him. Being witless, the hapless May meekly obeyed.

Recovering his senses Wiley implored Betsy.

"Look Betsy I got somethin' else which is worth a lot to the sheriff here and I'll gladly share the reward with you if you help."

Wiley told Betsy that in his bag, hung on his horse, was the head of Captain Mason the leader of the river pirates who he had slain one night and made off with his partner in crime, the fool James May who had helped him and had been lookout. Wiley's plan was to convince the sheriff that the head he possessed was his own and that he had slain Wiley Harpe himself as a certain John Setton. This half-baked plan he figured would free him from any further suspicion and guilt. May thought it brilliant but then he was retarded, that was for sure.

"Go then and mind I'll be watching you. We'll split the reward fifty-fifty." Betsy warned Wiley and stared fiercely into his eyes.

Wiley and May proceeded and went into the sheriff's office. After they walked in passed the other lawmen who were becoming curious as to what these two starngers were up to, Wiley pulled the grotesque head out of his bag and proudly showed off to the sheriff the head of the notorious Wiley Harpe, who indeed did look similar to Mason and confidentally awaited confirmation and due reward.

No sooner had they done this than Betsy walked in pushed past the two brigands and informed Sheriff Doolan that before him was not John Setton but the hated murderer and outlaw, Wiley Harpe.

Wiley immediately denied it saying that his name was John Setton not Wiley Harpe.

"This lady is mad!" he pleaded.

Betsy looked sternly at the sheriff, who she had met on a few occasions before when her husband had reason to make a complaint or consult with him. She asserted.

"No I'm not, just tear off his shirt at his chest and you'll see the famous scar he has from the Independence War Sheriff. He served with Tarleton and the British, he's a traitor!"

Sure enough Doolan who knew about the scar from descriptions circulated in the territory, ripped it away and before him was revealed Wiley's long scar. A feature all knew he had. Without further delay he called out to the three deputies.

"Put these two men in irons!"

Doolan immediately ordered and the three deputies quickly binded Wiley and May, even as May pleaded, to no avail, his innocence.

"But I ain't had nuthin' to do with with these killings...tell them Wiley!" he squeeled in terror.

Recovering his more usual confidence and arrogance Wiley retorted.

"Ha! Stop you're squeelin' May!"

Then added contemptuously.

"Afraid of dyin'? Ha ha!"

"Hang us both and to Hell with you all ye Yankee bastards!" he shouted to Doolan raising his fists.

With that both were dragged off into the jailhouse, bound and now gagged to prevent Wiley shouting any further profanities. Tears of sheer terror rolled down the pathetic face of James May, a fool and duped idiot boy.

It took a mere two days for a trial to be arranged and Judge Morris summoned to officiate. The jury took little time to find both men guilty of piracy, murder, robbery and numerous other felonies which shocked all who were in attendance. They returned to the court without delay to deliver the inevitable verdict. After the judge had completed outlining the evil perpetrated by them both, and with particular emphasis on Wiley's crimes, both were sentenced to death by hanging. They were then bundled unceremoniously out of the courthouse to the jail to await their fate. May wailed all night declaring to Wiley that he was innocent and that Wiley should speak up for him, especially as it would..."break my ma's heart, I'm too young to die!" Wiley merely spat at him saying with contempt.

"Shut yer mouth boy, I don't give two hoots 'bout you laddie, nor yer whore of a mother. To Hell with all of ye!"

May sobbed more but if he thought that Wiley Harpe would help him, then he was more of a fool than he already most certainly was.

Wiley and May were escorted out, were hanged the in the early morning, watched by a baying crowd and with satisfaction by Betsy Roberts, who now was free of all implication. Wiley had one last outburst before the platform board was kicked away.

"Go to Hell ye damned Yankees!!" he yelled.

May froze in horror, speechless with terror with urine visibly dripping down his trouser leg. He had stumbled his way to the gallows pleading his innocence all the time, sobbing uncontrollably then at the last moment before the noose was placed over his head he seemed to accept the inevitable and stood stiff to await his end,

The executioner did his job pulling the lever, then both men swung freely from the beam, legs kicking awhile before death claimed two more souls. Wiley's soul no doubt on its way to join his brother in Hell.

With the demise of Micajah and Wiley Harpe, Americans had seen their first known serial killers. Next day after the excitement of the hangings which were the talk of the town, soon the whole territiory, Betsy's actions were hailed as brave and commendable, and her husband John Leiper basked in the admiration held by all for this remarkable woman who had helped to bring the hated Wiley Harpe to justice finally.

He vowed immediately to let Moses Stegall know of these events and rode to his cabin a few days later to tell him what he thought was the good news. Unfortunately he found Moses in a drunken stupor, unable to properly take in the news of his hated foe. He had neglected himself to such an extent that John almost did not recognise his old friend. His cabin was now a shambles with empty and broken bottles scattered about, his clothes torn, unwashed, an old letter from Jane which he read and reread over and over again was all he had left to bring some measure of solace to his broken heart. Even later when he began to sober up it had little effect on him, his grief was too deep and palpable.

"Thank you John...but nothin' can bring my Jane back...my beautiful boy...damn them, damn them!" he raged as he stared forlornly at John Leiper.

"I know Moses, but you must try...for their sake." Leiper implored to little avail.

There was nothing more to be done sadly so with a heavy heart John left his friend feeling a profound sadness, also realising that Moses was never going to get over his terrible loss, indeed he was found dead a week later on the floor of his cabin with a broken bottle of liquor nearby, his only succour during those dark times.

John Leiper rode back to Lexington where the townspeople displayed their gratitude to Betsy on ridding the territory of the remaining Harpe brother in various ways, one being a reception laid on where Betsy was toasted by all as a heroine. It made John feel proud but Betsy took care not to overplay this situation which made her feel uncomfortable at times, and even feigned embarrassment so that her true feelings and complicity in the crimes of Wiley Harpe could be safely forgotten.

CHAPTER 38

Around one month later in early June as life resumed its dreary monotony and memories of Wiley Harpe's demise faded, Betsy made her move after contemplating her options during a sleepless night. Early in the morning she arose from her bed and took her trusty knife, and while John lay sleeping stabbed him through the heart in one swift deadly action. She covered his face with the sheet in order to avoid looking into his eyes, for despite doing what she did, Betsy knew him as a man of honesty and decency who had never wronged her. Leiper had no chance to resist, only twitching slightly after the knife was plunged into his heart and mercifully died quickly, knowing nothing about his wife's evil action.

Killing this man meant little to her now as she had become immune to anyone else's existence except her own and of course her son, Joshua. She made the house look like it been ransacked by outlaws or maybe Indians, and left clothes and belongings strewn about the place hoping that no suspicion would fall on her, and that anyone would assume she and her son had been kidnapped which was not uncommon even within a settlement or town.

Betsy quickly collected her son Joshua who was asleep from his room, a placid, obedient boy of four years old, then packed her things methodically, making sure she took John Leipers's new rifle and two pistols, loaded them up on to their horse and buggy that she had readied beforehand. She left with

Joshua in the early hours of the morning, without raising any alarm. The rising sun was just appearing above the horizon and casting its feeble rays over the town as she looked back for one last time. She had comforted her son, made him comfortable in the buggy next to her, then as she moved off breathed a big sigh of relief. Her first port of call was to head for Pharris Inn which took her most of the day in order to collect the three stashes that Wiley had told her about. Sure enough they were located under the rocks as described by him. Betsy needed no assistance thankfully in pulling out the saddlebags, indeed she had the strength of many men her age and was able to load them onto her buggy without too much difficulty. Joshua looked on curious as to what his mother was doing. Betsy looked at him and smiled.

"This will help us get set up good and proper when we get to where we're going dear son." she reassured him.

With considerable relief and satisfaction at her achievmnets she then whipped the horse and embarked on her long, long journey to the growing metropolis which was New York, a city she had many times heard about and which, she reckoned would offer her and Joshua the life that she really sought. Betsy Roberts was going to make a new life and nothing would stop her, neither arduous journey nor any man.

PART TWO

A NEW LIFE

CHAPTER 1

1807

Betsy's journey to New York from Lexington, Kentucky, was harder than she ever anticipated, not just with the rough, dangerous trails with their mixture of wild animals always present if rarely seen, murderous outlaws lurking off the trail and ready to set upon unsuspecting travellers, but also the possibility of landslips, damaged roads with yawning gaps at the side of the road, blockages by fallen trees, rocks and unfriendly Indian tribes looking to vent their rage on unsuspecting migrants, easy prey for some of them. Luckily Betsy had the Harpe brothers to thank for reducing this potential problem, thanks to their time spent with the Chickamaugas with good relations especially against a common enemy; white settlers. This stood her in good stead.

Betsy, now in her twenties, was a fully mature woman. Her natural beauty was still very much evident, her blonde hair, her rosy full lips, full sensuous figure, together with her pale skin, all these alluring qualities conveyed a rare attractiveness which she was well able to use to her advantage when the opportunity presented itself. If that was not enough she possessed the most gorgeous deep blue eyes which seemed to mesmerise and penetrate the soul of anyone engaged in discourse with her, or more pertinently the men who attempted to attract her attention. Many of these men looked on with concealed lust but conversely few ever attracted her attention, the only one of note being James back in Lexington of course, with whom she took her lustful pleasure secretly. This only added to Betsy's excitement, her husband blissfully unaware of her adulterous activity.

As well as attracting the attention of sundry men, she also elicited the unwanted jealousy and envy of some of the ladies of Lexington, who gossiped amongst themselves and gave her looks of unconcealed contempt on occasions. This merely amused Betsy. Added to her beauty was a character of incredible strength, she possessed a tongue which could cut to pieces with ease anyone who had the temerity to make a derogatory comment or give her a such a look. The majority of the ladies of the town thus avoided provoking her face to face, and the men contented themselves with lustful, desirous thoughts.

Betsy was a formidable woman. Her time with the Harpes had taught her many things, her relationship with Wiley had made her immune to some extent to physical contact whether sexual or not. She did, however despite all this, retain at least a carnal attraction to any lucky man who was able to display character as well as good looks. Her selection of the man was a matter of when and who she would decide was right for her, there was to be no other way.

Before departing Lexington Betsy had locked the Harpes's stash, which she had collected courtesy of Wiley, in a formidable wooden box, approximately 2 feet by one and a half feet, hidden away under the seat of the buggy with her other personal bags on top and at the rear of the buggy. Several chains and padlocks were used to secure this valuable collection, it was her and Joshua's future and she would guard it with her life.

Accordingly for the trials and tribulations which inevitably lay ahead, if there is one woman who had the wherewithal and courage to deal with all this, it was Betsy Roberts. Her experience over years of hardship, survival and brutality with Micajah and Wiley Harpe had made her tough and unflinching. She had much less fear of what might happen and the ability to deal ruthlessly with brigands than even most pioneers of these times. There was no template or training which could compare to her time with the Harpe brothers. Nothing was going to impede her progress or dampen her resolve to make a new life for herself and her dear son, Joshua.

Armed with this Betsy and Joshua stoically made their way along the Cumberland Pass, their wagon rattling and rolling with the pitted trail, at times it felt so uncomfortable that Betsy had to stop to rest the horse and check her buggy for damage.

Betsy aimed to reach Charleston, West Virginia via the local roads and trails of which she was familiar with from her days with the Harpes, as well as Indian trails which existed at this time and were well used by those pioneers and families traveling, mostly Westwards to what they perceived as the promised land. Thankfully on the advice of George Washington, Virginia commissioned the James River Company to upgrade these trails into roads. One of the company's largest and most important road projects was the James River and Kanawha Turnpike. The turnpike traversed the frontier from Lexington, Kentucky to Charleston, West Virginia. This is where Betsy headed for since she knew that Charleston was a growing centre of business, especially the with the notorious but burgeoning slave trade.

Her first destination along this route was to be the small settlement at Huntington, some one hundred and thirty miles from Lexington. At that time the journey could often take several days whether by horse, mule, wagon or walking as many travellers had to do. Some newly established turnpikes were gradually appearing enabling improvements to the roads but these were few and far between at this time.

With Joshua at her side she doggedly continued her journey passing by certain creeks and rivers where the Harpes had dumped the disembowelled bodies of their victims. Occasionally she shuddered at the recollection of what she had actively participated in, memories of innocent, poor souls who had had the misfortune to cross the path of these murderous brigands. She felt no such remorse for others particularly the foolish, Langford who she reckoned deserved his fate. Indeed she felt a certain pride in dispatching him. Joshua of course knew nothing of his mother's past criminality and simply was totally devoted to her.

"Ma how long are we going to be?" he asked.

"Don't you worry my boy, it's goin' to be a long journey but we have the good Lord with us, my maps, my two pistols, and your father's carbine to deal with any trouble. He may not be with us in body son but his spirit will always watch over us. You will be fine, believe me Joshua."

"I know ma, you can count on me."

"I know I can son, you're my rock."

Betsy put her arm around the boy lovingly. She felt a mother's love and devotion toward this young boy and would move heaven and earth to protect him come what may. Any feelings of guilt for what she had done in the past were submerged in what she had to do now.

CHAPTER 2

Before embarking on her journey Betsy had taken care to take her husband's two pistols, his Nock double barrelled carbine, which he had 'acquired' from a British prisoner during the War of Independence and hunting knife, a sharp an instrument as could be found in Virginia. The Nock carbine rifle was his pride and joy, much admired by many fellow hunters, not least his friend Moses who had failed to take one from the few that were available from certain prisoners, officers mostly. Betsy was well acquainted with it as she had practised using it on several occasions, even embarrassing Leiper once with her skill as a markswoman. She also armed herself with her trusty knife, a short blade of fearsome sharpness.

With these useful weapons Betsy felt reasonably secure, the privations of her journey were made a little less unpleasant thanks to her incredibly practical way of dealing with such things as toilet arrangements and living off the land. Occasionally luck would lend her a hand in the form of wild turkeys, deer and nuts, mushrooms presenting themselves and which she looked for. Wiley Harpe in particular had an encyclopaedic knowledge of all things related to living off the land and passed on much of this knowledge to Betsy which she always thought would be useful at some point in her life. Micajah was also occasionally useful in his skill as a hunter, amazingly stealthy stalking prey, given his ungainly, huge size! On one occasion Wiley took her to one side and impressed on her how important it was to learn these skills.

201

"You need to pay attention girl if you want to stay alive!" he implored Betsy on more than one occasion, Betsy faked indifference but nonetheless took it all in. Micajah had no such concerns, his suspicion and contempt for all the women, including Betsy, was all too evident at virtually every stage of their time together, his treatment of them and his children even was nothing short of barbaric.

Armed with all this experience Betsy forged ahead with her journey traveling twenty miles in the first day before resting up in a small clearing just off the trail. She slept but little, her main concern was comforting Joshua who despite everything slept well, secure in his mother's arms and always keeping an eye open for any potential danger.

Luckily the March weather was set fair this time and apart from a light shower, the rains were kept mercifully at bay for the first few days until she reached Huntington. Her main worry at this early stage apart from the obvious, was that the buggy would keep steady and not lose a wheel in one of the many ruts and holes along the trail. She preyed for this not to happen.

"Good Lord! Have mercy on us!" she exclaimed on several occasions as a wheel slumped into a hollow or was bounced out of a rut or juddered violently.

"Hang on Joshua we're going to hit a real hard bit now!"

"Oh no ma!"

But Joshua got used to these discomforts and made his mother secretly proud of him even joking.

"This'll make your bones strong boy!"

Joshua spent much of his time looking out for wild animals, scanning the forest, which Betsy had asked him to do.

She wisely kept him distracted and purposeful.

"Look ma, a bear!"

"I can't see any son, they rarely bother folks unless they are desperate or just plain mean in disposition. But keep your eyes peeled Josh."

Betsy smiled and reminded him that no bear would get near them, especially with her Nock double barrelled carbine, two pistols and a sharp hunting knife.

After the first two days traveling when no other travellers were seen on the trail, except for an old pioneer/hunter who clearly was heading for the Ohio River or one of its' tributaries in search of beaver most likely, but he disappeared no sooner was he in sight. It was on the third that they passed two men mounted on mules, with two

more mules in tow carrying heavy bags strapped to them. On seeing the men coming towards her and Joshua, Betsy slid her two loaded pistols under her skirts so that she could employ them at short notice.

The two men proved no threat as they politely enquired as to where Betsy was heading. She lied to them stating that her husband was following not far behind and they were on their way East .

"Well you take care of yerself lady and you too sonny, there's plenty of bad folk and wild critters lying in wait"

The older of the two bearded men advised. He looked at Betsy with some concern which instinctively Betsy regarded as sincere. The other man who had a patch over his eye and was of lesser stature nodded in agreement but said nothing.

"We will and I thank ye for your warning but I know this trail fairly well since I been along it with my husband before."

She smiled and ruffled Joshua's hair.

"I've got my boy to help me too."

The first man continued.

"Well at least them villains the Harpes ain't no more thank the good Lord. I hear them and their wicked women folk robbed and killed more than fifty innocent men, women and children. Vermin so they were, hope they rot in Hell all of 'em."

He spat out some tobacco that he had been chewing.

Betsy kept her thoughts closely in check but reddened slightly though she showed no emotion.

The man adjusted his tattered hat not noticing Betsy's discomfort, thinking instead that it was a rather inappropriate comment, given that this young woman and her young child were all alone.

He looked on with some embarrassment as did his companion.

Betsy broke the temporary silence.

"Well I guess we must get going but good to speak with you gentlemen and good luck with your trading." she said pleasantly.

"Thank you lady, we're heading to Lexington with some provisions. We need to get going so I'll bid you both good day"

Both men tipped their hats. With that the two men took their leave and Betsy breathed a sigh of relief and continued on her way.

CHAPTER 3

After three days of exhausting travel Betsy and Joshua encountered more travellers heading West, but thankfully they did not stop to investigate what she and Joshua were doing on the trail, such was their determination to reach their destination some hundreds of miles further on. Only the womenfolk showed any interest but their inquisitiveness was subdued by the need to make haste in their quest westwards and to reach Lexington to re-supply. Betsy neither encouraged discourse nor asked for any help at this point. When Joshua saw other children around his age he asked his mother if they could stop so he could play with some of them. Betsy discouraged this immediately.

"We need to hurry boy, no time for playin' you'll get plenty of time to make new friends when we get to New York, I promise son."

"Yes ma." he muttered plaintively.

On the fourth day, now reaching half way or more to Huntington, they came across a lone traveller who straight away Betsy determined was going to be potentially troublesome. The man was riding a mule with a rifle slung over his shoulder with a pistol and large knife tucked inside his belt. He looked in his thirties but could have been younger, time had not been kind with his grizzled beard, scar above his right eye and weaselly features suggested an unpleasant disposition. He rode up to the buggy and seized Betsy's horse, which was clearly tiring and undernourished, and looked Betsy over before saying in a sly tone.

"Well, well what have we here, a fine pretty young lass."

He laughed and then suddenly attempted to grab her, lunging forward but nearly falling off his mule. Losing his balance momentarily gave Betsy the opportunity to react as saw a split second opportunity to turn the tables on this villain.

Joshua screamed but before the man could go any further Betsy had whipped out her trusty blade and thrust it into his side.

"Knife!! Damn you bitch!!" he yelled.

He fell off his mule clutching his side as blood trickled down his thigh. He groaned pathetically looking at Betsy in total consternation and fear.

The thought that a young woman might not only resist but defeat him had never occurred to this opportunist brigand.

Betsy turned on him with contempt.

"You bastard, I'll kill ye if you as much as move!! You'll live more's the pity but get yourself out of here before I finish you off like the filthy hog you are!"

Betsy thrust the knife at his throat, then the man struggled to his feet swaying but with difficulty managed to get on his mule.

"I didn't mean no harm, just tryin' to be friendly."

Bearing his rotten teeth and groaning with the pain he managed very slowly to board his steed which had become disturbed and was bucking vigorously, making life for him all the more painful.

"Maybe this'll teach you. If it don't I hope someone else

will do what I nearly did and send you to Hell! Now get your miserable carcass out of here!"

Betsy then grabbed one of her pistols and made as if to fire.

"No no, I'm gittin' out of here woman!" he pleaded holding up his free hand and with the other hand clutching his side, and then rapidly and miraculously taking the reins of his mule, he made off.

When further on along the trail he turned and yelled.

"Damn ye bitch, I'll kill you if …." then his voice faded into a painful whimper as the pain of his knife wound returned with a vengeance. He clutched desperately at his side as he rode away.

"Good riddance to him." Betsy affirmed then looking at Joshua with concern said affectionately.

"Are you alright Joshua?"

"Yes mamma, is that ugly man gonna die?" he asked.

"I don't know son but he's gone now and we won't be seeing him ever again, I promise." she said reassuringly.

After putting her pistol and knife away safely and making sure all was well and in order, they climbed aboard the buggy and continued on their way, Betsy looking back occasionally to make sure they were well away from danger.

Further up the trail, some three miles on, once again Betsy sensed danger and paused to see what was the cause of her concern. This instinctive feeling was confirmed, when from what seemed like nowhere, a group of native Indians rushed her and Joshua quickly surrounding the buggy. One of the braves jumped aboard and dragged her off, while another took

Joshua in his arms. The band were Chickamauga renegades so it seemed to her as she struggled to break free but this fearsomely strong brave yielded not an inch.

"No, no please. We are your friends!" she shouted with a few words in their native language which she remembered from Wiley, she then called out Dragging Canoe's name. This mention of their respected chief caused the men to stop and look to their leader, an impressive young man who mercifully released Betsy from his grip.

"I was Wiley Harpes wife before he was captured, friend to your tribe with his brother Micajah. You remember?"

The young brave stared at her and for a brief second Betsy feared the worst as he seemed to go for his tomahawk, then smiled at her pointing to Joshua said.

"He…Wiley son, yes?"

Betsy lost no time confirming this lie, though Joshua frowned but thankfully said nothing.

"Yes he's Wiley's boy." Betsy quickly nodded.

"Wiley dead I hear and Micajah. White soldiers kill both, we take revenge on white demons as did they!"

He held up his tomahawk as if to strike and the others in the raiding party followed suit.

"You go in peace and may your God protect you."

The brave, who was in fact Doublehead, grandson of Dragging Canoe and leader of the tribe, then turned away but before leaving with the rest of the party, turned and said.

"Your boy is fine brave, grow up to be like his father."

Betsy secretly felt sick but nodded.

"Thank you, he will."

With that the Indians melted away into the forest, the rich, bright Spring undergrowth quickly concealing them.

After thinking deeply Joshua blurted out.

"Ma I'm not Wiley's son! He's not my daddy! Who is he?"

Betsy breathed deeply feeling pangs of guilt but replied tenderly.

"No my dear boy he is definitely not your father but I had to say that for a reason, to save us from danger. I promise I will explain some day when you're older. Now no more questions we must resume our journey before nightfall comes."

Joshua frowned but understood despite his young years, that his mother knew best. His trust in her was implicit.

Betsy had to conceal her true feelings on many occasions, sundry thoughts from her past years, as well as temper her reactions to events and sights which might well reveal a side to her which she most certainly wished to keep to herself. Joshua must never know the ruthlessness behind her loving, tender motherly persona, a persona which was genuine and exemplified in her love for her son, and her in day to day dealings with people. The further now she could get away from her past the better, she yearned for a new beginning.

Thus once again mother and son wearily ascended the buggy which had become filthy and now looked a sorry sight. Betsy took the reins, then gently but firmly whipped the horse resuming their way through the long, arduous trails. Exhausting work for her but she possessed a steel will and toughness borne of previous hardship and depravation.

CHAPTER 4

After five days of traveling Betsy and Joshua came across a group of families traveling West in five wagons, along with several mules and horses tethered in tow. The mules tethered together in line, were all carrying various boxes, bags and such like, the three horses were being rested after their use in pulling the wagons in pairs. Some of the men and older boys walked alongside the wagons, and two of the men rode ahead. The womenfolk and older men steered the wagons and some of the older girls sat beside their mothers, while others joined the boys walking along often making mischief as young folk tend to do.

It was the two men leading the party that Betsy encountered first as she rounded a bend in the road, their presence initially caused her concern but after looking closely at them as they stopped, she decided instinctively that their was no cause for any serious worrying, the two men had the appearance of honest individuals, their bearing straight, their clothes relatively modest, not the attire of your typical pioneer, outlaw or hunter most likely to be seen at this time.

Since the trail only had room for one wagon or carriage to pass Betsy pulled up and called out.

"Good day, can you let me pass?"

"Yes but we're about to make camp in this clearing ma'am." He pointed to where there was indeed a clearing not far from a creek which could just be seen through the trees.

"You and the boy are welcome to join us, we have food a plenty and would welcome your company if you so wish. Our intention is to rest overnight and then go on our way."

"Where you headin' if you don't mind me inquiring?" Betsy asked realising fully now that the men were harmless and indeed appeared courteous and helpful. She noticed that their clothes were not of the type worn by villains, their hats looked quite new, they were dressed in black. The rest of the party now appeared with the womenfolk and children which suggested to her that they were one of a number of Christian families seeking a better life out west. It was common during these times as many pilgrims sought opportunities to establish new communities and to spread the word of the Lord. This was confirmed as the man, obviously their leader and spokesman, continued.

"We have a long journey ahead of us and need to conserve as much energy as we can."

"Well thank ye, my son and I would be glad to stop a while with you.

Betsy pulled over to the clearing where the party were gathering as the two men indicated.

"I'm Emmet James."

He announced in an accent which at first Betsy did not recognize but with a sudden chill she remembered that the Harpe brothers spoke in a similar manner, a dialect emanating from Scotland, the Borders to be precise. Their voices reminiscent of Emmett's dialect, and especially Wiley's way of speaking, would remain with her for the rest of her life.

The man announced taking off his hat and bowed courteously.

"These people are good folk making their way West to find a new life and community. We've heard exciting things that folk have made their fortune there and established new towns and settlements. I'm guiding them there, where are you going miss?"

"It's Mrs for I am a widow and I'm not sure yet. Headin' east maybe New York" Betsy replied, keeping her cards close to her chest though she felt comfortable nonetheless.

Emmet immediately realised his mistake in calling her 'miss' but was somewhat perplexed at her vagueness concerning where she and her son were heading.

"Sorry lady, you're welcome to come with us, but you if I may offer you some advice, meanin' in a respectful way, I would dispense with your buggy and use the horse instead to ride on. I can sell you a couple of mules to carry all your belongings lady but you will have to get rid of the buggy, it'll slow you down on these roads, that's for sure. I'll show you how to pack up the horse tomorrow."

He pointed to the horse.

"Sit at the fire if you will with your boy and eat with us".

Betsy complied, grateful for the rest and the temporary 'safety in numbers' feeling of security she felt for the first time since leaving Lexington.

"I thank ye sir, we will be much obliged to you and your people for your offer of hospitality. I must admit being weary after the journey we have had up until now."

"That's not a surprise. May I ask your name?"

"It's Mrs Betsy Leiper, my husband died not so long ago, a fever took him, leaving me a widow and my son Joshua fatherless."

Emmett slowly shook his head and looked at the other man knowingly.

"I'm sorry to hear that Mrs Leiper, must be hard especially in these times not to have a man to protect and care for you."

Betsy smiled and nodded not wishing to go any further with the conversation, she turned, looked at the other man, a stocky, bearded fellow who seemed to emanate good humour as some folk do.

"And you sir what is your name if I may inquire?"

"You may indeed lady, it's Robert Guthrie and pleased to make your acquaintance ma'am."

"Well I'm please to meet both of you good gentlemen, my son misses his pa terribly so it is good to meet decent, upstanding men such as yourselves."

Emmett and Robert Guthrie took off their hats respectfully and seeing Betsy was obviously tired and no doubt hungry invited her to join the rest of the group who were by now making camp for the night and resting the horses and mules. The women were busily making a fire with wood collected by the men and boys. It was a well organized procedure, well practiced and with every member of the group knowing exactly what to do.

Emmet and Robert led Betsy and Joshua over to the camp and hailed the rest of the group introducing her and Joshua in a most welcoming manner which was responded with smiles and offers of help from several women who came over to her without any prompting or hesitation. Food was prepared quickly and three or four men including Robert Guthrie posted as lookouts.

After eating a frugal yet satisfying meal, preceded by

Emmett saying grace in a rather long winded prayer; "We give thanks to the good Lord above who with his eternal grace has provided us with this plentiful meal of which we, poor pilgrims are unworthy of receivin'..." Betsy almost started to eat but Emmett continued, he was in full flow... "But we thank ye good Lord, most sincerely from the bottom of our hearts dear Lord above...we unworthy sinners who are not fit to receive your blessings, the blessings of our Saviour the Lord Jesus Christ himself..."...and on it went until even Emmett became aware that it was time to finish with... "Amen!"

After the meal Betsy politely made conversation with Emmet, Robert Guthrie and other members of the group, she then gratefully accepted the offer of stopping overnight in one of the wagons.

A comfortable bed of sorts was made up her for with Joshua by her side, they soon fell into a deep sleep, secure in a covered wagon generously vacated by one of the families. Surrounded by boxes full of provisions, clothes of all sorts folded and stacked at the rear of the wagon, and such like articles, the familiar sounds of the forest; it's noises and rustling, together with a gentle breeze softly and rhythmically flapping the tarpaulins ensured it provided a serenade of sorts to reassure our two travellers.

CHAPTER 5

Dawn broke, the first rays of sunlight casting a dull, misty glow inside the wagon where Betsy and Joshua awoke together. A gentle breeze rustled the canvas above creating a restful ambience.

"Are you awake Joshua?" Betsy inquired.

Joshua stretched and nodded.

"We must get dressed and quickly wash and be on our way. It has been kind of these good folks to help us but we must not be delayed any more, We still got a long way ahead son."

Hastily they dressed, Betsy had kept her dress on and helped Joshua put on his shirt, britches and jacket, then the two of them climbed down only to see a purposeful activity ensuing with the whole community quietly going about the business of breaking camp and preparing themselves to continue their long journey west.

Emmet James appeared as soon as they were standing on the ground, he had saddled Betsy's horse for her and provided a mule which she had purchased from him, laden with their belongings. Suddenly she realised that the box containing the stash for the Harpes was not among the packed items.

"I must go and collect a box underneath the seat as there are some personal belongings and valuables."

"Of course Mrs Leiper, do you need any help?"

"No I'm fine thank ye."

Betsy quickly retrieved the treasure chest, Emmett tied it securely to the mule and turned to him saying in polite but firm tone.

"I will most likely not see you again but I wish you a safe journey and may the good Lord protect you and all you good folk."

"Thank you, I reckon so He will" Emmett replied.

Emmett paused then said to Betsy.

"You are heading to Winchester I know, I have a friend there, Augustus Bede, a good man. He may guide you if you wish, give him my name if you see him. I would feel better knowing that Augustus would do his best to ensure you safely reach your destination. He knows these trails and rivers like few others, him being a trapper formerly and scout for the British."

"I will look out for him, I do assure you, but you have no need to worry too much, I am well used to gettin' around on my own." Betsy replied.

Emmett nodded and scratched his head quite amazed at the confidence and obvious knowledge of this young woman. He wished that Betsy would join their party on their journey west as she would be a very useful extra hand but realised that this was a forlorn hope. At the back of his mind was a tentative thought that she might even become his wife. His hopes alas would have to remain unfulfilled.

Betsy then waved at the people who had gathered to bid her farewell, mounted her now rested, fed and heathier looking horse, took Joshua who Emmett handed to her, then a last wave continued on her way East. The small crowd that had gathered looked on with some surprise and not a little admiration at the obvious competence Betsy displayed in

216

mounting her trusty steed. She effortlessly set herself in the saddle with little Joshua sat in front and without hesitation made her way back on the trail, mule trotting behind, tethered to her horse. Emmett stood awhile staring at her as she rode into the distance, quite amazed by this extraordinary woman, the like he had not witnessed before and almost certainly would not encounter again. He turned to Robert Guthrie and murmured.

"Well I'll be, what a woman."

He stroked his beard in contemplation, momentarily lost in thought.

Robert smiled, fully aware of the effect that Betsy had had on his old friend but refrained from making any remark lest it disturbed Emmett's steadfast faith.

CHAPTER 6

Not surprisingly given the nature of travel during the late seventeen hundreds and early nineteenth century, this had been the first large group of people that Betsy had met on her expedition to New York and hoped for wealth and security. She had seen no way to take advantage of them, she had decided to set off on her own with Joshua as soon as possible without revealing anything of her past and what had happened in Lexington to her husband. Her resolve was now such on this journey that she would take no truck with fools or vagabonds, protecting her child like a mother bear. Betsy made good progress on her sturdy, faithful horse and Joshua enjoyed being close to his mother, watching everything of any interest as they made their way mile after mile, until late afternoon they stopped to rest to take food which had been generously been given to them by the good folk they had left behind.

Betsy dismounted and carefully put Joshua down, the boy had fallen asleep and she stood him up gently rousing him from his slumbers, quickly he woke up with startle.

"It's alright son we're just resting a short while to give the horse and mule some rest and oats. We can take something too. Are you hungry?"

Joshua nodded, rubbing his eyes.

They sat down after Betsy had tethered the horse and mule and proceeded to take some food and drink, a welcome respite after three hours of hard riding over what amounted to a road but in reality was little more than a rough path. No travellers were encountered but Betsy always kept a lookout for anything or anyone who might be lurking in the trees, her past experiences with the Harpe family had taught her never to be complacent. Not only were the brothers Wiley and Micajah adept at ambushing poor unfortunate victims,but were also at every moment aware that they could easily be prey to the law entrapping them and even other renegade outlaws and Indians attacking or ambushing them.

"How long have we to go ma?" Joshua asked.

"We've got a long ways yet Joshua but I know how proud your pa would be of you knowing what a brave boy you have been. I promise that when we get to New York we will live in a fine, big house with servants and you'll have lots of friends to play with."

She smiled affectionately at him and he perked up suddenly jumping up, looked around and seeing a large oak tree started climbing it.

"You be careful Joshua, don't you climb to high!"

But Joshua paid no heed and before long he had foolishly climbed to near the very top of this mighty tree. As he was attempting to get across to another branch the little boy suddenly lost his grip and fell.

"Joshua!!" Betsy screamed.

With amazing speed she rushed underneath where he was falling and caught him just in time before he hit the ground, his fall broken but causing Betsy herself to fall to the ground with her son slipping from her arms and hitting the ground also. Joshua cried and howled in some pain but luckily he was uninjured except for a few bruises. Betsy had twisted her ankle in falling but other than that was likewise in one piece.

"What did I say you stupid boy!"

She shouted at him. "You could have gotten us both killed!"

Joshua whimpered a "sorry" and Betsy instantly hugged him, relieved that the outcome could have been so much worse but thankful they had both apparently survived with minor injuries. She shuddered to think what would have happened if Joshua and been seriously injured or worse died, and she had become lame. The thought was quickly dismissed and a feeling of relief and gratitude took it's place. Betsy checked for any hidden wounds on Joshua but found nothing of any consequence except for a few bruises. She looked at her ankle and decided that her ankle was sprained, she next applied some water then bound it with cloth torn into strips as a bandage.

"That will do, it'll take more than a hurtin' ankle to put me off." She muttered to herself.

Turning to Joshua she gave him a stern few words.

"That'll teach you to disobey your Ma and go off climbing trees. You could have gotten' us both killed boy. Thank the good Lord we both survived but next time if you disobey me you'll get a hidin'."

Joshua whimpered but nodded.

Soon Betsy decided it was time to be off, looking at the sky which had begun to look threatening with dark clouds gathering some way off, she was concerned that they needed shelter further along the road. She remembered that a few miles further on there was an old, deserted cabin which she hoped was still the case. Memories of her time with the Harpe brothers sometimes came in useful and she was aware that they had used this shelter once before when on the run from the law. She felt that it was unlikely that anyone else would have taken over the cabin, cut off and away from the roadway as it was, so Betsy decided to take the risk and stay there for one night hoping that the cabin was still unoccupied. It took her over an hour to reach her destination and the rain was now falling heavily making the journey through pathways treacherous at times, rivulets appearing and undergrowth hampering her progress. Sometimes the mule had to be urged on by yanking the beast but they made it and on seeing the clearing with the cabin in the midst of it, Betsy stopped to observe the scene before her.

It was pretty obvious that no-one was inhabiting the place since there was no sign of life, just overgrown vegetation and remnants of broken wood scattered about, the only window could barely be seen such was the dilapidation around it. The door was closed which seemed slightly odd to Betsy and on looking more closely she perceived a thin whisp of smoke coming from the outlet on the roof of the cabin.

"That's strange Josh, I'm thinking that there might be someone in there so I need to take a look."

Betsy dismounted and tucked her two pistols into her belt, then after telling Joshua to stay still and be quiet, tying the horse and mule to a sturdy tree branch, she made her way cautiously to the cabin, keeping low and taking advantage of the late afternoon shadows to conceal herself.

As she got nearer to the cabin she made her way around to the door and with a firm push it opened easily. She quickly entered and to her surprise and shock looked upon the sight of what appeared to be an old woman lying on a rough wooden bed, covered in filthy blankets and apparently either dead or sleeping heavily. The room was dark since the only grimy window emitted little light but she could make out a table, one old chair and some boxes piled up against the wall. There was a fire which was dying rapidly and smoke filled the room causing Betsy to cough and cover her mouth. As her vision improved midst the gloom she noticed that the woman moved slightly.

"Hey who are you?" Betsy inquired placing her hand on one of loaded pistols just in case.

The old woman raised herself slightly and through gloom smiled a macabre smile exposing her two remaining black teeth, a scrawny filthy face, screwed her eyes and stared at Betsy with a piercing look. She was covered in rags, the sad remains of clothes she had obviously worn for years, that were soiled so that it made her appearance that of a wretched rag doll, with a tattered shawl partly covering her grey, matted head. She suddenly let out a scream and shouted something incoherent at Betsy which made no sense but made a fearful noise which caused Betsy to stumble back. This was followed by her trying to raise herself without much success but caused her to fall back.

"I ain't gonna hurt you woman, just here to take shelter for the night! Stop your wailin' before I shut you up good and proper ye damned bitch!"

Betsy had no time for pleasantries, she approached the woman and saw that she was in a bad way with stains on her blankets and her now groaning with obvious pain and discomfort. She attempted to shout.

"Leave me be…I'm…dyin'…are ye Beelzebub?!"

"No I ain't the Devil." Betsy replied.

Betsy leaned over her but on seeing the cataracts in the woman's eyes realised that she was blind or virtually so, also her foul breath had the odour of death. Despite this in a flash the old woman thrust a knife at Betsy which she concealed beneath the blankets her aim wild but her intent deadly.

"Yaargh, kill....ye." she croaked loudly but Betsy swiftly grabbed her wrist, twisted it and the knife dropped onto the floor.

"You evil old crone, you can go to Hell now!!

The woman suddenly groaned, fell back and lay dead, Betsy looked on amazed at this expired corpse, covered her with one of her blankets and picked up the knife. With relief she went outside and called Joshua, summoning him inside.

"Ma what was the noise? What's that on the bed?"

"Don't worry son it's just an old lady who's passed on, she called out in pain but there was nothin' I could do. Now just you ignore her, she's with God now, we need to collect some wood, light this fire and eat. We'll sleep on the floor tonight, ain't nothin' else for it but at least we'll be inside, dry. Tomorrow we'll be on our way again'."

With that they went outside and collected some wood before it got too damp, made a fire and ate. Betsy did not risk using the pot which was hanging over the fire, it looked pitted, grimy and she imagined it was holed. The two of them ate a cold meal keeping warm by the fire which was now emitting a welcome heat. They had brought in their own blankets and coats, made up two places away from the old woman and slept on straw.

The sounds of the night which could be heard clearly, consisting of the many creatures both large and small as well as the many insects of the forest, kept Joshua awake for a while but soon he inevitably fell asleep, Betsy kept one eye open for as long as she could, alert for any danger but she too fell into a deep slumber capitulating to the long, hard toils of the day. Danger might come in the from of a roving, hungry bear, wolves, bobcats or more worryingly vagrant bandits who could well be of the same evil mind as the Harpes. The eerie sound of coyotes was ever present with their screeching howls always unnerving her, something she never got used to. The sound of these dogs seemed to act like a terrible reminder from which she could not escape her past experiences with the Harpes, her shared guilt, all of which combined to tarnish the hope and propitious expectations which she so dearly sought. It would never escape her completely.

***

Morning brought a sunny start to the day with birds singing their dawn chorus and a shaft of sunlight bravely illuminating the shack. Spring was establishing itself evermore joyfully. Fortunately the night had passed uneventfully with no intrusion by either man nor beast, henceforth a reassuring calm permeated the shack with the sunlight streaming through progressively, even from the one grimy window which all in all created a scene of some calmness.

On waking Betsy moved quickly to arouse Joshua, they ate a simple breakfast of bread and some of the cheese that she had with her, which had been given by Emmett James along with some other useful provisions. She tidied herself and Joshua as best she could, washed, then packed her things before hastily leaving the old woman where she lay and the cabin behind.

The horse and mule were grazing lazily, unconcerned until

they both saw Betsy and her son coming toward them, instinctively the two beasts of burden readied themselves until Betsy loaded up the belongings they had, mounted the horse and set off, retracing their steps until they reached the trail. The ground was now sodden after the previous day's rains which tended to slow progress but at least provided some give underneath, making the journey a little easier on their rears!

Betsy headed East thinking that another days' travel would see them reach Huntington with it's promise of replenishing their supplies. She had been once before to Huntingdon, when with Micajah and Wiley and the other two women Susan and Sarah, they had all planned to steal whatever they could get a way with. They had sneaked in at night via an opening of the stockade, held up the two soldiers asleep on guard duty, knocking them both out viciously with their rifle butts, then made off with their arms as well as some hastily gathered provisions from the stores. All this was achieved without rousing the rest of the stockade who slept unawares through this raid. The two soldiers were duly punished the next day.

On descending a steep incline carefully, methodically, lest the horse and mule slipped, she recognised this modest little settlement with it's wooden stockade surrounding it. Feeling a trifle nervous she turned to Joshua and said.

"Now son we can get some rest and food here until tomorrow when we will have to move on."

Joshua nodded but sensing that his mother was not quite herself in some peculiar way which understandably given his young age, he was unable to perceive. However he was pleased that they would have the opportunity to see something different to the seemingly endless mile after mile of their journey along the Cumberland road.

"Can we stay here awhile mama?" He pleaded.

"We will stay for as long as we need to boy, only as long as needed, we have to keep goin'."

Betsy stroked his head reassuringly and motioned to move ahead.

CHAPTER 7

Huntington or more accurately Holderby's Landing as it was then at the time of Betsy's journey, was little more than a stockade in a large clearing in the forest, with a few wooden houses, more like cabins, within it's boundaries. It actually consisted of a large building or barracks where the company of soldiers that protected the place lived, maybe as few as twenty five or more, an armoury, stores, washhouse, barn, stables and what was clearly another wooden building where this modest settlement's captain lived with his wife and three children. The founder of this place was John Holderby who was a farmer and now lived within the stockade tending his land beyond it's boundaries with the help of his sons and daughters as well as some of the settlers of mostly French and British descent, and various travellers, waifs and strays within the fort. Holderby's house was of some substance being part wooden and with a stone chimney suggesting a more imposing and permanent structure.

The commander of the stockade was a certain Captain William Evans, originally of Welsh descent, who had fought on the British side in the War of Independence but had joined the American forces soon after the defeat and pledged his allegiance to this newly victorious state. He was a canny individual of some fifty years, who was capable of sensing the tide of change and adapting to it with some ease. His wife Emily, who was from an English pioneer family was some ten years younger, she was a sturdy, brunette and serious woman who ruled her family with a rod of iron. The children, two boys and a younger girl, had learned that it was better to obey than face the wrath of Mrs Evans who was prone to fits of temper which even her husband found fearsome.

Evans himself was a tall, rangy man with long, grey hair and whiskers which gave him a certain wild appearance but whose eyes had a softness about them suggesting a softer soul within. His worn blue uniform from the war had seen better days but all in all he cut a quite impressive figure with an obvious impression of authority.

It was to this place that Betsy, Joshua, her horse and mule entered much to the surprise of the stockade's inhabitants who looked on with surprise and curiosity. She looked weary, bedraggled with her boy walking by her side and wasted no time tethering the animals, then made her way to Captain Evans who was in the middle of giving orders to a group of soldiers. He looked at Betsy, took off his hat and welcomed her and Joshua, then inquired as to where they had come from and where they were heading. Betsy quickly dissembled a measure of distress, appealing to him in the most subtle imploring manner of which she was expertly capable of.

"I'm a poor widow Sir who is making her way east to New York in

Search of a better life for me and my dear boy Joshua. We won't trouble you long, we just need a little rest, clean up and some provisions if you'll be so kind….I have some money with which to pay for these things."

Evans looked kindly on her replying.

"Why sure lady we can most certainly help you with what you ask for but ain't you risking great danger by travelling by yerself, especially with your young son?"

"Why no, my late husband, God rest his poor soul, taught us how to survive and look after ourselves, Although I am a woman please do not think that I cannot protect my little loved one. Why in our time further West and in Lexington we've, I'm meanin' my husband John, and I have fought with Indians, bandits and wild critters and come out on top…"

Betsy stopped and looked at Captain Evans straight in the eye. He replied hesitatingly.

"I surely don't mean to question your ability but New York is a long way lady…many hundreds of miles…"

"I know Sir which is why I intend to seek help in Winchester further down the trail. There's a good man named Augustus Bede who will help us on the rest of the journey so please don't you worry unduly, we'll be fine and I know how to use pistols and a carbine Captain."

The captain unfazed, continued.

"Evans ma'am at your service. Well bearin' in mind what you tell me I guess I can help you."

"You're very kind and be assured Sir we can pay for anything we need, we ain't here to take charity."

"Charity no lady but I'm sure we can help with what you need. However if you are carrying money about ye, do be careful. I'm know there are some evil brigands out there, not includin' Indians!"

"I'm aware and I can take care of them."Betsy stared fixedly into his eyes.

"I figure you probably can."

With that he walked off and set about finding some temporary accommodation in an unused cabin which he reckoned would do for one or two nights, then arranged for her and Joshua, (who all this time had been fascinated by Captain Evans and others, mostly soldiers and other folk who had started to take an interest in proceedings), to get cleaned up by way of the bath and laundry house where the two ladies who ran it proved to be most helpful. Their clothes were immediately washed and hung out to dry over a fire and some dry clothes provided for Betsy and Joshua to wear while this was being attended to.

"I'm most obliged to you good ladies." Betsy remarked appreciatively.

"We're only too please to be of assistance to you both." One of the two stout ladies replied, looking with consternation at Betsy and wondering what was going on.

"Are you here long?" she asked.

"Oh no just a day or two, we've a long journey ahead, now you won't mind if I go and see Captain Evans about some things we need will you?"

"Why no, your boy will be fine here." The older of the two women replied.

Betsy left, leaving Joshua with the two ladies, who quickly made a fuss over him and provided him with some company other than his beloved mother.

It seemed strange to Betsy to be without Joshua even for a short period of time but she quickly went about her business visiting the Captain, who willingly directed her to the stores where she was able to replenish their supplies for the continuation of their journey at least until the next stage of it. Money was not an issue as Betsy had plenty hidden away in her secret box, so she made sure that they would all be well provided for for the next week or more, including the horse and mule.

CHAPTER 8

After collecting what she needed from a helpful storesman, who attracted by Betsy's looks, was more than generous with the supplies she needed, Betsy collected Joshua and made for her accommodation for the night, She found that a fire had been lit and some food left for her. She and Joshua enjoyed a meal of beef stew, assorted vegetables and a loaf of fresh bread, such a treat with coffee included as well. Just as they were finishing their meal Captain Evans appeared through the door with his dog, a large wolfhound who he called Behemoth or 'B'moth' in it's easier version. Joshua immediately withdrew behind his mother in some trepidation but the Captain quickly reassure him.

"He won't bite you boy, why he's softer than me and much friendlier, see he's wagging his tail. I reckon he likes you already."

Joshua tentatively came forward as the dog did seem friendly as Evans assured him. He even patted Behemoth on his head at which the dog nodded his head in appreciation which caused Joshua to smile.

"I think you've made a new friend there." observed Evans.

Betsy smiled and was thankful that her son had connected with the animal who now was slumped at Joshua's feet.

"You've been very kind and generous to us Captain, it has been a welcome relief to receive such hospitality here after our long, tiring journey."

"My pleasure ma'am. I hope you'll stay a little longer with us."

"That would be very tempting for sure but I fear if we did then we might'nt never get going again!"

She smiled one of her beautiful smiles.

"Well if we can't get you to stay perhaps you'll allow me to provide an escort for the next leg of your journey. I'm sure we can spare maybe two or three of our men to make sure you get to where you're going. If I'm not mistaken you're headin' to Winchester which is a good two days ride from here."

Betsy blushed slightly, irritated that possible interference with her plans and the possibility of someone or other of the soldiers might discover her cash and valuables rejected his offer.

"I thank ye again but we really will be fine, no need to inconvenience you Sir. I have plenty of supplies now thanks to your generosity and that of the storesman. We'll take our leave in the morning and won't forget your kindness I assure you."

"Well if I can't persuade you lady to accept our hospitality and offer of safe passage I guess I'll bid ye farewell. I'll see you in the morning before you go, that's the least I would hope to do."

"That would be most appreciated Captain, now if you'll excuse us my son and I would like to turn in early." Betsy replied.

Captain Evans at this point was torn between maintaining a gentlemanly disposition or taking the risk, with all it's horrendous consequences, of making a move for Betsy who exuded as was usually always the case, an alluring physical attraction. Evans was fully aware of the sensuous beauty of her even though she displayed not a square inch of her skin clothed as she was with a long dress, but he still felt the natural inclinations stirring within him....but he hesitated, which in retrospect was a merciful outcome given the wrath he would have most certainly have sustained from his dear wife, should she become aware of this potentially inappropriate behaviour "dear!".

At this moment as Evans was contemplating his intentions, Betsy turned away looking at Joshua who was now stroking the dog.

Betsy then smiled again, recovering her confidence and Captain Evans sensibly took his leave with Behemoth reluctantly following, tail wagging and looking back at Joshua, sad at leaving his newly found friend.

Betsy quickly arranged the two beds and packed her things including the provisions she had bought, then she and Joshua bedded down for the night as the light faded and a quiet suffusion permeated the stockade. They soon fell asleep for once feeling secure.

CHAPTER 9

N ext morning the two travellers wasted no time in readying themselves for departure, with a group of several people and of course Captain Evans on hand to see them off safely. Some of the soldiers had entertained hopes of going with them, no doubt looking forward to a welcome change of routine especially with so fair a young lady to protect. Their hopes were dashed as Captain Evans brusquely informed them that it was not happening.

"You'll attend to your duties as normal..." then thinking more added...

"...but perhaps we'll send out a patrol later to make sure all is well. You never can tell if there's any trouble out the on the trail."

He nodded and walked away contemplating if there was any way he might yet persuade her to change her mind. Alas no.

Mrs Evans merely scowled at Betsy, aware that her husband had visited her last night and was none to pleased about that, she had berated him accordingly.

So Betsy and Joshua, together with their horse and mule, made their way out through the gates of the Huntington stockade and settlement to continue their long journey East. Behemoth barked a canine farewell as Joshua turned to look back, the dog wagging his shaggy tail. Captain Evans waved but faintly as Mrs Evans gave him her nenowned ferocious glare which caused some amusement amongst the soldiers in attendance. A burly sergeant remarked.

"That woman scares me more than the Captain…that's for sure. She'd have you flogged for twitchin'."

The others agreed.

Betsy had some feelings of regret at departing especially as the folk there were so helpful and no doubt she could have established herself in the community as a significant force, seeking opportunities to take advantage of the expansion that was taking place at Huntington like so many other new settlements. They all provided the chance to make fortunes and make a name for oneself, but she had bigger ambitions than that and Huntington would never give her the means to become very wealthy as New York would, or so she believed. She had not survived the Hell that was her time with Micajah and Wiley Harpe to settle for anything less. Betsy had a resolve which would not be broken no matter what lay ahead she had learned via her time with those infamous brothers, that the only thing that mattered out in this frontier wilderness was mental and physical toughness, combined with ruthless determination.

Her complicity in their heinous crimes tainted any genuine feelings of warmth, softness and even compassion. So many of the terrible events from that time; murders, torture, brutal robbery, beatings and other sundry violent episodes especially from Micajah, would never leave her memory no matter what would happen to ease her life and that of her son. She had witnessed the horror of Big Harpe even killing his own child, displaying only at the end of his life any shred of remorse. He exhibited no remorse whatever for his other appalling murdering, Wiley too in some ways showed even less concern though his cleverness would sometimes be used to dissemble, whenever useful to him, an outward empathy to Betsy particularly.

CHAPTER 10

The journey to Winchester proved fairly uneventful, though arduous as usual, they were helped by having taken shelter, albeit for one night only, enjoying some good food they had brought with them from Huntington. Betsy was fairly familiar with the route, she found a cave they had used in the past with the Harpes when a thunderstorm made them seek shelter for the night. It served it's purpose during the night when torrential rain pelted down followed by the most dramatic thunder and lightning which illuminated their dark cavern. Joshua huddled up to his mother frightened but reassured by Betsy's soothing words and warm body next to his. At one point a stream of rainwater rushed through causing them both to seek a drier, higher part of the cave where they remained for the rest of the night. The tethered horse and mule brought in also needed regular reassurance from Betsy who needless to say slept little during the night, especially as Joshua could not really settle even with Betsy's calming words.

The morning brought a welcome contrast with brilliant rays of sunlight streaming forth from the entrance to the cave, the rain had abated before dawn thankfully though leaving pools of water both within and without as Betsy, Joshua and the two beasts of burden were brought outside to resume their travels. Betsy packed them both and they headed for the trail relieved that the storm had passed.

"Let us hope that the heavens don't open up agin' Joshua, it's hard enough without us getting no sleep."

"I don't like it mama."

Joshua nodded still frightened.

Betsy turned to him.

"It's gone now dearest but we have to get used to such things in God's creation."

They slowly made their way along the trail, careful to avoid slipping in the mud nor falling down, any serious injury could well prove a disastrous occurrence for such an apparently vulnerable duo.

The meadows along the trail by the roadsides gave opportunity for the horse and mule to graze and for Betsy and Joshua to take rests as well as food. They would walk alongside the animals to give them rest and using her skill as a horsewoman, negotiate several tricky narrow passages hewn through the hillsides, since by now in 1804 the Cumberland Pass had been improved in several places as more and more travellers, mostly heading West made it necessary for local settlements and the State authorities to make such improvements. These consisted of road widening, levelling, even excavating several tunnels to avoid the more dangerous ravines as well as shortening the route. The early eighteen hundreds saw a major effort to effect improvements and make passage to the Western territories much easier, the young nation demanded growth not just for its increasing population but to increase conquest West and seek out natural resources.

For Betsy though it was to the East where she sought a better life. Her dreams could only be fully realised in New York she believed, the town of which she had heard so much about.

Along the route Betsy now going along the Shenandoah Valley, encountered several groups of people, mostly families heading West but also travellers seeking fame and fortune wherever they could in this vast growing nation. One family who she came across not far from her destination of Winchester, West Virginia, were from the West Country in England. She recognised their accents and way of speaking from the way her mother and father spoke, her father many times reminisced about their previous life in Devonshire with it's beautiful rolling hills, lush green landscape. He would sometimes mimick the unmistakable drawl, the vernacular mannerisms which were still fresh in his memory and caused much amusement to Betsy and her sister Susan before Susan disappeared. Her loss turned him from a previously cheerful character to a more depressed, introspective man unable to fully articulate his inner feelings, though Mrs Roberts did her best to cheer him up and keep him positive. Betsy became his focus which not always played well with her as a headstrong girl who did not firstly care too much for Susan, often expressing indifference to her elder sister, even resentment that she had left her to do all the work and bear the brunt of her parent's moods. During the journey Betsy often reflected on what had gone before with the Harpes but just as much with her life before them. She missed her ma and pa and now wished she had been more helpful. Alas too late it was of no use brooding and regretting past failings, she shook herself out of such reveries when sadness overcame her. The travellers from England were delighted to meet her and bombarded her with many questions, coming as she was from the West. This merely irritated Betsy who wanted to move on to put this part of her life behind her.

With this thought she evaded their questions and even their helpfulness, preferring to continue her journey. Her answers became short and eventually these good people, full of enthusiasm left her be, moving ahead to their destination.

It took another two days of travel through periods of bad weather, the Spring rains not only making travel treacherous at times but also encouraging early vegetation growth, hosts of flowers, undergrowth, trees bursting with life and colour which West Virginia, more accurately the Shenandoah Valley, was renowned for. It became known as the 'Mountain State' due it's situation within the Appalachians with it's many hills and old mountains, beautiful, scenic but unfortunately at this time difficult to navigate even with the improvements to the road, and ideal country for vagabonds, as well as Native renegade bands of Indians. These were most notably Shawnee.

Betsy had little time to admire the lush scenery which she was already well familiar with and as she neared Winchester she was relieved to see the first signs of civilisation as well as Fort Loudon with it's guns visible along the fort's walls pointing outwards as if the War of Independence still held sway. The road which improved gradually ahead, revealed a few odd settlements where folk were tilling the land and rearing livestock as a more domesticated scene became more prevalent. As well as this the nearer she got to Winchester she encountered a patrol of seven or eight soldiers, led by a beefy sergeant. They had been dispatched from the fort to reassure the local settlers.

CHAPTER 11

Betsy arrived at Winchester, welcomed through the fort's open gate, once again arousing the curiosity of the soldiers and townsfolk who were busy about their business, as by now it was late morning, the sun was shing brightly and there was a bustle about the small town. Women with small children, soldiers, men, women, youths, collecting provisions from the General Stores, groups of men discussing matters at the fort's office, horses being attended to, some being led to the stables, some being tethered, wagons being loaded as people arrived then departed with their wagons loaded for the continuation of their journey. The town gave the appearance of a young, busy, growing little metropolis with sense of optimism as well as relief that at last there was a semblance of peace and some security.

Betsy quickly joined the throng making for the stables with Joshua in tow to arrange for her horse and mule to be fed, watered and cleaned since both creatures had thick, cloying mud all about them. She then made for the stores to buy some more provisions, though less this time as they hadn't used as much as before which was a relief to her. She did not want to delay too long with her main objective being to locate Augustus Bede and hire him for the rest of the journey. Going into the stores Betsy had to wait a while before the storekeeper got round to attending to her.

"What can I do for you lady?" he asked in a jovial manner.

Betsy gave him a list.

"Well now let me see....sure I reckon we can provide you with everything you need. Where you headin' my dear?"

"My son and I are on our way to New York so you'll understand we've got a long journey ahead of us."

The man looked at Betsy lost for words for a moment.

"Well lady that sure is a long way, my my."

He then muttered something in German though she caught "Mein Herr" which she understand but not the rest, he continued.

"By yourself...and your boy of course?"

"Yes we've made it this far and we ain't turning back. You must understand my husband died leaving us with nothing so I decided to take a big risk and head to where I hear there's opportunities to make a life for oneself.May I ask you if you've heard of an Augustus Bede, I was told that I could find him in Winchester?"

"Bede? Why sure but I'm sorry you've missed him. He left two days ago bein' hired by a merchant, some Frenchman, to take him and some goods

East to Charleston. He had six mules laden with goods which he intended to sell when he got there."

"That's a blow I was hoping to enlist his services as he was recommended to me by some kind folks I stayed with on the trail."

Betsy looked irritated.

"Sorry lady, I hope you find him, I too would agree with what your friends say, he's a good man always willing to help out and through his scouting days with the army he knows the territory as well as anyone or any of them Indians. I'm told he's been to your New York as well."

He muttered some more German beneath his breath, none of which Betsy could understand.

This confirmation by him however was reassuring to Betsy and reinforced her determination not to waste much time here in Winchester so she decided to head off later that day much to Joshua's disappointment.

"Oh ma can't we stay just a bit longer." he pleaded.

"No son we need to move on, I cannot afford to miss Bede next time, you'll understand when you're older."

Betsy made haste, packed the provisions she had purchased and departed without so much as a word or farewell. Some surprise was expressed and warnings from various folk but she brushed off these concerns without so much as a comment.

CHAPTER 12

B etsy and Joshua made haste leaving Winchester behind, seeking out the road which headed east, and which was recently improved making it easier to navigate. She had no difficulty in following this Cumberland Road since she encountered teams of workmen on her journey going about the business of improving the highway giving her cause for some reassurance. Not that the road, or more accurately trail, was yet anything like a highway, it's route was at times still dangerous what with rockfalls, flooding, craters still unfilled, not to mention the still lurking danger of outlaws, renegade Indians and wild animals always a present worry. Betsy was pleased that she had taken the extra mule bought from Emmett along with her horse rather than the buggy she started out with, given these precarious conditions.

"Well Josh, we makin' good progress my boy. Soon be in Charleston where we can lay up for a while and get us a guide."

"Yes mama." Joshua smiled.

Further along the Cumberland Road Betsy noticed something unusual down by the bank of a creek they were traveling along. Recently some heavy rains had washed up debris by the side of the waters but what she saw looked different. She dismounted telling Joshua to stay put while she went down to the riverside, stumbling a little among the rocks and stones and other debris.

On reaching the shore she looked in horror as she recognised the white leg, in fact the left leg, naked, of what she reckoned was a man since from it's rough shape it was highly unlikely to be female. It gently rocked with some driftwood which partly obscured this limb but at the same time seemed to caress it as it moved to and fro. Betsy also noticed that some of the flesh had been torn off, no doubt by pike or catfish each taking a bite of this free food. Not their normal diet but welcome nonetheless. Betsy by now was wondering if this leg or more accurately bone, was part of any of the victims of the Harpes, maybe she had lured this unfortunate man to his death. The sole piece of evidence was inconclusive though, giving her some relief from her horror at what she had discovered. Betsy quickly left the scene hurriedly scrambling back to where Joshua was, who by now was becoming concerned as to where his mother had got to.

"What did you see mama?" he asked.

"Oh nothing son just some part of a tree, a branch which looked funny."

"What do you mean?"

"Nothing son, nothing to concern us. Let's move on I don't like this place."

With that they carried on along the trail but Betsy could not help thinking back to her part in those terrible murders, much as she tried to erase the memories from those times there was always something that caused such thoughts, nay guilt, to return.

Camp was made as evening broke in a cave just by the road, it had been used previously as evidenced by some remains of burnt wood and animal bones which was not unusual at this time. With the sun now settling down behind the trees, birds singing their songs of mateship on this Spring evening as Betsy went about making a fire and preparing some food for herself

245

and Joshua as well as oats for the horse and mule, there was a sense of wellness which pervaded even if fleetingly. Joshua as usual dutifully helped collect as much dry wood as he could. This was not too difficult in these woods thankfully and soon a fire was blazing as the two of them settled down for the night.

***

Next morning camp was broken and they resumed their journey on to Charleston, an expanding town by this time, in order to get fresh supplies and rest up for a few days much to Joshua's relief though this was not necessarily Betsy's plan.

The journey to Charleston took Betsy past many large plantations which she had heard about and witnessed on a relatively modest scale in Lexington and beyond, but the scale of these was something which she was surprised to see. Hundreds if not thousands of Negro slaves could be seen toiling mostly in the numerous rice fields, bare footed and what shocked her most was the sight of young children put to work as well as men and women of all ages. Slave owners and traders in and around Charleston, had begun this enterprise in the late sixteen hundreds and this had swelled to more than twenty rice plantations along the Cooper River. Overseers dutifully looked on at the back breaking workers looking for any sign of slackness or dissent and at one point she witnessed the beating of a male slave, the poor young man bound by ropes to a wooden post and whipped by a most brutish looking foreman with two onlookers shouting abuse at him. His naked upper torso revealed the bloody effects of this cruelty.

Betsy did not stop to watch this awful spectacle, not least as Joshua asked questions as to why this was being done.

246

"Ain't none of our business Josh, now look away we ain't got time to inquire or get ourselves involved. I guess this black man had broken the law anyways or done something bad."

She averted Joshua's eyes away as the crack of the whip continued and the cries of the unfortunate man rang out. With this explanation she pushed on hoping that there would be no more such incidents.

Fortunately there were no such incidents and the two travellers plus horse and mule continued along the steadily improving road to the outskirts of the town which by now was spilling out beyond the fort which protected it.

Following this trail to Charleston which when they entered impressed Betsy with it's fine brick built houses and harbour by the bay created by the confluence of the Ashley and Cooper rivers. She quickly sought lodgings at an inn located on the main street, King Street in fact, with it's fine houses, bustling population to be seen walking along, gazing at the many shops, stores, outfitters, ladies of all ages enjoying the security which the town now offered, along with it's attractiveness. Children could be seen with their mothers or nanny's, boys and girls smartly dressed, men going about the business, soldiers from the fort occasionally passing by or on their way out to patrol the outlying areas where there was still a chance of trouble.

After settling in at the hotel next day Betsy made her way to Chalmers Street and noticed an auction was about to take place with a group of men, some in uniform, in attendance. She was curious and walked over with Joshua and to her surprise saw that this was a slave auction with five black slaves shackled together.

A notice outside proclaimed:

PUBLIC SALE OF SLAVES!!

MALE & FEMALE!

'To be sold on Tuesday 12th April outside the Slave Mart on Chalmers Street a choice of Twelve Negroes consisting of Seven men, Four women and One Childe. The utmost care has been taken to keep them FREE FROM SMALLPOX they all be fit, healthy specimens but surplus to the needs of their Master.

Austin, Laurens & Appleby'

With some trepidation but consumed with a curiosity Betsy entered the building and was immediately met with a noisy group of men all dressed finely and talking exuberantly. They stood around waiting for the first slaves to be brought in and placed on the large table set up to give an effective view of these poor wretches. The Negro slaves were soon brought in in a line but were displayed individually or in groups of two as auctioneers, planters, traders and curious onlookers watched, expectantly seeking the best specimins. Their only concern was whether their acquisitions would perform well. Smoke hung in the air as pipes and cigars were taken frequently. Betsy coughed suddenly which illicited the attention of the men who turned to inquire, on seeing her some tipped their hats others frowned disapprovingly.

"What is this woman and her child doing here?" she heard said.

"Most disagreeable William." the other replied

This ain't no place for a woman!"

More grumblings were heard but soon their attention was guided to the matter in hand and the group turned away.

Betsy merely ignored their comments as well as their disapprobation, both of which she treated with contempt.

As the slaves were brought in and stood around bereft of dignity she noticed that two of them appeared to be together, apparently a man and wife looking despondent, as they desperately attempted to cling to each other, hoping no doubt that they would not be separated. The auction began with the first four slaves purchased by different buyers. The auctioneer, and his assistant, a burly, darkly bearded man with cudgel and whip quickly threatened two slaves who hesitated when pushed forward on to the improvised platform. At that point suddenly Betsy remembered her own dreadful captivity with the Harpe brothers and felt some empathy for these wretched people, especially the young woman who intuitively struck her as not only being naturally attractive even in her wretched, ragged state, but also possessing a strength of character to be discerned in her manner which suggested a certain dignity. Betsy perceived this in her husband too, sound qualities that seemed obvious to her even at so early an encounter and under such appalling conditions. He had a physique both impressive and attractive to her eye.

Impulsively she decided on a whim suddenly to bid for the man and his "wife", her instincts suggested to her that they could be of considerable use and anyway she felt a growing sympathy when observing the terrible plight of them both. She could not help the other ten slaves sadly, they must accept their sorry fate and make the best of it.

Bidding commenced for the two slaves as a pair fortunately and a well dressed man named Colonel Horace H. Hunter, an elderly gentleman, attired in his uniform with it's gold epaulettes, sword, being a plantation owner, bid for both.

"Sixty!" he called out.

"Sixty-one!" Betsy replied causing surprise and irritation to Hunter who had never expected to be challenged by a woman.

"Sixty-five!" Hunter responded firmly, no doubt expected this bid to put an end to any further competition from this young woman.

Betsy was disconcerted but not put off called out.

"Seventy!"

At this Horace H. Hunter removed his hat stared at Betsy and hesitated but then turned to her saying. "Lady I have never been outbid by a woman but why do you do this? Do you really want these black savages? I am surely confounded."

"I do Sir and would be most obliged if you would give way as I need them as servants and helpers as I am heading East to set up home and business. Be so kind therefore."

Betsy then smiled one of her alluring smiles which immediately had the desired effect on Hunter. He stood staring at her momentarily then bowed courteously. Betsy's female wiles appealed to him further that her need for help was certainly greater than his.

"I need a couple, male and female for my own use." She continued. "...I must say that using my female intuition I know that these two would appear to suit my purpose most satisfactory."

While this discourse was going on the rest of the crowd

were becoming impatient at the delay. The auctioneer signified to Hunter to bid again or give way.

"We don't have all day Sir." he insisted.

Horace H. Hunter then gave way and stopped bidding against her, acceding to Betsy's charm, good looks and charisma so much so that he relented and gave way to her, tipped his hat in respect, and no doubt appreciating her beauty and magnetic character commented respectfully.

"The slaves are yours ma'am."

No other bidders were able to match her price so the two slaves were sold to her. Betsy signed the document, paid a deposit, gave a commitment to return forthwith with the balance.

After leaving to collect the rest of the money she owed, more Negroes were displayed individually and in groups of two within the building as auctioneers, planters from mostly rice plantations, traders and curious onlookers watched.

The two purchased slaves were called Solomon and Esther, they were indeed married recently when in captivity. They had fared reasonably well considering the nature of the work they did, indeed the plantation owner a Scotsman named Angus MacBride had allowed the two slaves a brief ceremony to get married, even giving them one day off to celebrate the occasion. As far as plantation owners go and there were many who would never have entertained such generosity, MacBride was a rare exception, a man of genuine Christian principles, being brough up as a strict Presbyterian. This did not prevent him from overseeing hundreds of slaves who worked his rice fields suffering in the heat and bad weather and living in the most rudimentary conditions. He was a businessman first and foremost, emigrating two decades ago from Scotland, having served for King and country in the British army, now with the intention of making a fortune.

Despite this his charges fared better than most, it had to be said. Therefore compared to the majority of others, they were better fed and shown at least a modicum of compassion and consideration so long as his profits were not unduly affected. As a consequence of this Solomon and Esther were in better condition than many of their ilk were.

This factor undoubtedly influenced Betsy's decision to purchase them and she quickly set about getting them lodged in the stables at the rear of the inn where she and Joshua were staying. The innkeeper at first was none too keen and had to be persuaded with extra dollars to look the other way, especially his wife who expressed disapproval vociferously.

Solomon and Esther understood that they had been fortunate to be sold to this young woman, their prospects were improved they surmised, better their chances in domestic work as opposed to a life in the fields with all the dangers of injury, mistreatment and illness, especially as they wanted to start a family of their own.

Later that day Betsy came to see them at the stables where they had made a bed for themselves and were tending the horse and mule of Betsy's, feeding and watering them both.

Betsy called them both over.

"You both belong to me now, I paid a good price for you, you understand?" she said looking pointedly at them both.

They nodded obediently. "I expect you to work hard, be loyal, obedient, you will behave at all times and maybe in time if you both honour your promises I'll consider giving you both

252

your freedom."

They look at her in some disbelief, nodding in agreement. Both become attentive to Betsy realising that this is a God sent chance for their salvation and freedom.

"We will miss, you can you be sure of that. Me and Esther never will cause you any trouble, we promise."

Esther nodded in accord, they both bowed.

"Well that's good. You keep your word and you'll find me a fair minded mistress. You don't and you'll be back where you started. Understood?"

"We do missy." Solomon asserted."Fine. This is my son Joshua who you'll get to know. He's a good boy so I hope you'll be friends eh Joshua."

All three nodded in agreement.

Betsy then set about feeding them both firstly by bribing the innkeeper to cook some dinner for them and later she provided them with some decent clothes that she purchased alone with Joshua. As she anticipated the simple clothes for both Solomon and Esther fitted fine and they both expressed their deep gratitude, this had never happened before.

Without any encouragement from Betsy who noticed that Esther was immediately taken with Joshua who, for such a young child in turn, seemed to take to her. Solomon too seemed to like the boy in a natural, respectful way. Betsy noticed this easy bond between them and smiled to herself.

Solomon and Esther

CHAPTER 13

After two days in Charleston Betsy became wary of being alone and decided to find some help there from the guide recommended to her by Emmett James. Joshua was left with Solomon and Esther who even at so soon a time were becoming fond of the boy with Solomon showing him some new tricks that he had learned from his days at the plantation, mostly with stones, making one of a group 'disappear' much to the boy's incredulity. After making some enquiries Betsy finally discovered one Augustus Bede in a rough bar drinking alone, the failed Hudson Bay fur company trapper who Emmet had recommended. Betsy bravely walked up to Bede, firstly announcing who she was and then offered to pay him if he will guide her to New York.

At first Bede is taken by surprise, looking at her inquisitively.

"Are you serious lady? I sure never had such a fine lady ask me such a thing!"

"I'm serious Mr Bede and I'll hold you to be serious too. I was told that you could help me by a certain Emmett James, leader of a group of folks headin' west.

"Well I do know Emmett and he's right, I'm your man lady."

"I hope so Mr Bede as I don't take kindly to anyone thinkin' they can fool or take advantage of me just because I'm a woman, understand?" and Betsy stared him in the eye with one of those fearsome looks that she knew would have an effect.

"Why no ma'am I will do the job for you won't have any reason to doubt me I promise. Now where you goin' exactly?"

"My young son and I are headin' Northeast to New York. We have two servants with us who will be coming along too. They were previously slaves but they work for me now, they're good folks."

Augustus tipped his hat back, whistled gently and replied.

" Well, I'll be...Yep that's fine with me miss. I charge a daily rate as well as expenses and I ask you to pay an advance up front so if that's acceptable to ye we have a deal."

He spat on his hand offering it Betsy.

After a moment's hesitation she clasped his hand firmly and the deal was done.

Betsy then asked Bede if he had mules to which he assured her that he could acquire as many as was needed."For a total of five travellers and provisions we will need I guess at least six, accepting that two or three will be carryin' all our stuff and the others we'll use to ride on. Or I could get us a wagon which will save on mules, we would only need three in that case. Would you be for that miss...sorry I didn't catch your surname lady?

"It's Mrs Betsy Leiper, I'm a widow from Lexington, my son is called Joshua and the two servants, Solomon and Esther. I am unaware if they have a surname. In answer to your question, it would seem sensible but what of the roads, would a wagon not have difficulty?"

"Not so much nowadays" he assured her, continuing... "recently the King's Highway as it's known has been improved making travel a lot easier though there will be difficulties, but Mrs Leiper you have Augustus Bede at your service and I will get us all to New York safe and well!"

Bede brought his hand down on the table to emphasize the point.

"Alright we will do as you suggest, a wagon will do fine."

Now securing the deal with Betsy he became only too eager to guide Betsy to New York, he made no more demands on her but set himself to being as helpful as he could, no doubt hoping to earn more along the way.

Bede then questioned Betsy about the two 'servants' who he felt could be potentially troublesome since they had obviously been slaves and of a lower class.

Betsy looked at him pointedly.

"You'll do your job Mr Bede and be well paid, leave it me to make my own decisions, Solomon and Esther are my charges, I trust them so I don't need anyone givin' me advice I don't need. You don't know me or what I am capable of, you hear." she added somewhat threateningly.

Bede shrugged his broad shoulders, pondering for a few seconds and mutters.

"You're the boss miss."

"You can be sure of that Mr Bede....with respect." she added not wanting to get their relationship off to an unnecessarily tense beginning.

They both drank up with Betsy informing Bede where she was staying and to report to her as soon as he had got the things they had agreed on.

With that they shook hands, Bede bowing a little, removing his hat in a demonstrative way which slightly amused Betsy, they then departed going on their separate ways.

Two days later Betsy was ready to depart Charleston but

not after she had taken Joshua down to the harbour to watch the ships moored there. They were a fascinating sight for a young boy but also for Betsy herself and they spent a good hour or two taking in the sights of ships, the choppy sea, sailors going about their work. He observed the many stevedores loading and unloading the hardy sailing vessels, large items of cargo, barrels, but from one ship he noticed on the other side of the harbour a sight which shook him. The little fellow had seen a group of negro slaves being taken ashore shackled and pushed along by several overseers, the same types who were at the auction in Charleston.

"Why are those men in chains ma?" he asked.

"I guess they've been bad Joshua. Now look away…my, my, see those fine looking sailors going aboard that ship son."

She pointed nearby to deflect his attention from such a distressing sight which his young mind would not fully understand.

They tarried a while as Joshua looked on, then it was time to go when Joshua asked if he could be a sailor.

"Who knows son, you can be anything you want but all in good time, we need to get you educated first at one of them fine schools in New York I been hearin' about even when we were in Lexington. Come now we need to get back to the inn and get our things ready for our departure"

Joshua nodded obediently and they walked back to the inn, all the while the sight of the slaves in their wretched condition made an impression on the boy, something he never forgot. He thought of Solomon and Esther, their new 'companions' but did not fully understand the situation where they both were not free as he was but remained in servitude.

CHAPTER 14

Augustus Bede, Betsy's newly appointed guide, was a man in his mid thirties, tall, dark haired, slim with a beard. He walked with a slight limp caused by a musket ball embedding itself for a while before the army surgeon removed it, somewhat painfully he admitted. He had fought for the American Revolutionary army and was curious to know more about John Leiper who he figured might well have served in the same regiment as he did, the South Carolinas. Betsy deflected these questions skilfully, changing the subject and saying that her late husband was not one to talk about the War, it brought back too many hurtful memories.

"Sorry Mrs Leiper I wasn't meanin' to pry. I served under Colonel Pinckney, Old Pinky as we called him" he explained.

"You weren't but my dear John has gone now and I don't wish to speak no more, you understand."

"I sure do, I sure do. Those were bad times and I can never forget one time I witnessed one of our men murdered by a mean looking giant of a man, swarthy, bearded, he had a smaller fellow with him. Took a shot at the biggun' but missed, anyway I had to getaway afore' the British captured me. Wish I had killed him though Mrs Leiper, I heard those two beasts went on to become murderers with some women too. Awful business... "

"I'll thanks you to keep such things to yourself Mr Bede..."

Betsy flushed slightly as she well recognised who he was referring to, she held up her hand. Bede understood that further inquiry would prove fruitless. He wisely desisted.

Having acquired wagon and fresh mules and loaded up everything they needed for the long journey ahead, Betsy, Joshua, Augustus or Gus as he preferred to be called ("easier on the tongue miss." he explained amused.) plus Solomon and Esther who would accompany them in the wagon or aboard the mules when permitted, plus the mules, they departed Charleston. Bede planned to head North and East along the King's Highway which had opened up the way to New York mainly to facilitate postal deliveries, troop movement and travellers heading West. The journey was certainly made a little easier there was no doubt by using the wagon which Gus had purchased in Charleston. He had many contacts there which he used to good purpose. One thing that had impressed him were the pistols and Nock double barrelled carbine that Betsy had, which she kept inside the wagon along with her and Joshua's possessions and of course her sturdy chest containing her cash and valuables which she did her best to conceal under all their other belongings.

"Fine piece of weaponry there Mrs Leiper." he commented, looking admiringly at the rifle.

"It was my husbands which he used during the War Mr Bede."

Bede then tried to formalise more informal name terms in what he hoped

Betsy would agree to.

"Please call me Gus, everyone does."

"I cannot do that Mr Bede, I don't approve of any over

familiarity you must know. I am your employer and until we take our leave of one another, that is how it will be."

"Why sure I understand if that is your wish but it's going to be a long trek so I had hoped you won't mind."

"I do mind. I will refer to you as Mr Bede and you will refer to me as Mrs Leiper both in public and in private. Is that understood Mr Bede?" emphasizing his formal name.

"Sure thing Mrs Leiper."

"I trust you'll not be offended."

Betsy looked Bede in the eye which caused him to ponder what kind of woman was he dealing with, certainly he had never encountered such a strong willed, determined lady. He smiled to himself, accepting the way things were going to be and thought to himself mischievously.

"I'll bide my time." he mused.

This exchange did not escape the attention of Solomon especially who had quickly felt a loyalty to his mistress and watched for any unwanted attention from Bede. He would henceforth act as a protector to Betsy without her necessarily realising it, Esther also felt similar feelings, both realised that Betsy potentially offered them a better future and their best strategy was to support her as much as they could.

CHAPTER 15

In fact Augustus Bede proved to be a good, conscientious guide, who after a while became obedient to Betsy. He quickly realised that she was no ordinary female but possessed a strength of character, iron will and determination which was the match of any man Bede had worked for or ridden with. Not only that, he admired the way Betsy obviously was able to handle the horse with expertise, used her carbine when she shot a wild turkey unfortunate enough to stray near their camp one early evening. She then plucked, gutted and prepared the bird for supper much to Bede's amazement.

"Nice work Mrs Leiper, I couldn't have done better myself."

"Thank you Mr Bede. I learned much from my pa who took me hunting in Kentucky where I come from. He was a fine man."

"Is he still alive, and your ma?""No, both with the Lord now, lost them to an Indian raid some ten years ago. Chickamaugas, a renegade band I believe."

"Sorry to hear that ma'am, I heard of that tribe on my travels."

"I don't bear any ill will, no point Mr Bede, It does no good fillin' yourself with hatred and revenge. That's something I learned."

"The good book teaches us to forgive, but for me I find that hard for sure considerin' some of the evil things I seen

262

done." Bede commented.

"An eye for an eye just makes everyone blind Mr Bede. The good Lord teaches us that."

"That's true, you have a lot of wisdom Mrs Leiper for one as young as yourself…if you don't mind me sayin'."

"I don't but every day brings new experiences, we can always learn more. Now I'll take Joshua and we'll retire to bed. Good evening Mr Bede.

"Evnin' ma'am."

Betsy retired to the wagon with Joshua leaving Bede pondering further, lighting his pipe and finishing off the coffee which Betsy had purchased in Charleston. He slept in an improvised tent, more a piece of canvas strung from the wagon, but he made it comfortable enough. Sleeping rough was common practise for him, his time in the army, as a fur trapper, guide made him used to open sleeping, living off the land and surviving generally in this vast, hostile wilderness where man and beast often crossed paths and sometimes killed one another.

Solomon and Esther kept themselves to themselves during this time but now also set up their tent which Betsy had acquired for them. Such consideration was appreciated, it was something which had never been shown before to them especially on the plantation where they lodged in what was a tin shack basically with other slaves, no privacy, hot in Summer, freezing in Winter. As a married couple for the first time properly they enjoyed the company of each other…

Augustus Bede was not entirely happy with this arrangement. To him slaves and white folks should not be mixing together and he was troubled by this new familiarity as

263

he saw it. He wisely kept his opinions to himself though.

Next morning saw a steady rain coming down making visibility difficult, the fineness of the rain created a mist which hampered their progress along the King's Highway. Even Bede with his knowledge of all the trails found it difficult on more than one occasion to locate the right road. He had to halt the party in order to work out exactly where they were and where they needed to go.

Thankfully the rain and mist lifted in the afternoon making visibility easier once again. With their fresh supplies from Charleston, together with their new beasts of burden the difficulty of the journey was mitigated somewhat. This was until one of the wagon wheels became stuck fast in a large muddy pothole which resembled a crater more than a pothole. Here Bede displayed his experience and strength, making good use of the mules as well as some wood which he cut to free the wheel and with the help of Solomon who immediately came to his aid, and with Betsy lending a hand as well, much against his will, they freed the wagon. This combined effort enabled them to continue their journey north and eastwards.

Solomon's strength impressed Bede when lifting the stuck wagon wheel with some ease, taking over from him when it became evident that he was not going to manage it by himself.

He looked back at him a little later on along the trail when Solomon came forward to give him water that Betsy had filled his canteen with, and commented in a rather condescending manner.

"Pretty impressive there boy."

Solomon looked him in the eye and replied.

"Years working on the plantation Mr Bede, if you don't

pull yer weight you get a whippin'."

Bede nodded.

"Made a man of you at least." he laughed.

"I don't know about that sir, but I knows that I had no choice, neither did Esther."

"Life's tough that's for sure." Bede nodded.

Augustus Bede mounted the lead mule leaving Solomon to return to the rear with Esther.

CHAPTER 16

As the journey progressed Betsy noticed Augustus Bede very slowly becoming more familiar with her again, even using her Christian name on a few occasions which she reprimanded him for, softly at first but with greater vehemence the next time.

"I think I made it clear to ye, we will keep our protocol as agreed Mr Bede." she affirmed not a little annoyed with him.

He then immediately apologised for this but it was obviously an attempt by him to get closer to her. Betsy's natural beauty, her blonde hair which she tried to conceal as much as she could with both bonnet and shawl, combined with her blue eyes and womanly figure, could not but attract Bede's notice. After all he was a man, with needs which he supressed and apart from his limp, he cut a respectable figure himself. Under normal circumstances Betsy might even have responded to his interest but this was not a normal situation and the last thing that she wanted was a relationship of some sort. That was definitely not on her agenda.

She was indeed amused by this situation at first, even slightly flattered but it started to irritate her as time progressed and sure enough on day three of their journey as they stopped to make camp for the night Bede approached Betsy with the intention of helping her clean and put away the pots after supper. It was still light as the sun slowly set on this fine Spring evening, Joshua was playing by the wagon and Augustus Bede approached.

"May I give you hand with these chores Mrs Leiper?" he asked using the correct term of address.

Esther who was helping Betsy looked surprised.

"Why it's not necessary Mr Bede, I can manage just fine thank you."

"Oh but it's no trouble I just want to be of use you know, a man should always be on hand to help don't you think?" as Bede started washing the pans they had used for their meal.

"Like I said there's no need I don't need no help." Betsy begun to realise the true nature of Bede's "help".

Esther feeling a little uncomfortable but not having the confidence to say something, withdrew

She turned to him as he moved a little closer to her and looking him straight in the eye said.

"I do appreciate your askin' Mr Bede but once and for all I don't need any help. If I do you can be sure I will ask you. Now will you please attend to them mules before we all turn in for the night. Once again we agreed the protocol for this matter in relation to speaking with one another, and I don't recollect any changes to it."

This was not a request but a command which Bede realized was best to be obeyed so he pulled away obediently and quietly attended to his Business with the animals.

Later he came over to Betsy again saying.

"You're a mighty fine woman Mrs Leiper, you can be sure that Augustus Bede knows his place and has nothing but respect for his mistress."

Betsy smiled.

"I know Mr Bede and I do appreciate your helping us on our way but understand, I am a widow now who has no plans to seek another husband, at least not for a long time, if ever." she added pointedly.

"Oh I realize that now lady, you'll have no trouble in that respect I can assure you. Why I got a woman in Tennessee waitin' for me when I decide to retire from this work. She sure is a fine lady, half Cherokee, half German I believe but a good woman nonetheless." Bede mused relieved to change the subject.

"We plan to get wed just as soon as practical." he continued.

"She took on a Christian name when she was young, taken in by a Minister of the church and his wife so she's just like us you know Mrs Leiper."

"As you say she sounds like a truly good, God fearin' woman. I'm sincerely pleased for you Mr Bede."

She smiled and nodded approval, easing the atmosphere between them.

"Thank ye. I intend to stay loyal and true to her even though a man can be distracted by so many temptations in this country, I know of some men who have not stayed true and then regretted it when their women have ended up with someone else."

"That's a pity so I hope that it doesn't happen to you."

Betsy put her hand over her mouth as she yawned, told Bede that it was nice talking but time to take her rest.

They then parted company for the night as Betsy collected Joshua and headed inside the wagon, relieved to escape Betsy's attentions and musings.

This episode with Augustus Bede did not escape the attention of Solomon and especially Esther who remarked to her husband.

"I'm a thinkin' that this Bede has taken a fancy to the mistress Solomon, I'm also thinkin' he ain't goin' to get anywhere with her."

"You're sure right, mistress Betsy ain't goin' to takin' a shine to him that's for sure."

They smiled at each other, Esther shaking her head and sensing that there might be trouble ahead.

"I know one thing for sure Esther, we won't be takin' sides with Bede if it comes to that. Our loyalty is with mistress Betsy." Solomon added.

Esther nodded.

CHAPTER 17

Next morning the party move on, a somewhat disparate a group of travellers, but now bound together more than ever by Betsy's force of character which she had now demonstrated more than once, and of course her wealth which had become more obvious as she had purchased with ease anything they needed in Charleston.

Bede now became curious as to this source of wealth but sensibly realised that his curiosity was best kept to himself. His forays into attracting the attentions of Betsy had proved futile so he focussed rightly on the job in hand, navigating shorter routes occasionally which he knew of from his scouting days, also taking the rope ferries across rivers and creeks where available to make the journey quicker. Only once was the ferry apparently too small to accommodate their wagon, or so they were told by the ferryman, an old, cantankerous man who with his sullen grandson proved impossible to reason with at first. He leaned against the wooden post smoking a clay pipe and occasionally spat streams of tobacco into the still river causing gentle ripples on the dark surface of the waters. He wore a battered hat which shielded his eyes from the sunlight which lit up the riverside bank. The boy simply stood glumly by his side ready to obey whatever command was issued by him. Both the old man and boy had noticed Solomon and Esther which further made them less than helpful.

"We ain't having no Negroes on my raft boy." he muttered to the lad, shaking his head.

Bede knowing full well that the wagon could easily fit on to their wooden ferry raft, apart from the attitude of them towards the two slaves, turned to Betsy shaking his head then glared at the ferryman.

"The wagon will fit on your raft old man, now get on with it!" he shouted at the man.

This outburst merely antagonised the man who took out a pistol.

"I'll blow yer brains out ye young scoundrel, we don't have no negrus on my ferry d'ya hear!" he yelled, waving the pistol in his direction ominously.

"Now steady on old timer. Let's just work this out." now realising the potentially dangerous situation.

"Git out of here, take yer wench, slaves and all of ye get the Hell out!" The man shouted and pointed the pistol at Bede now more threateningly, though Bede, judging from the condition of his pistol which looked as if it had seen better days, actually doubted that this old pistol was loaded or in working order.

Betsy was by now becoming concerned not just for Bede's safety but Joshua's and her own as well as Solomon and Esther. Solomon had looked at Esther, then Betsy, readying himself to intervene to help deal with this annoying and dangerous old man. Betsy noticed that the boy seemed also to be carrying a sidearm as well as a knife. She felt for her own pistol and readied herself to deal with them both should they make one wrong move. Just before the situation could get any worse, Betsy moved forward catching the attention of the old ferryman, then took out her purse and produced some gold coin which the ferryman noticed immediately. The sight of money glistening in the sunlight immediately attracted the attention of the ferryman and his son.

"What's that you got there woman?" he asked, his curiosity aroused.

"I will pay you most generously if you oblige me and my party by taking us across the river on your fine ferry Mr..? I did not catch your name sir."

"My name ain't yer business." he replied in a surly but slightly less combatitive way.

"Please forgive me bein' inquisitive." Betsy said in a most feminine, pleasant tone.

She then took out some gold coins displaying them in her hand so he could see.

"Five dollars for you if you will oblige."

She then closed her hand teasingly, gripping the five coins firmly.

Bede, Solomon and Esther observing this, smiled subtly to each other realising that Betsy would get what she wanted without anyone getting hurt.

"Ten dollars and we'll git ye all across."

"Very well sir ten it is." she agreed knowing full well that he would demand more and having enough in her hand already.

"You'll pay me now lady 'fore I do anythin'"

"Five now and five when we all across."

Betsy took out the first five coins quickly and handed them over staring one of her stares right into the eyes of this old fool.

The man bit on each coin then pocketed them all quickly

changing his mind, deciding that it was indeed perfectly workable for him and the boy to pull her wagon and mules across the waters which were calm at this time.

"It'll take two or maybe three crossings to git everything across lady …and you'll pay more if my ferry gits damaged by this damned wagon, so you will lady."

He nodded at Betsy

"That's fair, may we proceed now?" she asked staring brightly at him.

He hesitated, startled but indifferent to this woman speaking to him directly again, something unknown to him before this day. He then allowed the wagon aboard.

The ferryman and his boy who displayed great strength, though slow, managed the crossings with some ease, then the mules, together with the rest of the party crossed next, then Betsy, Joshua, Esther, Solomon and Bede who returned after securing the mules.

"Just made it, lucky for you lady." the ferryman grumbled.

"I'm much obliged to you." Betsy replied looking at this scrawny old creature and his miserable son, then handing over the remaining coins.

"We'll be moving on." she affirmed.

Bede made ready and the party continued on their way, somewhat relieved.

Later on they stopped by a clearing and Bede, like Betsy, who was an expert marksman, which proved his usefulness when stray deer, boar, turkey and other abundant edible creatures crossed their path, giving welcome fresh meat for their diet. It happened that he spotted a wild boar rummaging amongst the undergrowth seeking tasty truffles, then taking his musket he very stealthily crept up, took aim and brought down the beast, which twitched until Bede finished it off with his knife, slitting it's throat. The blood ran profusely into the grass turning it black, Bede then expertly skinned, gutted and prepared the carcass for dinner.

"This hog will keep us in good victuals for two or more days Mrs Leiper." he called to Betsy.

Similarly he knew which herbs, mushrooms, root vegetables could be safely consumed and so that evening for supper they enjoyed a hearty feast, roasting the hog over a blazing fire, Betsy proving an excellent cook with Esther lending a hand as well. It became obvious that she had cooking skills which Betsy noticed by the way she expertly went about preparing the food.

"Why I believe you can do some of the cookin' in future Esther." she smiled.

"I'd be glad to miss." Esther smiled back.

The meal was set out and was devoured with not a little relish.

"It's been a while since I tasted anything as good Mrs Leiper, you're sure a fine cook."

"Thank you Mr Bede, I learnt the arts of cooking from my late mother, but you can thank esther here as well." She said looking at Esther.

She added.

"…and as you will be aware I can handle any firearm and hunt thanks to my dear father."

"I don't doubt it." Bede replied.

Bede took out his pipe after they finished eating and walked away a little, finding a log to sit on to light his pipe.

Betsy decided to take go for a swim since there was a pool nearby which looked tempting, she yearned to wash herself and Joshua too who accompanied her to the edge of the pool then turned the other way while his mother undressed and then took a leisurely dip in the waters. Betsy found the water cold at first giving her a start, but quickly her body adjusted to the temperature, she washed herself then returned to the bank.

"Your turn now son."

It was indeed and Joshua needed no encouragement, he jumped in at the shallow end. Betsy completed the washing of clothes got dressed with dry clothes that she had brought along, then returned with her boy to the wagon, hanging out the clothes to dry overnight.

All this time Augustus Bede initially was unaware of Betsy's dip almost naked as she was but soon he was aware that she was to be seen very slightly through the trees and bushes. He could not help but have his interest aroused and very carefully he approached nearer to where she was swimming.

"My God."

He whispered this to himself observing the white, smooth figure of her and when she arose from the waters he almost fell back, desperately hoping she wouldn't know how near he was to her. Thankfully Betsy was blissfully unaware and Bede was able to return to his seat and finish smoking his pipe which in his excitement had gone out. The sight of this beautiful near naked woman created a dilemma for him, one which caused frustration and carnal thoughts occasionally. Nothing new there.

The morning brought a most extraordinarily beautiful sunrise, with the sun's golden rays shining through the leaves creating a most wonderful sight, revealing the colours of late Spring, early Summer which in West Virginia were unrivalled. It's natural lushness could be seen expressed through the bursting carpets of flowers of all colours, carpets of bluebells everywhere, yellow Black Eyed Susan, Wild Blue Phlox, daffodils, tulips, cherry blossoms, magnolias, peonies, azaleas and spring ephemerals like the famed Virginia bluebells. Flowers of all shapes, sizes made one feel the joy of living was within one's soul.

Birds were busy, bees buzzed incessantly, insects of all kinds were at work constantly moving around and like the other creatures frequently fighting over territory and breeding rights, flocks of wild turkey were an especially welcome sight for hunters, it's meat possessing a strong, gamey flavour.

It was to this life enhancing sight that the five travellers awoke and after taking in this natural splendour, with Joshua fascinated by the myriad effects of nature, they soon broke camp and resumed their journey. Bede now advised a return to the King's Highway which made it's way to their next port of call which was Morgantown was situated along the Monongahela River some ninety miles away.

"We need to follow this trail for a few miles which will lead us to the highway. I know this route well Mrs Leiper you can be sure."

"I have a notion that I have a memory of it too Mr Bede."

"That right?"

"You would be surprised how much I have had to travel these last years, sometimes under hard conditions."

Betsy was thinking back to the many trails, tracks some barely recognisable as pathways, which she went along with the Harpe brothers usually on the run from a posse or the army, cruelly pushing the women and children along in their desperate attempts to evade capture. She kept these thoughts to herself.

"You are right Mr Bede, let us head for the King's Highway and continue on our way to Morgantown which I believe would be a good place for us to stop for a day or two." she asked him.

"It would be so, Mrs Leiper, I know folks there who would provide hospitality if we need it for certain."

"That's kind but we will not require it as I believe there is a fine new hotel in the town where we can all stay."

Bede eyed Solomon and Esther.

"These two would not be welcome staying at no hotel miss. I can tell you that."

"Oh no don't you be fearin' about my two servants Mr Bede, provision will be made for them both I can assure you of that!"

"You know best." Bede affirmed.

After this discussion they resumed their journey North and East heading for the King's Highway with Bede navigating some obscure trails created firstly by wild animals and then by Native Indians.

CHAPTER 18

After a journey of just over one week when they eventually located the King's Highway thanks to Augustus Bede's navigation and his ability to avoid potential dangers by sometimes taking a detour off the beaten track, they arrived in Morgantown. Like many similar settlements in West Virginia and beyond, Morgantown was by now a growing community with an increasing population which increasingly had to be catered for thus; shops, hotels, saloons, stables and such like emerged quite rapidly to service this new demand. It had been chartered in 1785, founded by Zackquill Morgan who built a homestead there some forty years previous to Betsy's entry in the town. The fort stood within the town, other forts, or more accurately stockades surrounded the town, since it nestled in hilly terrain, surrounded by the Appalachian Mountains which still provided refuge for Native Indians, outlaws, renegades and the like.

Around midday, wet and weary with the rain coming down in disconnected showers typical of late Spring, the group of five entered Morgantown witnessing a place of not unpleasant sights. Many buildings were being constructed, mostly of wood but some now being built of stone, mostly sandstone. Their eyes explored all this activity with interest, though Bede was more familiar since he had been there not so long ago.

"It's a fine place Mrs Leiper!"

He called out from aboard his mule, smiling to himself and looking forward to meeting up with some old friends from his days in the War, no doubt also to the saloon which looked so inviting as they passed it.

Betsy merely acknowledged him with a nod, she was more concerned with finding decent lodgings for herself, Joshua, who looked unwell and badly in need of some rest and proper nourishment as well as a good bath, as they all did, and of course Solomon and Esther. The two 'servants' as they had now been described and referred to by Betsy, not 'slaves', looked at each other not knowing what this new place would hold for them. Fear remained within their hearts, they knew not what awaited them here since already two men from the town had looked at them in most contemptuous manner, renewing the terrors of before.

Betsy ordered Bede to halt then beckoning him over she enquired.

"Where can we lay up Mr Bede since you assured me that there was respectable hostelry in Morgantown?"

"Sure is Mrs Leiper, why further along the high street and on the right is a new hotel, just been built these last two years. I'm sure you will find it satisfactory."

Betsy nodded then instructed them all to move over to the hotel which on arrival looked quite impressive with it's veranda, it's three floors and grand entrance which looked welcoming. She quickly arranged for the mules to be stabled, the wagon was laid up and cleaned shortly after, and on arrival (Bede took his leave after being given instructions to report first thing tomorrow morning) she paid in advance, much to the delight of the hotel manager, a youngish man who went out of his way to be as helpful as possible. Thus Betsy found him courteous, attentive, but with a tendency toward obsequiousness which irritated her.

"It's such a pleasure ma'am to have so impressive a fine lady stay with us at our new hotel." he announced bowing to her.

"I hope you will enjoy your stay and please send for me if there's anything you require. I am at your service at all times." he drawled in a voice which feigned respectability but failed to impress Betsy.

"Thank you Mr..? I didn't catch your name."

With some embarrassment the manager replied.

"Why begging you pardon Mrs Leiper, its Gerald MacDougall, my family is originally from Scotland, a fine country so I'm told."

"Yes I'm, aware of Scotland's beauty from others who came from it." She remembered the stories that Wiley Harpe told her, embellishing them with tales of his family who proudly fought for the King George both in the Independence War and before.

"Now I have two servants with me as you can see; Solomon and Esther who will need lodgings as well as me and my son Joshua."

The manager looked uncomfortable but Betsy interjected.

"I'm aware of course that society dictates that it is not possible for them to stay within the hotel, correct?"

"Yes ma'am but I can arrange comfortable lodgings by the stables at the rear of the hotel, I will also arrange for food and refreshments to be provided for them, though there will be extra to pay, if you are willing?"

"That will do fine, now please show my son and I to our room, and Solomon and Esther…that is their names for your

280

information Mr MacDougall, to their abode."

"Most certainly Mrs Leiper all will be attended to you have my word of honour as a gentleman of West Virginia." he assured her most extravagantly, bowing once more.

Betsy and Joshua settled into their room which was basic but comfortable with it's window looking down on to the busy street below.

After unpacking their things which were carried up by a old porter who Betsy tipped generously much to his surprise, this unusual, rare event left him lost for words, stuttering a vague thank you as he turned and left hobbling down the hallway.

"I have some business to attend to Joshua, how would like to see Solomon and Esther? You could help them with the mules."

"Yes mama." he replied with enthusiasm.

Betsy took Joshua down to the stables where she found her two servants making themselves as comfortable as they could. They were delighted to see their mistress and her son who they welcomed joyfully. Betsy left them all content in the knowledge that he would be happier with them than with her.

CHAPTER 19

Betsy returned to her room ordering hot water to bathe herself and make herself look presentable as she decided to explore Morgantown and see what it might offer, if anything

After dressing she made her way downstairs where the hotel manager on seeing her bowed once again behind the counter, displaying a toothy smile which she found not a little repulsive.

"May I be of assistance Mrs Leiper?" he enquired looking admiringly at Betsy.

"Why no Mr MacDougall, everything I need is quite nearby, so as the weather is pleasant I am going out to do a little exploring."

"Yes ma'am, I hope you will be impressed with our modest little town of which we are all very proud."

"I'm sure I will." she affirmed.

Betsy departed leaving MacDougall staring admiringly after her.

"Sure is a fine, fine lady." He mumbled to himself.

***

Betsy made her way down the main street which now boasted an array of new shops and stores with several ladies, some in groups of two or three, some with husbands, some alone taking in the warm Spring air and looking in the shops.

Betsy decided to go and find the town bank out of curiosity, wondering if she should deposit her cash and valuables which she had hidden away in her room at the hotel. She soon found the town's only bank, the grandly titled Washington Trust Company Bank, recently established and built of stone with a fine Neo Classical façade. On entering her attention was drawn to a finely dressed gentleman who was making a deposit at the counter. It was obvious that this was a man of some importance due to the deferential manner with which he was being dealt with by everyone in the bank. His portly form, expensive attire, fine whiskers combed in such a manner as to suggest a certain coquettishness caught the attention of Betsy who looked at him with some interest. Her thoughts turned to mischief as she wondered whether to engage with this gentleman or simply ignore him. He could after all be of use, not simply as amusement but as a source of acquiring more wealth.

Her mind was made up suddenly as the man, on seeing Betsy, immediately came over to her, took her hand courteously and exclaimed.

"Well if I have not seen anything or anyone in all Virginia as beautiful as you dear lady, my, my. Please allow me to introduce myself; I am Cuthbert Bullitt the Second at your service, and who do I have the pleasure, indeed great pleasure in meeting?"

Betsy feigned a little blush and replied in her soft feminine tone.

"Why I am Betsy Leiper, a widow."

"I am honoured indeed Mrs Leiper and allow me to express my most sincere condolences at the loss of your husband. May I inquire as to how he left this troubled world?"

Bullitt replied expressing sympathy in his manner of speaking, but also looking at Betsy and taking in her extraordinary beauty, these impressions inevitably led to him thinking about less than gentlemanly possibilities with her maybe later on if he played his cards right. Bullitt, something of a 'ladies man' had had some success in his carnal conquests, using his position as Chairman of the Bank, town Clerk and general man of importance and wealth. Bullitt full of pomp, gave the impression to many ladies, less gullible than Betsy, that he is indeed wealthy, and of great standing in the community.

"My dear John lost his life fighting of renegade Indians near Lexington, from where I come."

Betsy somehow produced a tear which had the desired effect on Bullitt straight away.

"I am so sorry madam, your loss grieves me too. Indeed it does, I am confident enough to say that Mr Leiper was a fine, fine man, a hero like many in our land. A land of great beauty but a troubled and dangerous place at the same time. Verily I say this with great sincerity, if you'll mind me good lady."

He said this with considerable emotion, worthy of any traveling Shakespearean actor, of which there were many touring the small theatres and saloons at this time, plying their trade with a considerable dose of ham and falsity.

"I am most appreciative Mr Bullitt."

"Please may I call you by your first name, if I may be so forward?"

"You may call me Betsy when not in formal company." Betsy agreed but in her manner implied that this was an honour for him, something he should be grateful for.

Cuthbert Bullitt now full of confidence at winning over this beauty, or so he believed, went further and offered to escort her to the new Tea Rooms, set up to replicate a typical such English establishment in Morgantown.

Betsy gave him her arm putting aside for now all thoughts of banking, and the two newly acquainted friends made their way to the Tea Rooms with Bullitt exuding good manners and impressing on Betsy how important a person he was in the town and how his reputation had spread through the state, indeed the whole nation, such was his exaggerating personality.

Betsy said little but giving him plenty of line as one would to a fish, allowed him to carry on, she even pretended to be impressed commenting occasionally with gentle remarks such as.

"My, my Mr Bullitt, I do declare." or "That is so impressive. Really? Oh goodness me"

There was no woman in the whole of America better skilled at dissembling than Betsy Roberts, she was well practised from her days with the Harpes, and Bullitt fell for her charms hook, line and sinker.

In reality Betsy of course saw a gullible fool, there for the taking and the more he was increasingly taken in by her charms, the easier it became for her to manipulate the situation to her potential advantage. She realised from quite early on in their relationship that Bullitt was a charlatan, prone to extreme exaggeration, a fake, much to Betsy's hidden disgust.

"He'll pay for this." she mused.

Her thoughts turned to taking advantage of him and an urge, mainly suppressed in recent years began to re-emerge, to not only punish him for his pomposity and arrogance, but also to relieve him of the wealth he so demonstratively boasted about. She commenced setting about planning his demise, Bullitt's days were numbered. Fortunately her emerging plans were given a boost when he invited her for dinner in the evening at another recently established restaurant just off the main street. It served fine food in an intimate setting and was managed by one of Bullitt's associates so he assured her of a most pleasant evening. He would send his man to pick her up at 6.30pm in his buggy which the man would drive, and they would eat at seven. Betsy at first declined his invitation but after some pleading from

Bullitt agreed to go along.

"I might as well enjoy some good food and we'll see what happens." she thought to herself.

"Well that's settled, I am most honoured to have you as my guest this evening, it is a rare honour I do declare."

Bullitt then escorted her back to the hotel, then with an extra spring in his step, full of the joys of Spring combined with thoughts of burgeoning love or more accuarately lust, something he had little or no real experience of, he went home to the finest house in Morgantown, his day now made exceptionally rewarding.

CHAPTER 20

On returning to the hotel and avoiding the attentions of the manager who hovered around her in expectation of being of some assistance, Betsy quickly made arrangements with Solomon and Esther to take care of Joshua for the evening, who was more than happy to remain with them both, such was the growing attachment between them all. Betsy then took to her room to prepare for what would be, she hoped, a profitable evening with the Honourable Cuthbert Bullitt. She selected her best dress, bonnet and shoes and then oddly slipped a small dark bottle into her purse.

True to Bullitt's word the buggy arrived on time and Betsy was whisked away to the rendezvous agreed. The journey was short and on arrival Bullitt was on hand to help down from the carriage in most courteous, gentlemanly manner, such was his desire to impress Betsy. He was dressed in the fashion of the day, no doubt purchasing clothes from London and Paris via New York, fine breeches, coat, hat and the most dandyish silk stockings which revealed a finely turned calf. Betsy smiled to herself feigning approval, whilst she herself had taken trouble to put on one of her best dresses, revealing a teasing glimpse of her full bosom, lovely bonnet and a pair of shoes she bought in Lexington just before she left there in a hurry.

"May I say Betsy, if I may, you look a pretty picture, why I would go further and say that I know of no great painter who could create so beautiful a picture, none who could do justice to you my dear."

Betsy smiled replying.

"Why thank you Cuthbert, I don't recall anyone other than my late, dear husband giving me such a compliment."

Betsy used his Christian name with a slight emphasis to suggest an increasing fondness with him, which of course in reality did not exist.

True to his word Cuthbert Bullitt wined and dined Betsy, extravagantly going out of his way to impress once again, boasting of his wealth and status and suggesting that if he married then his wife would become not just rich, but well respected within Morgantown as well as the whole territory.

This amused Betsy but she concealed her contempt for him by pretending to be impressed and of course enjoying a good meal with wine for the first time since she left Lexington, at no cost to herself, Bullitt going out of his way to ensure that she could chose anything she fancied with what the restaurant could offer.

"I am most grateful to you Cuthbert, it has been a while since I enjoyed such fine food, and I may say such pleasant attentive company."

Bullitt, taken aback at such a compliment replied.

"The pleasure is all mine my dear." he gushed, by now feeling a tad inebriated.

Betsy realised that he was becoming more careless in word and action, indicated as he gave the surprised waiter a most generous tip when they had finished their meal.

After consuming more wine together with Cuthbert's favourite digestif, a French brandy recently acquired from Charelston as it happened, Bullitt boldly invited Betsy to his room which he rented there specifically as a place where he could seduce any willing or unwilling female. It had been a very satisfactory arrangement.

Betsy feigning giddiness, agreed to go with him to see his especially "unique collection of English jewellery" which his dear late mother had left him, but before embarking on this visit Betsy, unbeknown to Bullitt had surreptitiously slipped several drops of arsenic from her small bottle into his brandy, which he consumed with a flourish as they departed.

"Excellent." she said to herself.

She then promptly accompanied him up to his rented room, or more like a suite of three rooms, consisting of a lounge, bathroom and bedroom with it's large four poster, sent to him from New York. Bullitt had staggered upstairs and was hazily thinking he had drunk too much. Indeed he had and shortly after entering the rooms he collapsed on the bed writhing increasingly in convulsions and abdominal pains. Betsy laughed saying to the unfortunate Bullitt as she stood over him.

"You thought I was interested in you..fool! You'll never know who I really am or what I've done, especially to men like you!"

Bullitt opened his eyes wide for an instant, gasping desperately, then trying to say something to her but quickly fell into a fog of pain and unconsciousness.

Betsy observing what she hoped would be his final agonies, grabbed a pillow and pushed it down on to his face so that he would it would hasten his demise. After doing this and exclaiming.

"Die, damn ye!"

She then left him to die alone, which actually occurred a short time after her departure, his sudden expiration left him sprawled across the bed, an undignified end to Morgantown's wealthiest, most eligible bachelor.

Betsy quietly slipped away going down the back fire escape stairs to go to Bullitt's house. Bullit where he foolishly had previously told Betsy the location of his valuables and money. She removed the keys from his coat pocket. On entering the house which was fortunately deserted found the locked cabinet but on seeing it's contents Betsy shook her head, disappointed with the amount, but nonetheless placed them in her purse including a few gold coins, jewellery, which was what Bullitt had told her was his mother's but in fact was little more that some earrings, a necklace and two rings of modest value.

Without delay she slipped back to Bullitt's bedroom suite via the fire escape and pushing his prone deflated body on to the floor she settled down in his bed sleeping soundly though not without some irritation, disappointed at the amount of money he actually had. Cuthbert Bullitt had revealed himself to be not just a philanderer but also a liar to boot.

The next morning brought a sunny day with the sun's rays shining brightly through the large windows of Bullitt's bedroom. Betsy had slept soundly but now hastily dressed, washed, composed herself and ran downstairs shouting for the landlord loudly to come and see Bullitt.

"Help, help me, please!! Something terrible has happened…it's Mr Bullitt…I…dead!!"

She cried hysterically, putting on a show worthy of her and startling the poor man, who acting on her cries, went upstairs and to his horror found Bullitt lying apparently dead on the floor. He ran downstairs finding Betsy distraught on the floor and being alone at this time in the morning did his best to comfort her shaking body.

"There, there now. I'll get you some water, make you feel a

little better. Such a terrible shock. Do you know what happened lady?"

"We went to his room…" she spluttered, "he wanted to show me some items….oh dear we became intimate…we slept…you must understand I ain't no….."

More profuse tears and wailing followed, the landlord not being able to cope with this display of emotion, assured Betsy saying.

"Not my business lady. Now I'm going to get the doctor, old Doctor Robertson. Here, sit yourself down, I'll be back before you know it."

The landlord returned promptly with the doctor who demanded a drink first, then lit a cigar.

"Whisky will do fine Mr Brook."

"Well I do think you should attend to Bullitt doc." the landlord protested.

Looking at Betsy who was quietly sobbing, crouched on the floor the doctor turned to her asking.

"Pardon lady I believe we haven't met before."

"Please sir, can you go and see if Cuthbert is alive, you may be able to save him." she implored.

"Too late he's most certainly done for, now don't upset yourself no more girl, I'm goin' now."

Doctor Robertson finished his dram, stubbed his cigar and went upstairs to attend to his new patient, taking his time up the stairway. He was not as fit as he used to be due to his drinking, smoking his cigars and felt more keenly his own various ailments.

After around twenty minutes, during which Betsy had gone into a near catatonic state, the doctor returned declaring.

"I'm sorry to say there's nothing to be done. Our esteemed Cuthbert Bullitt has left this world. I will arrange for our undertaker to collect his person forthwith."

The doctor bade farewell confirming that he would visit the local undertaker to make arrangements for the body to be collected as soon as possible, especially as the room needed to be fumigated.

Thankfully for Betsy, Bullitt's demise was henceforth put down to a sudden heart attack by Robertson, who all along had seemed more concerned to avail himself of more whisky which the landlord with some reluctance had supplied him.

"Well I'm not surprised, he had it comin' with his drinking and womanising." the landlord muttered.

Betsy nodded and returned to her room at the hotel where she was greeted by the manager Mr MacDougall, Solomon, Esther, Joshua and Augustus Bede who had heard about these events. Bede looked at Betsy, who continued to appear distressed, not willing to say much to anyone, and wondered to himself what on earth had been going on with Cuthbert Bullitt and his employer, there was something not right but he kept his thoughts to himself.

CHAPTER 21

Next morning after a largely sleepless night Betsy collected Joshua who had been with Solomon and Esther, paid her bill promptly, much to Mr MacDougall's disappointment as he and hoped she would stay longer, sent for Bede, and all together once again they moved out of town to resume their journey.

Augustus Bede who was now becoming aware of Betsy's unusual actions, but caring nothing for Cuthbert Bullitt, (who he had heard of from previous viists to the town) had noticed that there was much talk about the town about the demise of Bullitt but little sympathy was evident for him fortunately for Betsy. Bede decided that it was not his concern even when a drunken fool challenged him, accusing him of shooting Bullitt. He didn't even get the cause of death right claiming that Bede had stabbed him in the back! Bede soon saw him off by laying him flat out with his fist, much to the amusement of several onlookers who merely commented.

"He had that comin'!" they laughed.

Bede knew where his loyalty lay, both for monetary reasons and also his genuine growing affection for Betsy, who fascinated him more and more.

****

They all travelled onwards East through Elizabeth Town, Cumberland, Harrisburg and on to Allentown. The trail was easier now as they headed nearer to the growing towns of New York, Philadelphia and Boston. On route Betsy stopped at a town called Cumberland where she killed another wealthy man with her trusty knife, on that occasion. He was a foolish shopkeeper who tried his luck with her when there was no-one in the stores and attempted to molest her. In a flash she thrust the knife into his side, twisting it with great ferocity.

The unlucky man collapsed in a heap, the wound fatal, Betsy then wasted no time taking cash from his till, made her escape and left town with Bede, Solomon, and Esther wondering what and happened to make her want to leave in such a hasty manner.

"Is everything alright Mrs Leiper, I figured we'd be stayin' a while longer?"

"All's fine Mr Bede, but we need to get moving, time and tide wait for no man...neither does the Devil!" she added quizzically.

"Well you're the boss ma'am."

"I most certainly am Mr Bede."

That was all she was prepared to offer by way of explanation, so any further discussion was pointless, as Bede knew by now.

Bede henceforth wasted no time, readied the mules, wagon and instructed Solomon, who likewise wondered what Betsy had been up to as he whispered to Esther.

"Missy must have done somethin' bad or had somethin' done to her for her to be in such a hurry to leave."

Esther merely smiled. She had a feeling that her mistress

had been 'up to something' but even at this early stage in their relationship, felt a keen confidence and trust in her as to not question her actions

It became obvious to them all that Betsy was hell bent on taking any advantage whenever the opportunity arose for her to act in a compulsive way, especially with any man who crossed her path whom she had reason to deal with decisively. Betsy herself felt an even greater confidence in her own abilities but realised the need to take care to avoid unnecessary risks especially with Joshua to consider. Her compulsion to take revenge when appropriate, seize an opportunity to gain in anyway possible either via wealth or power or both, as well as a growing ambition to make a name for herself was becoming something that she had to keep control of but she felt it to be a struggle within herself. Only Betsy herself knew the reasons for her actions, she confided in no-one.

CHAPTER 22

At Harrisburg named after English trader John Harris, this attractive settlement sits prettily on the Susquehanna River, and was an important resting place and crossroads for Native American traders, as the trails leading from the Delaware to the Ohio rivers, and from the Potomac to the Upper Susquehanna intersected there, Betsy at last instructed the party to lay up for a much needed respite. Harrisburg at this time was a busy, bustling place due to the many travellers heading West. They had mostly travelled by river there, but thereafter continued the rest of their long journey by road, the same road that Betsy and the rest of her group had arrived in Harrisburg both to and from.

All this time on the trail Betsy was pleased to see her son Joshua getting on so well with both Solomon and Esther, to such an extent that he sought their company as often as possible. Solomon showed the boy his many conjuring tricks usually involving stones or an odd coin, playfought with him which Joshua enjoyed greatly, especially as he taught the boy some useful moves. Esther too played with Joshua which brought out her latent maternal instincts, forming a bond which would last a long time. She was an attractive woman herself and despite the rough treatment she had received at the plantation unfortunately from other slaves mostly, she retained a gentle disposition. It was Solomon who intervened on her behalf dealing brutally with another slave who had tried to rape Esther, he beat the man to a pulp and warned others what the consequences would be if anyone else tried his luck with her.

Esther though proud, could not be but grateful especially as Solomon made no moves on her, indeed behaved in a considerate, polite, protective way…he was handsome too which attracted Esther's attention. Their love blossomed steadily over the months ahead and they gradually became inseparable taking every opportunity to spend time together despite the difficulties.

Betsy once more arranged for them all to stay at the town's finest inn, insisting Bede also stayed there, once again the two slaves had to make do with the stables again but were grateful nonetheless for her taking care to provide decent facilities. She insisted that they had makeshift beds of sorts instead of merely straw, plentiful water and food for them at regular intervals.

***

On day two of their stay Betsy robbed another gentleman, this time a bank manager who fell for her charms and foolishly fell for a trap laid by her with Solomon for the first time innocently participating in. He was initially astounded at his mistress's violent behaviour but saw a chance for some revenge on his hated white oppressors. She had dealt with this man in a way that astonished Solomon initially by thrusting her sharp knife to his throat and acting intuitively Solomon then grabbed the fellow pinning his arms back, Betsy seizing his wallet and helped herself to the contents, a not inconsiderable sum of cash.

"If you utter a word about this, you can be sure me and my helper will find you, cut your throat and get your family. You got me?" she spat out.

"Yes, please let me go, I promise…I won't say a word…believe me lady, I…I won't say anything…"

The man sweated, terrified at this sudden violent attack, fearing his life was going any minute.

"Let him go." Betsy instructed Solomon, who slowly released the wretched man, who fell to the floor clutching his throat.

Betsy and Solomon made their escape with not a word spoken, Solomon understandably amazed, but at the same time totally in awe of his mistresses's actions. Little did he know how she had learned all this from her years with Micajah and Wiley Harpe, a schooling which although horrific had made her partly what she was now.

From then on with Betsy's guidance he became more and more Betsy's willing accomplice, using his strength, guile and keenness to exact at least some retribution for what he and Esther had had to endure over their years of captivity. Even with their previous owner's better treatment he was still often beaten, worked hard and had to live in the most rudimentary conditions, wooden shacks – stiflingly hot in Summer, bitterly cold in Winter, it was little better than what the owner's hogs lived in.

"You done well Solomon, now say nothing to Esther, Bede nor 'specially Joshua, ya understand?"

"Yes ma'am I decidedly do, you can trust in me ma'am." he enthusiastically assured her.

"Good then we will become friends, just realise that I have scores to settle…like you do I guess?"

Solomon nodded firmly.

"You let me down mind, and I promise that you will both

regret it…I promise." she added threateningly.

Solomon was quick to reassure her on that point!

They returned to the inn with Betsy, barely displaying any indication of what had occurred, hiding her stash in the room in a locked cabinet along with her other valuables. A tidy sum was mounting up in addition to the what she had from before, but she now preferred to keep the cash and valuables nearer to her to avoid any suspicions. She then took Joshua out treating him to some sweet pastries that she had seen in the town's bakery shop. They then walked down to the riverside admiring the view across Susquehanna River, all the while Joshua threw stones skimming along the water of the river, as Bede had shown him some days before at the pool where Betsy had bathed.

At that moment Bede appeared walking along the riverbank and catching sight of Betsy and Joshua strode over, tipping his hat.

"Beautiful river ain't it Mrs Leiper." he commented looking across it's majestic wide expanse, with vessels going to and fro which caught the interest of Joshua. Bede took the opportunity to explain to the boy what each of the boats were, some sailing boats, some flat boats, some ferries going across the river, where he figured they were going to and how many sailors were on board some of the larger ships. Joshua was fascinated with Bede's descriptions and stories of when he was younger and was on board a riverboat with soldiers of the Revolutionary Army attacking British forces but suffering a defeat at the Battle of Brandywine.

"I had to make my escape pretty quickly 'fore those redcoats could get me!" he rejoined.

Joshua sat entranced with Bede's adventures but Betsy started to get a little concerned that he was influencing her son too much, and quickly they took their leave, returning to the inn, leaving Bede alone by the river bank.

Before leaving Betsy feeling slightly guilty turned to him saying."It's been nice meeting you here but we gotta go now Mr Bede. Please be ready to depart tomorrow."

"Sure Mrs Leiper." he replied, looking a little disappointed since he had much else to tell the young boy.

Betsy speedily returned back to her room with him and catching sight of Solomon and Esther, called out to them to prepare to leave by evening. She wasted no time in packing all their things, sending Solomon to find Bede and instruct him also to make ready to depart. He found Bede still by the riverside sat smoking his pipe, then promptly passed on his mistresses orders which almost immediately raised Bede' hackles. He was unused to receiving instructions from such as a slave, especially as this was not the first time Betsy had relayed messages to him, and feeling somewhat aggrieved he turned to face Solomon who stood his ground.

"Who are you boy, telling me what to do, I don't take no orders from a slave, you understand?"

"I'm just telling you what mistress told me to tell you." he replied frimly, looking Bede in the eye then smiling a little.

"I'll wipe that smile of yer face, so I will. When we get to New York I advise you to keep away from me, understand, I'll teach ye some manners boy!" Bede snarled, feeling the urge to strike Solomon.

"Thank you for the warnin' sir, but I believe I can take care of myself, and Esther too. Yer understand...sir." he replied, looking Bede again straight in the eye and slowly squaring up to this man who truth be told was not going to be a match physically for Solomon...and he knew it.

With that Bede strode away, seething with indignation.

Solomon smiled to himself relishing his first victory of sorts over this symbol of white oppression. He too returned to the inn and with Esther prepared for their departure.

CHAPTER 23

It was late afternoon before they all departed from Harrisburg. The wagon had been packed full with fresh provisions, baggage, the mules freshly fed and watered and the five travellers in their places with Augustus Bede leading the way. This was not an ideal time to get going but Betsy was determined to make as much ground as possible before the sun set and further progress impossible in the dense forests that had accompanied them all on every mile. He advised Betsy to trust him with finding a quicker route to Allentown, which was their next main destination, the trail ran near to the King's Highway though not parallel, but would avoid the turnpike with it's guard and any curious townsfolk who might come after Betsy seeking answers to the bank manager's unfortunate experience. That is if he had foolishly disobeyed her warnings and reported what had happened to the authorities at the fort.

The new trail selected by Bede proved difficult, the road little more than a narrow pathway with overhanging undergrowth, fallen branches and the occasional tree blocking the way. Here Bede with Solomon's help, using his trusty axe, cleared the way. Betsy kept her carbine close to hand fearing ambush at any point but fortunately it proved unnecessary, the only other living person was a traveling fur trader they encountered who wisely let them pass without comment. He was an unkempt, French pioneer who had been forced to turn his skills to trapping beaver, bears, wolves and any other creatures he could capture. His sole mule carried the pelts, tied together with rope, attracting the interest of Bede who himself had hunted extensively throughout Tennessee, Kentucky, Virginia and as far east as Pennsylvania. It turned out to be a lucrative occupation for the Frenchman due to the ever increasing demand for furs in the growing settlements, which were springing up all around the territory.

"Au revoir! Bonne chance!"

Bede shouted to him as they passed.

The Frenchman merely nodded nervously especially when he saw Solomon. This was an extremely rare sight even in these parts away from most of the plantations, the sight of a black man dressed well, obviously healthy, was something of a shock to this world weary pioneer who was more used to encountering Native Indians than what he assumed were free slaves.

The party moved on, laying up three times overnight before they resumed their journey on the easier King's Highway. Betsy was unsure if they had actually reduced the length of the route since it seemed to take an eternity on the trails that Bede had taken them on.

"It's cut ten miles off where were headin' and avoided turnpikes Mrs Leiper." he assured her when she commented on this.

"I trust you are correct. At least we're safe thank you Mr Bede."

"It's only around fifteen miles now to Allentown, we should make it with ease by tomorrow."

"These last days have been hard Mr Bede so I'm sure lookin' forward to restin' up that's for sure."

Betsy then ordered Bede to lay up while she washed by a creek near to the trail. She went in to it's cool waters first with

Joshua, who splashed about joyously, then allowed Esther, Solomon and Bede, in that order, to take their turns. Once again Bede felt some grievance that the two slaves were allowed to go before him but bit his tongue.

Next day the party neared their next destination as Betsy had decided to take a respite in the growing town of Allentown which was some ninety or so miles from New York, around four day's journey away.

Allentown had been founded some half a century before by William Allen a wealthy shipping merchant, former mayor of the city of Philadelphia and then Chief Justice of the Province of Pennsylvania. It is likely that a certain amount of rivalry with the Penns prompted Judge Allen to decide to start a town of his own in 1762 especially as he saw the possibilities of this area for development and riches.

She checked into an hotel, the impressive Compass and Square Hotel, another recently built establishment which offered a reasonable level of comfort in it's twenty odd rooms, complete with bathing facilities and of course stables at the side. Without any discussion she insisted that Solomon and as well as Bede of course, be given rooms also, sparking protests from the owner, a finely dressed man named George Morley, an Englishman from Harrogate in Yorkshire originally, who had carefully made a small fortune by speculating in this virgin land. By force of character and financial inducement she got her way, and the two slaves were given a room at the rear of the hotel, discretely out of the way so as not to offend the other guests. Also realising Bede's growing resentment and also showing him a level of appreciation she felt was due, she insisted on him staying in one of the best rooms.

This the owner/manager agreed without complaint. "Aye lass your wish will be respected, brass always does t' talkin'." he

304

said in his slightly gruff Yorkshire accent.

Betsy wasted no time in going out, this time without the attentions of any manager since the hotel was quite busy with the comings and goings of folk who were either on their way West or involved with trade of various sorts. Betsy having left Joshua with Solomon and Esther who were always glad of his company, took to exploring Allentown to gather as much information about it's wealth and any potential business to be had.

It did not take long before she was impressed with the hustle and bustle of the place with it's newly opened shops, market, hotels and businesses. She noticed an advertisement for the licence of a "house of entertainment" pinned to the town square's notice board which contained all sorts of business ventures, offers of work, those seeking work, stores advertising their wares, wanted posters (one of which caught her attention was a rough looking individual who reminded her of Wiley Harpe!), notices of land purchase, for sale, municipal notices, and much else besides. Betsy's attention though was directed to the "house of entertainment" notice advertising a large property just off the main street, the information pointing obviously at selling a house or more accurately inn of dubious repute, which was being sold for 40lb of silver.

Quickly realising the potential of such an establishment or almost certainly a brothel, not just economically but for potential blackmail and extortion purposes of gullible fools who might easily be taken in, she made haste to the agent. The office was nearby and without hesitation she purchased, it placing a deposit with all the cash she had, then collected the silver from the Harpes' stash kept in her case from the hotel, to complete the sale.

One of the other customers at the agent's office was a

local penniless entrepreneur and adventurer called Isaac Sturn, one of the many German immigrants of Allentown, who despite his lack of money for some reason impressed Betsy with his manner and look. Though having seen better days recently he gave the impression of confidence, his appearance cultured, wearing as he was a suit of some class and wearing spectacles. He was a man in his thirties with black hair, short and carefully combed, his physique slim and his manners evident as he bowed to Betsy on seeing her, removing his hat immediately. His voice suggested evidence of his German roots but was clear, possessing some authority and obvious intelligence. Keen to impress Besty he introduced himself without delay.

"Good day ma'am I have not had the pleasure of meeting you before.

New to Allentown?" he said in his slight German accent.

"Indeed I am, and who might you be sir?"

Quickly Stern introduced himself properly then set out his credentials, careful not to exaggerate unlike the foolish Cuthbert Bullitt, but making it plain that despite his recent run of bad luck, not uncommon in these times, he impressed Betsy with his ideas and energy. After further discussions and taking lemonade at a nearby hostelry to enable a continuation of the meeting, Betsy with unusual haste formed a business partnership with him to manage her future affairs in Allentown, stating that she will remain as a silent partner, something which he agreed to do. She was not prone to impulsiveness concerning business but she felt instinctively that this man had something about him which she found attractive as well as potentially useful.

"You may not know me Mr Sturn as we have only just met

306

today but you will quickly learn that I am most determined woman, a woman who gets what she wants, suffers no fools and deals with any treachery in a most decisive way. Understand?"

Sturn, with similar intuitive powers like Betsy herself, agreed with her, giving his word that he will work tirelessly on her behalf.

"You will not regret for one moment Mrs Leiper." he answered confidently.

"I trust not. We will draw up a suitable contract just to cement our arrangement. I noticed a lawyer down the street, can you recommend him Isaac?"

Betsy used his first name without hesitation and allowed Sturn to call her Betsy as well. A sure sign of her feeling of confidence in this new partnership.

"I can Betsy, his name is Josef Kleinwitz, a good, reliable lawyer." Sturn assured her.

They agreed to meet again next morning at the Kleinwitz office which Sturn would arrange for 9am.

"I look forward to seeing you in the morrow Betsy. I will make enquiries on your behalf as to the property and it's use." With that both parties took their leave.

Sturn acting decisively located a madame to run the house, since it was more than obvious what it's primary purpose was to be. He found a woman he knew of named 'Blue Sally', so named from a gunpowder burn on her right cheek. She had acquired this mark because of a gun backfiring as she attempted to shoot an aggrieved customer in her previous establishment. Blue Sally was a skinny harridan, in her forties, reddish hair, wearing a smart dress with bonnet jauntily cocked at an angle, she was something of a firebrand by all accounts but possesed a shrewd business brain. She possessed little compassion for the girls under her charge who she regarded as more of a commodity to be exploited rather than individuals with feelings, but despite this if you were fair with Blue Sally she would be fair with you. She always rewarded those who 'worked' hard and would give the ladies under her charge time off if they appeared a bit too 'battle weary'.

She tolerated no nonsense from customers and employed two burly minders, who were not averse to beating the living daylights with the cudgels they carried at all times, of any customers who attempted to avoid paying or abused the girls. Sally had no time for bullies consequently her reputation as a fair if tough madame was widely recognised not just in Allentown but other places where she had done business.

Betsy recognised that though Sally was a hardened operator, she was someone who could be trusted to do a job, and commensurately Sally herself realised that Betsy was not someone to be taken lightly, there was something about this out of the ordinary woman which not only fascinated her, but also she knew instinctively that she would deal decisively and ruthlessly with anyone who attempted to cheat on her. Both women had learned lessons the hard way, both women pledged to work together to make the business successful, though Betsy warned Sally not to allow any abuse or mistreatment of the women employed there, she knew from experience what that felt like.

"I don't Mrs Leiper but neither do I put up with any malingering, they may call me Blue Sally caused by the unfortunate accident I had with that damned firearm, but you can trust me!" she asserted, rising from her chair.

"I believe I can." Betsy replied looking her straight

between the eyes which slightly unnerved Sally.

"I'll start right away and pay you every week on Fridays your share. Isaac knows me. I never miss payments." she affirmed.

"I can vouch for that Mrs Leiper." Sturn confirmed, nodding in agreement.

"Well we have our deal and so long as we stick to it there's good chances for us all to make some money." Betsy said confidently.

Like Blue Sally, Sturn too was warned amidst this and immediately assured Betsy of his dedication and loyalty to her once again. She made clear that close contact would be maintained between the three of them with Betsy keeping a careful eye on proceedings. With these rules in place the new business venture would quickly become a very lucrative enterprise between the three of them.

All this she kept secret from the rest of the group, she was fearful that especially Augustus Bede might prove a problem should he get wind of Betsy's business dealings in Allentown. It was a problem she could do without, but one which she was prepared to deal with should Bede stray beyond his role as scout, which was what she had hired him for.

After completing the deal at the Kleinwitz legal offices with both parties signing the contract, and later meeting to go over the arrangements which included regular reports and contact between Betsy and Sturn, once again she gathered together the party of five and made ready to depart, feeling satisfied with the business she had done in Allentown.

Betsy Roberts' mission had only just begun, there was a whole world out there waiting for her to take her share of the riches which beckoned her.

'Blue' Sally

CHAPTER 24

After leaving Allentown Betsy almost subconsciously began to call Augustus Bede, with greater frequency, "Gus" more from convenience than anything else. Her mood was full of optimism after Allentown and she unusually became a little careless. Bede not unsurprisingly saw this mistakenly as the beginning of some form of affectionate relationship, something he had hoped would happen. Thinking he was entitled to do so, he attempted a tentative.

"Betsy... I was wonderin'.."

Only to be rebuked sharply.

"Mrs Leiper to you!" Betsy sharply replied.

Bede was not deterred, his perception of Betsy Roberts was imperfect to say the least and tainted by his attitude to all women, even though he knew that she was not like any women that he had encountered before.

Thirty miles from New York Betsy gave instructions for the group to lay up for the evening by a quick flowing river, which with it's wide banks would be a perfect spot to rest up before the last assault of their great trek eastwards. Bede had noticed it's ideal location and had pointed this out to Betsy.

"I remember this place from last Fall when I got as far as this on the trail of an escaped slave who had gotten away from his master's plantation, 'bring him back alive Bede so I can whip his hide!' I was told."

Bede stared at Solomon who could hear his comments as Bede purposely stared at him with a withering look.

"Thank you Mr Bede, we don't need to know any more." Betsy snapped at him.

"Well I found the critter Betsy…"

"Enough!"

Betsy had had enough of his familiarity, his taunting of Solomon had gone far enough.

With an uneasy atmosphere they parked the wagon and mules and made preparations to rest up for the night which was quickly drawing in. An eerie silence descended on them all with only Solomon whispering to Esther that he would settle matters with Bede as soon as he was safely able to do so."Now you be careful husband, I don't mean to be left a widow, ya hear me." she warned him taking hold of his collar to emphasize the point.

"I'll be careful sweet, no fear." Solomon relpied reassuring Esther with a kiss on her cheek.

It did not take long before all were sound asleep, Joshua who was tired from the day's exertions soon snored, Bede under cover as usual also snored loudly, only Betsy was awake, planning her next move which had been decided for her earlier. She figured correctly that Bede's use was now superfluous to her, the way ahead was clear and she knew from speaking to Isaac Sturn in Allentown that the road ahead became easier the nearer you got to New York and Boston beyond. They had passed through several settlements and small towns en route for her to gather information about her destination, and Bede's knowledge gradually became less vital especially as he had only once ventured anywhere near New York. She decided that a course of action was now necessary to be rid of this man who had become more a thorn in her side and who had obviously, to her way of thinking, planned to make a move to rob her of all her wealth. She did not trust him, her sole concern was the welfare of her son, Joshua, also Solomon and Betsy, who she had become fond of, and the riches she possessed which had increased considerably since her previous nefarious activities.

With these thoughts in mind Betsy waited until Bede was sound asleep and judging from the progressively loud snoring coming from him, it was an opportune moment to make her move. She checked that Joshua was sleeping soundly and slowly, stealthily crept up to Bede who lay face down with just his blanket covering him. Breathing quietly Betsy took out her trusty, sharpened knife, gently pulled his head upwards and slit his throat, the knife sliding easily through his jugular vein. Bede merely spluttered slightly as the blood spurted out but such was Betsy's expertise with the knife that he was unconscious, then dead before he knew it. Just then Betsy was aware of someone behind her.

It was Solomon who had been awoken, sensing that something was going on that he needed to investigate. He stood up and seeing what had happened he swiftly went over to the Betsy who had completed her task. She looked around slightly concerned at being discovered, but Solomon nodded approvingly now that he was aware of what had been done to Bede. He then willingly helped her having developed an intense dislike to Bede, who had refused more and more to call him by his name when Betsy was not around, but referred to him callously as "slave boy".

"I can help now miss." Solomon whispered to Betsy

" I'm obliged Solomon but you must not breathe a word of this. As far as

Joshua is concerned this critter up and left last night, he went back West. Understand?"

Solomon nodded obediently and pulled Bede's body as quietly as he could away from the wagon, clearing as much blood as he could using Bede's shirt and breeches.

"He won't be needin' these now miss."

"That's for sure, now we need to dispose of him. Ever gutted a hog before" Betsy asked him.

"Sure."

Solomon looked Betsy in the eye, realising what she was getting at.

She nodded.

They soon finished stripping Bede, who rolled over at one point staring at them both, his dead right eye slowly opening due to the movement and momentarily freaking Solomon, but not Betsy…then using a larger knife that she had removed from Bede, proceeded to gut him. When this was done, thinking back to the Harpes, she collected some rocks from the riverbank, placed them inside Bede's corpse and got Solomon to roll him down the side, pushing him into the Lamington River. The mortal remains of Augustus Bede's body slowly and remorselessly sank into it's waters.

After clearing away any remaining blood and disposing of Bede's clothes also in the river, the two of them, without a word said, returned to sleep. Betsy slept soundly. Esther merely turned over and sleepily asked where Solomon had been.

"I heeded a call of Nature my sweet."

CHAPTER 25

Next morning which heralded a fine late Spring day in Pennsylvania, Betsy woke up first, attended to her toilet, then woke Joshua and the two slaves who she now regarded more decidedly, not so much as slaves, but as 'servants'. Thanks to their increasingly invaluable assistance to her and evident good natures, both Solomon and Esther had made a favourable impression on Betsy, if not on the deceased Bede, but then he had paid the price for his attitude.

It did not take long before they were all ready to leave, Betsy duly dealt with Joshua's inquiries as to where Bede was, saying.

"He had to go back home son."

"Oh I liked him mama." Joshua said in a plaintive, hurt voice.

"Well that's how it is son, you make friends then sometimes folk have to move on but don't be worryin' we're going to be in New York soon and you'll make lots of new friends there I promise."

"I will?" he answered becoming more content.

Esther then looked at Solomon with some consternation.

"Business had to be taken care of Esther." he merely stated, not looking directly at her.

"Well I guess you did the right thing husband."

316

"We did, Miss Betsy wanted it that way."

Esther nodded not fully understanding what had been going on but she did not wish to explore this enigma any further.

***

The rest of the journey to New York minus Augustus Bede proved fairly uneventful as she had hoped, especially as the road became more easier to travel on. It had been levelled so that passage for wagons and wagon trains could make movement less troublesome and the route more obvious from then on.

They stopped once in Philadelphia to stock up with provisions, but could not help but be impressed with the town's size, especially noticing in passing the Presidents House, an impressive Georgian mansion once home to George Washington and John Adams more recently. Betsy was tempted to stay longer given the business potential of this growing commercial hub with it's port, full of sailing ships from the East and other parts of the country but resisted figuring that she could at a later date explore commercial possibilities. "It can wait a while." she mused.

Solomon and Esther were amazed on seeing the large number of people about, noticing particularly that black slaves seemed less wretched than from where they had come from in the South. There were still many plantations in the territory that they passed with obvious signs of exploitation, but overall in comparison to the Southern plantation conditions, they appeared not quite as severe.

317

NEW YORK

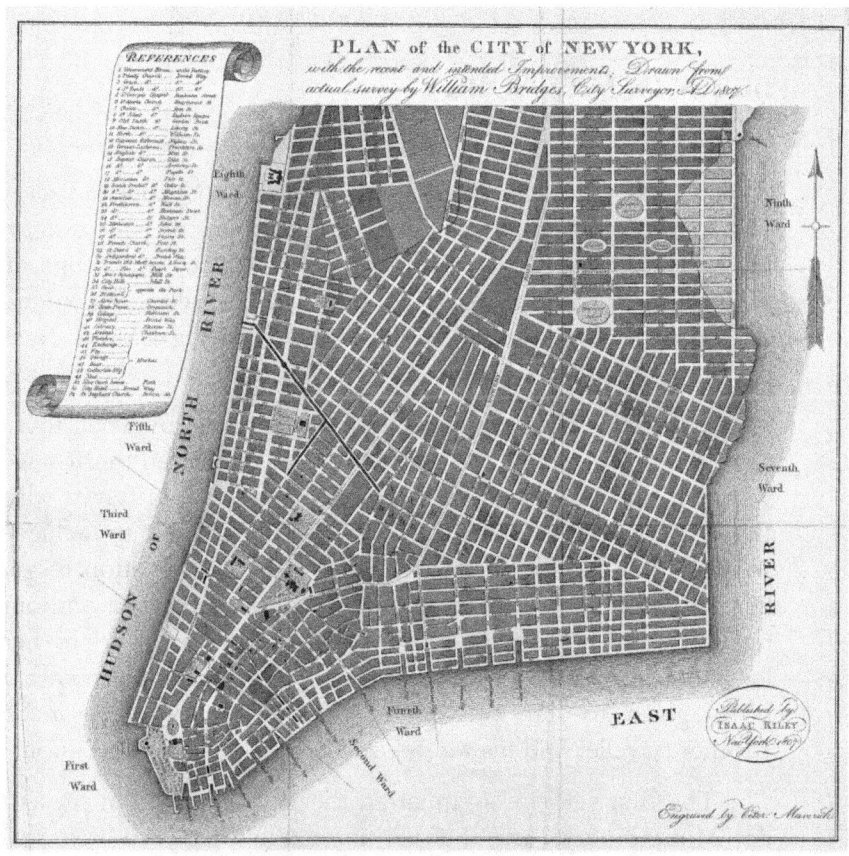

1807 New York street map

CHAPTER 26

BETSY IN NEW YORK

A growing sense of excitement grew as the four travellers neared New York with more and more wagons, wagon trains, mule pack trains, single travellers, and groups of men on horseback, pioneers passing them by, all going to and fro, on their way mostly West but some traveling East, to their chosen destination.

Many times it was a struggle to simply pass by when there were wagons comings toward them with little intention to give way, and on more than one occasion tempers were frayed with Betsy having to employ all her feminine wiles to achieve passage. Her pleading combined with her determination to get her way in almost all cases achieved the desired result without resort to any violent means, only once did she resort to her husband's carbine and pistols, with Solomon armed also with a pistol given to him by her. His impressive physique made another traveller and his wagon move over in quick succession!

The first sight of Manhattan they witnessed from present day Montgomery Park, then an uninhabited forested area, was such that it was something of an anti-climax since that morning it was shrouded in a mist, only the vaguest forms were visible across the wide Hudson River. Betsy pulled up the wagon and mules and stared across for a while, thinking to herself with a mixture of pride having achieved her goal of reaching New York, and some foreboding as to what lay ahead, not just for

319

herself but especially for Joshua and indeed Solomon and Esther, who likewise looked across with some trepidation, They both had put their trust and their futures in the hands of this woman, admittedly having little choice, but they both felt gratitude to Betsy, not just for their escape from the plantation through her purchasing them both, but also for giving them opportunities to reveal their true worth, something which would never have occurred should they have remained working in the fields like thousands of other poor souls. The relationship they had developed with Joshua was something they both treasured and could never have imagined until now, also of equal value the growing respect that Betsy had for them both, she no longer saw them as merely slaves but as real people who she could rely on. This was something that they could never have imagined in their wildest dreams, previously 'white folks' were their enemy by and large, used to exploiting and beating them and their compatriots who and been unfortunate enough to be enslaved.

Solomon turned to Esther and softly said.

"We don't know what's ahead Esther but the Lord has been kind to us and Miss Betsy too."

Esther nodded.

"She's a fine woman that's for sure husband, I say God bless Miss Betsy."

Joshua jumped up in excitement now, especially after being told by his mother on many occasions, what a fine place they were heading to and what great prospects lay ahead.

"I can't see it ma!"

He looked ahead keen to get a glimpse of what he imagined would be an enormous metropolis.

"You will soon Joshua, the best things are revealed in their own time be sure."

She called out.

"Well we made it, just this river to cross now so let's move on and find a ferry to get us across safely, be a shame if we get stuck here having come so far!"

Ahead by the shores of the Hudson River Betsy could see many sailing vessels going to and fro, some with one, some two sails, she also noticed large flat boats, ferries in fact which were common all over the country but here there were some especially large boats, big enough to carry them all as well as their wagon and mules, across to New York itself. There were also sailing ships which carried goods across the river and sailed up and down, so Betsy headed for a landing stage down by the river shore. A steady fine rain typical for this time of year fell and the mist seemed to thicken as they approached the jetty where two flat boats were moored, one larger than the other.

Two men operated the ferry and looked with some surprise when the wagon approached complete with mules laden with bags, with Betsy at the front handling the reins expertly with Solomon and Esther by her side. The sight of two slaves sitting with a white woman caused consternation but Betsy soon allayed any doubts with her usual charm and of course money which she offered to them above the actual fee. Without further ado they were all loaded on to the lager flatboat which only just took their weight.

"This is the most we took on this 'ere boat lady!" complained the boss ferryman.

"I appreciate your help so long as we don't sink halfway across!" Betsy laughed.

The ferryman was not amused and spat tobacco spittle into the deep waters.

"It's calm today lady but some days the river ain't so kind, why I seen men drown in these waters, so I have!... he continued...some days it can take over two hours in windy and rough conditions but today maybe less'an half that time. If ye don't respect this lady it'll deal with ye harshly for sure."

With three sturdy Negro helpers or slaves most likely, beckoned from the riverside cabin, the boat was slowly manoeuvred into the calm waters using long poles to steer the vessel, then made it's way across the wide Hudson River. In fact the first ferry service proper on the Hudson River commenced in 1700 when the First Earl of Bellomont, an English merchant granted a charter to Samuel Bayard for a ferry between Weehawken, New Jersey and Manhattan. This primitive service lasted over one hundred years, later to be replaced by steamboats making the journeys much easier, with greater capacity and the capability also of carrying more cargo to furnish the demands of the growing city.

After landing in South Manhattan near to the busy shipyards and thanking the ferry men and slaves who had worked tirelessly ensuring a safe passage, their skills with the guiding poles most impressive, Betsy and the party of four entered the growing, bustling city of New York and with information gladly given by officials at the landing stage as to where they could take lodgings, they headed off North along the partly paved and flattened dirt road known as the Bowery which was the main thoroughfare at that time. which at that time in reality was little more than a town of mostly wooden buildings, dirt roads, squalid districts of overcrowded houses. The fire of 1776 had destroyed over half the houses in the city with consequence that after this there was a huge expansion of building with many more houses and buildings being constructed of brick and stone, many fine houses built to accommodate the flourishing wealthy classes who demanded amenities befitting their standing and wealth.

New York at this time was dwarfed by European cities such as London, Paris, Berlin but rapidly caught up over the next century turning it into the equal or near equal of even London with it's enormous commercial business, financial power and cultural life rivalled by only Paris at that time.

As they had come nearer to the shore of Manhattan, they began to realise the actual size of the city with it's many large buildings, churches notably the fine Georgian cathedral of Trinity church with it's tall spire pointing skywards, various other structures many built of stone and brick for merchants, banks companies of all sorts and domestic abodes, all of which created a breathtaking skyline the like of which was something they had never witnessed before. Scores of people thronged the thoroughfares, going about their various means of employment or seeking places of entertainment, inns, shops also which sold everything imaginable, cattle, and sheep being driven to the main slaughterhouse on the banks of the Hudson River, the noises of the poor beasts displaying the distress they felt, some said that even from a distance they knew what their fate was to be and could scent doom and soon Death.

Not unlike most cities there was always the ever present chance of fights and disputes breaking out as the lower classes, which were being swelled at this time by influxes of immigrants arriving from all over Europe and beyond but mostly Britain, Germany, France, Holland, Belgium, Italians, Jews mostly from Eastern Europe, Irish immigrants who would come in greater numbers later in the century, victims of the terrible famines, Chinese coolies and many more of all colours, races and creeds…a melting pot of humanity was in the process of being created, it's variety only surpassed by London at this time and for the next one hundred years until New York, like London possessed a uniqueness with it's incredible mixture of such cultures, a melting pot of humanity, but a refuge for those escaping tyranny, extreme poverty, for those seeking a new life, fortunes to be made in what became known a s the land of the free. Many were to be sadly disappointed as much of the same causes of their desperate flight to America were to be found there, often to be replaced by even greater poverty, misery and exploitation. Disease and disasters were all too prevalent taking many victims just as they had done all too infrequently before.

As they made their way up the Bowery road slowly taking much of this. In and wondering what lay ahead, a man shouted out to them from a crowd of passers-by.

"Look there, a wench with two negrus!!"

Betsy seethed inside but kept silent, Solomon and Esther feared that here in New York, things would be the same. It appeared that much of what was bad from where they came from had followed them and was ever present in their new home.

CHAPTER 27

After struggling through the traffic mayhem for around an hour, Betsy eventually found her destination with much relief, especially as Joshua was becoming restless with fear especially never having experienced so much noise and occasional verbal abuse directed at them. New Yorkers were a rough bunch not afraid to express annoyance or disapproval whenever the circumstance arose and Betsy's appearance with her entourage was no exception to this behaviour. They were also a mass of people looking for opportunities to better themselves, gain for themselves anything of value or prestige, often at the expense of other weaker individuals but also they possessed an amazing ability to be generous, helpful and ingenious. Betsy sensed this very early on and it encouraged her to seek for herself as much advantage as this metropolis could offer. Unlike most women she was more than capable of achieving what she sought without anyone else's help.

After arriving at her destination much to the relief of everyone Betsy took lodgings at an Inn, the grandly impressive Bull's Head Tavern set by the Bowery main street, and once again she insisted on a room for Solomon and Esther. This was agreed by a convivial manager, a ruddy, stout, Irishman with impressive whiskers, named Fergal O'Rourke who had recently taken over the Inn and was keen to make it the most renowned hostelry in New York City. Fergal went out of his way to make Betsy welcome, giving her the finest rooms and made no objection to Solomon and Esther being given a comfortable room at the rear of the inn. Naturally Betsy's good looks and personality took the eye of Fergal who felt he was a ladies man with the charm necessary to prove this, her beauty succeeded in achieving her objectives with Mr O'Rourke.

"Such a pleasure my dear young lady to have you gracin' our humble inn, to be sure it is." he announced to Betsy in his most agreeable, charmingly spoken Irish brogue.

"I'm delighted, and most pleased with the location here." Betsy smiled and shook his offered hand.

"Now do let me know if you need anything Mrs Leiper, I'm at your service at all times."

"That's good to know Mr O'Rourke."

"Oh now please ye will call me Fergal, to be sure I never go with these formalities, especially with such a beautiful lady as yourself. Why it gladdens mi' heart to have you stay with us." he went on keen to impress our Betsy.

"Fergal it will be then, I'm content with that."

"Grand! Now is there anything I can gat you or help you with?"

Betsy thought for a moment and replied.

"I believe you can Fergal... she hesitated then continued….I assume you are acquainted with many lawyers, merchants, business people and the like, am I correct?"

Betsy was wasting no time in weighing up were worth making connections with, she was in a hurry to exploit as many business opportunities as she could, as well as establishing herself in the high social circles.

"Why sure, they all come here to dine, drink and make merry, Fergal O'Rourke runs the grandest place in this here

326

New York City. I can't begin to tell you who's who, who is worth getting acquainted with…is it a husband you seek if you don't mind a fool like me asking ye?" he enquired tentatively.

"Oh no, I have not long been a poor widow and still grievin' after my poor John, struck down in his prime…She faked sadness….No, no it is much too soon to think about such things Fergal, why I have a young son Joshua to care for and my responsibilities to my two servants Solomon and Esther."

"Oh forgive me Mrs Leiper, sure I put my foot in it, sure I did, my sister Mary would curse me if she was here now!"

"Don't upset yourself, you were not to know, I forgive you. I believe you are a good man and I think we'll get on just fine, you'll be a big help to me, a widowed lady new here to this town."

Betsy feigned a blush, dissembling some innocence, realising this rather naive man could become of great use to her. He stared at her with a mixture of admiration as well as attraction but even at this early stage in their relationship was aware that any move on his part would be doomed to failure. Sometimes one knows instinctively that there are some women and men who are beyond reach. Betsy Roberts now Leiper was one such unattainable gem.

"Nothing would give a true Irishman greater pleasure lady." Fergal continued then offered some food and refreshment to her and her entourage, permitting the two servants a table with food and drinks provided. Both Solomon and Esther were taken aback at this totally unusual hospitality, the first time in their lives that anything like this had occurred, but making up to a small extent for the abuse they had witnessed on their journey here. Joshua just got on with devouring his meal and later enjoyed some sweet candies given to him by a generous Fergal who clearly took a liking to this young boy.

***

Later in the day when Betsy and the others were all settled at the tavern, she again left Joshua with Solomon and Esther to investigate the surrounding environs and explore what New York had to offer. She took care to dress modestly before venturing out, tying her bonnet tightly on to her head to conceal her lovey blonde locks, and wrapping herself in a favourite woollen shawl that she selected for this purpose. Soon she was out amongst the crowds of nearly all men, few women to be seen, at first making her feel a little uncomfortable but she was well used to being in the company of men. At this time, like everywhere in this new nation, women were very much in the minority due to the thousands of men who rushed to work here, explore and seek fame and fortune. It took another hundred years before the gender balance became more equal as the country stabilised making it more law abiding and safer for women and children to co-exist. However Betsy was one of the exceptions, more than capable of fending for herself and more resourceful than most of the male population around and she was out to prove it!

Making her way along the sidewalk where most men treated her with respect, making way for her in a courteous manner, she noticed a lawyer's office, advertising the services of one Elijah J Gilbert of Broadway Street, as Broadway was known at that time, the letters of Gilbert's name painted finely in gold on its upper window, also displaying his impressive legal qualifications. This impressed Betsy and she decided to make a call on Mr Gilbert to inquire further, after all a trusted lawyer like Kleinwitz in Allentown was something essential to her quest.

On entering the offices Betsy was taken with the hustle and bustle of the place with several obvious assistants, clerks and office helpers going about their business. Going up to the desk she introduced herself revealing her beautiful golden locks and obvious stature.

"I would like to see Mr Gilbert please. You may announce me as Mrs Betsy Leiper of Lexington, looking to establish businesses for herself in New York."

"I believe Mr Gilbert is very busy currently, you will need to make an appointment in order to see him I'm afraid Mrs Leiper." The nervous, bespectacled young fellow replied.

"You inform him that it will be of great interest and possible benefit to him. Now go inform him right away young man."

"Very well miss."

He got up from his desk and entered Elijah J Gilbert's office, returning shortly afterwards saying.

"Mr Gibert will see you now, please go through this way."

The young office junior or apprentice lawyer immediately showed Betsy through. She was greeted by a tall, impressive looking gentleman, greying hair with pince nez spectacles, clothed in black, standing up from his leather upholstered chair and offering his hand in greeting.

"A pleasure Mrs Leiper, I am not acquainted with either you or your husband. May I inquire as to the purpose of this meeting, you will understand that I am very busy man with many clients to tend to. Business is growing all the time now."

He seated himself after offering Betsy a chair opposite and fresh water to drink, which she declined.

"I am pleased that business is developing Mr Gilbert, this is why I am here as I intend to further considerably it's growth. You may not know me but I must inform you that I am recently widowed, now in receipt of considerable funds that my dear late husband left me as well as my own wealth which I fully intend to invest in several ways. I already have invested in other businesses, other places before I came here. Thus your help, contractually speaking would be useful to me…do not think for one moment that because I am woman that I am inexperienced in business matters, to do so would be a great mistake Mr Gilbert, a great mistake." she emphasised.

Elijah was a little shocked by her comments but realised that here before him was a lady quite unlike any of the ladies, including his own wife and two daughters, that he had ever know before.

"What is it I can do for you then Mrs Leiper?"

"You may be of service to me primarily in matters of contracts but also in helping make connections with the right people. I also need a place to live or at least rent for the time being….Here Betsy leaned forward emphasizing to Elijah J Gilbert….Let me emphasize to you Mr Gilbert…money is no object, you will find me a generous client but one who expects a job done for me is done well. You understand?"

"I understand perfectly and if I am to represent you Mrs Leiper be assured, be assured most certainly that I will look after your interests in the many ways you describe, most diligently. I am also confident that if you have any doubts about our integrity and due diligence you may only make the necessary inquiries in this city, I'm sure anyone who we work for or knows, will verify as to my, our competence, nay reliability, honesty and yes due diligence. Our reputation is second to none Mrs Leiper!"

Eilijah smiled now certain that his new client was someone who was going to be well worth getting to know. He quickly ordered an agreement, in principle, to be drawn up right away, to be signed tomorrow and informed Betsy that one of his clients was an estate agent and property developer by the name of Kurt Vanderhausen, who dealt with many properties which would be well worth her looking at.

"I will speak to Vanderhausen later today when we meet up and will inform him of your plans Mrs Leiper if I may?"

"That will be fine, I do not wish to stay at the tavern for as long as I have to. Ask him to look for a property sufficient for myself, my son Joshua and my two servants who will be living in with me. Also spacious enough for me to entertain guests. If you will do this for me , I will of course pay you for your troubles."

"There is no need for you to pay me anything dear lady, it will be my pleasure to help."

Elijah was keen to be as helpful as possible the more he realised the nature of Betsy's ambition.

"I have a junior partner working with me, his name is Nicholas Cross, he's just matriculated from law school with first class honours in Boston, I will update him on our conversation and instruct him to be available at all times to assist whenever I am away or attending to other clients. I hope this will be satisfactory for you madam?"

"I'm sure that will be fine, I trust in your expertise, now I must bid you good day, I have other business to attend to Mr

Gilbert, a pleasure to meet you and thank you for seeing me at such short notice." Betsy smiled offering her hand to Elijah who bowed respectfully.

"The pleasure has been all mine Mrs Leiper, I most certainly look forward to our next meeting tomorrow, shall we say at one o'clock if agreeable to you?"

"That will be good."

With that Betsy departed but not before a young man was quickly summoned and briefly introduced to her on her way out. He was the aforementioned Nicholas Cross, a diminutive chap in his early twenties, who wasted no time in attempting to make a good impression to her by bowing and smiling. Betsy acknowledged his presence but headed out in a business like manner.

It's worth noting at this point that Betsy's wealth, mostly gained from what the Harpe's had left behind when she collected their stashes thanks to Wiley's information, as well as her late husband's money, was in the region, in today's cash value, of more than ten million dollars, not including some treasured jewellery items which she was reluctant to sell due to some sentimental value. John Leiper had been a generous husband and had purchased necklaces, a diamond ring as well as other gold rings, broaches, earrings and other trinkets for Betsy, who despite the way she had murdered Leiper, felt some remorse and even gratitude to him. He had not deserved his brutal end, and Betsy knew it.

CHAPTER 28

Business having been completed, Betsy returned to the Bull's Head Tavern where she was greeted by Fergus O'Rourke delightedly informing her that he knew of a good lawyer, a certain Elijah Gilbert of Broadway Street. Betsy smiled and informed him that she had already met him and was seeing him again tomorrow at his offices.

"Well I'll be....Fergal exclaimed in complete surprise....you met him Mrs Leiper? Well stone me if ye will!"

"Yes but I thank ye kindly. Oh don't be put off if there are any other people you think I should meet."

"To be sure I will, to be sure. Now can I get ye anything dear lady, anything at all."

"No I'm fine, thank you."

Betsy smiled at Fergus who blushed unashamedly, returning to work aghast at Betsy's alluring smile.

Betsy then went to see Solomon and Esther to sort out a more formal arrangement between them. She decided to employ them both on a suitable wage which she felt they would be more than happy with, it was time to tie them both down as they had both proved valuable assets to her. She needed a proper personal maid and though Esther had no experience as a lady's maid Betsy previously, she believed that with a modicum of training Esther would be perfect. Solomon also, she believed would make a good manservant, but possibly more than that, a right hand man she could trust to do most any task, questionable and otherwise, he had already shown his willingness to assist in her more nefarious dealings!

Sure enough an arrangement was made with little fuss, both slaves as technically they still were were delighted to agree to work for Betsy full time and Betsy told them that a proper contract would be drawn up to seal the arrangement. A salary of five dollars each per week was settled much to the amazement of Solomon and Esther, clothes, meals, lodgings via live in provided free, and they were both told what their duties would be especially when a house had been acquired where they would all live together.

"Thank ye kindly missy Leiper, Esther and I will work hard for ye, ye can count on us missy."

Solomon told her with unconcealed delight, the first time he had expressed such emotion since Betsy had bought them both from the slave market.

Esther was speechless at first but soon joined in with expressing her gratitude and loyalty.

"You can count on both me and Solomon, Mrs Leiper, we'll work hard for you, the Lord willing until our last breath."

Betsy nodded and shook the hands of both of them formerly but tenderly to emphasize the new bond which had been struck.

Later supper was ordered and the four of them ate together as a special treat sealing the new arrangements.

***

Next morning Betsy went to the stables next door to the tavern to check on her mules and wagon, both of which items she now wanted to sell, having no further use for them. Solomon, usually accompanied by Joshua had been tending to the mules and keeping an eye on them in case of any felons who might think of stealing them. It would not be long before all were sold to a dealer known to Fergal, Betsy was not too concerned about haggling over a price and allowed the trader to take them for a more than fair price, this would not be the normal template for future business however.

As Betsy came away from the stables she noticed a blacksmith's foundry next door the stables which aroused her curiosity, so much that she wandered in to observe what was going on. On entering she saw Nathaniel Green, the blacksmith and farrier working away at the anvil with hammer and brazier adjacent working on horseshoes, he didn't see her at first but when he lifted his head to plunge one of the horseshoes in to the cold water, his eyes found the lovely form of our Betsy, who likewise had noticed this impressive looking man with his torso bare except for his leather apron. Genuine attraction occurred, something which owed it's cause to some instinctive feeling latent within a man or woman's being, lust yes, but more than that a feeling that this person was special in some way!

Nathaniel stared at Betsy then smiled saying with some embarrassment.

"You'll forgive me lady I'm not dressed decently."

To which Betsy also smiled replying.

"I noticed Mr?"she said coyly feeling more and more attracted to this quietly spoken blacksmith who now wiped his hands respectfully.

"I'm Nathaniel Green. Can I help you lady? I must confess

I have not had the pleasure before, indeed I haven't seen such a beautiful woman before…if you'll forgive me bein' forward"

"I forgive you, you may call me Betsy and I'm staying at the tavern next door. Do you work for Mr O'Rourke?"

"I work for myself but I do services for him and many of his guests who need horses, mules and cartwheels fixin'" he said.

Betsy was struck by his way of speaking which suggested a man of some character as well as handsome looks, his black hair unkempt but not ugly, his looks and personality for once caused her some confusion and at the same time a desire to get to know this handsome man. It had been some time since Betsy had given way to her carnal desires, back in Lexington in fact with her then lover James Weller, since then she had subdued such feelings not wishing to be distracted, but she was a young woman in her prime and here was a man as attractive as James had been.

Nathaniel explained what his workshop was about but as he was pointing casually to the many items he had crafted, Betsy caught his eye and natural passions took over, she fell into his arms, they kissed passionately and to Nathaniel's surprise she came on to him with little inhibitions, her womanly body responding to this man's firmness and tenderness, he pushed her up against the wall behind the anvil and they made love until Betsy realised the dangers of her situation suddenly preventing full entry.

"No Nathaniel, not this time… forgive me.." she breathed.

Nathaniel obeyed apologising.

"Don't apologize, there's no need. I'll arrange another meeting if you will?"

He agreed and after some tender, slightly embarrassing moments Betsy departed leaving a totally bemused but delighted Nathaniel Green to ponder on the events of the last few moments.

The two lovers got to know each other more as several other exciting, illicit meetings occurred and a genuine bond developed going beyond mere lust. Soon Betsy for only the second time in her life fell in love with this man, a love of physical passion combined with a love of Nathaniel as a man, a strong and decent man who had an easy manner and even treated the horses he shod with a certain affection. They met on several occasions as their passion for each grew more and more intense, so much so that Betsy had difficulty keeping this secret from others especially of course Joshua which was not too difficult given his innocence and young age, but more importantly Solomon and Esther who she did not want to know, at least at this stage of her relationship with Nathaniel. There was still some remaining doubt lingering within her as to whether this was something that Betsy really and truly wanted for herself permanently. But she was close to deciding yes.

What determined her positively as the short but intense relationship grew was Betsy's attitude, she even began to ponder a more lasting relationship between them such was her desire for him. She was struck by the fact that he appeared not to show any interest in her obvious wealth but loved her for her character as well as her beauty. Then tragedy struck!

One afternoon as everyone was occupied at the tavern and Solomon had been sent to purchase some things, Betsy watched him fit new shoes to a recently purchased stallion belonging to a wealthy merchant who wished to race him. Nathaniel displaying his expertise with horses set the animal up to be shoed taking hold of it's leg, but immediately the horse now becoming unsettled violently kicked out with his rear right leg catching poor Nathaniel in the head, blood streamed from his head, he fell heavily on to the ground, killing him instantly.

"Nathaniel!! Oh my God!!"

Betsy screamed and rushed to Fergal for help.

"It's…Nathaniel, blood, he fell…a horse has kicked him..oh please help!"

Fergal immediately rushed to Nathaniel who lay motionless on the ground, the horse agitated, cocking it's head back and forth.

"Get a doctor Fergal..quickly please!!" she implored before feinting.

Fergal now had to check Nathaniel's pulse, attend to the prone Betsy, quickly he sent a boy for Doctor Wilson who fortunately was nearby at his surgery. He came right away but could only confirm that Nathaniel was dead, giving salts to Betsy who gradually regained consciousness.

She implored Doctor Wilson to help Nathaniel.

"Is there nothing you can do!?!" she pleaded desperate for a miracle.

"I'm sorry lady there's nuthin' I can do for this poor man, now you must rest yourself. I insist."

Doctor Wilson's concern had switched to Betsy who was shaking but obviously trying to compose herself as much as she could. Betsy with tears streaming, suddenly with a mighty effort, managed to compose herself and returned to her room in the tavern. Fergal looked at the doctor perplexed, then returned himself back to the tavern, Doctor Wilson left to deal with poor Nathaniel's body which was later removed by a local undertaker.

Returning to her room alone Betsy fell on to her bed in tears, devastated. Her dreams of a true loving relationship shattered. Full of grief she vowed never to get emotionally close to any man again, only to use them to her advantage.

CHAPTER 29

The next morning after a troubled night's sleep, a young man appeared at the tavern with a message for Betsy requesting that she attend the offices of her new lawyer Elijah J Gilbert at ten. Betsy duly composed herself descended the stairs, and asked Fergal to order a cab to take her there for ten o'clock.

"Why it'll be a pleasure Mrs Leiper, just leave it me." he effusively promised, glancing at Betsy to see if she was feeling alright.

"A terrible thing to happen to the poor lad, Lord knows! Now are you sure you wouldn't like to rest some more?" he enquired.

Betsy looked at him, breathing deeply.

"No Mr O'Rourke I'm fine I can assure you, yes a most terrible accident, he seemed a nice man, I hope he hasn't left any dependents."

"No, one good thing so far as I know he lived alone with no family, a small blessing to be sure."

Betsy nodded feeling a pang of hurt, thinking briefly what a shame, what could have been. She quickly dismissed any further thoughts as she had done many times in the past, hardened as she had become to anything life threw up at her.

On time her cab arrived, a one horse buggy run by an Englishman called Ned or 'Nip' Nateley, who had plied his trade in London previously until the lure of the New World beckoned this wiry, bow legged coachman. Before that 'Nip' had actually been a successful jockey having come second in the famous St Leger classic race at Doncaster racecourse, England, but unfortunately a serious injury dubiously caused, had ended prematurely his racing career. Fortunately his love of horses combined with an uncanny control, nay empathy with his equestrian charges made him a near perfect coachman, something Betsy soon became aware of as she herself had always had a fascination for these fine beasts.

She now climbed aboard Nip's buggy, relieved to escape any further questions from Fergal O'Rourke. She arrived at Elijah J Gilbert's office to be greeted by Nicholas Cross who courteously accompanied her onto the office of his employer. There before her as well as Elijah was another man smiling broadly and looking at Betsy approvingly, he was the man that Elijah had mentioned; the agent and property developer Kurt Vanderhausen, a rather grim looking elderly gentleman dressed in the old fashion manner, wearing a three cornered tricorn hat, with silk stockings showing off a calf he was obviously proud of, and probably imagined the ladies would notice, as well as his powdered wig marking him out as a man of distinction.

"May I introduce Mr Kurt Vanderhausen Mrs Leiper, land agent, property developer of New York. I can without exaggeration recommend this esteemed gentleman to help you find what you are looking for in terms of a suitable property."

"Delighted to make your acquaintance Mrs Leiper, I sincerely hope I may be of assistance to you." he said, speaking with a slight Dutch accent which betrayed his place of birth some sixty-three years before.

"I sincerely hope you can Mr Vanderhausen."

Betsy seated now with all her faculties listened to what Vanderhausen had to offer. This consisted of several houses in New York but also out of town in the popular environs which were springing up like the rest of this extraordinary city, also some apartments which she could either rent or purchase.

Betsy interrupted.

"I have no wish to rent any property Mr Vanderhausen, I am looking to purchase only."

Having clarified this point it came down to three houses all within the bounds of the city itself. Betsy arranged to view all three over the next two days and Vanderhausen promptly made the arrangements for viewing these properties.

Betsy thanked the two gentleman, smiled teasingly at young Cross on her way out and took the same cab back to the tavern. The afternoon was spent shopping for new garments for herself, Solomon, Esther and Joshua, all three she determined must now be dressed according to their needs and station. Solomon and Esther tried on their new practical clothes and were amazed that Betsy had judged correctly their sizes. Solomon was given possession of a top hat with Esther two bonnets and shawls which she expressed delight with, Joshua, less enthusiastic as young boys tend to be, nonetheless expressed reluctant enthusiasm.

"My Joshua what a handsome young man you are growing into!" she exclaimed, much to his embarrassment.

"We'll have to find a school for you, a private school for young gentleman, I can't leave it any longer son."

Joshua none to happy at this idea mumbled morosely.

"Do I have to go to school mama?"

"You must, I want you to become a gentleman who will make a mark for himself in this world."

Betsy then decided to make inquiries as to a suitable school so she could get him enrolled as soon as possible, she feared that he would get too used to rough ways and idleness if this important matter was not dealt with quickly.

Next day Betsy took a cab, Nip's in fact who she specifically called for and who was delighted to carry her wherever she desired (no doubt Betsy's generous tipping had helped!) went with Vanderhausen to view the three properties and very quickly made her mind up which one she desired to be her permanent residence.

It seemed to possess everything she needed; spacious in prospect, an enclosed rear garden with apple trees which would be good for Jashua, a large loft divided into three rooms, suitable for servants quarters, lovely drawing room, large spacious lounge with clavichord included, dining room, study with bookshelves inbuilt, reception room to receive guests which she anticipated would be frequent once she had established herself on the social scene, expansive hallway, large kitchen and scullery, all of the house decorated in the modern fashion with lush carpets, a grand front door and porch, set back from the street. The house was built some fifteen years previous on the Lower East Side near to the East River with it's views out to sea, something Joshua would appreciate, with ships aplenty to be viewed and exciting voyages to be imagined by the young fellow.

It was going to be hers and when a price was agreed after intense negotiation which was akin to prising a something from the barnacle character of Vanderhausen who was representing the previous owner, a widow who no longer need such a large abode, the contracts were duly drawn up and Betsy, much to the incredulity of both Vanderhausen and Gilbert paid the full amount in cash, the princely sum of five thousand dollars which she had anticipated and as such she had brought the cash plus more in case she was forced to pay more.

It was then that Betsy after completing this important transaction placed all her monies in the recently opened Washington Trust Company bank on Wall Street where she already had an account. She had realised that Wall Street, which of course was to become the financial centre not just of New York but of the entire nation, was without doubt a place she would frequent to negotiate deals, speculate and so forth, and now aided by the 1792 Burtonwood Agreement which brought some measure of control over financial dealings which had not existed before, gave her the confidence to pursue her dream of greater wealth and influence.

Her presence there initially aroused much curiosity combined with a degree of disapproval, after all women were not supposed to be dealing in such matters, this was men's business, but some of the younger men found her presence fascinating and naturally her looks helped to confirm that interest. Especially at first Betsy had to fend off attentions which were not related to business, this she expected, but gradually as she made several lucrative investments which shocked some, she gained their respect at least grudgingly from some.

Comments such as;

"Well I never!"

"Who the devil is this woman!?"

"Lord spare us from this harpy!"

"This is outrageous, who let this woman come here!?"

And similar expressions of surprise, outrage and contempt.

None of this had any effect on Betsy, she used all her female wiles and persuasion to outbid, outmanoeuvre, outwit these foolishly outraged men on many occasions.

One man who caught her attention was a decent, helpful and quite handsome gentleman probably she thought, in his forties, was a certain John Hoffman Junior, a very wealthy banker and stockbroker with many business interests who she discovered by overhearing conversations marked by a mixture of envy and admiration by fellow businessmen. She discovered that he was even richer than her by some distance in fact. Naturally this aroused Betsy's interests and soon they got on well, going even further with Hoffman advising her what to invest in and how to manipulate the market. Their relationship would consequently flourish in due course.

As they became more acquainted and as Betsy contemplated the future

prospects of some kind of union between them, either commercially or personally or maybe both with him, she decided to proceed circumspectly naturally not wishing to involve herself too deeply, unless she was one hundred percent certain. Ostensibly he seemed an investment of sorts that Betsy considered worth making.

CHAPTER 30

After a week of preparations with the help of Solomon, who now accompanied her on all her outings, purchasing fittings, furniture, paintings, including some original works by Ralph Earl and Gilbert Stuart, notable painters of the day, curtains and the finest porcelain, cutlery and so forth that money could buy, Betsy was ready to move into this handsome house. She was determined to make her home a special place to live in and also crucially to become what she hoped would be a fashionable salon for the upper echelons of society to gather, where meetings, soirees, music evenings could take place right in her home. It had to exude class and impress people as soon as they entered the house, to be greeted by a smartly dressed Solomon and other servants who Betsy was intending to seek out and employ.

The matter of Joshua's education was also settled even before they all moved into this wonderful new house, Joshua was enrolled into the recommended, recently established Alexander Robertson School, a private Presbyterian establishment well situated to nearby Columbus Avenue by what is Central Park today, but then was a wooded parkland with no specific boundaries. It was another thirty years or more before Central Park proper was created for the benefit of the good citizens of New York City.

Nip the coachman, it was arranged, would carry "Young Master Leiper" both to and from school each day. This was something that he was delighted to do given the uncertainty of income in New York with it's often quite brutal competition between coachmen, to have a regular income like this was a godsend to him, also the envy of many of his competitors!

"Well bless ye Mrs Leiper, I'll be ready for ye whenever ye have need of 'ol Nip and his sturdy horse 'Rosy'!'"

Betsy nodded agreement.

Thus after settling her bill with Fergus O'Rourke, who was deeply

sorry to see Betsy depart, the day of moving descended on them all.

"Oh Mrs Leiper I'm so sad to see you leavin' us to be sure. You're presence here has been a true delight, please come back whenever you're passin' this way I tell ye there'll always be a warm welcome for ye all, as long as Fergal O'Rouke is me name!"

Fergal bowed, watery eyes evident as they appeared on his craggy face causing him some embarrassment, but Betsy was genuinely grateful for all his hospitality and helpfulness, not least toward Joshua, Solomon and Esther, the latter two experiencing for the first time in their lives a modicum of consideration and even respect from this bluff Irishman.

"Be assured Fergal, you have a new friend, indeed friends now, I will not forget you, of that you can be certain…as long as Betsy Leiper is MY name!" she smiled.

They departed on the best of terms with Fergal waving somewhat forlornly outside the tavern, a few of his customers coming out to see what was going on complete with tankards of ale.

"Why lookee here, Fergal's a blubbin', I reckon he took a shine to that fair lady!" one of his regulars commented whilst

347

downing his ale.

With that Betsy spent the day moving into her new home, with hired hands carrying in the rest of the furniture as well as all else she had acquired, Nip conveyed her and Joshua to Lower East Side and soon they were all ensconced in their new home. The excitement could not be measured with Joshua delighted to have a garden to play in together with some new toys, including a rocking horse that she had found on her travels to Broadway, Solomon and Esther too were amazed at what they found, their new quarters were something they would have never dreamed of at the old plantation with it's depravations.

CHAPTER 31

The next few weeks were spent in the joyful experience of 'settling in' to the new home, with everyone lending a hand, Solomon doing the heavy moving of furniture, arranging and then rearranging these items until Betsy was satisfied, he also cleaned, tended the garden and went on various errands as Betsy decided she needed this or that to enhance their splendid abode. Esther was an invaluable helping hand to Betsy as a good servant come maid could be, she enthusiastically joined her mistress on various shopping expeditions, helped her arrange all the fittings, curtains, organising the kitchen which now had a cook and kitchen lackey to prepare each meal. With Betsy's guidance she became more and more her personal maid as she learned the arts of the female toilet, helping Betsy to dress, undress, bathe, arrange her hair, jewellery, personal effects, indeed Esther learned so rapidly that she became a valuable appendage to her mistress, someone who she would call upon to assist in even the most private matters. It was obvious that Betsy had discovered in Esther and her husband Solomon, two thoroughly reliable, invaluable servants whose loyalty and devotion she never felt the need to question.

Joshua was packed off to his new school where he settled in well, glad to make new friends with a few of the boys already there, his education came on in leaps and bounds much to the delight of his mother.

During the second week of their tenure at Betsy's new house, an incident occurred which reawakened old fears.

Solomon was returning one evening from an errand that he had been sent on by his mistress, when he was set upon by three rough looking thugs who had laid in wait ready to ambush some poor unsuspecting person in order to 'relieve' him of anything worth robbing. The three brigands had been drinking in a notorious inn off Broadway Street; 'The George', frequented mostly by thieves, down and outs, prostitutes, and other assorted ner' do wells. As chance would have it the three of them spied a tallish figure coming toward them.

"Look 'ere, it's a black 'un."

One of the thugs muttered to his two compatriots.

"We'll do him!"

He gripped a black cudgel ready to render the unfortunate figure a blow to the head.

As Solomon came near to them, ready to pass, he became aware of a presence, a danger which quickly manifested itself with the three desperate thugs jumping him, one of them attempting to strike him with the cudgel while the other two attempted to restrain him. Solomon quick as a flash turned, broke free, then smashed his fist into the thug with the cudgel, shattering his jaw.

"Aaargh!!!" the ruffian screamed in agony, then shouted.

"Kill the slave bastard!!"

The other two hesitated slightly on witnessing the blood and screams of their comrade now clutching his broken jaw which hung down dislocated from the rest of his skull, but just enough for Solomon, who possessed a much stronger physique and skill than any of the three ruffians, to rush at one of the other louts. The third thug panicked, he had had enough and ran off like a jack rabbit, unwilling to take on this black colossus who was now in the process of hammering both his fallen accomplices.

"Help, murder!!" screamed the one in flight, but no-one else was around to assist, what law there was at this time was not to be found in dark places such as this but was in it's infancy mostly made up of watchmen, vigilantes and constables privately hired to maintain some protection of lives and property of the wealthy classes.

Solomon exacted a severe revenge raining punishment on the two remaining thugs who now pleaded with him for their lives.

"Damn you, damn ye!!"

Solomon shouted at the two louts as he pummelled both of them mercilessly, both wretches now desperately attempting to fend off his blows. The one with the shattered jaw coughed blood and had no chance of defence.

"Please I'm dun for." he spluttered pathetically.

The other one lay semi-conscious now merely groaning in pain, his arms involuntarily attempting to defend himself, but with no success.

Solomon suddenly realised that he needed to stop, he had meted out enough punishment and if he continued with this beating the two of them could well perish, this was not something he knew would be good, it might also bring trouble to Betsy. With this thought flickering in his head, he stopped suddenly, looked over them both saying contemptuously.

"I'll finish this if I ever see ye again, to Hell with ye!" Solomon walked away with just a few blood stains on his clothes but unharmed, he felt a sense of satisfaction at what he had dealt out to the three dregs, who after all were intent on robbing him and in all likelihood murdering him.

On returning home Betsy immediately noticed the blood stains on Solomon's shirt and jacket as well as swelling to be seen below his eye. Esther too looked on in horror.

"What happened Solomon, looks like you been fighting, I hope not." Betsy asked him.

"Oh no ma'am just set upon by some drunk fools. All's fine, I saw them off, no damage missy Leiper."

"I surely hope not Solomon, can't afford to lose you now can I?" she smiled, feeling reassured.

Esther still worried tended to Solomon berating him at the same time.

"I find out you been causin' trouble my man....and I'll whip your hide, so I will!"

Solomon smiled and patted Esther affectionately.

"Now you'll come with me so I can bathe that swellin', if that's alright Mrs Leiper?"

Betsy nodded ascent and both husband and wife went out, with Esther leading Solomon by the hand.

Next day, a fine early Summer's morning in May, after Joshua had been duly collected by Nip who had taken to calling him 'young Master', and taken him to school, complete with new satchel, Betsy set off on Nip's return to Wall Street with a little part of her hoping to run into John Hoffman. She had no real attraction physically to him even though as a good looking, bachelor he was much sought after by many of the ladies of New York society, more for his advice and possible companionship. Betsy had made a few notable acquaintances but they were all ladies, mostly wives of businessmen, and had arranged tea mornings and meetings at each others houses. This was all very pleasant, serving a purpose as it did for her but such ladies, though extending her influence wider and wider, were not going to help her directly achieve the huge wealth and power that she sought in this increasingly powerful city, now outstripping all other cities in America, even Boston, Philadelphia and her initial place of investment, Allentown. Betsy Leiper or Betsy Roberts as she now thought of herself as, was ready to extend her interests and Hoffman seemed just the man to assist her in this objective.

Much to Betsy's pleasant surprise, Hoffman was there and immediately invited her to dine with him at midday, she accepted and during their lunchtime meal they discussed possible investments and purchases which he was happy to advise her on.

"You must tread cautiously Betsy, I have found that patience is usually rewarded in these affairs. Combined with that though it must be admitted that sometimes I have seized an opportunity even throwing caution to the wind if the situation called for it. Why don't it say 'strike while the iron is hot'? though not always!"

"I have a mind to follow what you suggest John, my late husband left me well provided for so I'm minded not to squander what I possess so foolishly."

Betsy smiled at him one of her smiles which John Hoffman was not one to miss, he immediately read it as a sign of favour but being a sensible, cautious man, single for all his life, he did not act on this straight away, but wait until he had a better knowledge of this beautiful woman.

"You are wise Betsy and I would be pleased to help if I can or more appropriately if you wish me to."

"Yes of course, I hope we can become good friends." she affirmed with another gentle nod and smile.

"Perhaps you would permit me to see you one evening, there are one or two theatres now in New York which you might like?"

"I would like that very much John."

Lunch finished they departed with John Hoffman taking Betsy's hand and kissing it tenderly.

Betsy returned home via Nip who politely inquired if she had... "had a good meetin'?"

"Oh yes Nip, most deifinitely." she replied with a hint of mischief.

Nip smiled to himself and set Rosy his faithful mare on course for home.

During their meeting Betsy had observed with some admiration John Hoffman's easy but calculatedly determined manner in achieving what he desired, gaining all the time financial advantage and wealth. It was obvious that he possessed a shrewd, far sighted attitude, one not prone to recklessness but an attitude which had gained the respect of all his competitors in the circle of financial speculation and business in general. She figured at a guess that his worth must be quadruple hers, in fact his wealth was much greater approaching as it did six times what she had, acquired it must be admitted over many years.

Her thoughts turned to the possibility of a union between

the two of them, at least at some point in the future she mused. After all he was single, rich, of good character and disposition, very attractive qualities in a potential future husband, though there was one caveat, she was a widow with a child. Not many men would consider such a match…but then she was Betsy Roberts.

CHAPTER 32

As her connections expanded not just with other women but with certain gentlemen as well as John Hoffman and business interests gained ground, Betsy realised more opportunities in the burgeoning city of New York, her new lawyer Elijah J Gilbert, a man of mean but shrewd disposition who diligently looked after her growing portfolio of business over the next months was a significant partner to her in this process. Betsy with her wealth, all her own from the Harpe days and from her deceased husband, John Leiper, invested in several legitimate businesses, buying a newly built restaurant 'Le Revolution' which specialised in French cuisine situated on Broadway Street, a haberdashery shop, dress shops and dry goods business. She also continued to wisely invest in several companies on the new American stock market on Wall Street. The friendship with John Hoffman was proving very lucrative as well as John, despite his natural reticence and shyness, becoming more and more attracted to the softly manipulative Betsy who herself responded to his attentions in a measured but genuinely friendly way.

John's feelings were such that he was a frequent visitor to her home, calling to spend evenings with her, enjoying recitals given using the clavichord, with occasional singers to entertain him and her other guests in the evenings. Betsy had been learning to play, practising religiously and receiving music which included popular American and British folk songs of the day but also works by such European masters as Mozart (the 'Rondo Alla Turka' form his Sonata K310 was a particular favourite of hers), Haydn, Vivaldi and Boccherini. They also went out in his newly purchased Buggy this time driven by his own coachman, much to the chagrin of Nip, picnicking if weather permitted this early Summer and for walks where they discussed intently the business of the day.

One evening John suddenly called to see Betsy, he clearly was in a nervous state which he failed to conceal, Esther noticing immediately but he was greeted by Betsy with surprise and pleasure.

"May I speak with you privately Betsy...There's something I need to ask you ...of a personal nature..you'll understand.." he stammered out desperately attempting to control himself.

"Why of course John, what is it that brings you here unexpectedly"

Betsy wondered to herself if there was something terribly wrong or he was going to confess something awful to her. Just then John went down on one knee bowed his head saying with more confidence now.

"Betsy, will you do me the great, most amazing honour and accept my humble proposal...to you...to err...be my wife...." he stumbled again but continued with Betsy staring a little wide eyed at him "...you do not have to give your answer straight away my precious...but please think it over and please don't be mad at me if you'd rather not...I err hope we could carry on being friends even if you refuse me."

Betsy breathed a deep breath, took his hand and replied softly.

"John please stand up, you do me a great honour and I will most surely give you my answer as soon as I can. This is such a surprise, but not an unpleasant one"

John felt relieved, she had not said 'no' which gave him hope that he would win her hand. Having accomplished his mission albeit without a definite answer one way or the other, he took his leave bowing again and kissing Betsy's hand.

Esther and now Solomon looked on in mystification, wondering what had occurred between their mistress and John Hoffman.

Later Esther turned to Solomon and quietly told him.

"He's proposed to our missy, I'll wager anything you like Solomon dear."

"Well I be..."

"You be right to listen to me husband." she laughed.

Next morning nothing further was said, Betsy had been thinking during the night unable to sleep much, about John's proposal. She genuinely could not decide, arguments for and against the match went through her thoughts. Firstly she liked him and valued greatly his companionship, he was also quite handsome, would no doubt make a loyal husband and father to the children she hoped to rear, as much as for companionship for Joshua as anything, he was very wealthy and would create an empire for them, especially her, but on the other hand she was loathe to give up her hard won independence, she was wealthy anyway, did she really want greater riches...well the answer was yes to that she knew, she would also have to keep control of her husband so that nothing would upset her ambitions. All in all much to ponder!

Having said all this Betsy decided to accept John's proposal, she was convinced after two days of deliberations, as would a jury in a court of law trying someone for a capital offense would, that the benefits clearly outweighed any concerns she might have. Her confidence in herself was steadfast, so with her decision made Betsy sent a sealed note to John Hoffman via Solomon aboard Nip's buggy, requesting him to visit her as soon as was convenient. His reply came back with almost unseemly haste, he would call to see her later that afternoon, a fine late May day.

Full of nervous expectation John Hoffman arrived at Betsy's residence duly excited but with a feeling of foreboding, mostly fearing he would be met with a negative response and so taking a deep breath, rehearsing how he would respond himself to such disappointing news, with dignity he had decided, he arrived and entered her home only to be met with a smiling Betsy Leiper, waiting for him in the drawing room.

She arose as soon as he entered quickly dispensing John's worst fears.

"I would love to be your wife John Hoffman, nothing would fill me with greater joy."

John's eyes lit up.

"Well…what can I say Betsy…other than the fact that you have made me the happiest man in the whole of America!"

The two soon to be man and wife embraced, with Betsy keen to discuss the wedding arrangements, who to invite, where to have the ceremony, the reception and honeymoon.

John had already given this much thought in the hope that he would not be rejected.

"If you're agreeable my love, I would like to have our wedding at St Paul's on the southern part of Manhattan where we have been before on one occasion, do you remember?"

"I do and that would be just fine with me John. When do think would be a good time for this?"

John hesitated for a moment stroking his chin, looked at Betsy, then asserted.

"I would most sincerely wish for us to be married as soon as the necessary arrangements can be made...that is if you don't think it's too soon?"

Betsy hesitated for a moment and taking his hand tenderly replied.

"No dearest I would be most happy to go along with your suggestion, let us not delay especially while we have the lovely late Spring weather to make it a special occasion."

"Wonderful, I will go right ahead, you will have a day to remember with everything due to such a beautiful bride as you Betsy!"

They embraced and John took his leave, excited to let everyone hear his good news, his only concern was what the reaction of his elderly widowed mother would be. Betsy had met her once only, only to receive a less than cordial reception.

Betsy duly informed Solomon and Esther who could not conceal their joy at their mistress's good news, Esther congratulating Betsy effusively.

"Why Miss I'm so happy for you, there won't be a more beautiful bride in all the United States of America so there won't!...if ye don't mind me saying Mrs Leiper?" she added.

"No Esther not at all, I guess you will have to get used to calling me Mrs Hoffman soon." Betsy laughed.

Betsy only concern was what effect this news would have on her only child, Joshua, would he be alright or worryingly upset? Her answer came quickly when she called Joshua and told him the news, to her relief the boy was delighted and as she expected as he had liked this pleasant gentleman who talked to him and even played with him sometimes on his frequent visits to their home. Added to that Joshua had not known his real father, John Leiper very long, he had been away for much of the boy's life only intermittently being around to join in with Joshua's games and expeditions.

Betsy Roberts, as she most definitely thought of herself as, seated herself in the garden, sent for some homemade lemonade which Esther duly brought to her, and contemplated her future as the wife of John Hoffman Jr with all the possible benefits that would accrue. She planned to be a good wife to him, faithful and obedient, at least as long as it suited her, to use his extensive connections with the rich, influential people that he had cultivated for so long, vast wealth and good, respectable name to further her own ambitions, and also of course bear him children which would also be potentially a big advantage in many ways, not least in securing her reputation in New York and beyond. She took delight in anticipation of her being the mistress of the Hoffman residence, a house twice the size of her own, located in the rural area of Washington Heights outside the city, the many servants she would control, though she had insisted on taking Esther and Solomon with her, to which John gladly agreed.

She shivered with anticipation at all these prospects as he sipped her lemonade, prospects which not so long ago seemed merely a distant, forlorn dream.

CHAPTER 33

The day of Betsy Leiper and John Hoffman Junior's wedding arrived, the weather was kind with not a cloud in sight, birds sang merrily as if they were rejoicing this most splendid of occasions. Betsy had made for her a stunning white and pastel coloured dress for her wedding in the latest fashion, made from fine lightweight material with her bosom revealed a touch provocatively as was the fashion of the day. It was made from muslin which had been sent from Paris and purchased from New York's finest dress shop on Broadway Street. She had it fitted with much care at home, attended to by several ladies from the shop to ensure it fitted perfectly, a simple, flowing wrap made in India from soft cashmere lightly covered her slender shoulders. She purchased her shoes, made of thin, soft leather and a hat trimmed with feathers and lace, from the milliners also on Braodway Street. Long white crumpled lace gloves adorned her slender arms. Her hair was carefully styled in the Greek fashion with masses of curls, was pulled back into a bun, satin and silk ribbons adorning her a plenty.

A more beautiful, resplendent picture could not be imagined, Betsy Roberts a woman in the prime of life, without a hint of the suffering she had endured those years ago at the hands of the Harpe brothers, no residual hint of any abuse, looked at herself in the mirror when she was fully dressed and smiled to herself a smile which expressed both pleasure as well as total confidence, only to be found in the most fortunate of women.

"Oh my, my Missy you look such a picture, I never seen such a more lovely sight, no never in all my days. Why Mr Hoffman is a very lucky man I do declare!"

Esther proclaimed joyfully as she dutifully assisted Betsy with her preparations.

The coach pulled by two magnificent white horses arrived on time

at 2pm for Betsy and a smart looking Joshua, with Esther who was acting as Betsy's bridesmaid, a significant honour for her which she had been very nervous to accept at first, but after some gentle persuasion from her mistress agreed and also Solomon, to be conveyed to St Paul's chapel as the service was due to commence at 3pm.

The service was a grand affair with many of the high society of New York in attendance, some appalled to see a black bridesmaid with Betsy and some to concealing their displeasure at such a sight. Betsy aware of some of this disapprobation, chose to ignore it, she was determined to enjoy her special day and make an unforgettable impression to everyone present. John Hoffman, bedecked in top hat and the finest black suit he could have made for his wedding, was more concerned to not look foolish by making any errors during the ceremony, he was aware himself of disapproving comments coming from friends and family alike toward Esther who bravely ignored it all, his own mother had berated him the day before. To his credit he stood firm merely commenting.

"If Betsy wants her as bridesmaid then Betsy will have her wish."

Mrs Katrina Hoffman shook her head, disapprovingly but knew that her son, though amenable to her in most matters, was not going to change his mind on this one.

"Well, I ain't happy John, that's all I'll say."

"I know mother but it's what Betsy wants, you'll see ma, you and her will get along fine I promise."

"Pah!!" she cried agitated and shifting uncomfortably in her chair.

Mrs Hoffman said nothing more after her outburst, keeping her feelings to herself but seething inside, she had taken a loathing to Betsy.

And so the wedding took place in the chapel of St Paul's, a fine Georgian classical building with hymns sung heartily, the organist a scholar from New York's music academy playing several Bach choral preludes, as well as his cantanta 'Ich Habe Genug' a favourite of John's. All went according to plan, with gasps of admiration coming from the packed congregation on seeing the stunning figure of Betsy Roberts, seemingly glide along as if whisked along by some tender zephyr, escorted down the aisle by John's brother Arthur, a quiet thoughtful fellow, younger and in thrall of his elder brother.

The ceremony now completed, the newly wed bride and groom were quickly greeted outside the chapel with flurries of rose petals cast over them by dozens of well-wishers who had gathered to witness this most wonderful of marriages. The wedding party (which included Betsy's few guests; Elijah J Gilbert, Kurt Vanderhausen, as well as three new female friends that Betsy had made since arriving) made their way by coach to the reception which was to be held, once again at Betsy's request, at the New Bull Tavern much to the obvious delight of it's landlord Fergal O'Rourke who rented out the upper rooms for her.

He greeted the guests, some of whom were none too impressed with this choice of venue, dressed in his finest suit with servants, which now included Solomon and Esther who Fergal was happy to meet again, all of them ready to escort everyone inside.

"I can't tell you Betsy how honoured we are here in my 'umble tavern to entertain ye all, to be sure." he said to Betsy as she slowly passed him by arm in arm with John who nodded politely but stayed silent, not wishing to offend by making a negative comment.

"Blessed Jesus, Mary and Joseph, don't ye look the most beautiful lady in all our great nation!" he waxed lyrically in his Irish tones.

Betsy smiled, leaving Fergal to scurry around issuing instructions to his staff to make ready for the dinner and entertainment.

Thankfully the evening went well, even most of the high society guests admitted to enjoying the night especially the fiddler, the string quartet playing popular dance tunes of the time, dancing the quadrilles which was common at this time, and of course consuming plenty of alcoholic beverages, indeed more than one guest had to be helped out before the end due to excessive inebriation!

John's brother Arthur made a decent speech welcoming Betsy into their family in a slightly serious but sincere tone, then John himself expressing his total happiness at securing such a catch, Betsy feigned a blush or two much to the amusement of most of the guests. Toasts were made to the main party especially Betsy now Mrs Betsy Hoffman, dedications to the United States constitution and the President who was currently Thomas Jefferson and thanks to Mr Fergal O'Rourke for putting on 'most acceptable reception', John Hoffman was not prone to any excessive compliments unless they were for Betsy, his wife.

"I must be the most fortunate man in our United States let alone our great city of New York to have as my wife the…now…Mrs Betsy Hoffman." he proclaimed a little nervously but he took a deep breath as all the guests watched…and continued bravely…

…"She has honoured me this day more than she can ever realise..and I promise you Betsy as your husband now…I will be ever faithful to you, protect and care for you…just I promised at our wedding service…now all of you please be upstanding and raise your glasses in honour of my wife Mrs Betsy Hoffman!"

Without hesitation everyone present stood and toasted the beautiful, blushing bride. Esther with tears in her eyes turned to Solomon who was stood by her side and whispered.

"This is the happiest day of my life Solomon, I feel sure, the Lord willing, that missy has found true happiness herself."

More tears of joy duly streamed forth from her, Solomon himself felt decidedly pleased for 'white folks' for the first time in his life, but more a feeling of anticipation of being part of a rich family which could benefit both he and Esther in many ways. They both resumed their duties as soon as the toasts and dedications were completed.

The evening came to an end and the happy couple departed to John's home to spend their first night of married life together. Another new chapter in the life of Betsy Roberts was beginning!

Betsy on her wedding day

CHAPTER 34

The first night spent together in the new impressive four poster bed that John had purchased, went well. Betsy found John a tender, if not very passionate lover, but at least better than the her previous husband, the generally incompetent John Leiper. At least this John had some idea as to how to please a lady which she responded to with enthusiasm, much to the delight of her husband! Betsy decided to be fully responsive to him, knowing all the tricks of love making and even shocked poor John with her ways of drawing passion from him! He had never experienced such pleasure before having only once previously had a rather unsatisfactory, brief affair with a servant girl some ten years ago which thankfully remained a secret. John Hoffman enjoyed the best that Betsy could serve up to him, he became overwhelmed by her soft but firm body which she used in almost every conceivable way to arouse him, sexual pleasure combined with the most sensuous eroticism was tenderly, but also forcefully laid out to him on a scale he had never dreamed possible. It was an experience that turned the proverbial boy into a man, sexually speaking, within a matter of hours.

Not surprisingly the next morning found him exhausted and not a little disturbed by the carnal activities he had experienced the previous night. His body ached in places, he was mouth sore and dry but he looked at Betsy on waking up amazed at this extraordinary woman who was now his wife. He mused to himself on what had made her such a sexual predatory entity, where had she learned all the carnal, erotic techniques that she clearly possessed? He decided to put such thoughts to one side, he was a lucky man...or so he believed.

Betsy soon also awoke then smiled to herself thinking that he was well and truly under her spell, if not control. She would reinforce this by attending to him as a dutiful wife whilst all the time extracting as much information and advantage as he could, she had no qualms adopting this quite mercenary attitude although she did feel sometimes a pang of guilt, though a guilty feeling insufficient to prevent her from furthering her own ambitions.

The weeks and months ahead during 1807 proved generally blissful with the married couple enjoying a brief honeymoon at a lodge owned by John's family near to Lake Wallenpaupack, a freshwater lake in North Eastern Pennsylvania, a full day's journey from New York. John enjoyed some fishing here while Betsy relaxed by the lakeside taking the occasional turn and reading some favourite novels recently acquired by her. The evenings were spent with just the two of them sitting by the fireside, with Esther who was brought along with them, serving the meals.

After three days of this blissful sojourn Betsy became restless wanting to return to New York to embark on her ambitious quest for power and influence, unbeknown to her husband who revelled in his wife's tender attentions but became aware that by day four the attentions had become noticeably less frequent.

"Is everything alright my love?" he inquired, noticing Betsy seemed a little irritated.

"Oh yes dearest, but should we not be returning home? I know how much you miss your work, you are such an important man."

"You are so considerate to me Betsy, but don't worry Arthur is looking after business while we're away..." but after thinking for a moment he continued.... "maybe you're right sweet love, it's the first time that I've been away for any period of time, Arthur has only been in charge for the odd day or two... so perhaps we should make our way back....tomorrow, would that be not too soon my dearest?"

Betsy smiled taking his hand in hers.

"If that is your wish John, I hope your not bored with me?"

"Oh no, mercy me! How could I ever be bored being with the most lovely, sweetest wife any man could wish for!"

"Well go if we must but I will treasure these few days all my life, so I will."

Betsy kissed him and arrangements were made the next day for their return with John again taking the reigns of their coach as they set off, Betsy linking his arm whilst Esther sat in the rear of the vehicle a little perplexed at the events of the last days of the honeymoon, sensing as only another woman can, that something was amiss in Betsy's behaviour toward John. It was something she thought about but could not come to any conclusion, and on their return when she mentioned it tentatively to Solomon, she was met with a more dismissive tone from him.

"I don't know what ye mean girl, master and mistress seem fine to me, stop yer worryin' he advised her.

"Well mark my words husband, somethin's not right, you're a man you wouldn't notice such things now would ye?" she replied staring him right in the eye.

"Well I'll be dun for Esther if ye look at me like that, so I will!" Solomon protested.

Esther laughed poking him in the chest then they returned to their respective chores with Solomon shaking his head in amusement.

"Was there ever a woman like my Esther" he thought to himself, chuckling at the same time.

***

As time passed and the heat of the New York Summer sapped energy away from most people though not, it must be said Betsy Hoffman who ensured that a daily routine developed which pleased John. He basked in the comforts which married life provided him as well as the orderly nature of the household servants Betsy controlled now which caused a certain hidden concern from some of the more long established members of his household, notably his retainer an old crotchety man named Benedict (he didn't seem to possess a surname and had always been referred to as Ben) ever since he had been employed by John's mother many years ago.Betsy remained attentive to her husband, subtly extracting information in their conversations, but also pleasing him with her feminine attentions and pretend ignorance of some of the more detailed business matters, all the time gaining more and more knowledge from this strategy for her own carefully disguised ends.

Joshua had found life at their new home much to his liking, John even took him fishing on the many rivers, ponds and lakes in the nearby countryside which still was mostly unspoilt, rich in wildlife and most beautiful in the Summer. During the

371

vacation Joshua also found much to occupy himself with, as always Solomon liked to have the eager boy help him with some of the duties he had to perform especially in the stables tending to the horses owned by Mr Hoffman. He liked to feed them, brush their smooth coats and sometimes, with Solomon's help ride the youngest mare who was gentle in character and minded not a jot when the boy eagerly cajoled the beast to hurry on. The Summer of 1807 was the most idyllic of their lives, a contrast to the turmoil both Betsy and he had endured in the years before.

As the Summer reached it's inevitable end and the Fall drew in bringing cooler weather, mixed with thunderstorms, Joshua returned to his schooling which he at first he dreaded like most young schoolboys, but which rapidly occupied his energies and attention.

Business too became more all encompassing with John Hoffman working longer hours at his offices in the city, consequently causing him to come home later than before. Betsy herself began to seek out opportunities for herself which she kept concealed from her husband but which she delighted developed, visiting her lawyer Elijah J Gilbert quite frequently.

It was around mid November that with Gilbert's studious advice and the connivance of her agent Kurt Vanderhausen that she met a man of dubious business acumen but obvious talents in certain ventures named Barton Grove, a portly man in his late thirties. Grove had built up a string of questionable businesses in the fields of entertainment, hostelry, racketeering and the like. He possessed a likeable but barely concealed violent nature which he used whenever anyone crossed him or owed him money. He had learned his dodgy trade originally when he came over from a place called Rawtenstall, Lancashire,

England, with a trading ship conveying goods to New York and then returning to Liverpool with cotton to feed the numerous mills of Lancashire which had flourished during their Industrial Revolution.

He rapidly realised the potential of the city which was expanding in so many directions, population, area, and not least in the scores of businesses which were feeding the insatiable demand of the population for all kinds of diverse things. The cunning Barton Grove was not going to miss out on all this virgin territory, ripe for him to plunder and make him a rich man. By his side during all these enterprises was a brute of a man who acted as his enforcer, a man named Jem Sowerbutts from Platt Bridge, another small village also in Lancashire, England, who was a strapping six foot two inches, bare knuckle prize fighter in his Lancashire days, and who had at first practised this brutal trade on arriving at New York with Grove as there was plenty of money to be had in the fairs, illicit rooms and fields in and around the city. There was no regulation of course and Sowerbutts laid waste many fellows foolish enough to believe they could beat this bull-like pugilist. Before that the two immigrants had spent a short time in Allentown with Jem Sowerbutts working for Blue Sally as one of her two enforcers. Few of Barton Grove's enterprises succeeded unsurprisingly, but it was Barton who brought to an end Sowerbutt's prize fighting career, not through any concern for his compatriot's well being, but he needed him on a permanent basis as more and more 'businesses' were acquired.

Betsy became aware of Barton's presence firstly through her friend Fergal O'Rourke who knew of him and Sowerbutts, both of whom frequented the tavern occasionally spending their ill-gotten gains with considerable relish. He warned Betsy, who he knew was interested in some of the areas of business that Grove was engaged with, that both Grove and Sowerbutts were men to be avoided.

"Y'll do well Mrs Hoffman, sure I do like your name now Betsy." he waxed lyrical...but continued earnestly... "...to give those two rascals a wide birth if ye don't mind me givin' ye some advice. I'm thinkin' they're a bit like wolves in sheeps clothin'..if ye follow me meanin', hopin' ye'll know where I'm cummin' from."

Fergal nodded wisely.

"Oh I do appreciate your concern Fergal, you're a true friend, but you need not worry on my account, I am more than capable of dealing with those two...not that I have any intentions mind you." she added hoping to allay the genuine fears of Fergal.

Betsy indeed was in no way deterred by this well intentioned advice from the Irishman and sought out Grove the following day to explore if there were any areas of interest worthy of her attention. She found him at the King's Arms, a well known inn where even theatrical performances were held, together with a huge brute of a man, the two taking refreshment. Barton Grove though surprised by Betsy's arrival at this place agreed to meet her. After Betsy left he turned to Sowerbutts saying.

"Well Jem what have we here? A lass looking for some excitement methinks, let's not us disappoint her I say."

"Aye, wench could be trouble...nowt...aye." Jem muttered barely intelligibly to which Barton Grove laughed and slapped his compatriot soundly on the back, Sowerbutts barely moved an inch.

Jem Sowerbutts bare knuckle fighter

CHAPTER 35

The meeting between Betsy Hoffman, accompanied by her manservant Solomon who Betsy had sworn to secrecy beforehand, knowing that he was now in no doubt of her modus operandi in these matters from previous experiences with her, which he acknowledged without any hesitation, and Barton Grove, duly took place at a restaurant on Nassau Street, east of Broadway, the burly fellow Jem Sowerbutts accompanying Grove, who looked smart in his newly acquired suit and top hat.

Removing his hat in deference to Betsy he revealed a balding head with his greying whiskers coming to a forlorn end above his smallish ears, a moustache of impressive proportions added a certain classic pugilist look quite common among such fighting types. Sowerbutts wore a cocked, rougher looking 'John Bull' type of hat, with his thick leather belt barely containing a fearsome bull-like torso with the arms of a gorilla, his biceps bulged, his face marked and scarred from scores of fights, only two large teeth, more like fangs in truth remained in his mouth, and his fists resembled two huge sledgehammers. The two sat opposite Betsy with Solomon by her side staring at them, both now had removed their hats respectfully with Barton Grove fascinated to meet this beautiful woman who had sought them out. He looked at Solomon with some suspicion but said nothing since it was not unusual at this time in New York for black servants to accompany rich ladies.

Thinking about the meeting due to commence he

pondered to himself.

"For what purpose?" he asked, even becoming nervous at the obvious presence of a woman of exceptional and obvious character, who seemed unfazed at his presence. He was struck not so much by her class and beauty, it was evident that he lacked the wherewithal to appreciate or take any advantage of, but by her eyes which seemed to pierce into a man's soul, even Grove's dull interior. Sowerbutts simply sat silently as would a huge faithful pit bull, unaware of any subtleties but nonetheless even he gradually became hypnotised by this extraordinary woman and the power she exuded.

All this spectacle, far from making Betsy herself nervous, merely amused her as she surveyed the two men.

Much to Barton Grove's surprise Betsy wasted no time setting out her interest and intention in staking her claim into taking advantage of the various growing businesses described already, she made it clear that she had wealth, power and influence and if Grove wanted to benefit from this and gain a level of protection himself due to Betsy's influence, he would do well to work for her. Failure to seize this unique opportunity would cause him regret which would leave him also without many of his rackets since she was determined to take control with or without his help.

Barton Grove was taken aback, startled at the force of Betsy's personality which left him speechless for most of their meeting, until towards the end he looked at Jem Sowerbutts saying to both him and Betsy.

"It appears you leave us with ner' much choice lass, I heard what ye say…thinkin' on…I'll agree."

Grove was a decisive man, not one to procrastinate unnecessarily and raised his mug of ale to Betsy as did Jem

Sowerbutts following his master's lead to signify assent. Betsy nodded lifting her small glass of liqueur which she had become partial to. Solomon remained seated motionless but having taken it all in.

Betsy remarked to Grove.

"We have a deal Mr Grove, I will arrange for it to be made legally binding, you will furnish me with all your business dealings and I will pay you handsomely whenever you work for me. Be warned though you will not under any circumstances, by your actions or words mark me, compromise me in any way. If that occurs I promise you that it will be the end of you, understand? You will work for me soley from now."

She proclaimed, again giving Grove a stare that caused him to visibly flinch. Sowerbutts who remained silent throughout the proceedings looked at Betsy with awe, his canine character instinctively felt a definite fidelity to her which began a loyal faithful relationship, such was the power of her personality. He was smitten! This bull of a man had become mesmerised by Betsy, not the first man to fall under her spell nor the last, he was unable to articulate his feelings not unsurprisingly, but he determined to do her bidding whatever she asked of him, even to the extent of going against Barton Grove, his erstwhile master until now.

Grove, not a little shell shocked after Betsy has laid down the template of their relationship to which he meekly agreed bade her farewell promising to do her bidding, Sowerbutts under her spell smiled the dullest smile he could, Betsy acknowledged them both and departed with Solomon again impressed with his mistress's performance.

Turning to Solomon as the left the restaurant such as it was, she remarked pointedly.

"You realise that what happened back there must remain a secret Solomon, I value your loyalty and you know I'll show my gratitude in return to both you and Esther, but NEVER discuss these matters with anyone, not even Esther…understand?"

"Count on me miss I will never let you down."

And so the two of them departed aboard Nip's buggy, Betsy feeling pleased with herself.

***

Over the next few weeks Betsy through the Wall Street gathering, word from Barton Grove and even via conversations with her husband John, Betsy found new avenues of legitimate business which she sought to exploit, These consisted of a haberdashers store, two dress shops, dry goods wholesalers, shipping merchant enterprise mostly dealing with cotton meant for the insatiable markets of Northern England, a new tavern by Wall Street which she saw as providing much needed food and refreshments for the many dealers in the area, she also, on taking John's advice, made some modest investments in the new stock market which she knew would please him. Something they could share, Betsy reasoned, would cement their relationship and show how much she valued his input in these matters.

In actuality the real excitement for Betsy Hoffman was in the rackets and dubious businesses she invested in with Barton Grove who quickly proved his worth by encouraging to put a stake in the numerous gambling houses, early casinos which were appearing with the promise of rich pickings, lending shops, insurance, theatres which were appearing in great numbers now as New York's population exploded during the early eighteen hundreds, and even protection rackets and prostitution following on from her investment in the bordello in Allentown run by Blue Sally. She had received regular updates via Isaac Sturn that her interests there were reaping considerable rewards, which pleased her but she also reminded him that a visit from her as well as her minder, would be forthcoming, significantly with no advance warning. This naturally was intended to keep them both on their toes.

On one occasion when visiting Barton in person at his lodgings on the Bowery, she noticed Jem Sowerbutts outside in the rear yard practising his pugilistic craft by punching a tree trunk, the intention was to harden his already iron like fists. The effect on Betsy was akin to one of witnessing pistons hammering against a rock, Sowerbutts's strength and hardness was something she had never seen before even during her years with the Harpes, who were hardened enough. The difference she discerned was that both Harpe brothers were sadistic, vicious brutes who usually used either a tomahawk in Micajah's case, or knife in Wiley's, Sowerbutts needed neither weapon, his sheer strength and fists were sufficient to deal with most any foe. Sowerbutts, Grove explained had gained much advice from another renowned fighter by the name of Bob Gregson, who he met in a tavern in Manchester, England, after Gregson had dispatched an opponent on a field outside the city on Platt Fields, beating the hapless fellow senseless within twenty minutes, much to the disappointment of the rowdy crowd who expected to see more action and blood. Later that year Sowerbutts took on the fighter regarded as world champion at that time, Tom Cribb, who defeated him and taught him a lesson in sheer hardness and brutal technique. It was Cribb who advised hitting a tree trunk every day as a sure way to turn fists into merciless sledgehammers!

380

"I'll wager there's ner' mon who could hold fer more than ten minutes against Jem, Mrs Hoffman." Grove proudly informed her. "I do not doubt you Mr Grove." she replied, fascinated with the awesome display put on by Jem.

After a short while Sowerbutts appeared with cloths wrapped around his fists, signs of blood seeping through but quickly he plunged them into cold water then vinegar to complete the training from the day.

He stared at Betsy, offered a sly smile in return muttering a tad nervously.

"Howdo ma'am." spoken in his broad Lancashire accent.

"Goodday Mr Sowerbutts, I come to see how we can develop our business here with Mr Grove."

Sowerbutts blushed slightly mumbling.

"Aye tis reet m'lady, ya know I'm alus 'ere to 'elp, alus."

Barely understanding his word Betsy discerned that this was a declaration of loyalty from this beast of a man. A man who could prove very valuable should there be any trouble to be dealt with, Jem Sowerbutts was perfect for the job. She anticipated Jem would prove a most loyal, subservient implement for her.

Returning to Barton Grove, Betsy made clear that henceforth all communication regarding the businesses they had established be done verbally by trusted messengers, which would include Solomon who she felt would be the perfect go between, not just for messages but to keep an eye on Grove. All money transactions were to be done in cash via her legitimate businesses thus creating a money laundering apparatus to conceal the dubious nature of what was going on.

Solomon in fact struck up a good rapport with Sowerbutts

who had some empathy with Solomon's background, since he himself had been brought up and exploited from an early age, even working as a child in the local cotton mill where children were exploited, working long hours in dangerous conditions for little reward, akin to slavery. This was aside from his bare fist fighting. Sowerbutts saw the irony in this with Solomon at the production beginning of the trade with Sowerbutts at the manufacturing end, both exploited ruthlessly by their wealthy masters who shared very little of the incredible riches they made. Barton Grove readily agreed to Betsy's terms proudly exclaiming to her.

"Barton Grove is a man of his word, Mrs Hoffman, it shall be done as you instructed!"

"I trust it will."

After saying that Betsy arose and took her leave with both Grove and his henchman Sowerbutts, left in her wake in some awe.

CHAPTER 36

The following weeks saw Barton Grove increasingly fall under Betsy Hoffman's spell, just had many others before him, he diligently operated the illicit, dubious businesses and with the trusty Jem Sowerbutts, collected the dollars with undue fuss, keeping half for himself as was the agreement. Betsy herself busied herself in much else, not least the running of the household and assisting husband John with his matters. One morning though Betsy noticed a definite sign of pregnancy, she had missed her period and had a notion of what was happening within her. Saying nothing to John she consulted the family doctor, a certain Doctor Kramer originally from Brandenburg, Germany, who after examining her, he indeed confirmed this happy condition.

"Congratulations Mrs Hoffman you are to be mother for the second time, now please do not overdo, you know not too much activity, ja? Not good for the child or you." the good doctor announced.

"Are you sure doc?" Betsy asked surprised, yet pleased at the same time, she had wanted another child so that Joshua would have a brother or sister to play with.

"Most definitely Mrs Hoffman, now will you inform your husband or shall I?"

Betsy paused slightly then replied confidently.

"I will as soon as he returns from his work this evening, I know he will be thrilled to know he's goin' to be a father."

"I will be here if you need anything Mrs Hoffman but I do believe that your pregnancy will go just fine. You are a healthy, strong woman as I can see from just looking at you."

The doctor duly declared looking admiringly at Betsy, who couldn't help but notice his eyes exploring her figure, with perhaps more than a medical interest.Despite this intrusion which didn't bother her, Betsy was delighted. To have more children was part of her desire to establish a dynasty here in New York which would serve to increase her power and influence, but also secure her husband's devotion even more than it already was. She returned home in anticipation of John's delight on receiving the good news, but said nothing to Esther or Solomon.

When John arrived home his main concern after embracing Betsy was to have supper.

"I'm famished my dear it's been a long day."

"I'm sure it has John but I have some important news dear so please sit down for a moment while I tell you what it is."

John seated himself in his favourite armchair wondering what was to come.

"I think I'm right in saying darling that you have always craved having a son or daughter for that matter, yes?""Why sure." he replied now a little nervous, realising what Betsy was going to tell him. He stroked his chin."You're going to be father John, I went to see Doctor Kramer today and he confirmed what I suspected...I hope this news pleases you my dear." she added pretending a little nervousness.

"Why Betsy I couldn't be more pleased or deligh...ted, oh my that's wonderful news!"

"I was hoping it would be." Betsy replied and was

384

immediately kissed by her joyful husband who proceeded to stride around the room in excitement, taking out his pipe but not lighting it in his ecstasy.

At that moment Esther entered the room to announce that supper was ready to be served but stood rigid as John Hoffman blurted out.

"I'm going to be a father Esther, Betsy will be theee...best mother in the world, can you hear me girl!"

Esther looked at Betsy in surprise, Betsy nodded to her in agreement and Esther burst into a big smile.

"Why Mr and Mrs Hoffman that sure is great news, great news... please allow me to congratulate ye both...if ye'll pardon me!?"

John turned to her and in a moment of unrestrained joy, rushed over to her and gave her a hug which caused the poor girl to blush in

embarrassment but also produced a smile as wide as the Hudson River.

"I think it would be good now to serve supper Esther, we'll be coming through very soon." Betsy informed Esther smiling and giving a surreptitious wink to her at the same time.

The joyful news spread through the whole household in no time at all bringing a good feeling to all the servants, also John's friends and business associates congratulated him on hearing the news.

"Always thought he had it in him you know." This was a typical refrain oft repeated. Joshua, after Betsy had told him the news, was delighted thinking he would have a brother...or maybe sister to play with, and John's brother Arthur, not one to express his feelings too much, told him how pleased he was…"'sepecially as our family name will be secured now brother."

Only his mother failed to join in the happiness, she immediately suspected Betsy of some underhand plan, she also resented the increasing hold that she on her eldest son.

"I'm pleased John but I cannot be but vexed at the same time dear boy."

She complained with not a hint of smile on her grim face, indeed a look of displeasure which disappointed John.

"But dear mother, Betsy is my dearest, mot faithful wife, my love…and to think you will have a grandchild, something you've always wanted for me and indeed our family."

"I would…but not with that schemin' hussy. She might fool you boy but not your mother, hear me, you don't understand the ways of women like her, this will end in tears, in tears, y'hear me!"

John on hearing this insult against Betsy could no longer restrain his displeasure and told his mother sternly.

"You must desist in your baseless assault on my dearest Betsy, desist I say mother!" John's anger became obvious now.In order to avoid further unpleasantness, John took his leave. Mrs Hoffman merely huffed and cursed Betsy Hoffman to herself as soon as he left the room. She was unrepentant, immovable in her opinion of Betsy sensing that this marriage which she did not approve of, was going to end in tears. Her agitation remained with her for the rest of the day, her anger directed at her maid and servants who wondered what had got into her. She repeated often to herself.

"In tears!"

She was best left alone when in such a mood.

John Hoffman, though agitated and troubled by his mother's reaction to the news, decided to ignore her and could not bring himself to visit her in her home which was a short distance away.

"Best if I let sleepin' dogs lie as my daddy always said." he thought, convincing himself that mother would eventually come round to appreciating her daughter in law. Betsy herself, aware of Mrs Hoffman's displeasure cared nothing. She had already decided how to deal with this irascible 'old witch' she would maintain a polite diplomatic attitude, giving the woman no clear cause for obvious complaint but Betsy had no intention of bending in humble subservience, this was not on the agenda for her.

***

Over the next few weeks, John Hoffman was as attentive a husband as one could imagine even to the point irritation for Betsy, she knew well from previous experiences what the dangers of childbearing entailed, but at least she did not have to reckon with the arbitrary violence of Micajah Harpe who had killed more than one of his infants in a fit of uncontrolled rage. Betsy needed no advice from John but sensibly held her tongue and dissembled the adoring, obedient wife.

"I'm fine my dear, no need to fuss so much, why I'm made of stern stuff John Hoffman, I was raised on my parents farm in Kentucky so you can be assured this baby will be as healthy as a spring lamb." she reassured him taking his hand.

"Well if your certain…but you will let me know straight

away if you need anything my love, my darlin' Betsy, won't you?" he implored.

"Of course I will, now you must stop fussin' and get off to your work, you know Arthur needs you there!"

John nodded in agreement, leaving in haste at the thought of his brother Arthur at the helm.

Later that month on an early October morning Betsy set off with Solomon in tow to meet Barton Grove at his lodgings to look over their shared businesses, recent lucrative progress excited her and she was in no way going to be a silent partner in this unusual arrangement. She was now looking to expand her portfolio of enterprises further and wanted to look at what Grove had in mind for her, but also to examine which rackets were problematic or losing money.

Entering Grove's rooms she was greeted by the usual effusive welcome with Jem Sowerbutts looking on in awe. Whenever this ox of a man was in the company of Betsy he suddenly became this totally compliant, servile lap dog to her, ready to carry out any command with immediate effect. If Betsy threw a bone, no doubt Sowerbutts would have chased after it! All this amused Solomon but he and Jem had become friends of sorts over the last few weeks, combining forces on occasions to deal with certain troublesome individuals, who despite the threat of Sowerbutts looming form over them, still foolishly attempted to do Betsy and Grove out of money owed, or indeed not to admit at all to the true earnings they had made.

One recent business Betsy had her eyes on involved a popular burlesque, music hall on Fifth Avenue run by a dissolute and loathsome character by the name of Simon Crook, originally from London, who came to New York, bringing with him his own brand of salacious entertainment akin to a music hall, with dancing girls, singers and revues. Crook was a man in his fifties who had the appearance of dissolution, his hair was grey, he had a face resembling a grubby fox, a sneering manner with a tongue which emitted the most foul of language which was meant to make any underling feel small; an effect he took great pleasure in. He had a reputation for dishonesty and exploitation especially of those weaker and in debt to him. He had abused many of his employees back in London but coming to the New World he had reckoned on making his fortune, he brought with him a collection of dancing girls, some of whom he forced into what was little more than prostitution, various other entertainers, all of whom he had paid the fares for on the voyage across the Atlantic Ocean. These unfortunate people were now in debt to Crook who had informed them that although he had paid for their passage he would want repayment from them either they worked for nothing basically until the debt was paid off or they would earn it by working for little or nothing. He gathered this motley group together on arrival at the theatre he had purchased on Pearl Street, before setting sail, and announced to them in a sneering, condescending manner.

"If any of you imagine that I run a charity for you fools, I'm sorry to disillusion you all. You will pay me back, any of you who don't or won't I will see to it that you will be ruined...ruined.. here me!! I'll have you thrown on to the miserable scrapheap of humanity to fester and die!"

"But Mr Crook, beggin' yer pardon guvn'r how am I goin' to live and the other gals as well?" Inquired one of the bolder females there.

"That is not my concern you stupid hussy, but having said that I can think of a way to earn sufficient money to live by…yes I can!"

"The girls looked at each in fear but knew well that they had no choice but to obey him. Hobson's Choice was the only option unfortunately.And so Simon Crook began his work in New York putting on shows to entertain the lower classes who enjoyed the dancing girls cheekily revealing more than what was normal at that time, singers and comics dressed in the most ridiculous outfits made rude jokes and sang songs that no censor would ever pass, smoking, shouting, drunkenness was not uncommon and Crook would use pistols to restore order or his beast of a dog 'Ripper', a huge, slavering brown mastiff, to intimidate any customer looking to argue with him. It was not uncommon for prostitutes to operate especially in the upper tier where sexual activity was openly engaged in, this often involved the dancing girls themselves who had to pay off their debts to Crook. This form of exploitation was something Crook enjoyed to observe himself, and on a few occasions used it to blackmail some of the customers. He was also not averse to taking sexual favours from a few of the girls who caught his eye himself, promising them that their own debt would be paid off much faster if they did his depraved bidding, the cad got his wicked way more often than not especially when two of the girls witnessed Crook viciously beating a certain pretty girl, Irene, after she rejected his advances. She was left battered with a fracture to her arm and badly bruised but was still forced to perform the next evening. A dreadful atmosphere ensued with all his employees fearful but full of loathing for this evil creature.

As news spread of Simon Crook's 'theatre', Barton Grove quickly got wind of it all, as a dubious operator himself he was vaguely aware of Crook from his own days in London where he remembered that Crook operated a similar venue in the East End near Whitechapel, a place which itself would become notorious as the scene of the Jack the Ripper murders some eighty years later.

Being aware of this venue with it's regular clientele and profitability, Betsy decided to encourage Crook to accept her organisation's protection, and Barton Grove was dispatched with Jem to accept this arrangement, which he was told would be to his benefit. After some bartering he accepted realising that he was becoming more and more vulnerable to take over by the many other impresarios operating in the city, and agreed to make weekly payments in cash which they would collect each Monday. This worked well for the first few weeks but soon after payments became infrequent and despite warnings, they stopped altogether before two months were up. This enraged Betsy who also found out that Simon Crook was regularly mistreating badly some of the girls who worked for him. She was unaware of the full extent of this abuse until one day a young lad, scruffily dressed with holes in his trousers, ripped, dirty shirt and in bare feet delivered a message from Crook, requesting more time to pay the week's protection. Betsy and Solomon were present at the time. She opened the sealed letter looked at it, her left eye raised on reading it's meagre contents.

It read:

My dear Mrs Hoffman,

'Sincere apologies but I will not be able to pay anything until the end of this week. Cash flow not good, takings down over the past week.

Simply not possible!

Your humble servant,

The honourable Simon Crook

Betsy passed the letter to Grove who exhaled his breath in anger, raised his eyes to Betsy who said.

"So he won't pay this week will he? Cash flow indeed, we know for sure that's a lie! He needs to be taught a lesson Mr Grove, you will see to it that with Solomon's help and no doubt Mr Sowerbutt's, it will be a lesson he will never forget, the damnable scoundrel! Crook by name, crook by deed!"

Grove promptly replied.

"You can be sure, he will never be the same once we have finished with him Mrs Hoffman!"

Solomon and Jem looked on, no doubt relishing the opportunity to deal with the hated Simon Crook.

Next day under orders from Barton Grove who arranged the timing, but naturally more significantly Betsy herself, who despised the manner of Crook's operation with it's awful abuses, something she had of course endured herself, as had Solomon and Jem in different but equally terrible ways, Solomon and Sowerbutts were promptly sent to visit Crook.

Before leaving Betsy instructed them all.

"Teach that bastard a lesson but don't kill him, I would rather he was put out of action permanently so he don't harm any of those girls anymore, you understand?"

"We do Mrs Hoffman, he won't forget." Grove asserted.

Solomon and Jem nodded approvingly with Sowerbutts muttering.

"We'll do 'im gud an' proper. Aye we will."

The visit to Crook went ahead as planned when all was relatively quiet.

On entering his shabby office, littered with empty liquor

bottles, cigar butt ends, Simon Crook slouched in his old leather armchair and barely displayed any manners or greeting when the three of them entered, he merely remarked arrogantly.

"You got the letter? No more I can do as it states, now I have work to do so I'd be obliged if you'd all leave me in peace, I have other business to attend to…Maisie come here my dear! He shouted and within a few seconds the summoned Maisie appeared at the door, dressed in little more than a partly torn chemise.

Suddenly Barton Grove looked at Maisie and said.

"Maisie you can leave, we would not want you to witness what's going to happen next my dear."

Maisie scuttled off no doubt relieved.

Crook looked perplexed frowning as he regarded the three visitors.

"What do you think you're doing!"

But before he could say anything else Jem Sowerbutts hauled him out of his chair by his throat as if he was a doll, threw him against the wall behind, and proceeded to violently beat the shocked creature with fists that slammed into his body and face like pistons and sledgehammers.

Crook screamed in pain totally in shock at this sudden attack from the Lancashire pit bull. When Sowerbutts paused Barton Grove announced with satisfaction.

"I think Jem needs some support Solomon! Barton laughed.

Solomon took out his cudgel from his loose jacket and laid into the wretched Crook aiming for both legs, a definite crack was heard accordingly and Crook howled in agony, Jem finished his work now with two more colossal blows to Crook's face, and it was then left to Solomon to complete the punishment which ended with a violent kick into his rear end.

Blood streamed from his face which now was little more than pulp, teeth were missing, his mouth bloodied horribly, an eye was hanging limply from it's socket, one of his leg clearly broken hung at an angle, the other fearfully twisted. Crook could only writhe in pain around the floor, crying and moaning incoherently.

After the completion of the beating Barton Grove stood over Crook and shouted so that the wretch could hear.

"Listen you miserable bastard, you'll get the money you owe to us by tomorrow or we'll be back to give ye more severe medicine that'll take away your pain! You'll also be nice to those girls you abuse, you scum! As well as all your poor workers and you'll pay them properly, understand?"He lifted Crook's head to emphasize the point.

Simon Crook could only moan acceptance.

"Yue..shh!" he attempted to say, spitting blood in the process.

Grove continued.

"Now we'll be on our way but seein's I'm a decent chap, I'll get a doctor to come and patch you up. More than you deserve ya scoundrel...oh by the way my boss Mrs Betsy Hoffman sends her regards!"

The three enforcers left, pleased with a job well done.

Betsy was informed on their return as to what had happened which gave her uncontained satisfaction and next morning the money owed by Crook was delivered with a letter of apology enclosed.

It was no surprise that from then on a pathetic invalid, now wheelchair bound and much subdued, his right leg almost paralysed and his looks rearranged into a caricature of what they were previous to the beating, namely Simon Crook, ensured payment was made promptly, without failure.

The girls were now safe from his abuse and he became a more reliable, careful employer, thanks also to the attentions of Solomon and Jem who visited Crook frequently to ensure he did as he was told. He did. Betsy also took over direct running of the establishment and from then on it became one of her prized illicit assets offering further opportunities for more considerable earnings.

CHAPTER 37

After this incident news circulated as it tends to, that Barton Grove was someone not to be crossed, the evidence of Simon Crook's punishment became a source of gossip, with stories exaggerating the injuries sustained, some said he was a paralysed cripple unable to move or speak, some said he was dead and a new owner installed with the same name, other even more fanciful stories floated around Manhattan. Fortunately the name of Betsy Hoffman was kept out of all this thanks to Barton Grove's insistence that he was the responsible, no-one else, Grove wanted to send a clear message to his competitors.

For Betsy, life continued over the next months in it's by now well-worn routine, her pregnancy went smoothly with Husband John as attentive as ever though she had one brush with her irascible mother in law who accused her of "Gold digging" and being a "Brazen hussy!" with her not being good enough for her dear son John. Betsy kept her temper, politely denying these accusations and emphasizing her love and devotion to her dear son, reminding her also that she was carrying his child. Nothing changed Mrs Hoffman's loathing of Betsy and consequently Betsy felt nothing but loathing to her as well, indeed she began to think of ways of ridding herself of this troublesome old crone.

Thankfully her businesses both illicit and legal, continued to thrive and Solomon increasingly became her right hand man, studiously protecting Betsy's interests, even travelling to

Allentown for several days to meet with Isaac Sturn and Blue Sally. He discovered that Sturn had kept his word sending payments to Betsy as agreed and Sally, to all intents and purposes, was running the house efficiently, Solomon saw that the 'ladies' were happy, well looked after and seemed to enjoy their work, he was even offer free service which he declined much to the disappointment of one of the ladies who had obviously taken a shine to him. He left the next day.

"Shame ya have to leave son, Patsy likes ya y'know." Sally winked salaciously at Solomon who blushed replying.

"I thank you but I'm a married man…I must take my leave but thank Patsy, she is a mighty fine lady…" Solomon nervously replied.

"Well that's a shame fella, maybe next time yer here?"

"No thanks Sally." He took his leave swiftly leaving Blue Sally grinning then turning to Patsy she shouted. "Well I tried girl, we'll get him for ya next time!"

Solomon duly returned to New York to report to Betsy that all was well in Allentown.

Betsy's commercial empire expanded but not surprisingly John Hoffman became aware of at least some of the more dubious activities she was involved in, suspicions at first which he dismissed but the evidence mounted with one or two of his closest associates expressing some concern subtly suggesting Betsy was even compromising John's reputation.

"This is nonsense! I know my wife and she would not get involved in such affairs so I'll thank you to keep your insinuations to yourself!"

John snapped back indignantly, having complete

confidence in Betsy's good sense, after all there was not a shred of evidence to suggest that she was involved in anything but lawful activity. He assumed that it was the rumours spread by envious competitors keen to undermine his success and reputation that had initiated these slanderous comments.

Despite his confidence in Betsy he spoke to her later that evening delicately bringing up the subject by inquiring if all was going well with her investments and had there been any trouble with anything related to them.

"Why no my darling, I would speak to you straight away if there was, you know that. Why, has anyone been saying anything bad John. If so it's lies, lies, I would never compromise you, never"

Betsy affected hurt and tears magically appeared which had the desired effect instantly.

"Oh no my darling, I would never think that, it's some of my competitors, enemies more like, who will use any dirt to throw at me…us, forgive me, please forgive me, you know how much I love you, I couldn't live without you Betsy…!"

John pulled her toward him and kissed her passionately declaring his love, Betsy reciprocated.

After passions were sated Betsy asked John what he thought of giving Solomon and Esther their freedom, since she had been considering this move for some time she informed him, but she needed his assent of course.

"Why Betsy I have no objection, I must say I have been impressed with both of them and it seems right and proper to grant this…if you're sure.

After all we don't want to lose two good servants do we?

Betsy smiled and reassured him that both of them would

remain, of that she was convinced after all where would they go?

"Well it's settled then, do you want to tell them or would you like me to do it sweetheart?"

"I'll tell them John, I've known them longer so I figure it's my job to speak with them both."

The following day after some last minute soul searching, Solomon and Esther were summoned over to her.

"Come here both you" she said to them.

She told them to sit down which they did wondering what was coming, Esther looked nervously at Solomon as they were seated.

Betsy continued, looking at them both studiously.

"Now we're all here together I have been thinkin' about a matter which has occupied my mind for some time now. This is it; I intend to give you both your freedom."

Taken by surprise Solomon almost rose from his seat while Esther held on to his arm, both taken by complete surprise at this unexpected announcement.

Betsy continued.

"It's up to you both to decide what you want to do. I will arrange to get legal documents for your freedom if you decide to accept it, freedom which I believe you truly deserve. I must say that you both have served me well, been loyal and I can say honestly that I value you not just as servants but even as friends who I can always turn to if ever I need some words of comfort or even advice…maybe even rebuke."

Betsy smiled here pausing slightly before continuing to address a speechless Solomon and Esther who at first feared that they were being dismissed.

Betsy continued.

"We've been through a lot together so I sincerely hope we will continue to do so even if you accept my offer to you. I will arrange for the necessary documents to be produced by my lawyer Elijah confirming your freedom if you decide in the affirmative. Go away and think about it but don't take too long as I have much to do. This time tomorrow at the latest if you both don't mind." she added

Betsy stood up then dismissed the speechless pair who held each others hand as they left the room.

As soon as they were on their own Solomon and Esther briefly discussed their options.

Esther looked to Solomon saying. "Won't we just be slaves under a different name Solomon?" she said, thinking at first Betsy was not being totally sincere.

Solomon replied taking Esther in his arms.

"We got nuthin' now woman, we should go with her for time being and decide proper when we got our freedom letters. But I do believe that missy has been good to us if ye think about it."

Esther nodded in agreement, then replied more confidently.

"Well she's been good to us, least we can do is give it a chance."

With this accord they both decide to inform Betsy straight away.

Solomon feeling satisfied that a correct decision had been made, went to Betsy and informed her that they wish to remain with her as her servants.

"We both owe a debt to you miss, and we thank ye and the good Lord for your kindness and offer of freedom."

Betsy nodded telling them that she will still arrange for the documents to be drafted in case they change their minds. This consideration to them by her confirmed to Solomon and Esther their future course of service to Betsy Hoffman who would remain their mistress for the foreseeable future.

Betsy visited Elijah J Gilbert the following day, a rainy early Summer's day to give the necessary instructions to her lawyer. This initially cause Gilbert some surprise advising Betsy against this action.

"Are you sure Mrs Hoffman, they are slaves after all, why risk giving them their freedom with the risk of them quitting you at any stage? I would advise you, as your lawyer to at least wait another year or more, that would be the sensible thing to do."

Betsy replied somewhat irritably.

"You will do as I instruct Mr Gilbert. My mind is made up and will not be changed. Solomon and Esther have more than proved to me their loyalty, please proceed as I instruct."

She tapped her foot in irritation.

"Very well it will be done as you instruct, I will have a document drawn up before the end of the week and sent over to you via Cross, I hope this will be to your satisfaction?"

"It is and while I am here I have some contracts for you look over if you'll be so kind."

"Of course." Elijah immediately agreed, not wishing to

create any further dissention between them.

The legal documents were delivered by young Nicholas Cross as promised and duly signed with him as witness, Elijah J Gilbert had already added his signature, so it was left to Betsy to sign and then Solomon and Esther to add their distinctive marks. This done Nicholas returned to Gilbert's office for copies to be produced.

"I'm not happy with this Nicholas, between you me, those negroes cannot be trusted, I fear for Mrs Hoffman doing this, an unwise move in my humble opinion."

Nicholas dutifully nodded his agreement.

"You are right of course Mr Gilbert, though I must say there was a distinct good feeling when they all signed…"

"Good feeling be damned Cross, I care not a fig for 'good feelings, it's bad business I say!'

Elijah J Gilbert, Doctor of Law, LLB, was not happy.

Despite Gilbert's concerns, the next few weeks Solomon and Esther experienced more clearly how good a life they now had working for Betsy, their duties remained the same but they both experienced a definite increase in the respect shown to them. Betsy and her husband John, both proved to be mistress and master of unusual courtesy, treating them both fairly, paying them well, but also not afraid to reprimand them when the occasion calls for rebuke. This was rare during these times, as a strong relationship built on respect continued to be developed. Esther became more definitely Betsy's trusted, loyal maid, but more than that even as her increasing confidant. Solomon likewise becomes her right hand man, willing to do as she asks, not baulking at any request from her.

John Hoffman went about his business with a barely perceived satisfaction that all was running smoothly in his household, crediting his dear wife for this, what more could a man wish for? Betsy and John enjoyed rides in what was to become Central Park, but was now at this time an area of woodland with well worn trails for the well to do to take their carriages and horse rides especially during the warm early Summer.

CHAPTER 38

Over the next few months as the hot Summer set in, as temperatures reached over ninety degrees and the days sometimes became unbearable, the air dry, and as stillness descended on the Hoffman household, a kind of atrophy which extended even to matters of business, pervaded. Betsy spent most of her time during this period of heat in the shade taking lemonade which she had a great fondness for, iced drinks and reading the latest bulletins from Wall Street as well as messages for all her associates which needed her attention, mindful of her pregnant condition and consequently only receiving the most urgent of visitors, Barton Grove appeared mostly once a week dressed in his finest to reinforce the impression that he was a respectable businessman who Betsy had some important dealings with. His task was to update her on development, she had given him authority even over Isaac Sturn in Allentown with instructions to utilise Solomon as well as Jem more frequently.

"I trust Solomon so you will keep nothing from him, you follow?" Betsy instructed.

"Yes of course Mrs Hoffman I'll send Jem with him to Allentown just to impress on Sturn what'll happen' if he strays from the fold!"

"That will be good, Solomon has already been there so he's known to them all."

Grove stayed a short while then took his leave, leaving an exhausted Betsy to rest for the remainder of the day. She was satisfied that all was going well, pleased that she had settled matters with Solomon and Esther and looking forward to becoming a mother again.

***

As Summer drew to a close, mercifully to some who had to work in the heat regardless of how tortuous that was, the day of Betsy's confinement approached. The baby was not due until November but she sensed that this was a healthy, impatient child who did not want to hang about in his or her mother's womb, and not unsurprisingly she was given the first sign at the end of September, a false alarm as it turned out but enough to send the whole household into a flurry of excitement with John becoming ever more attentive and over excited at the prospect of an heir to his family. Only Mrs Katrina Hoffman expressed neither excitement nor approval at this forthcoming obvious, significant event. Betsy simply ignored her while John abandoned any further attempts to bring his mother round. She was immovable in her contempt for her daughter in law, going as far as telling John that she would play no part in the child's upbringing.

"I'm damned sure your wife, Jezebel as I calls her, won't want me interfeerin'!" she protested to him… "So I'm damned if I'll have anythin' to do with your child, I'll not be moved John, not be moved."

She emphasized the point by banging her walking stick against the floor, a sound which reverberated throughout the room.

"Very well mother so be it."John shook his head deciding to continue his distance from her, avoiding confrontation, assuring Betsy that things would improve once the child arrived believing his mother's heart would soften accordingly. Betsy

405

nodded but cared nothing.

It was in October, the sixth day at four in the morning, that Eleanor, Katrina Hoffman arrived without too much fuss mercifully for her mother. The child was healthy, weighing a good seven pounds exactly, with Dr Kramer expressing his satisfaction that both mother and child were in the best of health, he gave the child a resounding smack lifting it upside down as was the custom, the midwife washed and then presented young Eleanor who screamed loudly until Betsy comforted the little mite. The bond was well and truly established.

John was summoned and though feeling a tinge of disappointment at not being given a son, soon got over that and doted on his new daughter heaping his gratitude on his wife.

"She sure is beautiful Betsy, just like you my dear. Our Eleanor is going to be a fine lady, a fine lady." he repeated proudly.

The Hoffman household expressed their congratulations and joy at the new arrival but as expected Katrina Hoffman said nothing, choosing to ignore the happy event, not even attending the christening, making the excuse of not feeling well enough. However John's brother Arthur who was to become the baby's Godfather was delighted to attend, along with John's cousin and nephew who made the journey from Boston, staying with them for four days, as well as the usual friends. Solomon and Esther were permitted to attend as was Elijah J Gibert, but not Barton Grove or Jem, that would taking things a risk too far.

Betsy regained her strength quickly, she was a strong determined woman who did not want to waste time resting too much even despite John and Dr Kramer's protestations. Much to her surprise another piece of news came to her a week later when Esther announced that she too was to become a mother for the first time.

"Oh my Esther! When is your baby due?"

"Well miss I reckon next March but I ain't certain."

"I'll get Dr Kramer to look at you and you can be sure Esther that you will be looked after, why your child will become one of the family not too different to Eleanor."

"Oh miss, don't you go worryin' about me, I'll be fine, sure I will."

"You will be fine, because you'll be cared for, now I don't want to hear another word on the subject, d'ya hear Esther?"

"I do Miss Betsy, I surely do."

***

After the birth of Eleanor a routine set in and the weather in New York gradually changed to a cooler, rainy period as December approached. Betsy's businesses flourished but during these few months leading up to Christmas she devoted herself to caring for her new daughter who made excellent progress, feeding from her mother as Betsy wished. No wet nurse for her, she remember the pitiful conditions that Susan and Sarah had to endure attempting to care for their babies which they did as best they could, unfortunately no amount of care could prevent the deaths of at least two of the infants being brutally murdered during one of Micajah Harpe's violent fits. It was true, as Betsy witnessed at his death at the hands of Moses Stegall, that 'Big Harpe' expressed remorse at killing his daughter, which was the only time in his life that he ever mentioned any sorrow for these monstrous acts, Betsy was determined to protect and nurture her own children. John Hoffman could only look on in admiration at his wife's loving care, which was something new to him since he had had a wet nurse in his own infancy, as well as a nanny to look after him. His own mother had no intention of being hampered or restricted herself, she had a busy social life to reorganise, amongst other diversions, her husband Tomas was a rather distant, cold man who immersed himself in developing businesses and investments which established the power of the Hoffman family in New York.

Just as everything to intents and purposes had settled into a satisfying routine over the following year with Esther duly giving birth to twins, a boy and girl, both healthy thanks to the care promised, tragedy struck!

Joshua now seven years old, progressing well at school, loyal friends made and forming an ever more firm bond with his step father John, who took him on his fishing trips, went sailing, as well as other activities they shared much to Betsy's delight, suddenly took ill. He had caught a chill one day the following March which turned into pneumonia, leaving the poor boy bed-bound and suffering high fevers with intense coughing fits. Dr Kramer attended the boy every day administering cold compresses, medicines, leeches were applied with the intention of removing the poisoned blood, or so it was believed at that time, long before antibiotics were discovered. Betsy was distraught caring as best she could for her only son and John too was distraught at thought of losing his stepson, made worse because he was aware that survival from this terrible infliction was rare.

Tragically despite the best efforts of all, with Dr Kramer

shaking his head in disappointment that everything he tried failed to cure Joshua, the dear boy died on the evening of Thursday 12th March. Betsy was inconsolable with grief, her cries and wailing resonated throughout the household, the sorrow shared by everyone, Solomon and Esther both felt the despair of their mistress keenly as well but try as John, Esther and others did, Betsy was devastated unable, to respond to even the most tender sympathies expressed. She went into a virtual comatosed state, she could not speak, would not take any nourishment, she simply sat with her head bowed, dressed in black, weeping intermittently and holding Joshua's favourite wooden toy soldier close to her breast.

The funeral of Joshua was a held on a rainy day at St Paul's, Lower Manhattan, half way through Betsy collapsed with grief unable to cope with the loss of her son, the realisation that she would never see him again in this life, it was very hard to take. She had to be taken home by Nip even missing the final part of the service and burial of Joshua. An impressive tomb with angels carved was made and eventually it became a place of pilgrimage for Betsy, and others who had known this dear little fellow, she laid flowers each time she visited his grave , as did Solomon and Esther who held a special affection for Joshua, Esther particularly felt her mistress's grief.

As the days and weeks went on, John became increasingly concerned at his wife's condition, he tried to console her with little Eleanor in his arms, saying tenderly.

"Oh my love, I am so sorry, I truly loved the little fellow but you know he rests in heaven now with our dear Lord Jesus and all the angels, he is at peace my sweet. Please try to get over this, we all need you especially little Eleanor and your devoted husband who misses his beautiful wife so much."

He gently handed over their baby

Betsy smiled faintly, the sight of their helpless daughter lifted her despair slightly and she took her into her arms tenderly. Eleanor cried softly as she sought her mother's breast and Betsy thankfully responded to the little child's need of nourishment. This brought a sigh of relief from John.

"We can't manage without you my love." he said taking Betsy's hand and kissing it softly.

Gradually Betsy, if not over the loss of her most treasured son Joshua, resumed her normal routine with Eleanor being the greatest comfort to her, the little girl with her whispy fair curls never failed to bring some joy to Betsy's grieving, broken heart. Esther could not help but share Betsy's loss and while not attempting to offset that loss with the presence of her own two babies, and though it was rare for her mistress to be seen outside with all three infants, Betsy insisted on walking a short distance with Esther, their two wooden prams, the best that could be purchased causing much admiration from other nannies and mothers out with their little ones.

Betsy found herself with more time to herself as John spent some nights at his newly acquired town house in the Battery in Lower Manhattan. This was an up market residential area at this time which eventually would become Battery Park with it's many offices surrounding it in time. Now though the area was a pleasant green oval space, which John was delighted to purchase a property within, especially as it would prove to be a sound investment as property values increased considerably. Betsy too was impressed with their new property and occasionally used it as a base for her own mostly legitimate businesses. She was careful never to invite Barton Grove or any other of her associates especially while John was there or there was a chance he might suddenly appear, only Elijah J Gilbert who John knew of course, visited it's impressive building with it's classical portico and window painted in gold with the name of John Hoffman Jr proudly displayed on it.

Betsy after her period of intense grief suddenly threw herself into her business interests finding new ventures via Barton Grove but also some sound investments recommended to her by Elijah and her husband who thought it was a good idea for her to busy herself with work, Eleanor, to Esther's delight was left with her and seemed to enjoy the company of the nanny's own children. This relationship flourished over time and later that year Betsy found herself pregnant once again much to the delight of herself and John who barely restrained his joy at the news that he was to be a father once again.

"Wowee Besty this is just wonderful and I know...at least I've a feeling that we'll be having a son this time!" he declared clasping his hands together in delight. Betsy smiled but inside felt a pang of sorrow, nothing she thought could ever replace her darling Joshua, but taking a deep breath, she shared his happiness.

Mrs Katrina Hoffman

CHAPTER 39

SEVEN YEARS ON

The year1815 and New York City had expanded to the north of Manhattan and beyond remorselessly eating up more and more virgin land as it became the most important commercial centre in the whole of America. It's growth attracted thousands more immigrants who all sought a better life but needed housing which consequently saw more and more dwellings constructed most of poor quality which were little more than slums, exploitation of the masses of people seeking honest work but many falling prey to the gangs of thieves, vagabonds and ner' do wells who preyed on these unfortunates. People from all over the world flooded there seeing the first droves of Irish immigrants but also more, British, Dutch, German, French, Italians, Chinese…and many more races, creeds and colours adding to the kaleidoscope of humanity in this metropolitan crucible. It's population grew to half a million by this time but reach over a million by 1860, it included the Bronx to the west with it's long shoreline, and Brooklyn, Queen's on Long Isalnd, all mostly residential areas developed during the nineteenth century. A valuable description of the city before then by French consul Fernand Braudel is apt:

"Its inhabitants, who are for the most part foreigners and made up of every nation except Americans so to speak, have in general no mind for anything but business. New York might be described as a permanent fair in which two-thirds of the population is always being replaced; where and where luxury has reached alarming heights... It is in the countryside and in the inland towns that one must look for the American population of New York State."

This description accurately represented the condition of New York even before the 1840's when this impression was written because at the time of Betsy's life there, it would have been very recognizable to her and everyone else at that period of time.

It was within this seething metropolis that Betsy Hoffman's empire grew with her commercial interests almost matching her husband's in revenue and diversity. Her connections she still kept to herself only letting John know of her most legitimate enterprises, but gradually he sensed that all was not what it seemed to be regarding his wife's many dealings. Word got to him more frequently of her connections not just with Barton Grove, but with others now who saw her as a means to fund their questionable activities.

Apart from these goings on Betsy had brought more joy to the Hoffman house by bearing four more children over the seven years since Eleanor's arrival. They were two more daughters and two sons in correct order; Eliza, Richard, Bartholomew and Hilde, all thankfully healthy though Bartholomew (or 'Bart' as became known) seemed a sickly child, frequently ill which caused his parents some concern. Betsy relied more frequently on Esther, who herself had three children with another son added to the twins; Moses and Ruth, the new son was named Caleb, and a nanny and Governess Miss Pretty, a severe looking thirtyish spinster from Aberdeen in Scotland originally, who ruled with an iron fist, much appreciated by Betsy and John. The house was a very full place with Betsy's children bringing much life and energy, something which she was grateful for, if occasionally irritated by their wailing, shouting and arguments which erupted from time to time. The matter of Joh Hoffman's concern over his wife's activities in the city came to a head one evening when he challenged Betsy over what she was doing working with Barton Grove, someone whose reputation and consequential connection to Betsy could not be concealed any longer.

On arrival he went straight to his study and sent for Betsy who had a feeling that something was brewing between her and John. She entered the room, sitting down opposite to him and casually inquired.

"What is it dearest, can it not wait, why you haven't taken your supper yet?"

"Supper can wait Betsy." he began.

He hesitated, feeling uncomfortable at what he was about to say and not being someone who chose confrontation, especially with his wife.

"Betsy you must heed my advice...command as your husband...I have been hearing more regularly from many quarters over quite a lot of time, of your dealings with that man Grove. This must stop! My reputation is at stake dear...I cannot allow any more of this, I now expect you to desist with all your business dealings, I will take over them and you know I will ensure that you lose nothing financially...indeed I promise you that with me at the helm, well you will earn more. Yes I can promise that. Now I won't be denied on this matter Betsy, it's for the best...you will from now on conclude all, I say all, of this, what has become embarrassing dealings the extent of which I was not aware, least not fully cognisant of...and I don't want to hear any more you follow me?!"

John with a hint of annoyance, concluded his diatribe,

breathing heavily and taking out his pipe to gain comfort from the rich tobacco that he filled it with.

Betsy stayed speechless for a moment, she had not expected John to be so insistent on her abandoning all her business interests and handing them over to him. She had some notion of what was coming but concluded that he would at most urge greater caution, but she quickly adjusted her response, seeking to placate him but in no way to give up what she had worked so tirelessly and with such determination and skill to achieve.

"Why dearest, how can ye think there is anything unlawful or underhand in anything I am involved with? You hurt me, most grievously you do, but I do understand your concerns for me, though I maintain you are mistaken dear. But if this is what you wish yes of course I will pull away as you request…I only ask that you give me some time to conclude matters, would you agree John? It's all I ask."

Betsy looked at John imploringly as John sat puffing on his briar pipe, a man clearly uneasy. After thinking a while he replied with some undisguised severity.

"Very well my love, I would condescend to you doing what you promise…but it must completely sorted within one month from today, exactly how I have stipulated."

Betsy nodded her assent then left the room keeping her anger to herself. She muttered to herself; "I'll be blowed if I am giving up everything I damn well worked for, he can go hang himself!"

This was the beginning of the end of the relationship between Betsy and John Hoffman. His fate was sealed.

***

After two weeks Betsy came to a decision within herself that John Hoffman would have to go, "go" for her meant eliminating the father of their five children, but unlike her previous homicides it was a course of action she did not embark on or look forward to with any pleasure, indeed she was aggrieved that John would not change his mind one iota, indeed he hardened his attitude seeming to have gained greater confidence from their meeting. He was under the impression that Betsy was from now on going to be content to be the dutiful, domesticated, subservient wife who would gratefully let him take over all their joint businesses. Betsy was not going to let this happen, she decided which method of murder to utilise and she was helped by the fact that John was becoming more breathless, strained and in some discomfort. Thinking back to how she dispatched Cuthbert Bullitt back in Morgantown, it seemed that the method used there; poisoning, would be the most effective, less suspicious of all, though naturally it was not without it's risks, Dr Kramer was no fool. She still had a significant quantity of arsenic left which she kept locked away in her dressing table within another locked box and so decided with some regret to administer the poison at the soonest opportunity.

That opportunity occurred two days later before John was due to retire to his bed (they now slept in separate bedrooms), Betsy brought him his nightcap, a brandy which he enjoyed often before taking to his bed. She spoke to him most tenderly passing him the deadly tot of brandy.

"There dearest, this will relax you my love, you need a good night's sleep, so you do."

"Thank you Betsy…I'm sorry I spoke to you harshly last time…but I only want you to be safe, you know I love you my poppet." he yawned and the drank the brandy in one gulp, but after swallowing felt that something was not right about it.

"Goodnight John, sleep well, I will always love you."

Betsy said to him as she left his study, closing the door firmly behind her. She felt no satisfaction it what she had done, her thoughts were a mixture of guilt, sadness, unease, but also some relief, assuming the arsenic did it's job and no suspicions were aroused, she hoped that a new chapter in her life would open up.

Next morning pandemonium broke out as Solomon discovered the body of his master John Hoffman lying diagonally across his bed, his arms outstretched, one of his fists still clenched. Dr Kramer was sent for as Betsy screamed in horror at seeing her husband, she clung to him even having to be pulled away by Esther who herself cried in despair. Solomon after his initial shock, looked on with some bemused suspicion but not daring to say a thing, he glanced at Betsy who maintained her almost uncontrolled grief. After arriving and going straight to John's bedroom where he still lay, it did not take Dr Kramer long before declaring to Betsy that John had obviously suffered a coronary heart attack leading to fatal consequences.

"I'm sorry Mrs Hoffman but I had advised Mr Hoffman to ease off his work, it appears he was not able to do this. I'm sorry to say this is the consequence."

The good Dr Kramer announced as only doctors can in such situations.

Betsy tearfully nodded before retiring to her room to decide on how to manage the situation that she had created, her thoughts quickly turned from dissembled grief to planning for the future.

Funeral arrangements were made mostly by John's brother, Arthur who outdid himself by organising the most impressive service at Trinity Cathedral, Betsy was too distraught to be involved and gladly left everything to him. The occasion was a grand affair with Mozart's superb Requiem performed together with John's favourite Bach Choral Preludes, a choir sang and tribute were poured out by John's brother, other members of his family as well as many of his closest friends. Betsy dressed in black was treated with the utmost respect, outpourings of condolences, sympathy were heaped upon her as she displayed the sorrow of a grieving widow. Only Mrs Katrina Hoffman was notable for her absence but as she was displaying the clear symptoms of dementia as we know now, it was not a great surprise. Arthur had been taken aback by her hateful remarks when he went to see her.

"I will not go anywhere if that… evil bitch is there!" she exclaimed pointing her fingers demonstratively at him… "I told my dear boy nothing good would come of it…she murdered him ya hear, murdered my boy, damn that whore to Hell!!"

Arthur could not take in her hysterical outburst any longer and so took his leave saying to her on his way out.

"Well mother if you change your mind I will arrange for you to be brought and cared for, I'm sure John would want you at his funeral."

"Go away, ye useless clown, go away!"

Arthur left.

Five months later Mrs Katrina Hoffman passed away, embittered, broken and still ranting about that "evil whore!" and "that Jezebel!"

John was laid to rest in Trinity Church's cemetery a not far from Joshua's grave, convenient for mourners to come and pay their respects. Betsy visited the cemetery regularly to lay flowers and speak with her beloved Joshua, a tear would trickle gently down her cheek as she thought of her lost beautiful boy, but also to lay flowers at John's grave as well, she felt a sense of obligation given what she had done, perhaps to make amends albeit in a subdued manner but genuinely tinged with some measure of remorse.

CHAPTER 40

1825

Ten years later as Betsy basked for once in the comfort of her situation which after John's demise she had restored full control of, her wealth considerably increased not just through her own doing but also with the enormous fortune that her husband had left her she decided to divest herself of all openly illegal, illicit businesses. This had been an ongoing procedure with Barton Grove necessarily cut adrift, although Betsy rewarded him for his assistance by handing over several lucrative enterprises she owned. Matters though had become increasingly difficult for Grove as more and more immigrants flooded into New York, with some desperados forming gangs which began to challenge his power. What made his situation worse was that two years ago he lost the services of his 'enforcer' the mighty Jem Sowerbutts who was found brutally murdered when he was set upon by a gang of seven of Irish descent who clubbed him to death mercilessly. Jem had fought bravely leaving some of these thugs badly beaten but he had eventually been overcome by sheer weight of numbers with some of the Irishmen shouting abuse at this 'English bastard'. Solomon who had ceased his working with Grove expressed sadness at the news, as did Betsy herself who paid for his funeral and gave generously to Jem's widow, a Dutch dancing girl called Wilma, who he met at Crook's theatre who he doted on. They were married not but four years previous.

Barton Grove henceforth slipped into a period of steady decline, taking to alcohol increasingly and seeing his remaining businesses either taken over by force by rivals or simply gone to ruin. One of these businesses which he helped Betsy with was of course the theatre owned by Simon Crook, who like Grove had slipped into decline, his disability made worse through frustration at not being able to deal with the increasing contempt shown to him by his employees, Crook was found one morning slumped over his desk with congealed blood found in his unkempt, matted grey hair. The girls especially merely laughed, relieved that he had gone for good and thankfully when Betsy heard of this wretched creature's demise she promptly purchased the theatre creating a much better managed place of entertainment with Solomon put in charge. Something he was most delighted with as he set about making improvements and restructuring the running of the place. Esther had her reservations about Solomon spending time there but it was not long before he found a reliable associate to run the theatre on a day to day basis for him.

Betsy also heard from Solomon that in Allentown Blue Sally had been found strangled one night by an irate customer inside the Bordello she owned. The man had objected to paying for the services of one of the girls causing an irate Sally, who as usual had drunk too much, to berate this man who had struck the girl leaving her bloodied, Sally now demanded payment pulling out her small ladies Derringer pistol which she kept tucked into a pocket in her dress. Hamish, a drover in fact, originally from Scotland, a powerful rough type, seized Sally before she could use the pistol nor utter another word and brutally strangled her in matter of minutes leaving her lying dead on the floor of the landing. He leapt down the stairs and made off knocking several customers aside as well as Sally's doorman who had tried to restrain him. Later when Solomon heard of this from Sturn, he went immediately to Allentown with Jem Sowerbutts, just before Jem's death, who had previously worked there, without even notifying Betsy. Jem was enraged on hearing Sally's death and pledged revenge.

They quickly found the Hamish, the drover, drunk in a saloon, Jem dragged him out and hammered the murderer unconscious with his fists, not needing Solomon's help.

"We'll give th'hogs at t' back summat to feed on!" Jem suggested.

Solomon nodded agreement grinning in the process.

The drover who came to, then moaned weakly. He was carried to the back of Blue Sally's establishment, then thrown into the hog sty there only to be devoured greedily by six hungry hogs who tore him apart leaving only a few bones left. Hamish had been aware that his last few sacred moments on earth, were to be devoured by the hogs.

Jem laughed loudly as Solomon looked on. After this they returned to New York with due haste and the grisly incident was reported to Betsy who praised the good work of Solomon and Jem, but decided to to sell up her property in Allentown. Isaac Sturn was instructed to fetch a good price for it and pay off the girls with severance monies provided for by her.

Betsy had also to say farewell to her lawyer Elijah J Gilbert who passed away peacefully aged seventy-three...of natural causes. His younger associate the keen and able Nicholas Cross took over the firm and continued to serve Betsy diligently for many years.

Betsy thereafter, as she entered her late forties became, as age usually decrees, not quite the driven intensely determined, ruthless person she was when younger. She oversaw all aspects of her business but noticed that the elder of her two sons, Richard, appeared to have an aptitude for serious study, a head for mathematics and a disposition which Betsy thought he had inherited from his father – no bad thing she thought as she began to contemplate the future when she would have to hand over her businesses. Her youngest daughter Hilde on the other hand demonstrated a lively, almost ruthless willpower which often brought her into conflict not just with her other siblings but with authority…namely Betsy along with her nanny, who try as she might could never bring Hilde to heel completely. Betsy although rebuking her daughter when necessary, secretly admired the girl's spirit, no doubt sensing that some her own spirit had manifested itself in this wilful child. The other two children, Bartholomew and her eldest daughter Eliza as appeared normal as any, Bart gradually became stronger much to his mother's relief and went on eventually to serve in the U.S. Navy having a successful career as a captain.

***

As Betsy grew into the latter stages of her life, she witnessed the marriage of three of her four children in rapid succession, all except for Bart who remained a bachelor, devoted to his life at sea, Betsy became a proud, doting a grandmother, enjoying the fruits of her wealth by purchasing more property in New York, investing in further projects and here Nicholas Cross along with the rapidly increasing ability and interest of Richard, proved a valuable aide. She was pleased to observe her interests in good hands, with Richard eventually taking control of the family business from his father's office in Battery. He felt a sense of pride and satisfaction as he seated himself in his father's favourite leather chair. It suited him well. Nicholas and Richard became good friends with Nicholas providing all the legal assistance necessary as Elijah had done prior to his demise. But then a sudden event happened which shook Betsy Hoffman to the core.

CHAPTER 41

In 1843 just after her sixty first birthday, a visitor appeared unexpectedly one afternoon. A smartly dressed youngish man complete with top hat, knocked at the door and asked Solomon, who answered if he could see Betsy. Solomon asked if this man who called himself Patrick Collins, had an appointment with his mistress.

"No but I humbly suggest that Mrs Hoffman, as she is known now I believe, will most certainly wish to see me. Please announce me to her."

He spoke politely in a soft Southern drawl removing his hat in full expectation of being granted an audience. Solomon stared at Patrick Collins who he had never heard of or met before then asked him to wait in the reception room before going to find his mistress who he discovered was in the garden relaxing.

"Excuse me miss there is a gentleman who had just arrived who wishes to see you. Shall I allow him or send him on his way?"

"What does he want Solomon?" she inquired in some surprise since uninvited guests were an extremely rare occurrence.

"He didn't say miss but said you would want to see him, for some reason."

Betsy thought for a moment, intrigued a little, then instructed Solomon to convey the unknown guest to the reception room and offer him some refreshment.

"Better not be a waste of my time!" she said.

On entering the room Patrick bowed and kissed Betsy's offered hand, they then both sat down.

"Well Mr Collins what is the purpose of your visit? I'm curious to know as I never heard of you before or had the pleasure of meeting you."

Patrick took a deep breath and continued seriously.

"You're correct Betsy, or Betsy Roberts as I knew you via my mother Susan."

Betsy blanched visibly on hearing a name she had not used or thought of very much all these years. Her long, lost sister from days gone by.

Patrick continued.

"Susan my dear mother discovered from sources that you had married a man named Leiper who was murdered by who knows who, that you took off with his money and fled to New York where ya evidently and obviously…judgin' by this fine house and your other rich trappin's, have done mighty well for yourself. And I must say I fully admirin' how nice a place ya have here…"

"Why thank you Mr Collins." Betsy interrupted.

"Please allow me to continue Betsy Roberts…I mean Hoffman. You may remember all those years ago don't you, that my mother was left with nothin', a penniless poor woman at the mercy of fate, but fortunately she met a man who took pity on her, a hard workin', honest man, a humble farmer in West Virginia who married her and they had me and my brother and sister. We didn't have much but both my parents worked hard until my pa died in an accident leaving my ma a poor widow."

"I'm sorry to hear that Patrick, how is Susan now?"

"Thanks to the Christian charity of good neighbours, she manages. My brother and sister help run the farm. I'm glad to say that I am able to support her and my younger brother and sister too, as I have a good job now working in the town bank. But I'll get to the point Betsy Roberts, Susan feels you owe her, owe her big time for what she endured, what is hers from the riches you have gained, deserting her at a time of great distress, you cleared off leaving my poor ma, so you did! You got rich I found out through unlawful methods, yes word get 'round Betsy you think no-one can touch you now but you're mistaken, my ma wants rightfully hers…or maybe it's time everyone knew who the real Betsy is and what she's been doin'."

Here Patrick displayed emotion shaking his fists. The effect had little effect on Betsy but quickly she regained her thoughts after taking in this barely concealed threat, as it was, indeed it smacked of blackmail which she anticipated was coming.

Betsy paused slightly then replied.

"I understand your feelings Patrick, and those of my sister Susan, it's been so long and you should know that Susan made it very clear to me that she wanted nothing more to do with me, not to see me again so you'll appreciate that all this is something of a surprise…to say the least. However I will think over what you have told me and give you my answer tomorrow morning I promise. In the meantime I will be honoured if you will stay with us tonight as our guest…after all is said and done, you are my nephew." Patrick a little surprised to be offered this hospitality accepted but commented.

"This doesn't change anything Betsy but yes I will stay

427

tonight, thank you for that."

Betsy sent for Solomon who was instructed to take Patrick to the guestroom.

"He will be joining us for supper this evening Solomon so we must make him feel at home as is our Northern hospitality demands."

She winked at him, giving Solomon room for speculation as to what the final outcome of this man's stay would be.

Supper passed politely enough with little said but Solomon continuously filled Patrick's glass with the best Beaujolais French wine they had. Patrick, unused to such treats, downed several glasses before being offered brandy which Betsy had arranged for Solomon to add a 'little sleeping draught' to help him on his way. At one point Patrick looked at Betsy and blurted out barely comprehendingly.

"We'll..broker a deal tomorrow then!"

Betsy smiled and replied.

"Sure we will nephew, sure." After two more glasses of her fine French brandy Patrick duly fell into a deep sleep dropping his cigar on to the best Persian carpet. Solomon immediately picked it up, extinguishing it efficiently.Betsy nodded to him saying.

"My, my, our guest is the worst for wear Solomon. Perhaps you could take him to his bed and then you know what to do later tonight, I fear he will not wake up until the morning when there will be an unexpected surprise right next to him."

Betsy chuckled knowing what they had planned for him.

"Yes ma'am he'll sure not forget his stay here, Lord no!"

Solomon picked up the prostrate fellow and carried him

upstairs.

Later that night as planned Solomon's youngest daughter twelve year old Mary, a naturally mischievous girl, was called upon to get into Patrick's bed. It was explained to her what the plot was about and how it had to be done to protect everyone from something bad. She was promised a reward if she played her part well, though Esther had her misgivings but she too was persuaded.

"Well just leave me out of this, don't sound right..but if mistress thinks it's needed then it must be necessary."

At around three in the morning Mary slipped into bed next to a snoring, clearly oblivious Patrick, she was naked except for a torn, scanty chemise. Bruises were put on her face by way of makeup and scratches were to be seen, which she herself had created using rough twigs which she had scored on to her body.

Morning arose with the first hints of sunlight slowly illuminating a scene of depravity; a young girl sobbing in distress, calling for help.

"Help!! Help!! Mary screamed and shivered in distress, when a drowsy Patrick awoke to find a very young girl beside him in bed almost naked, sobbing, badly bruised and scratched. One of Betsy's maid conveniently appeared at that moment in and looking at this shocking scene, she called for help.

"Come quickly, help young Mary has been attacked!" Straight away Solomon rushed in, then Betsy herself following a little way behind.

"Damned filthy scoundrel!" Solomon yelled in anger hauling a totally shocked Patrick out of the bed, as Mary ran off howling as he did.

"He raped me papa, forced me into his bed!"

"Child rapist, damn you to Hell!"

Solomon pretended total fury and thrust Patrick who began to come to his senses but could not say a word only mumble protestations of innocence.

"No, no!" he pleaded

Betsy then walked in looking in horror as she discovered what had happened, as Solomon told her the details.

"Miss Betsy that's my daughter, this man must pay for what he done, he must answer, I swear I'll kill him!" Solomon still seizing him by the throat, shook him one more time before releasing his grip. Patrick in complete confusion turned to Betsy.

"I…have no idea what has happened…you must believe me!" he protested.

"It's clear nephew that you lost control after imbibing my wine and brandy, taking advantage of my hospitality to you and then…abusing, nay raping I'm told a girl of only twelve years. How dare you! You will pack your things and leave before I have you arrested and thrown in jail. So I will!"

Betsy fumed."Get yourself dressed and leave this house! Be thankful I don't turn ye over to Solomon who I promise will take a terrible revenge upon you. Blackguard that you are boy!!"

Patrick could not respond such was his state of shock, he dressed, collected his few things and prepared to depart but before he left, by now looking to get away as fast as possible, red faced and shamed, though not having an inkling of how and why this terrible thing had happened (only later did he suspect something amiss, especially when he informed Susan who groaned in dismay!), Betsy called him in the hallway.

"I'm ashamed for you boy, I never want to see nor hear from you again, do I make myself clear?!"

"Yes."

"But take this, it's for Susan, tell her I'm sorry what had gone on in the past but I trust this sum will make her latter days a little easier for her."

Betsy then placed an envelope into Patrick's hand. It contained the sum of ten thousand dollars payable to Susan.

"Now go!"

Patrick, speechless left, never to be heard nor seen again.

Betsy smiled to herself in relief but in some amusement too, she still enjoyed the excitement of situations such as what had occurred. Solomon knew it too.

BETSY'S DREAM

Betsy Roberts it has to be said could never entirely escape her past and there began, as she grew older, a troubling vision which came to her occasionally in the form of a dream or more accurately, nightmare. This occurrence was something which bothered her until her very last day. It was a recurring dream she had which caused her to wake up during the night in a panic leaving her soaked in sweat. It always started and ended the same way with the same person taking the lead role in it.

Betsy would be walking alone in New York down one of the many avenues which she often went on shopping or on business. She enjoyed the Summer breeze, nodding occasionally as she was greeted by the odd passer-by who she knew from her busy social life, ladies who like her liked nothing more than to take a turn along one of the avenues, often Broadway, to seek out some hat or new dress, admire the latest fashions from the East, meaning Paris, London, Rome mainly. It was in this relaxed, pleasant state while strolling casually along that her whole being was to be shaken to it's core.

She suddenly felt a hand on her shoulder unexpectedly, then a voice which she faintly recognised from the past would speak to her saying.

"Well if it isn't Betsy Roberts, so nice to see you agin' but maybe it's high time you came with me, we've unfinished business…wife!"

He then gripped her shoulder tightly and as she turned

around to see who this mysterious stranger was, she recognised the face of none other than Wiley Harpe! A bolt of fear took hold of her whole body as she turned around slowly and stared at him speechless, unable to free herself from his tight grip even though she desperately wanted to get away. Wiley glared at her then continued in a menacing voice.

"So you thought ye could turn me in did ye an' get away with it did ye? I've been waitin' for this day for so long so I can take my revenge on Betsy Roberts, a lyin', cheatin' whore. Here's my knife Betsy which I'm gonna use to carve up her pretty little face, haha!" he said venomously thrusting the knife at her face.

"No Wiley don't, I'm still your wife, don't you know, we can get back together again just like we were before. Don't do it please Wiley!"

She implored him, her knees weakening underneath her, her whole being wilting as Wiley Harpe then seized her by the throat, his knife coming nearer towards her, slowly but remorselessly. She felt helpless, no fight or resistance could she offer as she noticed Wiley was dressed not as a filthy, wretched pioneer from the seventeen hundreds, but in a smart black suit with a top hat. He still had the same dark hair, beard and evil look but he was dressed much tidier with a gold watch and chain tucked into his top waistcoat pocket.

"I been waitin' for this moment too long Betsy now it's time to finish ye here in this fancy city, New York well I never...haha! Who the Hell dee ye think ye are bitch! Oh wait...I think Micajah is a comin' over, I see him now Betsy...yer old friend Big Harpe, we can both have some fun with ye haha!"

The huge unmistakeable figure of Wiley Harpe came

nearer as if from nowhere, a wicked grin on his face. The image of him was vague to begin with but became clearer as Betsy stared in disbelief. She looked at him in terror and screamed out.

"Help, help please help me, murder!!"

Betsy was in a panic, something she had not experienced quite so much since that fateful day many years ago when she was kidnapped by the Harpe brothers, abused, violated. She looked around frantically for help but strangely all the passers-by that now appeared in her dream just ignored her as if there was no-one there. They all continued about their business chatting and linking arms in some cases, a blissful scene on this fine Summers day. Wiley then viciously ripped the front of her skirts with his knife as she stood shaking, frozen with fear as Micajah grinned, but strangely unlike Wiley he was roughly dressed, dirt smudged into his skins, has face as before swarthy, his hair filthy and matted, he then said to Wiley.

"Let's do her here Wiley, I'll go first!"

Wiley laughed and moved to one side to allow his younger brother to take hold of Betsy.

Betsy groaned but just then noticed Solomon with Esther standing just across the road looking on. She called out to them in desperation.

"Help me Solomon, help me will you, can't you see…I'm being murdered, raped!!

Solomon stared at her for a few seconds, slowly shook his head in an attitude of disgust, then turned away to speak with Esther who appeared to look at Betsy with a scornful, disapproving look.

"She's getting what she deserves husband, she done wrong

434

as we know now. She fooled us all into thinkin' what an upright lady she was when all the time she was a wicked murderer."

Esther said to Solomon with undisguised contempt, and as Betsy looked at them in abject despair, they both turned around as one and walked away not looking back or responding to her desperate entreaties.

"What you doing…help, come back!!" she called out but in vain as they disappeared from view.

Just then her Pa appeared as if from nowhere from out of the busy unconcerned crowd. Her eyes lit up, but no sooner than he saw her, his face turned to an expression of disgust and he turned away joining arms with her mother. They disappeared from view as quickly as they had appeared.

Betsy screamed.

"Pa!! Pa!!" but to no avial!

"Ain't nobody goin' help ye now bitch!" Wiley retorted as Micajah ripped her dress brutally, his hands grasping her breasts, clawlike fingers ripping her ….

Then suddenly Betsy woke up gasping for air, sat herself up in her bed, gradually she recovered her senses, relieved that this whole horrible vision was over. She would lie there in shock before eventually saying to herself. "It's just a dream Betsy, just a dream."

Unfortunately it was one that she experienced periodically until her last days, it would not be erased.

EPILOGUE

After the extraordinary events described previously it was a blessing that Betsy Hoffman nee Roberts was later able to lead a more normal, settled life. She became a beloved matriarchal figure enjoying the company of her many grandchildren, taking holidays with Eliza and Hilde and their children, six in all and also joining Richard for gentle rides in the newly laid out Central Park. Only one other incident upset her and that was when her devoted coachman Nip Nateley fell badly while mounting one of the horses, sadly shattering his hip. He died two days later, single and alone in his room. Nip had never married, joking as he did on many occasions.

"What need have I for a wife, I got my good mare Mabel anyway and she does as I tells her!" ...was his usual cockney refrain.

Betsy did visit him but was too late to see him before he passed away. She made sure however that her faithful coachman was given a good send off, attending his funeral with Solomon and Esther, and paying for his gravestone to be adorned with a carving depicting him riding the winning horse in one of the many races he won before he came to New York. She was sure he would appreciate it.

As Betsy grew into old age she often thought back to her youth, remembering the many flowers that she collected which she carefully made into posies. She especially loved the pretty, yellow Butterweed flowers which were in abundance in Kentucky. She thought of her Ma and Pa, but her joy would turn to sadness when she remembered the terrible events from that time, the loss of her family, the loss of her innocence. Gone forever.

Betsy lived to the ripe old age of eighty-eight. She had increasingly suffered severe headaches as she neared her last days, which could only be relieved by her faithful Esther applying cold compresses and settling her in her darkened bedroom. Esther was her comfort just as Solomon had been her support.

As the end approached, Betsy was surrounded on her deathbed by all her family which by then had grown into a considerable number. Before the end, Eliza noticed a small delicate tear on her cheek, Betsy's very last thought, unbeknown to all before she slipped into that last sleep, was for her beloved Joshua. She imagined she saw him with his hand outstretched motioning for her to come to him, smiling and happy, welcoming his mama into the next life. Her weak heart skipped a gentle beat on seeing her dearest boy, Betsy then passed away peacefully, a faint smile left on her lips for all to see.

Betsy's funeral was held at Trinity Church, once again Mozart's great Requiem Mass was performed. It was more a celebration of an extraordinary life than a sorrowful occasion, the life of a woman who had made her mark in the most amazing way. Bart had been given last minute compassionate leave from the navy to attend, and with that she was laid to rest in between Joshua and John Hoffman.

She had survived and prospered through her own willpower and strength of character. With the terrible Harpes left behind in the distant past, only occasionally during her life did she feel a twinge of fear or remorse for her part in those dreadful events all that time, many, many years ago.

Betsy Roberts had survived the hell of living with Micajah and Wiley Harpe, utilising all of her resources, many of which she never knew she possessed when she was brutally kidnapped. Through her ordeal she became progressively toughened, courageous, manipulative and gradually immune to the horrors she witnessed as perpetrated by the Harpe brothers. Ultimately she was inevitably scarred by this which is hardly unsurprising, she even exhibited an evil streak in her which developed partly as a survival technique, but undoubtedly it grew to be a significant part of her character something she even enjoyed at times. It enabled her to take whatever advantage she could out of even the most terrible circumstances.

Her battles with the Harpes however, her strange relationship with Wiley as his 'wife' had a profound, lasting effect on her; it actually left her stronger but inextricably tainted. No amount of imagining however strenuously evoked, by ordinary, decent folk, could come close to understanding the reality of what she went through and witnessed. Remarkably it did not prevent her from forging a new life for herself and establishing a dynasty in the burgeoning city of New York. Her family would grow into a powerful force in later nineteenth and twentieth century America with many of them achieving great wealth and power, notably a certain young lady who seemed to possess many of the traits and qualities of Betsy Roberts herself. She even had an undeniable look of Betsy which would surprise those people who had known our heroine from before...but then that is another story yet to be told.

THE END